GW00372019

Catherine Parry is in her late twenties and has been writing fantasy ever since she learned how to begin stories with 'Once upon a time'. Growing up in the North Wales hills, she had plenty of time to write when trapped indoors by the weather. A talent for science directed her away from writing as a career, and fear of rejection meant that very few people were allowed to read any of those early stories.

Catherine has just given up a successful career in engineering and moved to Australia with her fiancé, where she intends to spend the next few years writing on the beach and perhaps starting a family.

THE
ICE WITCH

Catherine Parry

The
Ice Witch

Vanguard Press

VANGUARD PAPERBACK

© Copyright 2002
Catherine Parry

A CIP catalogue record for this title is
available from the British Library
ISBN 1 903489 74 1

*Vanguard Press is an imprint of
Pegasus Elliot MacKenzie Publishers Ltd.*
www.pegasuspublishers.com

First Published in 2002

**Vanguard Press
Sheraton House Castle Park
Cambridge England**

Printed & Bound in Great Britain

Dedication

To my family, who always believed I could be anyone I wanted to be, and for Nick, who showed me I only had to be myself.

Chapter 1

Iceden, early winter, the year 2712 after Founding

Icy winds whistled through the corridors of the immense castle. From the outside, the castle looked like a slender white flame against the blackness of an icy winter's night. Inside, hoarfrost coated the walls of the colder passages and the servants shivered beside the dying fires in the kitchens.

High up in the castle's spire, a light flickered through a narrow glassed window. A shrill scream sounded out, followed swiftly by another. Even if there had been anyone to hear, the wind whipped the sound away.

A little while later, a woman made her way slowly down the winding turret stairs. Shivering violently, she wrapped her cloak of thick black fur closer around herself. She was very beautiful: long silvery hair swept up on top of her head emphasised the aristocratic lines of her pale face, and her eyes, an incredible amethyst purple colour. Her beauty was marred by one of those enchanting eyes swelling shut with a purple bruise, and a cut welling blood at the corner of her lip.

In the high tower room the woman had just left, two men sat talking, one of perhaps fifty and the other still a young man of about seventeen.

"I have waited long enough, Father!" the younger of the pair exclaimed angrily. "I must wait many years yet before I become Prince of the Icelands, but I am bored *now*! I need a bride to occupy my time!"

"And you shall have one, Sasken," the prince said, smiling. "Your mother accepts now what she must do. I was just your age when I took my bride."

"Who gave you only a useless daughter," Sasken jeered.

"Not so useless, son, that daughter bore me you and four fine daughters. You are lucky: you will have four brides in time. I only had two, and not together."

"I want one now!" Sasken snapped.

"Your eldest sister Saskia began to bleed two days ago. In two weeks she will be cleansed and fertile to breed, you will have her then. I tell you again, Sasken: you are lucky. At twelve she is very young to bleed. She will make you a fine wife and give you a strong son."

"I hope none of my sisters give me sons," Sasken said sulkily. "I want to be like you, Father, to purify the line further by fathering children on my daughters. And maybe even my granddaughters: who knows?"

* * * *

The princess stumbled on through the dark, cold corridors, fighting the weariness and pain that sapped her strength. She had been born in this castle and rarely left it: few knew Iceden's ways as well as she, and it was easy for her to avoid the guards who walked the passageways. At last she reached the place she was looking for, in a dark wall niche. She stepped inside and felt above her head for a small iron lever. The back of the niche slid aside with a low grating sound, and the princess slipped silently in. She had been planning this night for some months now, and felt confidently on a shelf for the lamp and firebox she had left there. After a few moments she had the lamp lit, and closed the secret door.

The secret passageway was, if possible, even colder than the rest of Iceden. The princess crouched down and gathered up some bundles she had left on the floor. Then she set off, walking steadily through the dark passages. Some way on, she stopped and pulled a piece of cloth away from the wall. Peering through the crack, she saw a guard leaning indolently on the wall by a door. A wine jug rested by his foot. Dropping the cloth, the princess continued on around a corner. Raising her lamp to peer in front of her, she hesitated for a moment, then pressed out a complex sequence in a pattern of blue and white tiles set into the wall. Another section of wall shifted aside, and the princess squeezed through the narrow gap and pushed aside the tapestry hanging over the opening.

The room on the other side of the gap was very dark, but the princess' lamp gave off quite a lot of light. She walked quietly over to the nearest bed and looked down at her sleeping daughter.

Princess Saskia looked very like her mother. A younger, fresher version, at just twelve she had not yet developed any womanly curves at all. Standing, though, she was half a head taller, and looked likely to grow more before she reached her full height.

The princess stooped down and shook Saskia. She awoke with a start.

"Mama?" she queried quietly. Then she saw her mother's bruised and bleeding face. "Oh, Mama, you're hurt again."

"It doesn't matter. Get dressed," the princess whispered. She laid a bundle of heavy clothes on Saskia's bed. "Put all these on. It's very cold outside."

Saskia got up and dressed. "We're going *outside*?" she whispered back.

"Yes. Your father told me tonight that you're to marry Sasken in two weeks. If we don't leave now, you'll never escape him."

"What about the others?" Saskia asked, tying her bootlaces.

The princess looked across the room at the other three beds, at her sleeping younger daughters. "Not tonight," she said softly. "It's your marriage, not theirs. Only because you have begun to bleed. They will be safe for years yet. I have a better chance of taking you out alone."

Saskia turned to look at her nearest sister, nine-year-old Iskia. "Issy," she said softly. "Can I say goodbye?" she pleaded with her mother.

The princess hesitated for a moment. "Just to Iskia," she said at last. "Don't wake the younger two. Iskia can tell them that we have gone."

Saskia kissed each of the younger two sisters; eight-year-old Riaskia and seven-year-old Liaskia, lightly on the brow, and her mother followed suit, whispering a silent goodbye. Then Saskia gently woke Iskia up, placing a finger to her lips to quiet her when she started.

"Mama, Sass," Iskia said. "What is it?"

"We have to go away for a while," the princess said, stroking Iskia's hair gently. "I should be back soon, but you may not see Saskia for a very long time."

"Why?"

"Your father has ordered that Sasken and Saskia get married in two weeks' time."

Iskia's small face hardened. "Then you must go, that must not happen."

"I know, honey." Saskia hugged her sister tightly. "I wish you could come, but Mama says it will be all right, that you are safe for years yet. I'll come back for you as soon as I can, I swear it."

"Promise?" Iskia said in a slightly trembling voice.

"I promise. I'll come back for all of you. Never doubt it." The two girls hugged, and then the princess kissed Iskia's brow.

"I'll see you soon, sweeting. If anyone asks you, you did not hear us leave tonight, all right?"

Iskia nodded. "Where are you going?"

"You don't need to know, sweeting. We'll be safe, never fear, and you will too. Sleep well now."

Saskia stared in astonishment as her mother led her back into the secret passageway. "I never knew this was here!"

"I spent years studying Iceden's plans as a child. As far as I know, I am the only one who knows about most of the passages."

"Where are we going?" Saskia asked as they crept on downwards.

"Away from Iceden, as far as I can take you," the princess replied. She held up her wrists: the thick gold bands on them flashed in the lamplight. "Your father locked these onto my wrists the day we were married. I cannot take them off. A sorcerer could trace them easily. So, I can only take you so far, and then I must leave you to throw them off the trail."

They got out of the castle by crawling down a long, dark tunnel Saskia thought would never end. At the far end was a small cave in a rocky slope: there the princess made her stop and put on more clothes: a heavy winter fur cloak and some thick gloves.

"It is freezing cold and snowing a blizzard," the princess reported after a brief foray outside. "I know you have hardly ever been outside Iceden before, Saskia, but you must stay close to me or we could get separated. We must reach the river before dawn."

It was a dark and blustery night. The wind blew blasts of freezing snow into Saskia's face as she stumbled close behind her mother. The trip no longer felt like an adventure, and she began to feel very afraid.

The two princesses reached the river just as the sky began to lighten and the snow to ease off. The princess led Saskia to a little boathouse, and together they dragged out a sturdy little rowing boat.

The Iceflow looked terribly fast and cold to Saskia. Only a few metres wide, still it was more water than she had ever seen. They launched the boat, and the princess showed Saskia how to keep it straight in the water using the rudder and an occasional pull on the oars. The current carried them quickly downstream. The princess stood up in the boat, and looked back at the boathouse, and the long marks on the bank where they had pulled the boat to the river. She lifted a hand and her eyes took on a distant look. As Saskia watched in astonishment, the gashes on the bank disappeared, covered over by unmarked snow.

"How did you..." Saskia began, then stopped as her mother collapsed. Saskia tried to wake her mother, then gave up and settled for making the princess comfortable, wrapping her heavy cloak tightly around her. She found a bit of clean cloth, wet it and dabbed carefully at the cut on her mother's lip. Then she settled down to wait, concentrating on keeping the boat in the middle of the river.

Saskia tried to remember the maps she had seen, and the towns along the river as it grew broader towards the sea. It was a hundred miles from Iceden to the sea, that much she did know. She wondered how far they could travel in a day. Faster than a horse in the snow, of that she was sure. They could stay ahead of the news that they were missing for a while. It would be at least noon before her father would be satisfied that they were not within Iceden. Then they would spend time searching for tracks, which would be all covered up by the fallen snow. Now that her mother had hidden the marks left by pulling the boat into the river, the only evidence that they had gone this way was the one missing boat. There had been so many boats that one small rowboat missing would probably not be noticed at all.

A couple of hours later, Saskia's mother roused herself. She groaned weakly. Saskia dipped a cup of water for her, and unpacked some bread and cheese she had found in one of her mother's bundles. They both ate greedily, then sat back and looked at each other.

"What did you do?" Saskia asked curiously.

The princess looked up at the dark grey sky. It was leaden with the promise of more snow to come. She sighed and looked back at her daughter.

"What do you know of Blood Gifts?" she asked.

"Only what I have read: that they run in bloodlines, that there are many different types and that the type of Gift is not what is inherited, but only the fact of being gifted."

"That's all quite true. What you do *not* know is that Gifts run in the Icelander royal blood. I was born with them, and your father. Your father has a very weak Healing Gift, which he only ever uses to cause pain. The Gifts can be turned in on themselves, you see."

"What are your Gifts, Mama? Do I have any?"

The princess hesitated for a long moment. "I was born with two Gifts, one strong and one weak," she said finally. "I have TimeSight in a fair measure: glimpses of the future are revealed to me. Sometimes I do not know what they mean, but every single one has come to pass. The other Gift in me is weak, and that is the Gift of Power."

"I have not heard of that before."

"I am not surprised, daughter. It is the rarest Gift of all. It is what sorcerers are born with, and is the only Gift that requires training to use. All of the other Gifts are for one specific purpose, but with Power you can do almost anything another person can do with any Gift. Power gives you the ability to manipulate objects, like I did to the riverbank back there, and to control the minds of animals. Even people, if they are weak. I have heard it said that memories can even be changed by a powerful sorcerer."

Saskia thought about it for a moment. "Is that what I have?" she asked hesitantly. "Sometimes – when I was riding last summer – I could almost feel the pony thinking. And I did not need to guide her: she seemed to follow my thoughts."

The princess nodded tiredly. "What is barely a spark in me is a firestorm in you. I have never heard of someone born with the Power using it without being trained."

"Do I have any other Gifts?"

"I don't believe so. Your brother Sasken was born with an uncanny amount of Luck, though: do not ever count on being able to trick him. As for your sisters: Iskia has a goodly amount of LongSight, Riaskia has more TimeSight than I could ever imagine, and a fair dose of Luck too. As for Liaskia, well, she has the hardest road of all to tread. She will be the greatest Healer in a hundred generations and she has Empathy that will make her task harder, for she will feel every man's pain even as she heals him."

Saskia looked quizzically at her mother. "Why did we not bring them, Mama?"

The princess frowned slightly. "Never think that I did not want to, but it will be hard enough for the two of us. Iskia is only nine and the other two even younger: there are three years yet before they could be in any danger, and hopefully longer. I hope that you will be able to bring my plans to bear before that."

Saskia wanted to ask her mother about the plans, but the princess told her to lie down and rest while she could. For three days and nights, they stayed on the river, taking it in turns to control the boat and to sleep. On the third day, a strange smell came to Saskia's nose.

"What is that smell, Mama?" she asked curiously.

The princess sniffed and frowned. "From what my nurse told me – I think that is the smell of a port," she said hesitantly. "Soon we should see a big town on the southern bank, that will be Terrport. We must pull in there, we will be joining a land caravan."

Saskia nodded. "Where will the land caravan take us, Mama?" she asked.

"Haven City. Can you tell me why the caravan will go there from Terrport?"

Saskia thought about it. "Because Terrport is in Haven," she said. "Haven City is the provincial capital. There must be a road. It wasn't on the maps."

"No, it's a new road. Twenty years ago there were only rough farm trails, but the Emperor built a new road to serve Haven City. Now tell me why that would be."

Saskia knew what her mother was doing: she was talking to distract them both from nerves as they neared Terrport. "Because Haven City serves the North Market City," she said readily, "and they might as well use Terrport as have everything go through Iridia and the Market."

"That's not a bad answer. Actually, it's because the Emperor realised that Iridia and North Market were becoming too crowded. So he sent many of the goods through Terrport, and the port has grown to meet the demand. It was only a small fishing port before: now, it's a thriving city."

They both looked towards the city, nearing now as they pulled on the oars. Night was falling, and lights were springing up all over the great town.

"Where do we go once we land, Mama?" Saskia asked.

"I am taking you to my old nurse. She still lives here in Terrport where she was born. She will be accompanying you to Haven City, while I take the ship for Eastport."

"Eastport? Why?"

The princess smiled faintly. "You are too young to understand, but I will tell you anyway. After Sasken was born, I fell in love with a young soldier. He was part of the escort of the Emperor, when he came to visit Iceden after the birth of a new prince. I never lay with Wesan, but your father found out we had met in secret. He went to the Emperor, and Wesan was dismissed and sent home. He sent a letter to me, through my old nurse, and told me he was working as a guard for the Duke of Eastphal, in

Highfort. So, I will sail to Eastport, and since I let your father find the letter years ago, that is the first place he will look for me. On the wrong side of the continent to find you."

Saskia was absolutely astounded by her mother's cleverness. The princess had always been a slightly diffident figure, cowed by her father's presence, busy with the younger daughters. The only thing she had instilled in Saskia was a love of learning, and a hatred of the incestuous slavery all the women of the royal line of Iceden had been forced into.

They guided the boat quietly into a small fishing dock. No one spared them a second glance as they moored and got out of the boat.

"Do you know where we're going?" Saskia asked.

"Roughly. See up there, on that hill? That's the keep. My old nurse lives in a house backing onto the walls."

They walked on up through the town. Dressed in their heavy clothes, they were hardly recognisable as women. Almost everyone was indoors already for the cold night, and they had no trouble. The princess counted quietly under her breath as they started along a street. At last she stopped outside a little house and peered at the door. A small symbol of oddly curved lines was carved into it just above the knocker.

"This is it," said the princess, knocking confidently.

The door was opened by a straight-backed woman in her late fifties. She was not tall, perhaps the same height as the princess, but seemed a great deal more robust and forbidding. She stared at the two princesses for a moment.

"Nurse?" said the princess timidly. "It's me, Saskia."

Saskia turned to look at her mother in astonishment. She had not known that they shared a name. Even her father called the princess "lady" when speaking to her.

The woman's face was instantly transformed from forbidding to welcoming. "My lady! Come inside, you must be freezing."

They entered the little house. It was blissfully warm after the cold days on the river. Saskia pulled off her cloak and gloves.

The nurse stared at her. "Ah," was all she said. She looked sharply at the princess.

"My eldest daughter, Saskia," the princess said softly. "Saskia, this is my old nurse, Rianna."

* * * *

Rianna fed them well on thick fishy stew and dark bread. Afterwards, she put Saskia to bed and sat by the fire with the princess. She had looked at the black eye the princess was still sporting, and took out a pot of ointment for her without comment. The princess had suffered cuts and bruises – and even a broken bone or two – so many times at her husband's hands that she never complained any more. Still, she took the ointment gratefully and rubbed it carefully into the puffy, painful skin around her eye.

"Are you still wearing those bracelets?" Rianna asked.

"They will not come off until my death, you know that. I have tried everything, but even with the Gift of Earth, I am not strong enough to remove them."

"Then you must be out of here on the dawn tide."

"I know, Rianna. You must take care of Saskia for me. Do you remember the plan?"

"Of course. But I thought there would be a few years yet. She cannot reveal herself before she is sixteen, or the Prince can just demand her back. She's what, not even thirteen yet?"

"No." The princess frowned. "Three and a half years will be a long time to hide her, Rianna. I have no one else to go to, and I cannot give her up to her brother. I *cannot*."

"You will never need to, child. What did you tell Saskia?"

"The truth. That she is Power-born and must be trained to use it. Not that you will train her, though: that is for you to say. That I am sailing to Eastport to hunt for Wesan."

"He's long dead, you know."

"Of course, but my husband does not. I'll lead him a merry dance all over Eastphal. You know what you must do with Saskia? She thinks you're going to Haven City, and from there to North Market."

"And you?"

"I have no idea where you're going, Rianna. That was our

agreement. If I had to guess, I'd say Summerlands or Envetierra: as far away from the Icelands as possible."

"You tell your husband that when he catches up with you. Get some rest now. I'll go down to the Sail Office and get you a ticket to Eastport. Two tickets – we want your husband to think you both sailed."

* * * *

Shortly before dawn, the princess woke her daughter. "I have to go now, sweeting," she whispered.

"Mama," Saskia clung to her. "When will I see you again?"

The princess stroked her daughter's bright hair. "I don't know," she said sadly. "You must promise to take good care, and do everything Rianna tells you. I put your life and mine into her hands: you must believe me when I say you can trust her absolutely. She has nothing to gain by betraying you."

"Mama!" Saskia wailed as the princess pulled away.

"I love you, sweeting." She kissed her daughter one last time. "Farewell."

Saskia cried for a long time. At last Rianna walked into the room. She looked down at the weeping girl with compassion.

"You have had even less freedom as a child than your mother did," she said gently. "I am about to give you more freedom than most people will ever know in a lifetime. It's time for us to leave."

Saskia gathered her courage, stood up and glared at the older woman. "Where are we going?"

"Not to Haven City."

"Where then? Or I'm not going anywhere." Saskia tried to be defiant, but only managed to look rather pitiful, with her face streaked by her tears.

"We're going to Clanhold."

"*Clanhold*!" Saskia rocked back on her heels, utterly shocked. "*Why*? It must be more than a thousand miles!"

Rianna smiled grimly. "That's right. We're going there because that is the very last place anyone will look for you. I am Clanborn, of the Clan Berenna, which not even your mother

21

knows. My clan will take me back happily, and you too until it is time."

"Time for what?"

Rianna explained. Until Saskia was sixteen, not even the Emperor could gainsay the Prince's rights over his daughter. No crime had yet been committed against her, and thus she would have to be returned to the care of her family. So she must remain hidden until her sixteenth birthingday, and among the Clans was a very good place to hide.

Saskia understood that well enough. She asked questions as she helped Rianna pack belongings. "How will we get there? Whiteport, I suppose, and then along the Dark Waters coast to Clanport."

"Nothing so simple. The Dark Waters coast is not safe, especially in winter. We are going overland."

"Overland!" Saskia thought back to the map in her father's study. "At least we will be travelling away from the worst of the winter," she said gloomily.

Rianna laughed. "It will take us three moons to get to Clanhold," she said. "Summer will be starting by the time we arrive. It's warm all year round that far south, though."

They set out a few hours later, after eating a hearty breakfast. Rianna had produced two fine horses from somewhere, far better than Saskia had ever been permitted to ride, and a solid cob to carry their packs. Rianna supervised the packing.

"Never leave anything on your packhorse you can't live without," she warned. "Carry your money on you, and food for a few days at least in your saddlebags."

"I have no money."

"Your mother brought plenty. Here, this is for you, your emergency money." Rianna gave Saskia a small cloth bag. It was full of silver pieces.

"I've never seen so much money!" Saskia exclaimed.

"Poor thing, you were kept on a tight rein, weren't you?" Rianna said gently. "Come now. It's time to go."

Saskia hesitated. "I don't really know how to ride," she admitted in a small voice.

"You've never been on a horse?" Rianna said incredulously.

"Well, a few times. The Stablemaster let me sit on Sasken's pony when nobody was looking."

Rianna rolled her eyes. "It's a good thing we don't have to outrun pursuit just yet," she said dryly. "Come on. I'll help you up. You'll just have to learn as we go along."

They mounted up, and rode south out of Terrport. The snow was starting to come down again, and they bundled up against the cold and headed south to the Haven Road.

There were villages and towns every few miles along the road. In the first large town they came to, Rianna dismounted and went into the smithy. She came back out a few minutes later, astonishing Saskia with what she carried: two longswords and several knives.

"What in the Light..." Saskia began.

"Shut up. Tie the horses and come with me."

Saskia obeyed, bristling slightly at being issued such peremptory orders. She followed Rianna into the tannery, and stood patiently while she was measured. The tanner put a swordbelt round her waist, and Rianna attached the scabbard of one longsword, and pushed the knife into a sheath at her other hip. Rianna had the same, with extra knives hidden in her boots and sleeves. Clad in travelling leathers and armed to the teeth, she suddenly looked exactly as Saskia had always imagined a bloodthirsty Clansman to look. Except – she had never imagined a lone female with grey hair.

The pair mounted up again and headed south. They stayed in the larger villages and towns by night, where people were less likely to remember two travelling women dressed in Clan fashion. Rianna had braided her grey hair in a strange manner, and secured it with a beaten silver ring engraved with the symbols of her Clan, the Berenna. She bound Saskia's hair up with a leather thong, marking her as being of the Clanspeople but not accepted into any one Clan.

"You look all wrong for Clan," Rianna said critically, looking at Saskia. It was the fourth night they were on the road. "No Clansman ever had hair that pale. And those purple eyes mark you as one of the Icelander royal line."

23

"These townspeople know no different," Saskia said, shrugging. "I know little of the Clans, and I have read a great deal. I doubt Clanspeople ever come this far north."

"Rarely. Only for a good reason."

"Why did you come to Iceden, Rianna?"

Rianna had been waiting for the question. She tossed another log on the fire in the small inn bedroom they were sharing. "I heard there was a princess born in the royal line. One who might need what I could give."

"And what would that be?"

Rianna tensed. "Training in the use of Power," she replied finally.

"Ahhh," Saskia said. "Now I understand. That is why my mother sent me to you. So you can teach me how to use the Power."

"That's right." Rianna caught Saskia's eyes with hers, a brown so dark they were nearly black. "You have more Power than any other born in a thousand years. You can use it to bring down Iceden around itself, to save your sisters and yourself. But until you are sixteen you can do nothing. Do you understand that?"

Saskia was quiet for a long time. "Iskia could have bled by then," she said.

"That is true." Rianna sat and watched her. Eventually Saskia shrugged.

"What choices do I have? None, that I see. I must wait, and hope, and trust that my mother will do what she can."

Rianna nodded. "Now you know why your mother sent you to me. I am to be your guardian and your teacher. That teaching will start tonight."

"What do I do?" Saskia asked eagerly.

"First of all, I will explain a little about the Power. There are four kinds, for the four elements, Earth, Air, Fire and Water. Most sorcerers can use any kind to some degree, but you will find that you have a particular affinity for one type. Mine is for Air; I can stir up weather, or clear away smoke, with the greatest of ease. Earth is the opposite of Air, so that is the hardest for me to work with. Unfortunately, that is what your mother has. I could teach her very little."

"What am I?"

"That we will find out tonight. I will give you four tests. One of them will be so easy, you will perhaps not even realise you have done it."

Saskia could not cleanse the cup of brackish water that Rianna gave her. The twig she tried to make grow leaves snapped in her fingers. Then when she tried to reverse the flow of wind stirring the curtain, it just flapped mockingly at her.

"Well, that leaves only one option," Rianna said. "You must be a Fire Power. We'll find out for sure." She led Saskia back to the dying embers of the fire, and handed her an unlit log.

"Make the fire jump up and light this," she said.

Saskia held the log out and shut her eyes. Rianna watched in disbelief as a slim spear of fire rose straight up out of the embers and the log burst into flame.

Saskia opened her eyes. "It worked!" she said in delight, tossing the log into the fire.

Rianna stared at her for a moment. "It should not have worked like that," she said slowly. "I expected a conflagration. That – that was almost like an arrow."

Saskia shrugged. "That's what I thought of," she said. "Did I do it wrong?"

Rianna shook her head. "No, no. But Fire magic – I don't know much about it. It's the most uncommon of the Power types, and everything I've read says that they are usually completely out of control."

"Well, I'm not out of control," Saskia said almost huffily. "That was easy. Can I try something else?"

Rianna laughed. "Eager to learn, aren't you? Well, we'll start with the hardest thing of all. I want you to sit down, shut your eyes, and think about what you saw when you lit the log."

"I just imagined it lit."

"No, not like that. Think hard. Just as you lit it, you saw the afterimage of something, on the inside of your eyelids, didn't you? What did you see?"

Saskia frowned, thinking, her eyes squeezed tightly shut. "It's like a river," she said slowly. "A river made out of fire.

Slow moving, sluggish. But then I grabbed at it and – threw – some to light the wood."

"Right, that's good. Think about the river again. Try to see it."

"I see it," Saskia said after a long moment. Rianna watched her fingers curl and uncurl. "It – wants me to take hold."

"It will. The Power is addictive. Now, I want you to think about sewing."

"*Sewing*?" Saskia opened her eyes and looked incredulously at Rianna. "What?"

"Trust me. It's the only way to work. Sewing is the most detailed work you will do. Imagine the threads, threading them into your needle, careful fingers making the exact patterns you want them to make."

It almost made sense to Saskia. But try as she might, the red river of fire that she saw as the Power would only form into thick, clumsy ropes.

"It will take time," Rianna said. "Few people could hold the amounts of Power that you grip there. Your mother can only work with the fine threads: she is an Earth power, but has so little that most things exhaust her. To you, the Power is like thick crayons. You need to learn to work with a brush a single hair thick, or you'll be setting fires everywhere you go, just as a side effect of everything you do."

Saskia stopped struggling and let the Power slide away. She felt truly exhausted.

The weather eased as they rode south. Each day, Rianna would give lessons in control and use of Power while they rode, and each evening they would spend half an hour working with swords and knives. Saskia had never so much as seen a sword fight before. The first time Rianna told Saskia to draw her sword, she got it stuck in the scabbard and ended up falling over in an ungainly heap.

Rianna could not stop her giggles. She was a patient teacher, however, and soon Saskia could draw and resheath the sword without falling over or cutting herself.

The hardest part of the journey for Saskia was the riding. She was saddle-sore, and for the first week could not stand after they dismounted for the night. The Power helped, giving her some insight into the horse, and why it was acting how it did. Soon she began to get accustomed to riding, and built a few muscles in her arms from swinging the sword.

Rianna despaired over her, though. "I am no teacher for this, and you are so unfit," she said dismally. "I fear you will have a hard time of it in the Clanhold."

On they rode, southward through Haven Province. They skirted Haven City: it was possible that someone there could be searching for them. Carrier pigeons could have flown from Terrport by now. They rode on and into ForstMarch. Half a day over the border, the trees began.

Saskia could not believe it. She had seen no trees in the Icelands, not like these. Some of the hill slopes in the Icelands carried tall pines, and she had seen a few trees on the Haven Road, but nothing like these giant, peaceful oaks and beech. They were off the main roads now, often following farm tracks, but always moving south. The weather was warming significantly, and there was no more snow.

Rianna liked to see Saskia free among the trees. She watched the girl romp laughing among the huge oaks as they rested, camping overnight, and smiled to herself. This was a very different girl to the frightened mouse she had met in Terrport. Travel had put some colour in her cheeks, and the thin child's body was gaining a woman's curves. For the first time it occurred to Rianna that this young woman was far too beautiful to let loose among the Clans.

"Then I'll just have to guard her with my life," Rianna said fiercely to herself. "This one, I'm going to save!" She had never forgiven herself for her inability to get the bracelets off the princess' wrists. She could not let Sasken lock them onto this beautiful, sweet-tempered child.

The only time they were challenged at all was in ForstMarch. Rianna had taken the precaution of laying an illusion of Air on Saskia as soon as she spotted the patrol on the road approaching them. The four riders saw only two Clanswomen, dark of hair and eye, one old and one young.

"May I see your identity papers, please," the officer

requested politely. Rianna produced the papers; one set carefully forged to give Saskia a new identity. While Rianna was speaking with the officer, one of the other men approached Saskia.

"Hello, pretty," he said, reaching out a hand to cup her chin. Saskia jerked back before he touched her. She wondered how a Clanswoman would react, and decided that she would be unlikely to tolerate any ill handling.

"Touch me and I'll chop your hand off," she snarled, putting one hand on her sword hilt and speaking carefully to disguise her Icelander accent.

"Hey, hey, I was only trying to be friendly!" the Forstian soldier said in an aggrieved tone.

"Leave her alone!" shouted his officer at that moment. "I swear by the Light, Eric, you hassle one more woman on my shift and you're out of the Guard!"

Rianna nodded approvingly at Saskia. Once the soldiers had gone, the officer still berating the hapless Eric, she patted Saskia's shoulder.

"You did well there. You accent still sounds a little peculiar, but that attitude was certainly Clan!"

"Were they looking for me?" Saskia asked anxiously.

"They had instructions to watch for two Icelander princesses, yes. Word has spread – but don't worry. We're nearly at the Clanlands border, and even if anyone there does realise who you are, no one would betray you. Historically the Clans have no liking for the Icelander Princes. They will certainly shelter you."

* * * *

When they crossed the border into the Clanlands, Saskia kept looking around her as though expecting to see Clansmen. The trees had petered out a day or two ago, and spreading out before them was hundreds of miles of rolling plain. Rianna was sure of her directions now. She turned them west at last, and after a journey which had taken them ninety-one days, they finally entered the Clan Mountains. The eight high, jagged spikes, tipped with ice, made her smile at last. Saskia was awed by the sheer size.

"The Icelands have mountains as high," Rianna said.

"But I've never seen them," Saskia replied, eyes reaching for the sky.

They had been seen from afar by Clansmen for days, but Rianna had put out signs of Clan travellers, and as was traditional they were not challenged until they approached Clanhold itself. The challenge, when it came, was a shock. They were riding peacefully through a narrow canyon when wild shouts came from all around. One moment they were alone with their horses, the next they were surrounded by archers.

"State your name," a young warrior ordered. Saskia stared at him. He was a handsome young man, black hair cut very short to his scalp. His clothes were made of leather dyed in shades of grey and green, to blend into the rocks and bushes of the hillside. His bow was nearly as tall as he was, and he held it drawn, an arrow aimed unerringly at Rianna's heart.

"I am Rianna ca'Berenna, and this is my companion, Saskanna of no Clan." They had agreed to keep Saskia's name as close to her own as possible.

The young archer moved closer. "Your business at Clanhold," he demanded.

"I go to see my brother, the Clanlord. Beyond that is no business of yours."

The archer bowed to her, and they all lowered their bows. "Honour to serve, Clandaughter," he said respectfully. "I will escort you and your companion to Clanhold if you desire." His hot black eyes raked over Saskia, and Rianna sighed.

"I have no need of an escort, Clanson," she said. "Return to your duties."

The young archer actually looked disappointed, but he gestured to his men and they melted back into the rocks.

Rianna took Saskia's reins from her to lead her down into Clanhold's valley. The way was steep and dangerous, and first-time visitors usually spent so much time looking at the Hold that they forgot to watch their footing.

Saskia was absolutely awed by Clanhold. She knew from her reading that it was even older than Iceden, second only in age to the Citadel itself, but she had never imagined that it would be so big. Iceden was one clean white spire reaching to the heavens. The Clanhold had a hundred towers and low sprawling buildings, all built of the same dark grey rock. It loomed forbiddingly, even viewed from above. The walls were so high that they looked utterly impregnable. Outside the Hold itself was the town, bigger than any Saskia had ever seen.

"Who knows about me here?" Saskia asked nervously.

"Only my brother. My nephew, Lirallen, the lord of Clan Berenna, will have to know also. Trust me, Saskia, you will be safe here. Home at last," Rianna added to herself. She smiled at Saskia. "I have not been here in over twenty years."

Rianna's brother, the Clanlord himself, came out to greet them, obviously summoned by a messenger from the scouting group. He was an old man, but straight backed still on a tall red warhorse, and his dark eyes still flashed as sharp as an eagle's. "Beloved sister," he said gruffly, holding his arms out to Rianna. "You never wrote me enough letters."

Rianna threw herself into her brother's arms and burst into tears. Saskia sat and fidgeted with her reins. At last the old warlord turned to her.

"You must be Saskanna," he said. "I am glad to have you here. The Clans welcome another daughter."

The Berenna warlord, Lirallen, the Clanlord's son and Rianna's nephew, came out to greet them also. He was a tall, serious man in his twenties, dark as all the Clansmen and very like his father with the sharp eagle eyes. For Rianna, though, he had a joyous smile. Rianna was amazed by him: barely a child when she left, she had not expected this grown, powerful warrior.

Chapter 2

Clanhold, Midsummer, the year 2713 after Founding

That first night in Clanhold, Saskia's hair was braided and secured with the engraved ring of beaten silver, as she was officially adopted into Clan Berenna as Rianna's daughter. She ate in the great hall at the Clanlord's right hand, and every warrior in the room fell in love with her. It was the day before her thirteenth birthday.

The following morning was not so much fun. Rianna was happy enough with Saskia's progress in the Power, but insisted she needed to get fitter in her body. She sent Saskia out running with the young women of Clanhold. Twice around the walls in the Midsummer heat and Saskia was gasping. Another girl slowed to keep pace with her.

"How far do you run?" Saskia asked painfully.

"Ten times or more around. Depends! I'm Liara. You're Saskanna, aren't you?"

"That's right." Saskia stopped, unable to run another step. "I think this is going to be hard," she said ruefully, when she finally managed to get some breath back.

Liara laughed. "You'll get there." She was very beautiful, small, with long dark hair and midnight eyes. A couple of years older than Saskia, she had an air of authority.

"Saskanna di'Berenna," Saskia said, remembering her manners.

"Adopted of Berenna," Liara said musingly. "I am Liara ca'Berenna."

"The royal line of Berenna," Saskia replied, with an acknowledging tip of her head. Liara must be the youngest daughter the Clanlord had mentioned last night, with an indulgent note in his voice. Liara outranked her by far. Not as a Princess of Iceden, of course, but that Saskia must keep to herself.

"I think I like you," Liara said. "Come on. I'll help you run."

Liara was friendly to Saskia. Saskia did wonder why, briefly, but at last worked it out: the older girl was lonely. She had friends, mostly daughters of other Clan Warlords, but none within the Berenna. In addition, they were not so much friends as sycophants, agreeing with every word the Clanlord's daughter spoke. Saskia was grateful for a friend, and Liara was good fun, always chatting and laughing. She liked to flirt with the young men about the hold, and was always in some mischief or another.

* * * *

On Saskia's twentieth day in the Clanhold, she at last managed her tenth circuit of Clanhold's walls, encouraged all the way by Liara.

Rianna nodded approvingly when Saskia came in, gasping and dripping with sweat. "Time for the swords," she said.

"But I have learnt the swords already, from you," Saskia said. "You have taught me a great deal: surely I need not train to be a warrior!"

Rianna shook her head. "Trust me, Saskia. If you do not learn the swords, one day you will be sorry for it. Let Liara introduce you to Erhallen."

"Who's Erhallen?" Saskia asked Liara during their midday meal.

"My half-brother, why?"

"Your half-brother, does that mean he's Lord Lirallen's full brother?"

"That's right, he's the Berenna Master of Swords," Liara shrugged.

"Lady Rianna has asked that you introduce me to him. She would like me to learn the sword."

Liara looked surprised. "You're very old to learn," she said. "I was using a sword by the time I could walk."

"Do you still practice?" Saskia asked eagerly, hoping to be able to learn with her friend.

"Light, no, I gave that up. Erhallen is just too hard a taskmaster, and I have no need for bulging muscles! I don't envy you at all. I'll take you to meet him later."

* * * *

Erhallen looked very much like Lirallen, though he was a few years younger at only twenty. A warrior born, he was the finest swordsman in his Clan. He looked critically at Saskia.

"Not much muscle on you, is there?" he said disparagingly, tapping her forearm. Saskia twitched away, unaccustomed to being touched by men.

"All right. Let's see what my aunt Rianna has taught you."

Rianna had confined Saskia's teaching to the most basic of moves: how to draw, hold and sheath the sword correctly, and how to swing it without chopping bits of herself off. Erhallen nodded finally in grudging approval.

"Good. Rianna has not taught you any bad habits at least! Now, we will start all over again. That sword is too short for you: Rianna bought one in her own length, but you are a half-head taller than she, and so you need a blade a half-hand longer. Come, we will go and have a look in the stores and find something more suitable."

Saskia followed the rather brusque young man docilely. He put several different swords into her hand and told her to move through a few simple steps with them. Finally he gave her one sword which might have been made for her: it balanced perfectly in her hand and was comfortable. An old blade, with a worn grip, still it was well polished and cared for, without any nicks.

Erhallen nodded approvingly. "Excellent," he said. "When I'm done with you, you'll be able to fight with any weapon that comes into your hand. That's your sword, at least for now until you grow some more. Keep it with you, and you'd better look after it or there'll be trouble. That was Lirallen's sword when he was a boy."

"Oh, surely some other, then," Saskia said.

"Why? It's too short for him now, and he has no son yet. Better by far for it to be used. Come. I want to see how well you move with it."

Now that Saskia had the right sword, she learnt more easily. Muscles built slowly onto her long frame. Luckily she was blessed with fast reflexes, but she had one failing: she feared to attack an opponent, not wanting to hurt anybody. Erhallen and Rianna discussed what they could do to break her of that. Finally Rianna decided a little bit of sorcery was in order.

* * * *

Saskia looked around in surprise when she entered the practice yard. Erhallen was normally there to greet her, but today there was nobody present. She took up her usual practice sword and sheathed it at her side. Of course, her real sword was too dangerous to practice with, and was kept safely in the armoury unless she needed it.

Tapping her fingers on the hilt of her sword, Saskia waited for a while. Finally she turned to leave and stopped dead, staring. Standing in the entry door to the court was her brother Sasken, a real sword dripping with blood in his hand.

Saskia could not think. Later she realised that she could have used Fire to fry Sasken where he stood. When he started for her, sword lowering, she ripped her practice blade from its sheath and went for him with a howl of rage.

Saskia did not hesitate. She went for the killing strike at once. But in moments she was on the back foot as her first reckless swing was parried with contemptuous ease. Saskia soon found herself fighting for her life, using every move Erhallen had taught her. Her rage disappeared and an icy calm settled over her as she began to calculate Sasken's weaknesses and try to turn them against him. Finally she disarmed Sasken, and he fell on his rump. Saskia did not hesitate for an instant. The practice sword struck for his throat – and at the last moment, jammed in the air.

Saskia howled with frustration, let go of the sword and went for Sasken, fully intending to kill him with her bare hands. Her hands were about his throat when his face shimmered and

34

changed. It was a young Clansman in front of her, one whom she knew, another of Erhallen's pupils. She had never been able to beat him.

Clapping started behind her. Getting to her feet, Saskia turned to face Rianna and Erhallen.

"Well done, daughter," Rianna said. "I do not think you will hesitate again to kill."

"You used Air to create an illusion," Saskia said. "Light, Rianna, I could have *killed* him!" The young Clansman was staggering to his feet behind her, clutching at his throat.

Rianna nodded. "The point was to see if you could. I knew the killing instinct was in you. Now think of this, Saskia. If I could make Irinnan look like Sasken – why could another sorcerer not make Sasken look like Irinnan? Or Erhallen, or even me? I chose Irinnan because he is close to your father's height and build, and I understand your brother is much the same. But a skilled bit of trickery with Air, and you might find Sasken disguised as a friend."

Saskia paled. "You are saying that I cannot trust anybody," she said.

"That's right. Nobody except yourself. You have Gift enough to detect Air illusions, even to make them, when you are thinking rationally."

"Rationally is right," Erhallen added. "You nearly lost that fight because you lost your temper. But then you got it back under control, and you started thinking. That's when you won. And now you know, you can kill even if you aren't in a berserk rage."

"I don't mind admitting you frightened the life out of me," Irinnan added. "Your eyes went so cold. I could see my own death in them."

"So will Sasken, if I ever get him at the point of my sword," Saskia said fiercely. "I have much yet to learn if I am ever to face him, though. Thank you, Rianna. I understand now what Erhallen has been trying to teach me. I will not hesitate to go for the kill again."

Saskia progressed very quickly after that. Irinnan could never match her again, and soon she was beyond the rest of

Erhallen's students.

Finally the day came when Erhallen took out practice swords for them both. "Come at me," he ordered.

Saskia obeyed, pressing the attacks as he had taught her. She was surprised to find that she had faster reflexes than Erhallen, despite his training. Finally though, his reach and strength told and she stood weaponless and sweating in the practice yard.

Saskia was astonished to hear applause. Turning, she saw the Clanlord, Rianna and Lirallen, all clapping. She looked back at Erhallen in surprise.

"Did I not tell you?" Erhallen said to them.

"What?" Saskia asked in confusion.

"She fights like one born to the sword," Lirallen said admiringly. "Saskia, Erhallen and I have seen many young men and women train with the sword, ever since they were big enough to hold a stick. But I've never seen anyone your age with that kind of ability. It's raw still and untrained, but you learn more in a week than a Clan warrior would learn in a month."

"I would not have believed it if I had not seen it for myself," the Clanlord said. "Your foster-daughter will bring honour to Clan Berenna, sister."

Saskia turned back to Erhallen. "You never said I was any good," she accused.

The young man's granite-hard face softened. "Foster-cousin," he said. "I did not want to speak until I was sure. I am sure now. You will better me with the sword before we are done."

* * * *

A little before Midwinter, Clan Berenna moved back to their hold, in the hills overlooking the Dark Coast. Saskia absolutely adored living at Berennahold. She missed Liara, who had stayed with her father at Clanhold, but had a new best friend in Erhallen, who became her self-appointed guardian as well as teacher. Saskia learned faster and faster with the sword, and grew somewhat taller as well as stronger. Finally she gave Lirallen's old blade back to him and chose herself a new sword, another half-hand longer. Her fifteenth birthday was the day she first bested Erhallen in the practice yard.

Then, one day not long after, all their lives changed forever. An Imperial rider came into Berennahold with a message. The Emperor was dead. He had been in Summerlands visiting the family of his dead wife, and an assassin had murdered him. The man was an Envetierran fanatic, from their heretical Church of Chaos. The Summerlanders had armed for war and sailed to South Envetierra. The Church of Chaos had been destroyed, and most of its priests executed.

The damage had already been done, though, and now the Empire stood without a crowned lord. The Emperor had a son, but the Ceremony of Earth in the Citadel had shown him to be false in his heart and hungry for power. The Crowning Stone had struck him dead. Most of the Lords of the Empire were riding in, distantly related to the Imperial line, to see who the Ceremony of Earth would accept as the Emperor.

"Clan Berenna has the right to go," Rianna said when Saskia asked her. "My great-great-great-grandmother bore a son to a younger son of an Emperor. I am of that line. You are not, but you must come with me anyway, I dare not leave you alone. We will stay at the Citadel until you are sixteen, and then the new Emperor will help you."

Saskia was astonished at the warlike way in which Clan Berenna had prepared and garbed, almost as though they were riding to fight a war and not to find their overlord. She asked Rianna why.

"When the Emperor is crowned, we will offer him our swords," Rianna explained. "Come, child. We go to Clanhold to meet my father and Liara. From there, it is not so many days to the Citadel."

Saskia was pleased at the idea of seeing Liara again: she had not seen her in a year and a half, since leaving Clanhold for Berennahold. She rode eagerly into Clanhold looking for her friend.

* * * *

37

Liara had changed very little. Saskia knew she was still unwed, the Clanlord wanting to keep his last child with him. She had not expected to find Liara lying at her ease on a couch in Clanhold's central garden, surrounded by a positive army of suitors, both Clan and outlanders.

"Liara?" Saskia said hesitantly. She had sent Liara a letter to say that she was coming.

Liara sat up. "Saskanna!" she exclaimed. She cast a disparaging eye over Saskia's scruffy riding leathers. "My dear, don't you want to get changed?"

Saskia felt like a fool. Of course she should have gone to her rooms and bathed before coming to find Liara. She stood, feeling rather embarrassed, unsure of what to say.

"My, my, who is this?" a young man dressed in ForstMarch green said. He strode towards Saskia and took her hand to kiss it.

"I am Saskanna di'Berenna," Saskia said, the lie rolling easily off her tongue after so much practice.

"I am *most* honoured to meet you, my lady. I am Erisien vos Verstadt, from Forstport."

Several of the other young men crowded around, introducing themselves. Confused, Saskia accepted the cup of cool fruit punch Erisien pressed upon her.

Liara stared. Only a couple of her most persistent admirers stayed at her side. What in the Light were they all fussing over Saskanna for? She looked dreadful: grown even taller since Liara had seen her last, she was on an eye level with most of the men and taller than a couple. Her ghastly silvery hair was escaping from her Clan ring, falling loosely around her face: her tanned face looked weird against the ghostly paleness of her hair. She looked tired and dusty, smears of road dirt on her hands and cheek. What was all the fuss about?

The men saw something entirely different: a statuesque, yet slender young woman, with magnificently unusual colouring and beautiful eyes.

Saskia was tired and a little unhappy. Her friend was looking at her with cold eyes, and all these strangers were fussing over her. At that moment Erhallen walked into the garden. His sword hand went up to grasp the hilt of the long blade slung across his back, but then he took in the situation and grinned.

"Sister," he bowed gracefully to Liara. "We have missed you at Berennahold, you have not visited your home in a long time."

Liara flushed slightly. "Brother, my home is with our father until I am wed. I accompany him on his travels, but he has no cause to visit Berennahold this year."

Saskia drank down the cup of punch swiftly and turned to Erhallen. "Erhallen, do you know where our rooms are, I need a bath?" she said.

Erhallen winced, hearing what the young men would be hearing, the implication that they shared rooms. "Your rooms are beside Lady Rianna's," he said politely. "I will escort you there, if you misremember the way."

"Thank you," Saskia said formally, realising what she had said. She tilted her head as Erisien took her empty cup, then bowed to Liara. "I am sure I shall see you at dinner, foster-cousin."

Liara's blood was up. What did Saskanna think she was doing, swanning in here as though she were truly Clan Blood royalty instead of some mere foundling Rianna had taken a fancy to? And to add insult to injury, Lord Erisien of Forstport and the handsome young Erinean lord had not even returned to Liara's side, but stood conversing quietly together. A couple of the young Clansmen moved away to join them even as she watched.

* * * *

The Clanlord was surprised to see his daughter in the middle of the afternoon, especially when she stormed into his study and slumped down in a chair.

"What is wrong, my angel?" he said indulgently.

"Saskanna."

The Clanlord frowned for a moment, trying to recall the name. "Oh, Rianna's adoptive daughter? What has she done, my sweet?"

"Why is she here with the Berenna to go to the Citadel? She

has no Imperial blood, and will only be a drain on Clan resources. Surely it would be better to have her simply remain here."

"If you would prefer that she did not come, daughter, of course I will tell Rianna to leave the girl here."

"Thank you, papa," Liara's pout was transformed into a smile. She kissed her father's cheek and ran out.

Rianna came in not long after to greet her brother. "You look tired, Livallen, you should get more rest," she said, hugging him.

"It's hard work, governing the Clans, sister," he said with a sigh. "Sometimes I feel very old."

There were almost twenty years in age between the two of them: there had been six sisters in between, but every one had married outClan and settled far away. Rianna and Livallen had not really become friends until they were both growing old. Even now, Livallen still had a tendency to treat Rianna as the baby sister who must be cared for. He smiled down at her now.

"This foster-daughter of yours," he said. "She is not of our blood, not of the Imperial lines. Leave her here when we go to the Citadel."

"What? I'm not leaving her anywhere, Livallen: have you lost your mind? She might not be of the Imperial blood, but have you forgotten who she is?"

"No, sister, I have not. But have you considered that there will be Icelanders in the Citadel, who will take one look at her and *know* her for what she is? She is not sixteen for a while yet, am I right?"

"A few months," Rianna admitted. "But don't you see, Livallen, I could stay in the Citadel with her after the crowning, present her to the new Emperor. It's got to be as soon as possible after her birthday, for her sisters' sake. Consider: what if a Berenna were to be chosen? Lirallen and Erhallen are both fine boys, they have as much of a chance as any to the crown."

Livallen paused. "The Ceremony chose a Clanlander once before," he said slowly. "Three hundred years ago one of Davria's was chosen as the Emperor."

"It is not impossible."

Livallen shrugged. "Oh, all right, then," he said irritably. "Bring the girl. But you can think up a good reason to tell Liara."

"Liara wanted her left behind?"

"That's right. I thought those two were friends?"

"So did I. I'll have to ask Saskanna about it."

Saskia was polishing her sword when Rianna walked in. She looked up and smiled. "Hello. Would you like a cup of tea?"

"No, thanks, dear." Rianna sat down and looked thoughtfully at Saskia's head, bent over the bright steel blade. "What did you say to Liara?" she asked.

"I beg your pardon?" Saskia looked up.

"Liara's in a snit over something. I was asked to leave you behind while we went to the Citadel. No, it's all right," as she saw a spark of fear in Saskia's eyes. "She does not know who you are, and I have told my brother he speaks nonsense. You're coming with us. What did you say, though? I thought the two of you were friends."

"I said nothing, I have barely seen Liara," Saskia said in bewilderment. She told Rianna about the incident in the garden. "I cannot imagine why Liara should have taken offence at that," she said.

Rianna could imagine only too well. She covered her mouth in amusement at the thought of her haughty niece taken down a few pegs.

"Me neither," she told Saskia.

Saskia frowned at her foster-mother, unsure if Rianna was being serious. Then she shrugged and returned to polishing her sword.

* * * *

The Clan group left Clanhold the following morning. There were thirty-eight Clansmen and women eligible to stand at the ceremony. Some of Liara's outClan suitors were travelling with them as well, most notably Erisien vos Verstadt, who made a positive nuisance of himself around Saskia. That drove Liara into an even bigger temper. She was already enraged that Saskia was along on the journey, but the total defection of the handsomest and most highly-titled of her suitors maddened her further.

Erhallen was riding at Saskia's side. The two of them were accustomed to having time and space to talk, and the constant presence of Erisien was an irritant. He rode cheerfully along on Saskia's other side, pointing out animals and birds she had noticed and recognised long before. After the third time Erisien said;

"Oh, *look*, Saskanna, there's a fox!" Saskia shared a look with Erhallen. She turned back to Erisien with a sweet smile and clenched the fingers of her right hand, gathering the Power to her.

Erisien's pretty bay mare suddenly twitched, then bucked.

"Oh, my lord Erisien, please!" Saskia said, fumbling with her reins. "Your horse is frightening mine!" she made her gelding rear up.

Erisien moved his mare away. She twitched and wriggled under him.

"What did you do to that poor mare?" Rianna asked fiercely, catching up.

"I just made her ears itch, like sweetoak itch. I'll feed her sugar tonight to make up, I promise, and it'll wear off in a few minutes. But if he points another animal out to me I swear I'll scream, and that would have made the poor thing jump much worse."

Rianna did think it was funny. Nevertheless, she shook her head at Saskia. "You shouldn't use it for frivolous things," she said.

"I know, and I'm sorry," Saskia said penitently.

"All right, child. How about I ride here, and then Erisien will not be able to bother you quite so much?"

Saskia's smile was brilliant with relief. "I would like that, foster-mother," she said.

It took them fifteen days to reach the Citadel. They were travelling slowly, aware that groups from other parts of the Empire would be converging, many of them coming from much further away. There was no need to hurry.

Saskia was utterly awed by the Citadel. She had seen two of the principal Empire forts, Iceden and Clanhold. Iceden, with its clean white spire reaching to the sky, was impressive in its way, and the sheer sprawling bulk of the Clanhold inspired awe. The Citadel was the oldest and greatest stronghold of all. Like Iceden it had been built all at one time and other buildings had grown up around the main fortress to make the city.

The Citadel palace was built out of golden stone that seemed to reflect the sunlight. It stood on a high hill, and the city sprawled down around it, spreading out over the plain below. The palace itself was as high as Iceden's spire, but with many great towers instead of only one, one tower for each province. From each tower flew a province flag, but the central, highest tower flew no flag, because the Empire had no lord.

"Recite the province flags for me," Rianna said softly to Saskia as they rode towards the city.

"Black for the Clanlands, green for ForstMarch, red for the Desert, purple for the Seal Islands, white with a purple star for the Icelands, blue and silver vertical stripes for Haven, blue with a white wave for Eastphal, red with a white triangle for Westphal, green with a golden wheatsheaf for the Summerlands, green with three grey mountains for the Roman'ii Tribes, grey and red horizontal stripes for Erinea, black with a red cross for Envetierra, grey and white diagonal lines for Zahennarra," Saskia recited. She could not see them all, not clearly from this distance, but the knowledge had been drilled into her, both as an Icelander Princess and in the Clanhold. "Why are the Roman'ii Tribes given a flag with the provinces when they own no land, Rianna?"

"The Roman'ii once had one of their own chosen Emperor," Rianna shrugged. "He gave the Tribes the right to be on an equal footing and formalised their laws. They may not formally own land, but it is their land nonetheless. No one else owns it, and they care for it well and give their fealty and their quota of fighting men to the Empire. They have as much right as the Clans. I think that perhaps they are not so different from us."

Saskia accepted that from what she had read. The Roman'ii were a southern people like the Clans, dark in colouring. They loved horses just as the Clan and Desertmen did, although some of their customs were strange, from what she had read. For one, their chiefs were allowed to take as many as three wives, if his first wife proved infertile! And marriage itself was a peculiar business: if a Roman'ii could steal away a girl who was unpromised and keep her with him for one full moon, they were wed as legally as though the ceremony had been performed in a Temple of the Light. But, romantically, he was not permitted to keep the girl by force, before he lay with her he had to place his knife in her hand and put it to his own throat, so that it was always her choice.

Saskia wished for that kind of freedom. She fell into a pleasant little dream, riding along, of some darkly handsome Roman'i tribesman, who'd steal her away and protect her all her days.

"Saskanna!" Rianna snapped. "Do look where you're going!"

Saskia jerked slightly. She had almost let her horse put his foot in a pothole. Glancing guiltily at Rianna, she smiled and took up her grip on the reins.

* * * *

They rode on down towards the river, the Empire Water, the trade route and lifeblood of the Citadel. There were houses around them now, the homes of those who did not wish to live in the city itself. They arrived at the ferry dock and boarded the waiting ferry. There were three: always one at each dock and one in transit. The trip across took them about ten minutes, and then they were in the city itself, riding out of the docking area and up to the city's great square, passing by the markets on the way.

Saskia had heard a great deal about the markets of the Citadel, and longed to go into the Great Market, where it was said anything in the world could be bought, or into the food market, full of exotic tastes and scents. They passed through the city square and rode on up the Empire Way to the Citadel itself, massive and brooding before them on its high hill. At the gates they were challenged, but finally they were allowed to enter inside the great ring fortress and ride all the way across it to the Clan tower.

The Citadel was immense, a ring of high golden stone walls

with the thirteen towers spread out along the perimeter. The central palace was a fortress within the fortress itself, with its own separate walls and gate, opposite the main gate into the Citadel. The palace gate was closed. Saskia knew that inside was a self-sufficient keep, with its own stables, servants quarters and kitchens. Between the palace and the Citadel's walls were various other buildings, more stables, the Guard barracks and grassy walled gardens. The rest of the area was cobbled, for the horses to walk on.

The Clansmen were staying in the tower that flew the black flag of the United Clans. The tower was the same as the other twelve, with living quarters, and its own kitchens. The rooms spread out through the walls on either side of the tower until they eventually merged into the neighbouring province's rooms, the Desert on one side and Erinea on the other. The group of Clansmen found that their tower was more than big enough for all of them, even Saskia had a private room of her own. Saskia was pleased that her room was right next door to the suite of three rooms allotted to Liara. She went in to greet her friend, hoping that Liara had forgiven her for being brought to the Citadel. Liara greeted Saskia pleasantly enough, especially when the younger girl helped her to unpack and hang up her clothes. Liara had no dedicated maid here as in the Clanhold, and was not looking forward to having to do nearly everything for herself.

Liara adored the Citadel, though. It was full of nobility from all over the Empire, and she, as one of the most highly born and beautiful among them, was in great demand. She had soon gathered a little group of female hangers-on, and a selection of new male admirers. She still resented the loss of Erisien vos Verstadt to Saskia, who persisted in ignoring the young man, with greater ease now that he was residing in the Forst tower with his lord the Duke of ForstMarch.

Erhallen and Lirallen had their share of admirers too, among Liara's little coterie. The two men took to spending most of their time with Saskia and Rianna, exploring the great city, meeting a few of the other people who had no wish to mingle with the crowd.

Chapter 3

The Citadel, Spring, the year 2716 after Founding

At last, on a warm balmy day in mid-spring, the declarations for the crown were closed. The Ceremony of Earth would be held on the following day, and the Imperial crown set on the head of the chosen one of Imperial blood. The Ceremony itself was held outside the Citadel, in a grove beyond the city consecrated to the Light. Saskia was forbidden to attend, as no Imperial blood ran in her veins, and even Rianna would not countermand that order.

The Clan party left in the middle of the night, as they had to be in the grove before sunrise. A few minutes later, Saskia sneaked quietly out of the Clan tower and down to the stables to get her horse. She had already scouted a route to the grove, planning to arrive just a few minutes after the others did.

Finding the place she had marked, Saskia tethered her horse in a concealed thicket before heading towards the centre of the grove. The centre was a shallow dish-shaped valley, with low hills around it. Saskia had picked out the hill furthest away from the route out that the new Imperial party would take.

Saskia crawled quietly to the top of the hill, staying well down in the tall grass. At last she saw the group below and stopped, lying still in the grass.

The Crowning Stone looked incongruous in the middle of the grassy grove, with the grass around it cut short. The Stone itself was about waist-high, black and squarish, with a flat top. From the top protruded the hilt of the Imperial Sword, and around the handle of the sword rested the Imperial Crown, a gorgeous thing of Desert diamonds and massive coloured gems.

Around the Stone, not getting too close, stood the Imperial Blood contenders for the crown. Saskia was surprised at how many there were within the required eighth generation of blood kinship: there must be a good three hundred or more people down there. In addition, there were three representatives from the Temple of the Light, the senior priest and a young priest and priestess to stand with him.

Saskia spotted the Berenna group, a large contingent, the Clanlord, his sister Rianna and his four daughters and two sons, with the contenders from the other two eligible Clans. Saskia was still watching them when the senior priest raised his hands and a tingle of Power raced along her bones. Saskia saw Rianna flinch: it must be quite a bit more intense down there.

There was a sudden scuffling noise behind Saskia, and then someone kicked her hard in the ribs and fell over onto her.

Saskia swallowed a scream and struggled. The person rolled off her.

"Gosh, I'm sorry, what are you doing here?"

Saskia looked into a pair of intense blue eyes. They were in the tanned, sharp-cheekboned face of a young man.

"You clumsy oaf!" she hissed, enraged, feeling at the tender spot in her side. "Why in the Light couldn't you look where you were going? Quite apart from anything else, you could have blundered straight into that little show!"

"I'm sorry, I'm not used to grass." He regarded her for a moment. "I'm Aleksandr von Chenuwska."

"Saskanna di'Berenna," she said reluctantly. Aleksandr had to be about two years older than her, she supposed. At a guess he would be not quite eighteen, not quite old enough to stand in the gathering below.

"I'm sorry I fell over you," Aleksandr apologised. "I hope you're not hurt. Berenna, but you're not a Clanlander, are you?" he looked her up and down, seeing a beautiful girl, slim and long-bodied, with a mane of pale silvery hair. Her pretty face was tanned to a pale copper, and eyes of the most remarkably pure purple colour stared back at him.

"I'm adopted," Saskia gave her standard reply. She looked him up and down in return. Dressed in tanned leather vest and trousers, his dark hair cut short, even if he had not made the comment about being unused to grass, it was obvious what he had to be. He was remarkably handsome: slim and muscular. Saskia was accustomed to athletic young men among the Clans, though: it was Aleksandr's blue eyes that fascinated her. She had not met anybody with eyes so pale since leaving Iceden.

"You're a Desertman," she said.

"I am that, Lady."

Cries and shouts came from the crowd below them. Both Saskia and Aleksandr turned and craned their necks to see.

The Imperial crown was floating in midair, flashing in the early morning sun. Two people were lying dead on the ground, and everyone else had drawn back from them.

"What's going on?" Saskia exclaimed.

"At a Crowning ceremony, sometimes there are those there with such lust for power that they will kill and kill again to get to the throne, to try to corrupt the Empire in the way of their choosing. The Crowning Stone will strike them dead."

The crown was still floating. It seemed to be moving in a slow circle over the heads of the assembled, almost as though searching for someone.

"It should have chosen by now," the young Desert lord said, puzzled. "Oh, look, it's hovering over my lord Jeskarin!"

Saskia knew that name: Jeskarin was the Lord of Firehold, a title that carried with it the overlordship of the Red Desert territories. She looked now, and saw a tall dark man with a kindly face. But the crown was floating onward. It hovered for a second over Lirallen and then moved on.

The priest increased the amount of Power he was channelling, Saskia could feel it, hot on her skin. The crown lifted higher, and at last sped up and floated purposefully away from the crowd of candidates towards the hill where the two young people lay concealed. An instant later Saskia understood. She took one desperate look at Aleksandr von Chenowska, and rolled hastily away, looking for denser foliage to hide in. The crown hovered for an instant over Aleks, lying in the grass, and then settled onto his head. The crowd and the priests began walking up towards him, craning their necks to try and see who had been crowned.

Aleks felt unbelievingly at the crown on his head. He

looked quickly around for Saskia, but she was gone. He stood to face the crowd.

"Lord von Chenowska!" Lord Jeskarin exclaimed, recognising him at once. He turned to the rest of the group. "May I have the honour of presenting our new Emperor, Aleksandr von Chenowska!"

* * * *

The priests led Aleksandr to the Crowning Stone for the final tests. With his hands on the Stone, it lit up and glowed from within. The sword slid free easily in his hands and a cheer went up.

Aleksandr glanced down in surprise as a girl appeared at his side. She was short, and very beautiful, with her dark curly hair. She curtsied to him, giving him a look at her generous cleavage.

"My lord," the dark girl said breathily, "I am Liara ca'Berenna."

"Honoured, my lady," Aleksandr said politely. She flashed him a smile, and then melted into the crowd.

Puzzled, Aleks turned to receive the congratulations of the Clanlord, who smiled indulgently. "That's my youngest, Liara. A good girl."

Aleks recoiled. Was he already having these women thrown at him, to gain power by association? Liara was indeed pretty, but the thought repelled him. Instead, he found himself recalling a remarkable pair of amethyst eyes. Who was she? A Clanlander: he debated asking the Clanlord about her, but then it occurred to him that the girl had obviously been forbidden to attend the ceremony, and he might get her into trouble.

Aleks clutched the Imperial sword in his fist and looked around nervously. He was good with a sword, very good, in fact. An old armsman had taken the orphaned boy under his wing and taught him everything he knew. The priests were approaching him warily, eyes on the sword and the competent way he held it. One of them wordlessly offered a scabbard. Another led forward a tall bay stallion.

* * * *

Back at the Citadel, the priests took Aleks to the throne room and seated him on the throne for the Council of Thirteen, representatives from each province, to kneel before him and offer up their rights to govern in his name. The Council only existed in the time between the crowning of Emperors, and now they would disband again.

The criers were already out in the streets, proclaiming Aleksandr as the Chosen Emperor. Archivists were looking up his name and lineage: they tutted over his youth, but the Ceremony of Earth chose as it willed and there was nothing anyone could do to revoke the choice.

Aleks was utterly bemused. The priests draped a costly blue and gold robe around him, showed him how the Imperial sword slotted into the side of his throne, and straightened the crown on his dark hair.

Aleks sat on the throne and looked down at the Council of Thirteen, kneeling before him. He spoke the brief words of acceptance as coached by the priests.

Now came the hardest part of the ceremony. Before all of the Imperial Blood assembled, Aleks knelt on the golden sunburst inlaid into the white marble tiles in the centre of the throne room. Sword in hands, he lifted it high, and spoke the words learnt by every child.

"Know, my country, that should an enemy ever profane your beloved soil, that each of your children was born a soldier, to fight and die in your defence, to uphold truth and the rights of all your people in the Light." He paused, and added the words the priests had hastily coached him in. "Mine to have and to hold, mine to protect all my days, I swear that my sword will be the first lifted in your defence, that I will be the one to lead your people for your glory, Light willing, with the last drop of my heart's blood."

* * * *

The throne room was deathly silent. Rianna shared a

surprised look with Erhallen, standing beside her. This young man, this young Emperor, spoke with true passion and belief. He truly loved the Empire. That, Rianna supposed, was why the Ceremony had chosen him. Watching, she stared in astonishment as Aleks slowly crumpled to the floor.

Aleks could not believe what was happening to him. One moment he was holding the sword aloft, and the next it was unbelievably heavy, dragging his arms down. The crown was equally heavy, and he blacked out for a moment. When he woke, two priests were kneeling, one on each side of him.

"It is all right, my lord, do not panic," one of them murmured. "What you feel is the weight of Duty. The Empire demands a great deal of her lord. You will grow accustomed to the weight in a few days."

Aleks could feel the weight, not just the crown and sword, but a pressure like invisible hands dragging down all over his body. With an effort he pulled himself to his feet and waved to the crowd.

* * * *

Two days later, Aleks was presented to the people of the Citadel. In the city's main square was the Palace of Justice, the law courts. On the first floor was a balcony, and there it was traditional for the Emperor to stand and greet his people, at the beginning of his reign and on the same day every year after that.

Aleks raised his hands, and the massive crowd gathered below the balcony cheered. He could not stop his eyes searching for a specific face, though he knew that he would never be able to pick her out of such a crowd.

Where was she? he mused. Since the crown had settled on his head, every lord and lady of any noble birth at all had trooped through the palace to pay their respects. When the Berenna clan came to offer their swords, he had looked for her, but she was not there. He had debated asking the Berenna warlord, Lirallen, about Saskanna, but suspected that the fierce young warlord would give him no answer.

Unbidden, an image of clear lilac eyes in a copper-tanned

face, surrounded by that mane of silvery white hair, rose up before his eyes.

Back in his office in the palace keep, Aleks sat down at his desk and took his crown off with a sigh. Putting it on the desk, he rubbed at his head for a moment. Frowning thoughtfully, he didn't realise he was drumming his fingers on the polished wood desk until his secretary Arryn spoke.

"My lord, I served the last Emperor with utter discretion," Arryn said gently. "I will do no less for you. Please, my lord, tell me what is bothering you. Maybe I can help."

Aleks sighed. "I have no one else to ask, and I will go mad if I do not know. There is a girl, Arryn. No, not like that!" as the smaller man's eyes widened. "I have only met her once. She told me her name was Saskanna di'Berenna. Find her for me."

"The 'di' prefix denotes an adopted Clanlander. Saskanna is a northern name, though, maybe Havener or Zahennarran."

"Find out. Find out who she is, who her family is, why she has been adopted into a royal old Clan."

"My lord." Arryn bowed and left.

* * * *

Arryn was quick and efficient. In the Hall of Records, all the records from all the provinces were kept, updated every year with births, marriages and deaths. The Clan records were divided simply by Clan, and the Berenna section was large and easy enough to find. There was only one adoption recognised in the last five years. Arryn took the thin sheet of parchment and began to read. He frowned slightly, turned the page over to look at the back, then frowned some more.

Aleks was not by nature patient, but when Arryn returned within two hours, even he was impressed.

"What have you found?" Aleks asked eagerly.

"I have found the record of her adoption. I copied out the certificate." Arryn handed over a single sheet of paper.

Aleks scanned the paper, and scowled. "But this tells me nothing! Her place of birth, the date, even her parents are listed as unknown!"

"She is a foundling, my lord, perhaps left in some temple to die."

"But it says here that she was adopted aged approximately thirteen. What in the Light took the Clans so long?"

"An intriguing mystery. Why don't you ask her adoptive mother, Rianna ca'Berenna?"

Aleks frowned. "I do remember *her*, I think, a formidable lady. Yes. Summon her."

Rianna wondered why the Emperor would be summoning her. Saskia had been too frightened to admit she had been in the grove and met Aleksandr. She had pretended illness the day the rest of the Clan went to the palace to present themselves to him. Rianna had shrugged it off, knowing there were only a few weeks remaining until Saskia's sixteenth birthday. Liara had been quite cruel, unknowingly, when she told Saskia how handsome the new young Emperor was.

"There's only a few weeks in age between us," Liara said, smiling dreamily. "And he's such a gorgeous man: such blue eyes, so tall!"

Liara's sycophants were already whispering of her as a potential bride for the Emperor. She would, after all, be a most eligible match: born of the highest blood in the oldest Clan. Added to which, she was young, beautiful, and born of a fertile line.

Rianna swept regally into the Throne Hall. Aleks was not seated on the throne, but standing by one wall, examining a beautiful tapestry there, depicting the wedding of the last Emperor and his lady, a southern lady from a tiny holding in Summerlands. The Lady Asparia had brought no dowry, being the youngest of five, no great alliances, nothing but herself. Rianna had known Asparia briefly when she came to Iceden with the Emperor, and could not remember ever seeing a couple happier or more in love.

But why was the young Emperor studying the tapestry of his distant cousin's marriage? Perhaps he had left his lady behind in the Desert, and hoped to bring her here as his bride. Rianna smiled fondly at the handsome young man.

"My Lady Rianna," Aleks said, returning her smile. He

53

shook his head when she made to curtsy to him. "No, my lady, do not stand on ceremony! I have seen too much of it these last few days."

"It must be hard on you," Rianna said sympathetically.

Aleks only smiled. "I had a hard childhood, my lady. The Desert is an unforgiving land, and my parents died when I was very young, leaving me alone to face my demons. A child grows up quickly when he must."

Rianna nodded, dark eyes probing his face. Why had he brought her here?

Aleks turned back to the tapestry. "Beautiful, isn't it?" he said, touching the woven threads that made up the Empress' blue and gold wedding gown.

"Indeed, my lord. I met them both, some years ago. The Empress was very beautiful."

"Oh? I never heard that they went to the Clanhold."

"They did not, my lord."

"Then you met them here in the Citadel?"

"No, my lord." Somehow Rianna could not lie. Those blue eyes were piercing, and she realised he was at least somewhat Gifted. In what? she thought frantically. Certainly not in the Power. In Charisma, maybe, that would explain why she felt compelled to tell him everything.

"Where did you meet them?" Aleks asked.

Rianna struggled against the compulsion. "Iceden," she said finally.

"*Iceden*?" He looked astonished. "That's a very long way from Clanhold."

Rianna struggled to smile. "Yes, my lord. I went there as a companion for the princess. I was there when the Emperor and Empress came for the new Prince to be presented at his Naming Day."

Aleks's thoughts suddenly went off onto another track. Purple eyes from Iceden – about the right age. He remembered all the searches that had been made a couple of years ago for a young princess who had run away from Iceden with her mother. The older woman had been taken back in Eastphal, but she had sworn the girl was dead. The continent had been turned upside down looking for her. Had she been hidden away in the Clanlands all this time?

"I met a girl," Aleks said after a few long moments. "She said she was of Berenna."

Rianna thought frantically. Liara, yes, it must be Liara. Aleks dispelled the notion.

"She told me her name was Saskanna, adopted of Berenna."

"Oh, Light help me," Rianna's lips moved silently. "Yes, my lord?" she forced a smile. "Saskanna is my adopted daughter, a sweet girl."

"Very sweet," Aleks smiled. "Who is she, Rianna?"

Rianna froze, trapped by the direct question, unsure of her ability to lie successfully to him. Aleks shocked her again a moment later.

"I think I know who she must be, and she's no foundling. She's of blood more royal than either of us, isn't she? Despite the Old Imperial blood running through our veins, the Icelander royal house has been on their throne a very long time."

Rianna just stared at him. "Oh, Light forgive me, I should not have brought her here," she whispered, tears welling up in her eyes.

"Why have you hidden her for so long?" Aleks asked gently. "I do not believe you would do such a thing without a good reason. What have you hidden her from?"

Rianna could not speak. She stared, shocked, up at Aleks. At last she shook her head. "It is not my secret to tell," she said reluctantly. "If you ask it, I will send for Saskia."

"Is that her true name?"

"It is. I will have her come to you, if you will, and tell you her story. We had hoped to remain undiscovered until Midsummer, because she would be safer then. But you would have had to know anyway."

Rianna made as though to leave, but Aleks caught her arm. "Oh, no, my lady. You will stay here with me. If I let you go to fetch Saskia, how can I know that you will not disappear with her? No, you will write her a note, tell her to meet you." He called for Arryn to bring pen and paper.

Rianna took the pen into her hand. "I will not write it to

Saskia, but to my nephew Erhallen, telling him to bring her here," she said. "Saskia would be too frightened to come alone. Erhallen will see her safe."

* * * *

Aleks read over Rianna's shoulder as she penned the brief note, then gave it to Arryn.

Half an hour later, Erhallen and Saskia were shown into Aleks' private study. Rianna sat in the window seat, pale and nervous. Saskia crossed to her at once.

"Foster-mother, are you quite well?" she asked gently. She herself went pale as Aleks stepped out from the alcove where he had been standing and into her line of vision. "You!"

"My lady Saskia," he said. Saskia did not miss that he used her correct name.

"Oh no, my lord, her name is Saskanna," Erhallen said in a forced tone. He too looked nervous.

"I think not."

"You _told_ him?" Erhallen rounded on Rianna. "_Why_? It's too soon!"

"I didn't tell him!" Rianna said. "He worked it out on his own."

Saskia stared in horror. Her hand felt at her side for her sword, but no one was permitted to carry a blade into the Emperor's presence. Aleks realised her distress and reached for her hand. "Princess, you have nothing to fear. I swear you are safe with me."

Seeing the expression on his face, Rianna and Erhallen traded looks. Rianna's was astonished, and rather pleased. Erhallen's was a study in pain. He had come to love Saskia, and though he had always known she was destined for greatness, had harboured hopes of winning her love in return.

Saskia shook her head. "How much do you know?" she asked in a voice barely above a whisper.

"I know only your name and your birth. Rianna has insisted that the rest is yours to tell."

Saskia braced herself. He will not look at me like this once he knows what I am, she thought. I am a child of sickness and incest, of a pure blood twisted beyond imagining. He will turn away from me in revulsion once he knows.

For all that, it was a relief to finally speak of it. Saskia had not spoken of her family since the day she came to Clanhold. Hesitantly she began.

"A few weeks after my twelfth birthday, my mother woke me up in the middle of the night. She told me that my betrothal had been agreed and I was to be married in two weeks' time."

"Twelve?" Aleks said, astonished. "That's not legal, not even in the Icelands."

"That is not the worst of it. The man I was to marry was my brother, Sasken."

Aleks stared at her speechlessly. "Go on," he said finally.

So Saskia did. She told him everything, the mad flight from Iceden, the revelation of her Gifts, meeting Rianna. Travelling to Clanhold, three years with Clan Berenna. At last she stopped, pausing for a long moment, then began again. "My lord – this incestuous union would not have been the first in the Icelander royal line."

Here Rianna took up the story. "Saskia's mother was married to her own father, who got her on his sister. The Icelander line have been marrying internally for three hundred years."

Aleks looked incredulous. "But how have they kept this hidden?" he said, astonished. "Surely the Emperor would have put a stop to it."

"Of course. It was very simple to hide. They just never announced the birth of daughters, they registered them as daughters of lesser Icelander Blood houses, so no one would come petitioning for an Icelander princess. When the princes married, they gave it out that they always married young ladies of Icelander blood."

Aleks shook his head at Saskia. "I understand now. You were hiding until your sixteenth Birthingday," he said. "After that, you would have the right to petition the Emperor against them."

Saskia nodded. "If they find me now, I will be forced to go

back," she said. "I will be forced to marry my brother, and I will never leave Iceden again."

Aleks nodded. "Then you will just have to remain hidden," he said. "Who else knows this secret?"

"My brother the Clanlord, my nephew Lirallen of Berenna," Rianna said. "Anyone you have told."

"My secretary, Arryn, knows something. I will keep him quiet. You will remain as you are for now, Saskia Cevaria. Erhallen, I charge you with the task of Saskia's safety. On her sixteenth Birthingday, you will deliver her to me here, and Light help you if you do not."

Erhallen nodded, a little sulkily. Aleks saw it and made a mental note to reward Erhallen somehow when this was all over.

Aleks dismissed them. Then he called Arryn in. "How long will it take to organise a coronation ball?" he asked.

"Oh, weeks, my lord."

"Good." Aleks smiled a wolfish grin. "I'm going to need some people to organise one for me."

* * * *

Invitations went out to every lord and lady in the Empire, including the Prince and Princess of the Icelands. On Midsummer's Eve, the Emperor would be holding a grand ball in the Hall of the Citadel. There would be over two thousand guests.

"What is he doing?" Saskia said in a low voice when she read the card, delivered to "Saskanna di'Berenna", that was her invitation. "That's my Birthingday."

"I think that might just be the point, dearheart," Rianna said, unable to stop herself from feeling a little smug.

The day rolled round astonishingly quickly. Saskia had to listen as Liara declared to her cronies that she was sure she would catch the Emperor's eye. Liara had a fabulous dress all in red and gold that her adoring father had bought for her. It was daringly cut, and the tiny dark girl did look very beautiful in it. Saskia thought a little forlornly of her own blue dress, quite simple as Rianna had insisted.

The day of the ball dawned bright and clear, and just before midday there came a knock on the door of the Clan tower. A few minutes later, a servant staggered into Saskia's room, laden down with bundles.

"What is all this?" Rianna demanded.

"Delivered for Miss Saskanna, my lady. There is no message."

"Put them on the bed there."

The two women began to open the parcels. Magnificent jewels tumbled out, a dress, shoes, and a long evening cloak. Saskia held up the dress in awe. It was made of a silver cloth that rippled and caught the light, soft to the touch. The dress was simply cut and the shoes were dyed silver to match it.

The jewels were fabulous too, a strand of thick white pearls to go around her neck and a longer, thinner strand interspersed with amethysts to pin into her hair, with studs for her ears.

The cloak, however, was quite plain, full length and high necked, with a deep hood. It was quite clearly intended to disguise Saskia entirely until the moment was right. The only extravagant thing about the cloak was its colour, the exact purple of Saskia's eyes. Finally, pinned inside the cloak, she found the note.

"I look forward to unmasking you tonight. Aleks."

"Oh, Light, what is he planning?" Saskia said. "I cannot go like this. Liara will kill me for the jewels alone."

"Liara won't know until it's far too late." Rianna smiled mysteriously. "Come on. You had better go and start getting ready."

Chapter 4

The Citadel, Midsummer's Eve,
the year 2716 after Founding

Rianna, Saskia and Erhallen walked across the Citadel's courtyards to the palace together. Rianna had deliberately made excuses to delay until they were very late. They were the very last group of people to walk into the Great Hall to present themselves.

Saskia nearly fainted when she saw her mother and father by the throne. Her mother looked pale and tired. Only Erhallen's strong arm kept Saskia from bolting when her father turned and looked in her direction. The Prince could not possibly have recognised his daughter, cloaked and hooded as she was, but that did not stop a choking fear rising up in Saskia's throat.

The little group walked slowly down through the centre of the hall to bow before Aleks on his throne. He looked absolutely magnificent: clad all in black and silver and crowned with Desert diamonds. His blue eyes flashed as they bowed to him.

"Declare yourselves," his herald said formally.

Rianna laid off her cloak. "I am Rianna ca'Berenna of Clan Berenna, and I offer to you my fealty," she said.

Aleks nodded in acceptance. Then Erhallen repeated the procedure.

"I am Erhallen ca'Berenna of Clan Berenna, and I offer to you my fealty."

At last it was Saskia's turn. Her hands were shaking so much she could barely undo her cloak, but she did, and gave it to Erhallen. Gasps went up around the hall at the beauty of her dress.

"I am Princess Saskia Cevaria of the Royal Blood of

Iceden, named di'Berenna for my adoption into that Clan," she declared formally, "and I offer to you my fealty."

Out of the corner of her eye Saskia saw her father start forward, but somehow there were Imperial Guards in his way. Aleks rose to his feet.

"I accept your oath, Saskia Cevaria," he said formally. "And I would ask of you more than fealty." He stepped down off the dais and took her hand. "Before these witnesses assembled here tonight and before your own kin, I ask you to be my bride."

Saskia's mouth fell open. She could hear the shocked gasps rippling around the hall. Then there was a scream of "No!"

Saskia turned, astonished. It was Liara who had screamed, her pretty face contorted with fury.

"She is no princess! She lies!" Liara shouted.

"Ah, but you are wrong there," said the Prince. Saskia shivered as her father came towards her and took her hand.

"Dearest daughter," he said poisonously. "You have blossomed since I saw you last. You should come home to Iceden." The look he cast over her was positively lustful.

Saskia finally understood what Aleks had done: that he had protected her in the only way he could. The moment she was declared, she was fair game. Her father could easily claim he was protecting her from fortune hunters by taking her home to Iceden. From there, she would never see the world again. Even had she married, her father could have had the man killed. Only if she married a man of equal or greater power could she be free. Aleks was really the only option.

Why? Saskia asked herself. Why had he done this, having met her only twice? Of course, there were political advantages: marrying a princess of the Icelands would bind the principality far more tightly into the Empire. She looked up into Aleks' bright blue eyes. There was really very little choice to make.

"I should be most glad and honoured to plight you my troth, my lord," Saskia said, with a graceful little curtsy.

Aleks smiled delightedly. "Good! My lord prince, will you bless your daughter's troth?" he said.

The Prince gritted his teeth. "Gladly," he said with a forced smile. He shook Aleks' hand rigidly.

Aleks turned back to Saskia and took her hand. On her finger he slipped a ring, a white Desert diamond surrounded by tiny amethysts. "With this ring, I plight thee my troth," he said gently.

"Oh my lord, I have nothing to give you," Saskia said, almost in tears.

Aleks laughed. "Then, my lady, I'll claim what you have to give: a kiss!"

Laughter and cheers rang out as he stooped to capture her lips. Liara stormed from the hall, and the Prince backed away. The Princess came forward, and clasped hands for a moment with Rianna.

"Well done," the princess said softly.

"Did you know?"

"I had a TimeSight vision of her crowned in Desert diamonds. I could not know who the man was, but for sure her brother would never have set diamonds on her brow."

Saskia heard none of this. She was held securely in Aleks' arms as he kissed her.

At last he let her go. "You're safe," he whispered, stroking her hair.

"Thank you," Saskia said. Then she spotted her mother. "MAMA!" she cried out, and ran into her mother's arms. "Oh, I've missed you so!"

Aleks was left standing by himself, looking rather ruefully after her.

* * * *

The ball began in earnest. The Prince left, claiming a headache, much to Saskia's relief. Dozens of people wanted to meet Saskia and her mother, and wanted to know how and why she had hidden for so long. Lord Jeskarin of the Desert came and swept the Princess away for a dance, and Aleks led Saskia onto the floor. Every woman there envied her: beautiful as a sunrise, slim and supple as a willow, she was by far the most beautiful woman in the room, and now betrothed to the Emperor.

Saskia could have danced all night, she was having such a

wonderful time. But at last she was dancing with Aleks when he drew her to a stop, then suddenly through a hidden door, up two flights of stairs, then through another door and out onto a little balcony.

"Oh!" Saskia exclaimed. It was a beautiful night: the stars and moons shone clearly in the night sky above the Citadel's golden walls. "How lovely!"

"Not half so lovely as you," Aleks said, his voice deep. He drew Saskia gently into his arms and kissed her for the second time. No chaste engagement kiss this time, this was a kiss of passion that seared them both to their souls.

When they finally drew apart, both trembling, Saskia looked up into his eyes.

"Why?" she asked.

"Why what, princess?"

"Why do you want to marry me? My blood is tainted and inbred. My father and brother will be nothing but trouble to you. Why me?"

"I loved you that first moment in the glade, with grass stains on your cheek," Aleks said. "All I could think about after being crowned was seeing you again. This seemed like an opportunity sent from heaven. You would *have* to marry me."

Saskia stared up at him in astonishment. "You love me? Already? But how?"

"I don't know." He lifted the Imperial crown from his head, and set it gently on hers. "But I know I want you to be my Empress. Now and forever. We're going to break the chain of Icelander blood. I'll force your father to give me your sisters as companions for you, and settle some pretty fool girl with a huge dowry as a gift for your brother. Your sisters will marry as they choose."

Saskia had no idea how beautiful she was as she stood there, all silver and gems flashing in the darkness. Her radiant smile warmed Aleks' weary heart. He held her hand and turned to look down at the city, quiet and peaceful beneath them.

"I do not know anything about how to be an Emperor," he said softly. "I was born to rule a holding in the Desert. You would like Chenova, Saskia: it is very peaceful. The craftsmen there make beautiful stained glass for the homes of rich lords. I manage Chenova easily: my people like me and we all work hard together to win a living from the sands. But I do not know how to rule an Empire. You were born a princess, brought up to command. You have what I do not: the ability to make everyone around you more concerned for your welfare than their own."

Saskia smiled very slightly to herself. "You have more at your disposal than you might think, my lord," she said.

"What do you mean?"

"Has it ever been said to you that Gifts ran in your family?"

"My mother had a touch of the TimeSight."

"You have more than a touch, my lord, and I don't think TimeSight is what you are Gifted with. You have a certain knack of drawing people's attention, of making them want to tell you what you want to know. You surprised Rianna with it. She believes you to be very powerfully gifted with Charisma."

"And what would Rianna know about Gifts? And you? I never heard that they ran in the Icelander royal family."

"Rianna is a sorceress, my lord, Gifted very greatly with Power. Gifts in the Icelander line have been thin indeed, up until the birth of my siblings and I. Rianna took me because I was the only one Gifted with Power, as well as the oldest daughter. And I am truly Gifted, it seems. Rianna says that I have more Power born into me than anyone in a thousand years."

Aleks shook his head in surprise. "Power-Gifted? Maybe that is why you have lit such a fire in my blood!" He kissed her again. "You said your siblings were Gifted also?"

"Yes, in different ways. Healing, TimeSight, Empathy, LongSight, my sisters have differing degrees. My brother Sasken is very powerfully Gifted with Luck. It is the most unreliable Gift of all, but he can never be underestimated."

They stood there for a long time, Saskia leaning against Aleks trustingly. She was tall for a woman, but he was the tallest man she had ever seen, towering over her.

"Who was that girl who shouted when you declared yourself?" Aleks asked suddenly.

Saskia stiffened. "My adoptive cousin," she said reluctantly. "Liara ca'Berenna, the Clanlord's daughter."

"She is young to be his," Aleks said.

Saskia nodded. "The Clanlord married three times, the last time to a very young girl. Liara was born of that marriage, and she is the apple of his eye."

"Why does she hate you?"

"I do not know, my lord. When I first went to Clanhold, we became friends, but just recently, she has turned entirely against me – I don't know why. The Clanlord can be silly where Liara is concerned, and gives her everything she desires. She asked her father to forbid me to come to the Citadel. Only for Rianna turning on her brother in fury, I would not be here."

Aleks nodded. "It is as I thought, she is jealous of you."

"Of me? But I had nothing, in the Clans. I could not speak of my true birth. Why should Liara be jealous of me?"

"Liara is a pretty girl." Aleks realised his mistake as soon as Saskia's head snapped round to look at him.

"Oh, Light," he said. "I didn't mean it like that."

"You were still looking," Saskia said, her voice a little frozen. "You say that you love me, Aleks, so why were you looking?"

"Saskia, listen a moment. If you are jealous when I happen to notice that another girl is pretty, how do you think I feel when I see you on Erhallen's arm?"

"Erhallen?" Saskia looked puzzled. "He is like a brother to me."

"Unfortunately, I think he feels about you the same way your true brother does."

Saskia shook her head. "It is not the same at all, Aleks. I never looked at Erhallen in that way."

Aleks sighed. "We are getting off the point here. What I originally meant to say, and you must hear me out, is that Liara is a pretty girl, and highly born. Before you came along she was probably the most desirable match in the Clans."

"She still is, my lord. I do not understand you."

"Liara is pretty, but pretty in the way of Clan women, dark and small. You, with your height and your hair, must have seemed like some rare exotic flower to those young Clansmen. Liara would have noticed the attention on her falling off, and quite rightly noticed that it was being paid to you. Even if you did not want the attention or even notice it, she would still have blamed you."

"You seem to know a great deal about the workings of the minds of young women, my lord."

Aleks grimaced. "I have learned more in these last few weeks. Even when I was only Lord at Chenova, I would have been a good match. Women have been trying to catch my eye since I was very young."

Saskia frowned. Aleks realised at once that his lady was going to be very jealous where he was concerned. He stooped to kiss her again.

"Don't worry, my sweet. I want no other woman but you."

Saskia blushed. "My lord," she began in a slightly trembling voice. "I have never noticed a man before I met you."

"That day I fell over you, you mean?" Aleks said teasingly. Saskia laughed.

"Indeed, my lord, that day I called you a clumsy oaf."

Aleks frowned down at her gently. "There is one thing to be settled between us yet, Saskia," he said.

"My lord?"

"That's exactly it. We are to be married. I don't want to go through the rest of my life lording and ladying each other. My name is Aleksandr, yours is Saskia, and I think we should use them. In fact I would like it very much if you were to call me Aleks."

Saskia smiled hesitantly. "When I was little, my sisters called me Sass," she said.

"Then Sass and Aleks we shall be, when we are alone. Speaking of that, I am sure I have quite ruined your reputation by keeping you with me for so long. People will think we have anticipated our wedding night."

Saskia could not help but laugh. "I care not, Aleks. But you are right, we should go back in. People will be leaving, and you must bid farewell to your guests."

"As must you! You're officially my bride now, and just as much a host here as I am! Everyone will be wanting to congratulate us both."

Saskia took the crown off her head and offered it back to Aleks. With a sigh he accepted it. "It looks better on you," he said ruefully, setting it back atop his dark hair. Saskia shook her head at him and took his arm, smiling.

* * * *

Inside the great hall, people were indeed preparing to leave. There was still plenty of dancing going on, though, and Saskia was drawn away for a dance with Lirallen. When he led her back to the dais, Aleks was gone. Saskia caught sight of him dancing with Liara. Her temper rose, and her eyes narrowed. To her surprise, her mother appeared at her side and caught her arm.

"Mama?"

The princess's eyes were curiously blank. "That one will be nothing but a trial to you," she said.

"Who?"

"The dark girl dancing with Aleks. There is poison in her soul. You must keep her from you both, or she will destroy you."

"Is that a TimeSight vision?"

The princess shuddered slightly, and her eyes refocused. "Yes, sweeting. But a strange one: there are many possibilities, and the outcome can only be decided by your actions."

Aleks was walking back to them, Liara hanging possessively onto his arm. She shot Saskia a vicious look.

"Foster-cousin," Saskia said with a gracious smile.

Reluctantly, Liara bent her knees in a tiny curtsy. "Princess."

Aleks disengaged his arm and reached for Saskia's hand. "Princess Saskia, will you come with me to bid farewell to our guests?"

"Of course, Aleksandr," Saskia said with a bright smile.

Liara curtsied deeply to Aleks, giving him a good look at her full cleavage. "I greatly enjoyed our dance, my lord," she said breathily. "I hope we may repeat it some time."

Aleks nodded dismissively, already leading Saskia away. Liara glared poisonously after them.

* * * *

Saskia and Rianna moved out of the Clanlands tower and into the palace itself. Saskia's father, in a rage, ordered the bags of the Icelander party packed and they departed the day after the ball. Before they left, though, Aleks summoned the Prince and asked, in such a way that it was an order, that Saskia's sisters be brought to the Citadel before Midwinter, when the wedding was to be held.

"I am sure they will enjoy seeing some of the world outside Iceden," he said with a charming, innocent smile.

"Are we too late for Iskia?" Saskia whispered to her mother.

"Not yet, sweeting," the princess replied. "She is maturing very slowly. I think Midwinter will be soon enough."

Saskia sighed a little with relief. "I will see you at Midwinter, then," she said.

The princess smiled at her a little sadly. "I may not be able to come," she said. "I – think your father will not wish to leave Iceden again so soon. He will probably send Sasken with the others."

"Oh, Mama," Saskia's eyes filled with tears.

"Don't cry for me, angel. I have done what I had to, and my life has not been so terrible. You will break the chain." The princess put her arms round her daughter and hugged her tightly.

Ten days later, they received word that the princess had died on the North Road to Iridia. The letter brought by the courier said that she had fallen from her horse and struck her head on a rock.

Saskia cried like a child, held in Rianna's arms.

"He killed her, I know it," she wept. "He killed her to take it out on her, because I defied him and will take the others from him."

"Hush, angel, hush," Rianna soothed. "I'm sure that can't be so. Your mother was not well, remember, and no horsewoman. She could easily have fallen."

"No. She Saw her own death in a TimeSight vision. I am sure of it, for she spoke as though she would never see me again. It was no accident."

Aleks came in at that moment, having just received the news. He had been out practising swords in the yard with Erhallen, with whom he had become fast friends. Wearing only a pair of old tan leather hunting trousers and a shirt unlaced to his waist, he looked magnificent, tall and muscular. He came to Saskia's side and drew her into his arms to comfort her.

"Are you sure about this?" he queried.

"Entirely sure! Mama spoke so strangely to me when she left. She knew he would kill her, and perhaps she saw other futures in which she lived and terrible things happened. She could have asked you to have her remain here, but she knew that she must not."

Aleks stroked Saskia's hair gently. "Then your mother made the ultimate sacrifice. Tonight we will honour her in the temple."

Saskia could not seem to stop her weeping. She clung to Aleks, sobbing into his shoulder. He held her close, relishing the feel of her in his arms. Aleks was actually having a lot of difficulty being around Saskia: he was too passionate by nature and she was so young, he did not want to frighten her into fearing her wedding night. He was quite sure that Rianna would give her sensible advice, but advice and actions were two entirely different things.

Six months until Midwinter was quite a long time to wait, but Aleks was absolutely determined not to dishonour Saskia by anticipating their marriage vows. He kissed her now and set her away from him with a little sigh. The palace of the Citadel seemed to be full of Berenna clansmen these days, Saskia's honour guard, who watched him with narrowed eyes. The Imperial Guards in return watched the Berenna clansmen closely, and there was a certain amount of tension between the two groups. Aleks had been Emperor only a few weeks, and was still getting used to the ways of the Court. He missed the silence of his Desert holding.

"Why don't we take a trip?" he said suddenly.

"What? Where?" Saskia looked up at him, hiccoughing a little. Her tears were finally drying. Aleks thought how remarkable it was that, despite crying usually turning girls into red blotchy messes, Saskia still looked beautiful, her skin still golden and her eyes deep liquid pools.

"I would like to take you into the Desert, to Firehold and to Chenova. An Emperor should be seen in the provinces, and though this year I cannot travel too far if I would be back before Midwinter, still I should like you to see my home."

Saskia clapped her hands in delight. "Oh, that would be wonderful! We could make a circuit and come back through the Clanhold: you would like to see it, wouldn't you?"

"I would love to. That would all take perhaps four months: we should be back here about the same time as your sisters arrive."

* * * *

The trip was carefully and swiftly planned. The group that would travel was not large: a company of Imperial guards, Erhallen and six Berenna Clan warriors with Saskia, Rianna and Aleks, and a few servants to see to their comfort. As they travelled south through the hills, gradually the land began to dry out and change to flat, thin grass plains where little grew. Soon even the grass stopped growing, and eight days south of the Citadel, there was nothing but sand to be seen in every direction.

They travelled mainly by night, and camped under canvas by day. Saskia could not believe how anyone could find their way: everything was so flat and featureless. So hot: even a Clanlands summer was not so hot as this. The only Northern-bred in the group, she suffered in the heat.

Aleks thrived in the burning Desert. His eyes flashed brighter the deeper they rode into the sands, and he led them to water in the most unlikely places. By the time they reached Firehold he had won the respect of even the hardiest soldiers in the group, for his skills and toughness in such a hard land.

Saskia was not much impressed by her first sight of Firehold. Far smaller than Iceden or the Clanhold, it looked from a distance like a low jumble of rocks rising out of the sand. She was, however, impressed by the quality of the horses on which the Desert lords rode out to greet them. Even the Clan warriors, proud of their horses, nudged one another as the Lord of

Firehold reined his dark brown stallion in before Aleks.

"My lord Emperor," the lord said, bowing deeply from his saddle. He was middle-aged, handsome and craggy, deeply tanned by the Desert sun. "My lady Princess."

"Lord Jeskarin," Aleks bowed in return. "My heart sings at the sight of Firehold."

"At the sight of my horses, you mean," Jeskarin smiled. "Welcome, all of you. It is getting hot today. Let us get into Firehold."

At last Saskia understood why Firehold was so low. They rode their horses in and down, along a long ramp. Most of Firehold was underground, in the rock caverns, far cooler than the sun-heated buildings above. Saskia remarked on it to Lord Jeskarin.

"The buildings above are an empty sham, Princess," Jeskarin said. "They were used as traps at the time of the War with the Clans. The heart of Firehold lies deep underground." They left the horses not too far from the surface, and continued on foot.

As they went deeper, Saskia was astonished to hear running water. "What is that?" she asked.

Jeskarin smiled. "It is what enables us to survive here, Princess: the Desert Water. It runs from here south to Fireport, fast and smooth all the way. We send boats down it carrying many of our goods. The river reaches the surface just before Fireport, and that area is the only fertile land above ground in the Desert. We could never survive without foodstuffs shipped in from Summerlands. Come, this way." He led them along a series of narrow passages, until at last they came out on a high ledge. A rail prevented anyone from falling. Saskia, used to the sea cliffs of Berennahold, stepped fearlessly to the edge and looked over.

Below, a vast cavern was lit up by thousands of lights. Along the floor of the cavern ran the wide Fire Water river, cut into a deep channel to make it possible for boats to dock. Hundreds of people moved about below, loading and unloading goods. On other levels along the cavern wall were cut ledges and stairways, and people moved up and down constantly. It was a magnificent sight. Saskia stared and stared, thinking that she could never tire of watching the ceaseless activity.

Aleks had been to Firehold many times before, and had some friends there. He slipped off to find them while Jeskarin entertained Saskia and Rianna. Not long before the evening meal he returned in low spirits, and came to find Saskia.

"Hey there, princess," he said, finding her reading in Jeskarin's library.

"Hello, beloved." Saskia set the book aside. "What is wrong?" she asked, seeing his face.

"My friends did not want to know me," he burst out. "They were afraid to speak openly with me there. Only one of them dared to remark on your beauty. The others all looked frightened when he spoke."

Saskia understood. Clansmen who had been friendly with her before Midsummer now did not speak around her.

"An Emperor can have few friends," she said.

"But *why*? Why does it have to be that way? I don't understand."

Saskia had been brought up as royalty. She understood. "Power is a strange thing," she said slowly. "Some people fear it, but most covet it. I think that the Crowning Stone will only choose those who fear power, because they are the ones who will use it wisely. Those who covet power will never have enough."

"What are you saying?"

"That your former friends envy your power, and fear it. They do not dare speak, because they understand the kind of power you have, which you do not, yet. You could have their heads off with a word, for daring even to look on me. They do not understand that you could never use it in that way."

Aleks shook his head. "I don't want people to fear me."

Saskia smiled. "And yet, that is what being a ruler is all about, Aleks."

Aleks scowled. "I never wanted to be a ruler," he said despairingly. "I don't think I'm very good at it."

"You are better than you know, truly." Saskia sensed that he needed her to reassure him. "Listen, Aleks, no one else can do what you can. You would not have been Chosen, otherwise. There is no way to fool the Ceremony of Earth."

Aleks shook his head. "I'm just so tired. Even here, away from the Citadel, I have paperwork and things to attend to every day. Half of them, I don't understand what they are. What if I'm signing an innocent man's death warrant? I didn't want this job!"

Saskia laughed, and reached up to take his face in her hands. "Oh, Aleks. Not one man in ten thousand would think of being Emperor in such a way!"

At last Aleks smiled. "I'll be Emperor, Sass, with you as my Empress. Any other way I think I'd want to give the crown back."

At that moment Jeskarin walked in. He smiled benignly at both of them.

"Young love, such a sweet thing to see," he said fondly. Then he remembered his business there and smoothed his expression. "I have a boon to ask of you, my lord."

"Of course, Jeskarin. What is it?"

"It's my sons. The oldest is seven now, a likely boy. I would like you to take him on as a squire."

Aleks stared. "But of course! What is his name?"

"Enniskarin. I will have him serve you at dinner. He has never left the Desert, and I would like him to see some more of the world."

"I would love to take him on," Aleks said sincerely. "It is a fine idea: I think that more lord's sons should be fostered out. They would learn far more of the world outside their own holding. I wish I had seen more outside Chenova."

"Ah well, I don't want to let him go, really, and my wife Ennesia will be sad. But we have two younger sons, and they will keep her occupied."

At dinner, they met Enniskarin. He seemed a nice boy, a little overawed by Aleks and struck dumb by Saskia. Aleks spotted a massive crush beginning, as the young lad forgot himself entirely and stared at Saskia with his mouth open when she asked him to pour her wine.

* * * *

The travellers left Firehold two days later, riding out

73

eastward towards Chenova. Before they left, Jeskarin gifted them both with Firehold horses, a red chestnut stallion for Aleks and a mare of palest silvery grey for Saskia. Saskia, for the first time in her life, fell completely for a horse, and insisted on racing the little mare across the sand as soon as they found a flat area.

"What will you name her?" Aleks asked as she pulled up, laughing, beside him. He thought privately that he had never seen Saskia look so happy, or so beautiful.

"Dawn, I think. She's just that colour that the sky turns before the sun rises. What about your red horse?"

"Sandstorm, I think. He has the speed of a sandstorm, and the ill temper of one, too! Stop it, you swine!" He heeled the stallion away from biting at Dawn.

They rode on eastward through the burning heat towards Chenova. Saskia wilted away from the cool caverns of Firehold, even though her gifts in Fire meant she rarely felt hot. The sun dried her out, though, and made her tired. Aleks watched over her carefully, and Rianna brewed up restorative potions for Saskia to drink. At last they reached Chenova.

"Light, look at that!" Saskia exclaimed as they mounted the final dune and saw the fortress. Chenova was a keep built for defence, and was a low, dun-coloured pile of stone in the red desert sands. But today it was covered in cloths of every colour imaginable, draped from the roof and hanging from windows to welcome their lord.

Aleks burst out laughing. He set heels to Sandstorm's sides and galloped on down to his home. There was a loud cheer, and the gates swung open. The people of Chenova came rushing out to meet him. In a northern land of the Empire, they would have draped him in flowers, but here in the Desert flowers were impossible to find. So instead they tucked rags of bright cloth into his clothes, his boots, his horse's harness. Sandstorm for once behaved himself and did not bite anyone, as Aleks swung down from the saddle and started hugging people.

Saskia followed at a more sedate pace, trading smiles with Rianna. As soon as they arrived on the edge of the crowd, she too was besieged by well wishers. Finally she came to Aleks' side, and was astonished to see tears in his eyes.

"My love, are you all right?" she asked in concern.

"I'm just so glad to be home," he said, a little choked. After a moment he raised his voice. "Come, my people! Let us get inside: my princess is too fragile to bear this hot sun for long!"

There was a laugh and a cheer, and they were swept inside the fortress.

Chapter 5

Chenova Holding, late summer, the year 2716 after Founding

Chenova was not grand, but the servants must have been working for many days to get it so clean. Every surface that could be polished gleamed. In the great hall, the wooden table was polished and a new carved chair had been set at the head, with a smaller one beside it for Saskia. The travellers were seated, and cool fruit punch served in magnificent blown glass goblets.

Saskia, knowing the reputation of the Chenovan glass-makers, admired her goblet before even taking a sip. The glasses used to serve Rianna, Erhallen and the soldiers were all of a plain design, green and gold, but hers had clearly been made with her in mind. The glass was tall and slender, blown out of violet glass, with silver wire wound around the foot and rim. Aleks' was even more beautiful, all blue and gold, with a design suggesting a crown set around the foot.

The keep's steward came to kneel beside Aleks. Aleks raised him up and shook his hand.

"Lyart, you have worked wonders here," he said proudly. "It is good to be home in Chenova again."

Everyone had crowded into the hall to hear him speak. Aleks smiled and turned to the crowd.

"Chenova has done me proud here today," he said, and the crowd fell into breathless silence. Aleks put out a hand to Saskia and raised her to her feet. "You have given a great honour to me," he said to the audience. "And so I present to you, Chenova's lady-to-be, the Princess Saskia of Iceden!"

A huge cheer went up around the room. Saskia smiled up at Aleks. When they quieted again, she spoke.

"I have longed to see my betrothed's home," she said. "Now I understand why he speaks so highly of Chenova and his people."

They cheered her again. Saskia sat, and Aleks spoke again.

"A great deal has happened since I last set foot on Chenova sand," he said.

"No kidding," a voice remarked dryly from the back of the hall. Everybody laughed.

Aleks grinned. "I did not ask for the honour to be made Emperor," he said seriously. "But I was Chosen, and I have sworn to do my best for the Empire, and to leave a lasting legacy for those to follow after me. The greatest blessing to come to me through being Chosen was my bride." He smiled down at Saskia, who smiled joyously back and reached for his hand.

Later on, they ate a magnificent meal in the hall. Everyone wanted to meet Saskia, and Aleks was happy to oblige by introducing her. After the meal, the tables were cleared away and the dancing began. Saskia was passed from hand to hand through one wild jig after another. At last she fell laughing into the arms of another partner, and looked up in surprise as the musicians began to play a slower air. She had come back, finally, into Aleks' arms.

"It's late, princess, are you tired?" he asked solicitously.

"Very, but I'm having such a wonderful time! I love your people, Aleks, they're so kind and welcoming. I could dance all night here!"

Aleks grinned. "Save some energy for tomorrow. I would like you to come round and meet some of the people."

The following morning, he woke Saskia early. Rianna grumbled about the impropriety of him walking in when they still slept, but Aleks just laughed.

"Get up, angel, there's something I want you to see."

"Ten minutes," Saskia said.

A little while later, she met him downstairs. Aleks was fairly bouncing with excitement. Outside in the courtyard, their horses were saddled.

"Where are we going?" Saskia asked curiously.

"Wait and see!"

Saskia could only laugh and gallop after Aleks. He led her out into the Desert, and they rode for half an hour before arriving in a narrow canyon. It dropped quite deep, and at the bottom was a square, obviously man-made cave. A light shone inside.

Aleks tied up the horses and took Saskia's hand. Leading her into the cave, they were met by Lyart, Chenova's steward. He bowed to them both.

"What is this?" Saskia whispered as Lyart led them both deeper underground.

"Chenova's wealth," Aleks said softly. "This is the reason so many of Chenova's people are able to spend their time blowing glass, and not struggling to smelt ingots. This is how we can buy our ingots, and the compounds to make colours for the glass, and plenty of food."

At last they came out into a central cavern. Tunnels lay carved out in several directions.

"What is this place?" Saskia asked, looking around.

"Come," was Aleks's only response, and he led her down one of the tunnels, towards an odd tapping sound.

At the end of the tunnel, two men were working, tapping away at a rock face with small tools. They threw most of the rock they broke off into a small cart behind them, but some few pieces they laid carefully into pots at their feet.

"I don't understand, what are they doing?" Saskia asked.

"Mining." Aleks took a piece of rock from one of the men's pots. They nodded to him and he passed the small stone to Saskia. She turned it over in her fingers, mystified: it looked like nothing, a small chunk of dark grey rock.

"They are only mined here," Aleks said. "Then they are carried to Firehold, to be cut and polished, and set. When the process is done, they will look more like this." From his pocket, he took out a glittering diamond.

"Diamonds!" Saskia gasped. "This is where Desert diamonds come from!"

"Not only here, there are a couple of other mines in the Desert. But Chenova produces the largest stones, and the clearest." He gave her both the cut and the uncut diamond. "They're about the same. I'll have this one cut and a pair of earrings made for you."

Saskia laughed, delighted, as they walked back down the tunnel. "Aleks, you spoil me. You need not do that!"

"But I want to," Aleks smiled. "Come on, back to Chenova. I have something else I want to show you."

In the Hold, he led Saskia to a locked storeroom. He took out two boxes marked with the seals of both Chenova and Firehold.

"I ordered these for you," he said. "I collected them at Firehold, but I didn't want to show you them until you'd seen Chenova."

One box contained a magnificent diamond necklace, centred on a huge teardrop amethyst. The other held a matching crown.

Saskia could not believe what she was seeing. "You ordered these – for me?" she said incredulously. "Why?"

"After we are wed, you will be crowned as Empress," Aleks said with a shrug. "I wanted something better than a mere gold circlet to set on your brow."

"Oh, Aleks!" Saskia put her arms around his neck and kissed him. "You needn't have done that. And the necklace is surely an extravagance!"

"Not really. I gave you a ring for our betrothal, but in some parts of the Empire it is traditional to give a necklet. I could not have my citizens asking why I put no necklet around my lady's neck, now could I?"

Saskia laughed, hugging Aleks close. He stroked her hair, smiling down at her.

"Come, princess. We should go to find Rianna." He took the jewels and locked them away again.

They stayed six days in Chenova before riding on to the Clanlands. They took the long route along the coast, to see Berennahold.

Saskia was amazed at the welcome the normally hostile Clanlanders gave to her and to Aleks. She had not realised how fully she had been accepted among them: to the Clans it was as if a born Clanlander was to be the Empress. Until now she had not appreciated truly what it was to be the Emperor. The Icelands had little to do with the Empire, being so far distant from the Citadel, and the Desert had welcomed Aleks as one of their own who had made the highest achievement. But the Clansmen bowed down before Aleks, and treated him with far more reverence than Saskia had ever seen the Clanlord treated.

At Berennahold Lirallen was waiting to greet them, and Saskia sighed to see Liara at his side. Also there was a pretty woman with beautiful long red curly hair, a Clanlander by dress. She stood at Lirallen's shoulder.

Lirallen bowed low before Aleks before reversing his saber over his arm.

"My lord Emperor, Berennahold is yours. May I present my sister Liara," Lirallen's mouth twisted slightly as Liara curtsied. She was wearing the tightest Clan leathers Saskia had ever seen.

"And, my lord, I would like to present to you my bride Mairi." As he spoke, the redhead curtsied too.

Rianna and Saskia both gasped. Lirallen smiled up at them both. "Sorry to spring this one on you, ladies. I've been asking Mairi to marry me for a couple of years now. Aleks' rather cavalier approach in not giving Sass much choice, inspired me."

Mairi accompanied Saskia to a guest room, far more ornate than her old room in the Hold.

"How did you meet Lirallen?" Saskia asked curiously. She looked Mairi up and down. The redhead was lovely: nearly as tall as Saskia and well made, with strong muscles but feminine curves as well. Her hair was incredible, like a river of red fire. Her face was strongly beautiful, and she was older than Saskia, perhaps as much as five years older, Saskia guessed.

"My family is from the ForstMarch – Clan border, my mother a Clan trader. She died some years ago and I have lived with my father since. We were at home on our breeding farm when Lirallen came to look over the stock."

"And he fell in love with you, how romantic," Saskia said.

"Well, that's not quite how it happened," Mairi blushed. "My father was out, and Lirallen tried to tumble me in the barn. I showed him that I would not be trifled with. He looked at me differently and begged my pardon. A few days later he came back and paid far more than they were worth for all the stock we would sell."

Saskia burst out laughing. "If that's not just like Lirallen! An overextravagant gesture to say he was sorry!"

"Indeed. He came back just a few weeks later with the offer of a swap for our stallion: ours was beginning to breed too close to the mares. Every few weeks after that he found some excuse to come back. When he asked me to marry him, I said no: he should have made an alliance with some other Clan, not with a Clanless. But, well, in the end he would not be denied, and we will be married now that the Emperor is here to witness." Mairi's smile was radiant.

"I'm so glad," Saskia hugged her impulsively. "Lirallen needs someone to take care of him. He's been the Berenna lord too long, he was only eighteen when he became Warlord, and he's never had any time for himself. He's a good man, Mairi, and he'll make you a fine husband."

* * * *

Lirallen and Mairi were married that very night in Berennahold's great hall. Aleks blessed them and gave Mairi a gift, a white shawl of Desert lace worth a small fortune. There was plenty of dancing, and quite a bit of drinking and merriment.

Rianna was not feeling very well. Saskia left the party early with her, to make her comfortable. Aleks stayed a little while longer, then bade Lirallen and Mairi good night and left the hall. Two Imperial Guards, his constant companions, moved with him as he headed for his room. At the door, one reached for the handle.

"Oh, no, my friend, I don't think there are any dangers to me in Berennahold," Aleks said. He opened the door himself and went in as the two guards took up stations on either side.

It took Aleks a couple of minutes to get used to the faint light in the room. He frowned, thinking that there should have been a brighter light left ready for him. Then he glanced over at the bed and froze. There, stark naked in a provocative pose, was Liara ca'Berenna.

"Are you not coming to bed, my lord?" she inquired

huskily.

Aleks stared for about five seconds. Then he backed up and opened the door, which had swung closed behind him. "In here, please," he said.

The two guards walked in and stared. Liara quickly snatched the sheet around herself.

"Get Warlord Lirallen, now," Aleks said to one guard. The other stood at his side and kept his eyes on Liara, hand on the hilt of his sword.

Lirallen was there within minutes, Mairi not far behind him.

"I'm sorry to ruin your wedding feast, Lirallen," Aleks said sincerely, facing Lirallen in the doorway. "But I don't think it fitting that a ca'Berenna should be trying to make a whore of herself."

Lirallen took one look at Liara in the bed and swore. "You stupid little bitch. What in the Light do you think you're playing at?"

"Aleks invited me here," Liara said. "Didn't you, darling?"

Mairi gave Aleks a suspicious look, but Lirallen only laughed. "Aleks, my friend, I credit you with better taste than that. Liara is neither pretty enough nor intelligent enough for you. And you'd never risk Saskia for a tumble with this little slut."

"Lirallen, she's your sister!" Mairi exclaimed.

"Half-sister. Her mother was a whore and she's no better. Liara, you've gone too far this time. No Clansman will wed you now: the story will be round the hold before dawn how you tried to put yourself into the Emperor's bed. To your room. Now."

The note of command was strong in Lirallen's voice. Liara got up from the bed, still wrapped in the sheet, and walked past them. She did not look at Aleks.

"Make sure she does as Lord Lirallen commands," Aleks told one of his Guards, who nodded and moved to follow.

There was a sudden hiss of rage in the hall. Aleks leaned out of the door, and saw Saskia there. She looked at Liara in the sheet, the Guard escorting her away from Aleks' room, and jumped to entirely the wrong conclusion.

Saskia lost her temper entirely. She spat at Liara and snarled a curse in Icelander at Aleks, before bolting off down the corridor.

Liara laughed and turned back to Aleks. "Looks like your Icelander princess doesn't trust you, Aleks. Are you quite sure you don't want to marry me instead?"

"To your room!" Lirallen roared. He and Aleks took off down the corridor after Saskia, Mairi gathering her skirts and rushing hastily along behind.

Saskia was quick on her feet, but could not match the speed of Aleks and Lirallen. They caught her before she had gone far. She collapsed sobbing in Lirallen's arms, but screamed when Aleks tried to touch her.

"How could you! How could you do this do me? With Liara, of all people, that – *katsbaia!*" She reverted to Icelander and cursed at him.

"A what?" Mairi asked, catching up. Lirallen shrugged at her.

"I did not, Sass, I swear it. I found her in my bed and called Lirallen: I was never alone with her, not for more than ten seconds."

"It's true, Sass, I promise. Aleks only left the hall ten minutes ago, and then one of his Guards came for me." Lirallen stroked her hair. "Foster-cousin, Liara tried to whore herself tonight, but failed."

"True?" Saskia lifted her eyes to Lirallen's. He nodded firmly.

"I would not lie to you, not about something this important. I have ordered Liara to her room and there she will stay until you are both gone from the Clanlands."

Saskia turned to Aleks. He looked down on her with a concerned frown. With a sob she threw herself into his arms. Her next words were a shock.

"I was coming to find you. It's Rianna, she's been taken very ill."

"What?" Aleks held Saskia, concerned. "Lirallen, do you have a healer in the hold?"

Lirallen shook his head. "Only a midwife."

"I know a little," Mairi volunteered shyly. "I have a touch of the Healing Gift."

Rianna was grey and shaking when they reached her, clutching at her stomach. Mairi laid hands on her and concentrated hard.

"Mairi has a little of the Healing Gift, Rianna," Saskia said when Rianna tried to pull away. "Rest quiet for a moment."

Mairi drew back, shaking her head. The midwife had arrived and she and Mairi put their heads together over the bag of herbs before giving Rianna a dose of something.

"That will quiet her pain," Mairi said softly, drawing Saskia aside. "But, princess, I am sorry, there is nothing more than that I can do for her. There is a growth in her belly, and it is not a new one."

"You must be able to help, do something!"

"Princess, there is nothing I can do. I swear it. My mother died of growths in her breasts. I could not save her, and I cannot save Lady Rianna."

"How long?" Aleks asked, coming to stand by Saskia and take her hands.

"I do not know. My mother died of it within a month, it had got into her lungs. I have seen this in others, though, and sometimes they have lived for years. It depends where the growths are. In Lady Rianna, they are big in her stomach. She will not be able to eat or drink very much, so she will get weaker quickly. Perhaps she would prefer to stay here at Berennahold, to rest and die in her home."

"My home is with the princess," Rianna said weakly from the bed. "I have known about the growths for weeks."

"Oh, Rianna, why did you not say anything?" Saskia asked plaintively, going to her side.

"I saw a Healer in the Citadel, who told me what Mairi has told you. I knew there was nothing to be done. But I wanted to see you safe, Sass." Rianna took Saskia's hand. "Your Desert lord is a good man. He will take care of you, as I have done. But I need you to take care of me now, Sass."

They waited two days, until Rianna was a little stronger, and then rode out for Clanhold. Aleks was impressed by the fortress, and the welcome they received there, but with Rianna's health in the balance they dared not linger and headed for the Citadel and its resident Healers at the best speed they could manage.

The Healers all shook their heads over Rianna. She sighed once, reaching for Saskia's hand.

"None of them are strong enough. If only your sister Liaskia were here."

"Strong enough for what?" Saskia asked.

"The Power can be channelled through another Gifted to increase their ability. I cannot do it because I would lose control as soon as the Healing began. And you are too strong: the amount of Power that runs through you would burn these Healers to a crisp. Control will come only with time. Until then, only the most powerfully Gifted could channel the Power you hold safely."

"And you think Liaskia is that Gifted?"

"All of your family are that Gifted, your mother says. Liaskia is the one with the Healing Gift, probably the only Healer alive strong enough to take the Power you could channel. But this is so bad – perhaps even that would not be enough."

Saskia frowned, thinking about that. "Liaskia will not be here for some time yet, Rianna. In the meantime, you grow weaker. Is there nothing I can do?"

Rianna smiled, stroking Saskia's hair. "Talk to me, child," she asked. "I want to be sure you will be happy as the Empress. Are you content to marry young Aleksandr?"

Saskia frowned, then shrugged. "Marriage was always something that I was going to have to deal with," she said honestly. "Aleksandr is a good man." She blushed very slightly, but Rianna noticed.

"There are plenty of good men about," Rianna said. "Do you love Aleksandr?"

"I don't know," Saskia mumbled in reply. "I've never been in love. I've never flirted like Liara does – I was too busy learning the sword."

Rianna sighed. "I know. I let you get away with it because I knew you could not marry a Clansman anyway. But you didn't answer my question, really – if you don't love Aleksandr, what do you feel for him?"

Saskia tried to put her thoughts in order. It wasn't easy – it seemed that every time she thought of her betrothed, her good sense seemed to desert her entirely.

"I want to spend time with him," she said. "I want to know him better. I was very glad to go to Chenova, where he grew up. A few times when he has kissed me, my head span and my knees went all weak."

Rianna smiled, satisfied. "He loves you already, I have heard him say it. From what you have just told me, I think that perhaps you will love him in time – a sooner time than you think. Trust in me, Saskia." She smiled wearily. "Your marriage will be a happy one."

* * * *

Rianna did not get any better. Aleks sent riders out on the north road, to find the Icelander princesses and hurry them along in the hope that Liaskia would be able to help. But no word came for days, and Rianna got steadily weaker. Aleks barely saw Saskia: there was so much that required his attention and she was always at Rianna's bedside. He did make a point of stopping by at least once every day to see them. One day he tapped on the door with a sick, sinking feeling, knowing that he was bearing terrible news. Enniskarin of the Desert stood at his side.

"Saskia," Aleks said softly. She turned to look up at him, her expression changing at the look on his face.

"What is it? What's wrong?"

Aleks shook his head. "I do not want to tell you," he said, "but I must. There has been an accident, in the Clan mountains. Jeskarin was visiting Clanhold to talk horses, and was out riding with the Clanlord. There was a rockfall, and – I am so sorry, Sass, but they're both dead."

Saskia took one look at Enniskarin and held her arms out to him. He ran to her with a muffled sob and clung to her. She rocked him, grieving: the Clanlord had been the closest thing to a true father she had ever known, kind to her always. And Jeskarin had made her feel welcome in the Desert, had treated her like the

86

daughter he had never had. She wept for both of them.

"Aleks says I must go back to the Desert, to join my mother and be proclaimed," Enniskarin sobbed out. "But I want to stay until after you are married!"

"All right," Saskia agreed. "It is only a few weeks until Midwinter. The Desert people know who their lord is, they will wait for him for as long as they must. You'll stay with me until then." She looked down at Rianna, sleeping peacefully. Saskia dreaded having to tell Rianna that her brother was dead.

* * * *

One morning, Saskia was sitting reading to Rianna, looking at the terrible grey shade of her skin. Rianna's breathing was growing weak and laboured, and even the painkilling drinks given to her by the Healers had little effect now. Both knew that the end was not far away. Hearing the news of her brother's death was almost the last straw for Rianna, and she seemed to have given up on living.

Rianna reached out slowly and pushed the book in Saskia's hand down. "Talk with me a little, child," she whispered. "There are things I must tell you."

"Save your strength, Rianna," Saskia said gently. Rianna shook her head.

"Heart's daughter," Rianna whispered, stroking Saskia's hair. "Such a fine girl, so strong. You will be the greatest Empress this land has known. Your lord will be proud of you. Your mama would have been proud of you too."

"I love you, Rianna," Saskia said softly, trying hard not to cry.

"Listen well to me now, Saskia. I have taught you everything I know of the Power, but you are so far beyond me, I think there is no one who can teach you more. You will have to make your own way now. Do not fear what you are and what you can do: learn to make use of it. Expand on what I have taught you, but be careful. You have not worked yet unguided: I hoped to have longer to teach you." She paused, struggling for breath.

"Do not exhaust yourself, my dear," Saskia said gently.

"You must rest."

"There is no more time," Rianna said. "If I rest now I will not speak what must be said. Before she left here, your mother and I spoke of many things. She had many TimeSight visions as you know: some she feared to speak of, others she told me, that I make sure they did not come to pass. There is only one that I must pass on to you, that you must make it come to pass."

"Tell me."

"Your brother Sasken must die by Riaskia's hand."

"Riaskia? She's eleven years old!"

"Nevertheless, she must kill him. Any other way will lead to ruin and death for all of you. She must kill him, when the time is right. You must prepare her to do it or she will not be able to wield the knife."

"What in the Light do I say to her?"

"That is for you to learn," Rianna smiled faintly. "I know it will not be simple, Sass, but you must do it."

"I will try," Saskia said at last, with a small shrug.

"I love you, heart's daughter. I wish on you every happiness." Worry clouded Rianna's eyes for a moment. "Just one more thing. Your mother never had any TimeSight visions of your children. She did not know if that meant you would have none, or if she just could not see them because your own future was so bright, with so many variations it clouded her vision."

"I will deal with that when the time comes," Saskia said.

"Yes, you will, child. You're young yet: barely sixteen, barely a woman. Yet you are a woman, and Aleksandr a man: you are both healthy and strong. I am sure you will be Light-blessed with a son." Rianna stopped and sucked in a pain-filled breath.

Saskia once again cursed her inability in the healing arts. She stroked Rianna's forehead. "Rest, beloved. Rest now."

"Rest forever," Rianna whispered. "I love you, heart's-daughter. Be well." She closed her eyes and her breathing slowed until finally, it stopped.

Saskia sat beside her foster-mother for a long time, holding the slowly cooling hand and keening softly to herself. At last there was a tap on the door and Aleks walked in.

"Sass! Your sisters have arrived!" He stopped, taking in the scene. "Oh, Light, no," he said. "Oh, no, Sass, I'm so sorry."

Saskia laid Rianna's hand gently down on the bed and crossed the room to Aleks. He folded her gently in his arms. "I'm so sorry," he repeated.

"Why, why," Saskia sobbed into his chest. "Why do all the good people have to die? My mother, the Clanlord, Lord Jeskarin, now Rianna. And all the while my father sits in Iceden like some kind of evil spider. Why can't he die instead?"

Aleks held Saskia, not knowing what to say. He was too young even to remember his parents, but Lord Jeskarin had been like a father to him, even as he had been to Saskia for the short time they had been friends. The old Clanlord had loved her like a daughter too. She was losing everyone who cared for her, and Aleks could do nothing to stop it.

"Come away, my love," he said gently. "Come away now."

Saskia could not stop weeping. It seemed to her that all the constants in her life were being torn away from her. She had only Aleks as a solid, reassuring presence, and clung to him fiercely.

"It's all right, love, I'm not letting you go," Aleks said. He caught the eye of one of his bodyguards. "Find my steward. Have him make the Icelander royals comfortable: I will meet them when I can. Ask him to make arrangements for Lady Rianna's body to be burned also."

Aleks took Saskia back to her rooms. He sat with her and washed her face like a child. She sat docilely and let him. "Did you hear me earlier?" he asked gently.

"Earlier what?"

"Your sisters and your brother have arrived," Aleks said. "I have just received word. The timing is terrible. I daresay you do not want to face Sasken yet."

"Definitely not," Saskia said with a shudder. "I do not have to greet them all together, do I? Could you not bring the girls here to me and make Sasken wait?"

"I suppose I could greet him formally," Aleks said. "After all, he is the Icelander heir. I'll see what I can do. Here comes your maid: why don't you put on a fresh dress and get ready for them?"

Saskia nodded almost mechanically and smiled a little weakly.

"I know this is tough for you, beloved, but you've got to be strong. Your sisters need you now." Aleks kissed her gently and left her alone.

Saskia did not want to intimidate her sisters by appearing too formal, but nor did she want to shock them by wearing her Clan leathers. In the end she settled on a plain blue dress and no jewellery apart from her engagement ring.

Chapter 6

The Citadel, before Midwinter, the year 2716 after Founding

Saskia was pacing impatiently when there was a timid knock on her door. "Come in!" she called.

The door opened, and three blonde girls stood there. Saskia stared at them. Two were small, and one somewhat taller, closer to Saskia's own height. They looked strange to her, unfamiliar after four years, and yet she could see her own mirror in their faces.

"Sass?" said the oldest girl hesitantly. She was tiny, her head not even reaching Saskia's shoulder, and she looked pale and thin.

"Issy?" Saskia said equally hesitantly.

"It is you. You've grown so tall!" The two ran into each other's arms. The younger girls held back, clinging together.

"Let me look at you all," said Saskia after a moment. "Gosh, Ria, you've grown!"

Physically Riaskia was the most like Saskia. Iskia and Liaskia were smaller and more delicate. They all looked tired and too thin to Saskia. She rang for her maid and requested tea and cake.

Saskia was horrified at her sisters' reaction to the food. Almost unconsciously, the other two waited for Riaskia to taste it and wait for a couple of minutes. Then when she nodded to them, they fell to with a will.

"What has been done to you?" Saskia whispered, horrified. "What do you fear in the food?"

"Drugs," Riaskia said calmly. "I am the strongest of us: so I taste just a tiny portion of everything to ensure it is safe."

"Why have you been drugged? Wait – am I too late? Are you already wed to Sasken?"

"No, we are all still virgin," Iskia answered after a long moment. "But we have been made to do – other things."

Saskia's hand went to her mouth. "Since when?" she said, horrified.

"Since Mama died. Father returned to Iceden in a rage and since then both he and Sasken have forced us to do – things for them. They used the drugs to make us docile."

"Oh, Light above," Saskia covered her eyes with her hands. "What have I done? I am so sorry. Sorry I could not help sooner."

Liaskia laid her hands on Saskia's shoulders. "Sister, you have done everything you could. We are here now, we are safe. The food testing – it was not meant to insult you. But they gave us drugs which made us see things which were not there." She shivered violently. "I do not want to remember. We have been so afraid that this is all a dream, that we would never reach the Citadel, or that you would not be here."

"I believed," Iskia said in a small voice. "I remembered you holding me that night you went away. You swore you'd come for us, one day, no matter what happened. I believed you."

"We didn't hear," Riaskia said. "I was only eight, and Lia only seven. How could we have believed? All we knew is that both you and Mama were gone. Mama did not come home for a very long time, and she swore that you were dead, even to us. How could we believe?"

Saskia was shaking. "I could not come before," she said dully. "I would never have seen you subjected to this. How could they? Lia, you're still only eleven years old! Iskia at thirteen, well, you're a year older than I was when I was ordered to marry Sasken. But still, too young for this!"

The three younger sisters were all close now. They all put their arms around Saskia.

"You did everything you could," Iskia said gently.

"You're not to blame."

"We're safe now."

"Everything's going to be all right."

The four girls clung together. When the door opened, though, it was Saskia who leaped away, reaching for the sword by the fireplace.

"Whoa, whoa!" Aleks said, holding up his hands. "Don't skewer me!"

Saskia smiled weakly. The other three huddled together behind her.

"Who is this, Sass?" Riaskia demanded.

Saskia turned to smile reassuringly at them. "This is my lord, the Emperor Aleksandr von Chenowska."

The three younger princesses gasped, and dropped deep curtsies.

"My lord, we owe you our deepest gratitude," Iskia said. "You have given us hope where before we had none."

"Princess – Iskia?" At Saskia's nod, Aleks bowed. "Your presence, and that of your sisters, graces the Citadel. I am pleased to offer you guest-right for as long as you choose to remain." He could not help staring at the young girls. They were all so alike. He supposed that was what inbreeding did to a family.

Saskia introduced the others and Aleks bowed politely over their hands. All three girls were somewhat awed by him. Aleks, sensing it, drew Saskia aside for a moment.

"I will leave you alone with them for now," he said, "but you will have to formally greet your brother tonight. You won't have to have him sit by you at dinner: the Duke of ForstMarch is here and outranks Sasken as a ruling lord."

Saskia sighed in relief. "What about Rianna's burning?" she asked.

"Sundown tomorrow. I have good news for you, also. Lirallen has been chosen Overlord of the Clans, and has named Erhallen as his successor to Clan Berenna."

Saskia was absolutely delighted. "How wonderful for them both! It must have been a surprise for Lirallen, so much younger than most of the other Warlords."

"He is very competent. I had word by pigeon today: both the brothers are on their way back to the Citadel. They will probably arrive tomorrow, which is why I put off Rianna's burning until then."

"She will be glad to have Clan Blood there," Saskia agreed.

"The only problem is, they're bringing Liara back with them. I think they're hoping to find a suitable husband for her."

"Light above," Saskia sighed. "This means we'll have to deal with her at the wedding. I hope she won't still be angry with me."

"I'll make sure she behaves herself. You're having enough trouble at the moment, with Sasken here."

"When should I come to greet him?"

"Two hours. He's coming in to formally greet me at the end of the Petitioners' Court. The throne room will be full. I want you there then."

"In front of all those people?"

"Would you rather face him alone?"

Saskia shivered. "The throne room will be fine," she agreed. "Will the others have to be there?"

"I'm afraid so: they have to be formally presented to me also. They will come in before Sasken so he will have to walk up to all of us." He looked at the three girls, dressed in plain grey riding dresses. "Do they have any more formal clothes? I suppose your things might fit Riaskia, but not the others."

Saskia nodded, catching his drift. "Don't worry. We'll put on a display."

Saskia found a couple of her ladies-in-waiting and gave some very specific instructions. Within ten minutes the Empress's suite was a hive of activity, as baths were prepared and clothes and jewels set out.

"What do you want me to wear?" Iskia asked.

"This should suit you nicely." Saskia held up a dazzling dress in blue and gold. Clothes for Liaskia and Iskia had been borrowed from one of her ladies' daughters. Saskia's things were too big for Riaskia's thin frame but they had found a lady-in-waiting around her size and borrowed a dress.

Saskia herself put on a smart violet dress she had never worn and a necklace of Desert diamonds. She raided the Empress's strongroom and found silver circlets for all of them to wear.

* * * *

In the throne room, Aleks smiled to himself when he heard gasps and whispers at the back of the hall. Saskia swept in, looking every inch a princess, and walked gracefully to Aleks's side. A high-backed chair had been placed there for her, and she seated herself as though she were already the Empress.

Aleks smiled across at Saskia, thinking how pale she looked. What an appalling day this had been for her: the horror of Rianna's death, the emotional reunion with her sisters, and now she had to face the brother who still threatened her.

The Icelander princesses were introduced together, and walked up to curtsy gracefully to Aleks. Saskia beckoned to them and they came to stand behind her chair.

Sasken was introduced. He had been kept waiting in a separate room to the princesses and so had not seen them. He walked into the throne room with a loose-limbed arrogance. Saskia looked him over, her fingers gripping white-knuckled onto the arms of her chair.

Sasken had grown taller too: he would be a half-head above Saskia now but was still short of Aleks' height. Other than that, at twenty he was still very much as he had been at sixteen, arrogant and sneering. He bowed to Aleks, the minimum depth for a prince to his overlord, and then raked his eyes boldly up and down Saskia's body.

"Sweet sister," he said softly. "It has been too long since I saw you at Iceden. You will visit after your wedding." It sounded like a command.

"My bride will never enter Iceden while you or your father rule there," Aleks said icily.

Saskia's head snapped round and she stared at Aleks in surprise. Sasken too was staring.

"My lord? You forbid my sister to visit her family?"

"Yes, I do. And furthermore," Aleks rose to his feet and drew the Imperial Sword from its sheath on the throne. "I claim the Princesses Iskia, Riaskia and Liaskia Cevaria as Wards of the Empire. Should any man wish to challenge my claim, he is to meet with me here on Midwinter Eve morning at sunrise to

95

decide the matter in formal combat." Aleks's eyes were cold and hard, and his expression was set in an uncompromising scowl.

An uproar broke out. Sasken stared up at Aleks dumbfounded. Then he turned and walked from the throne room.

"What have you done?" Saskia said to Aleks in shock.

"With any luck, your brother will have a pigeon heading for Iceden within the hour. There's no way your father could get here in time, and he is too old to fight anyway. Sasken will have to accept the challenge himself." Aleks smiled ghoulishly. "And then I'm going to turn him into mincemeat."

"You must not kill him," Saskia said.

"Why in the Light not? This may be the only opportunity I ever get!"

"If you kill him you will lead us all into disaster," Saskia said flatly. "My mother left another TimeSight legacy with Rianna. You must not kill him."

"Darkness take him!" Aleks sheathed the sword angrily. "I want him dead, Sass, he can be no threat to you then."

"He's not due to die yet." Saskia would not let herself look at Riaskia, twelve years old and destined one day to murder her brother.

Sasken did not show up for dinner, but sent his apologies. The younger princesses were very shy, sitting together and barely speaking. Saskia, stuck talking to the Duke of ForstMarch, smiled reassuringly at them occasionally.

* * * *

The following day, Rianna's burning was held at sunset. The younger Icelander princesses asked for permission to attend.

"We never knew Rianna ca'Berenna," Iskia said. "Nevertheless, we owe her our freedom. Without Rianna's help, Saskia could never have evaded capture. We would have remained in Iceden for the rest of our lives."

"We would like to honour Rianna with her friends," Riaskia added. "Our mother loved Rianna so much she Named me for her. I wish I had known her, but the best I can do is to stand at her burning."

So, at sunset, the four Icelander princesses stood together. Lirallen and Erhallen had ridden in with Liara and a large band of Clansmen just an hour before, and they too stood, tall and grim in Clan travelling clothes.

Lirallen lit the pyre, as Rianna's closest relative. He came to stand by Saskia and put his arm around her shoulders. She leant into him, trying to stifle her sobs.

Finally only ashes remained, as the stars stood bright in the sky. The group turned and walked slowly back to the Citadel. Saskia went to her room alone and wept long into the night.

The following morning, Saskia was contemplating the weather from her window. Only a few days before Midwinter, the sky was grey and overcast, looking like rain. There was a tap on her door.

"Enter!" she called.

"It's me, sister," said a small voice. Sass turned to see Iskia.

"Come in, Issy. Come and sit down. Would you like a cup of tea?"

"Thank you," Iskia seated herself. "I can't get over this weather," she said, looking out of the window. "It's so warm! Iceden was six feet deep in snow when we left."

Saskia smiled. "Perhaps I have been too long in the southlands. I barely remember what snow looks like. It never snows here or in the Clanlands."

Iskia shook her head in amazement. "I can hardly imagine life without snow." She took a sip of her tea. "I wanted to ask you, Sass, who were those people who came late to the ceremony last night?"

"Rianna's blood kin and my adopted family, the Berenna Clan. You saw the two tall men dressed in black?"

Iskia nodded. "One of them had a silver circlet on his head, and the other had a silver earring."

"That's right. The one with the circlet is the new Clanlord, Lirallen. The other is his brother, the Lord of Clan Berenna and my best friend, Erhallen."

"Your best friend?"

"Absolutely. Erhallen is the one who taught me how to use a sword when I was adopted into the Clan. He's looked after me for years now."

"They are very young to be lords in the Clans, are they not? I thought lordship had to be contested and won by the finest warriors."

"Well, Lirallen is older than he looks at thirty. But he is a superb warrior. You're right about Erhallen, he is only three-and-twenty, but again, such a fighter."

"Who was the dark-haired girl who stood with them?"

Saskia's lip curled up in a snarl. "Their half-sister, the Lady Liara. The old Clanlord's first wife gave him no children in many years. His second wife gave him Lirallen, Erhallen, and three daughters in between. She died birthing Erhallen, and the Clanlord took another bride who was only fourteen, shocking everyone since he was near fifty years old at the time. The Lady Kiara gave him one daughter only, Liara, and died in childbed. Of course the Clanlord blamed himself because she was too young. He spoiled Liara rotten, and she's turned out rather selfish because of it."

"You really don't like her," Iskia said in surprise. "What did she do to you?"

"She tried to steal Aleks for herself. I still don't understand everything that is wrong. We used to be friends, but I think she is too angry ever to be friends with me again. Lirallen has kept her in the Clanlands, but he had to bring her back for the wedding really, after all she's unwed and of the highest blood. I suppose he's hoping that she'll find herself a husband."

Iskia blinked. "Is she not rather old to be looking for a husband?"

"Liara's only eighteen! In most of the Empire it is not even *permitted* for a woman to marry until she turns sixteen. Only in the Icelands and the Clanlands are there exceptions to the rule."

"Sixteen!" Iskia said, astonished. "Truly? I had wondered why the Emperor had not married you sooner. Now I understand why you had to wait."

Saskia nodded. "Even you, Iskia, if you become a Ward of the Empire, cannot be married until you are sixteen, because you would be governed by Empire law."

"What if I wanted to marry sooner?"

"I am surprised you should want to marry at all! Have you an eye on someone already?"

"Oh no," Iskia said, too hurriedly.

Saskia refrained from asking any more questions, though she did look curiously at her sister.

* * * *

Midwinter's Eve dawned bright and cold. The four princesses had been up half the night preparing, determined to look their part. They could have no say in the proceedings, no matter what happened, but they would stand for Aleks.

As the sun rose in the throne room, Aleks stood in front of his throne, dressed in black Desert fighting leathers, his sword unsheathed in his hand. Saskia sat on her chair beside the throne, and the three younger princesses stood two steps below Aleks.

The throne room doors swung open, and the assembled onlookers gasped. Most of the great lords of the Empire were there, having arrived for the royal wedding the following day. But they were there today for the attraction of seeing their new Emperor prove himself with a sword.

Saskia had gone to Aleks before dawn to help him prepare.

"I fear for you," she told him simply, helping him lace his wrist bracers.

"Why, princess? Your brother is no warrior. You told me that yourself."

"He is still Gifted, Aleks, with Luck, the most unreliable and tricky Gift of all. Anything could happen there today: you could slip on the floor with your first step and find his sword through your belly."

Aleks shook his head. "If that happens, then it does. I must trust in the Light and my skills, Sass, I have no other choice. This is the only way to legally prevent him from ordering the girls back to Iceden."

Saskia frowned down at the floor. "I still don't like it," she said. "I always thought that I would fight him. I don't need you to fight all my battles for me."

Aleks grinned. "And well I know it, princess, you're better

with a sword than most men I've ever known. But by the law, you have no right to challenge him. He hasn't technically committed a crime that we can prove. If he had, there would be no need for this challenge: I could just declare the girls to be wards and that would be that. This one is my fight, Sass. If he wins, you can avenge me."

"That's not funny," Saskia responded fiercely. "If he wins, I don't want to live."

Aleks reached for her hand. "He won't, Sass, I promise." He took a deep breath. "I love you," he said.

Saskia hesitated, but then smiled in response. "I love you too," she replied. The smile that spread across Aleks' face melted her fear and kept her feeling warm inside – at least until the time came for the fight.

Saskia smoothed her face and looked out over the crowded throne room. The massive doors at the back swung open and Sasken walked in, unarmed. Two Imperial Guards walked behind him, one carrying a sheathed sword.

"I challenge you, Aleksandr von Chenowska," Sasken said. "I challenge you to single combat, for the guardianship of my sisters." He smiled unpleasantly at Saskia. "In addition, I received word this morning that my father is dead. As his only son, I declare myself ruler of the Principality of the Icelands. As the senior member of the Icelander royal family, I challenge your right to marry my sister Saskia."

Gasps went up around the throne room. Saskia felt nothing. The outcome of this fight would have decided her fate in any case. Either Sasken would lose and Aleks would claim her as his bride and the others as his wards, or Sasken would kill Aleks and they would all have no choice but to return to Iceden immediately.

Saskia considered that appalling possibility for a moment, then put it out of her mind. Her love for Aleks was too new and strong to contemplate losing. Without Aleks, she would not want to live. She felt for the sword she had concealed by strapping it along the side of her chair. It would not be too hard for her to fall on it after she killed Sasken.

Sasken walked up to face Aleks.

"I accept your challenge," Aleks said in a bored tone. He gestured with his sword. "Give him his weapon."

Sasken took his sword from the Guard, who then backed off to the edge of the circle.

Aleks laid his own sword across both palms and bowed. He had barely bent his head before Sasken's sword went whistling down towards his neck.

Gasps went up around the hall at the dirtiness of the trick. Aleks never even blinked. He leaned to one side with incredible grace and the sword swept harmlessly by. An instant later Aleks's own sword swung, and the two clashed.

Aleks never gave Sasken a chance. He had taken Saskia's warning about the Luck to heart, and realised that the longer Sasken had to fight, the more likely it was that Luck would affect the outcome. As the two swords clashed, he used his free hand to grab Sasken's wrist and swept one long leg in a swift arc to take out Sasken's ankles. A moment later Sasken's sword skittered away across the floor and Sasken was lying on his back, Aleks kneeling on his chest, sword edge on his throat.

Everyone stared in astonishment. Aleks had moved so fast that most of them had not even seen what he had done.

"What – how – " Sasken spluttered.

"Surrender," Aleks said in a deadly cold voice. "You will cede to me here and now all rights over your sisters, until they come to their majority. You will accept my right to wed your sister Saskia. And you will kneel to me as your overlord."

Sasken closed his eyes in defeat. "I will," he said. Aleks let him up and Sasken knelt under that drawn sword and spoke the formal words.

Saskia leaned back in her chair with a sigh of relief. And Iskia fainted, crumpling to the floor.

Surprisingly it was Erhallen who reached Iskia first, before any of the Guards. He put light fingers to her throat, then easily scooped her up. Saskia beckoned him back behind the thrones, where there was a door into a small series of private rooms. Erhallen laid Iskia on a couch. The other two sisters pushed in behind him and Liaskia put her hand on Iskia's forehead. She shared a quick, worried glance with Riaskia.

"What?" Saskia said, remembering suddenly that Lia's Gift was Healing. "What are you not telling me?"

Ria shook her head. "Iskia has been ill for some time. When they began to give us drugs, the first dose triggered a fit in her, like the falling sickness. Without being able to eat much because we could not trust the food, she has not been strong enough to fight the illness. Lia has done everything she can, but there has never been anyone to teach her what the Healing can do."

Saskia frowned down at her unconscious sister. She looked at Erhallen, standing by the door.

"Guard that door," she requested. Erhallen bowed his head to her, drew his sword, and stepped outside.

Saskia took Lia's hand. "Rianna told me that any Gift can be augmented by raw Power," she said, talking more to herself than her sister. "She said that to release the Power in raw form is very hard because your mind automatically begins to shape it for a purpose."

"What little I know of true Healing says that the strength must come from inside," Lia said nervously. "Perhaps you can feed Power into me and my Healing will be stronger for it."

Saskia closed her eyes and stilled her mind. She could feel the Power there, a raging river of lava just waiting for her to draw off what she needed. Instead of taking it for a specific purpose, she thought about just funnelling the pure lava.

"It will burn Lia," she thought suddenly. "Only the Power-Gifted can use it this way." She closed her hand into a fist, imagining the lava trapped within, and took Lia's hand, wrapping it over her fist.

Lia understood. She drew from inside herself, from the power contained within her hand. Then she laid her free hand on Iskia's brow.

To Riaskia, watching incredulously, their joined hands began to glow. Lia's other hand gleamed where it brushed lightly over Iskia's head. Iskia drew in a shuddering breath and opened her eyes.

"Issy!" Ria said, leaning over. "Are you all right?"

Iskia's eyes were unfocussed. Ria, Sight-Gifted herself, understood. Iskia's eyes were no longer seeing what was in front of her. Ria's Gift unleashed gave her visions of the future, but Iskia would be seeing other places, maybe far away. As soon as Lia lifted her hand away Iskia shuddered and her eyes focussed normally.

"What in the Light did you do to me?" she said faintly.

At that moment Aleks walked in through the door. "Sasken's on his way back to Iceden," he announced. "I remarked that clearly he would want to get back to receive fealty from his lords. Are you feeling quite well, Iskia?"

"I am much improved, my lord," Iskia got to her feet.

Erhallen came in after Aleks. He bowed deeply to Iskia. "Are you feeling better, my lady?"

"Yes, thank you," Iskia gave him a puzzled look.

"Lord Erhallen ca'Berenna carried you out of the throne room after you fainted," Saskia said pointedly.

"Oh!" Iskia swept him a deep curtsy. "I am most grateful for your aid, my lord."

"Princess Iskia," he inclined his head to her again. Saskia was suddenly amused by the size difference between them. Iskia's head reached only half-way up Erhallen's broad chest.

"Right," Saskia said in a businesslike tone. "We've all got work to do. You, my lord, had best go change out of those fighting clothes and bathe."

"I didn't get thanked yet," Aleks said in an injured tone.

The four princesses all curtsied to him. "Thank you, my lord," they chorused in unison.

Aleks smiled, then bent his head to claim a kiss from Saskia. The younger girls watched with interest until Erhallen shooed them from the room.

"What did Saskia mean, we've all got work to do?" Iskia asked as Erhallen shut the door firmly.

"It is the wedding tomorrow. Have you forgotten? Surely there are last-minute fittings and things that must be done." Erhallen shook his head when they clamoured for details. "I have no idea! Wait for Saskia."

Saskia rejoined the others a little while later and they headed for the Empress' suite.

"Where's your dress?" Iskia asked.

"Safely shut up. It was finished a while ago: I didn't want people seeing it. I won't get it out until morning."

Several of Saskia's ladies fussed over the younger sisters, fitting their dresses. They were to wear simple violet dresses with white lace sleeves, collars and hems. Lia in particular looked very doll-like in hers.

Saskia left them to it and went hunting through the Empress's strongroom in search of some good jewellery for all of them. She of course would wear the necklace Aleks had ordered from Chenova for her, and later he would crown her with the matching crown. Saskia looked at her hands. She wore only the betrothal ring Aleks had given her, and her right hand looked very bare. She went on the hunt for a ring. In a box hidden under many others, she finally found the perfect thing.

The gem was teardrop shaped. Saskia wasn't even sure exactly what it was. It was clear, but the colour changed from deepest blue to emerald green depending on how she turned it in the light. It was extraordinarily beautiful. She put it on her right hand and found it just the right size for her middle finger. Forgetting about it, she began hunting for jewels for the others to wear.

It was late when they finally slept. The four princesses were all sleeping in the same room. They ended up talking for hours before Saskia finally put the light out and they slept.

* * * *

The following morning, Saskia woke up before the others. She went into the ante-room and unlocked the cupboard containing her wedding dress.

The scream brought the other girls running. They found Saskia on her knees, weeping, surrounded by cut-up fragments of white and silver silk, none of the pieces bigger than the palm of her hand.

"Oh, Light," Iskia breathed. "Who has done this?"

Lia knelt, gathering her older sister close, unleashing a flood of Empathy and murmuring words of comfort.

"Only Sasken could have got close enough. He must have

used all his Luck to get here," Ria said.

"Aleks will go mad if he finds out," Saskia sobbed. "I must not let him know. Oh, Light, what am I going to do? It took months to make."

The four girls just sat for a while on the floor, holding each other, trying to offer comfort. Saskia shook her head finally, trying to quiet her tears.

"I do not know what to do," she admitted. "If I leave these rooms Aleks will know something is amiss."

"We had best look here then, hadn't we?" Ria said. She and Liaskia went through to the dressing-room and began to hunt through Saskia's wardrobe.

"I don't have anything," Saskia said miserably to Iskia. "Nothing is the right colour, or even the right style."

"What about using the Power?" Iskia said.

Saskia shook her head. "I wouldn't know how to go about changing something."

"How about *making* something? You've got all those bolts of cloth, in that storeroom where the strongroom door is. I bet there's something suitable there. Come on, let's go look."

"I wouldn't know where to start!" Saskia began as Iskia started unwrapping bolts of cloth for her inspection.

"What choice do you have, if you don't want Aleks to know?" Iskia responded.

Saskia could not help but agree. She began to help Iskia.

"Look, look!" Liaskia came running in. She held a length of incredibly thin white silk, stitched over with tiny silver flowers. "This veil's perfect!"

"I'd forgotten that!" Saskia took it from Lia's hands. "Yes, that's a good start."

"And here, look at this," Iskia held out a bolt of cloth-of-silver. "Now this would make a fabulous dress."

"But – how?"

"I don't know, Sass, you're the sorceress. Why don't we just have a go?"

They wrapped the cloth in an elegant draped style around Saskia and stepped back. She drew in a deep breath, shut her eyes and drew on the Power. A moment later she gave a yell of shock.

"What? What is it?"

Saskia was staring at her hand, where she was still wearing the ring she had found the previous day.

"It *tingled*," she said. "It tingled, and the Power came through it."

"Is it magic?" Riaskia said.

"I didn't think *things* could be magic, only people." Saskia experimented. She found to her amazement that she could pull more raw Power through the ring than she had ever been able to draw before. It was as though a pair of unseen, dextrous hands were helping her.

The other three sisters watched in amazement as Saskia ran her fingers over the cloth wrapped around her. It shifted and flowed under her hands.

In about half an hour, Saskia was wearing a most beautiful dress, moulded to her slender form. The dress was close fitting to her hips, and then the skirt fell in graceful flowing folds to the floor.

From a bolt of white silk, Saskia made a train, and using remnants of the cloth of silver, she used the Power to weave delicate, seemingly hand-stitched designs through it. The others gaped as her hands moved over the cloth in a stitching motion, and the patterns appeared there.

It took a long time for them all to get ready. They put Saskia's hair up and set her silver circlet carefully atop her veil. When the knock finally came on the door they were almost ready.

"One moment!" Saskia called, carefully setting Iskia's circlet on her piled pale blonde braids. "There! Are we all ready?"

"Your necklace, Sass," Ria said. "Come here." She fastened the massive diamonds and amethyst around Saskia's slender neck and smiled. "There."

Liaskia went over to open the door. Erhallen stood there, magnificent in full Clan regalia. "Princess Saskia," he bowed formally to her. "The Emperor had asked that I give you away, since your brother is not here."

Saskia smiled. "I would far rather be given away by my best friend, Erhallen. My family is well represented here."

Erhallen offered his arm. The younger princesses carefully gathered up Saskia's train and they proceeded down through the palace towards the throne room.

Chapter 7

The Citadel, Midwinter's Day, the year 2716 after Founding

The palace was eerily empty. Outside the throne room an escort of eight Guardsmen waited; but they were not wearing the usual insignia. Instead of golden crowns on the shoulders of their black uniforms, they wore silver lightning bolts. They were all young, but they had the hard eyes of skilled soldiers.

"Princess Saskia," their officer bowed to her. He had four lightning bolts on each shoulder. "I am Captain Evan Veravia. May I present the Empress's Guard?"

Saskia smiled, delighted. She took an instant liking to the young officer. He could not be many years older than she, and handsome, about her height with dark blond hair and brown eyes. "Captain Evan, I am most honoured to make your acquaintance. Will you announce me?"

"Gladly, my Lady." They all bowed to her. Then the eight men turned to the doors into the throne room and drew their swords. Evan rapped three times on the door with his sword hilt.

"Who goes there?" shouted a voice from inside.

"Princess Saskia Cevaria, Heir to the Icelands, Flower of the North!" Evan roared.

Saskia exchanged wondering glances with Erhallen. The doors swung open and eight Imperial Guards gave way before the drawn swords of Evan and his men. The Empress's Guards surrounded Saskia as she walked up the aisle in complete silence, followed by her sisters carrying her train. Enniskarin of the Desert walked before Saskia, throwing white rose petals into her path. Saskia smiled down at the boy, who smiled briefly back, but was concentrating on his task.

108

Aleks stood at the foot of the dais, Lirallen at his side, the Priests of the Light standing on the step above him. He smiled down the hallway towards Saskia.

The room was absolutely packed. Saskia did not recognise most of the finely dressed lords and ladies. Near the front she saw one face filled with rage, and sorrowed that Liara should be so unable to accept the situation.

Saskia's Guards sheathed their swords as they reached the dais.

"Who stands before the Light to be wed this day?" the priest intoned.

"I, Aleksandr von Chenowska, stand before the Light, of my own free will," Aleks said clearly.

Saskia's voice barely came out, she was so nervous. "I, Saskia Cevaria di'Berenna, stand before the Light, of my own free will," she said faintly.

"Does anyone here have any objections to this marriage? If they do, let them speak now or forever hold their peace."

Saskia tensed, almost expecting Liara's voice. But there was no sound throughout the packed hall.

Then came the part of the ceremony that would declare Saskia's fitness: a priestess of the Light laid her hands on Saskia's stomach. Saskia felt an odd shiver go through her.

"This woman is virgin," the priestess declared. "She is fit to be the Emperor's bride."

The priest nodded and turned back to the royal couple.

"Repeat after me, Aleksandr. I, Aleksandr von Chenowska, take you, Saskia Cevaria di'Berenna, as my lawfully wedded wife. I promise in the Light to love you, forsaking all others, so long as we both shall live. With my body I shall worship you, with my strength I shall protect you. I will care for you in sickness, and should the Light bless us with children, I will raise them as respectful and worthy of you."

Aleks's voice was strong and clear as he spoke. The priest turned to Saskia.

"Repeat after me, Saskia. I, Saskia Cevaria di'Berenna, take you, Aleksandr von Chenowska, to be my lawfully wedded husband. I promise in the Light to love you, forsaking all others, so long as we both shall live. With my body I shall worship you, with my hands I shall care for you. I will be your helpmate in times of trouble, and should the Light bless us with children, I will raise them as respectful and worthy of you."

Saskia repeated the words in a slightly trembling voice.

"Who gives this woman to be married to this man?"

"I do," Erhallen said firmly. He put Saskia's hand into the priest's.

"Who vouches for this man, that he will be a good husband to this woman?"

"I do," Lirallen said clearly.

The priest joined Aleks and Saskia's hands. "Do you have the rings?" he asked.

Enniskarin came forward, small face serious, and produced the two plain gold rings Aleks had ordered made.

"Let these rings be blessed in the Light, as a symbol of your marriage." The priest put a ring into Aleks' hand, and he slid it carefully onto Saskia's finger, to rest beside her betrothal ring. Saskia repeated the procedure for Aleks.

"Thus, Aleksandr and Saskia, I declare you to be lawfully man and wife. What has been joined in the Light, let no man try to put asunder."

Cheering erupted throughout the hall. Aleks reached out to flip back Saskia's veil and lean over to give her the traditional kiss. She smiled at him tremulously.

"You're mine now," Aleks whispered with a smile. "No one is ever going to part us again."

The second ceremony followed immediately.

"Saskia von Chenowska," the chief priest asked, "Do you, as Heir to the Icelands, revoke here and now any claim you may have on the Icelander throne in favour of your unborn children, excepting only your firstborn son?"

"I do," Saskia said firmly. She had known this would happen. No consort was ever allowed to retain titles of their own after their wedding, and no firstborn son of an Emperor was allowed any title other than that of Heir.

Aleks stepped down from his throne. "Then, as is my right as Emperor," he said formally, "I crown my wife as my consort, to sit at my side as Empress." He lifted the crown of amethyst and Desert diamonds. Gasps of awe and envy went up around the room as he removed Saskia's silver circlet and set the crown on her head.

"I present to you, the Empress Saskia!" he announced. The throne room erupted in cheering.

Saskia smiled, hand in Aleks'. She turned back towards the throne just in time to see a group of Imperial Guards setting a second throne beside Aleks' to replace the chair she had used before.

Aleks escorted Saskia to her seat before taking his own place. The procession of lords and ladies began, each coming up to kneel, swear fealty to the joint rulers and offer their congratulations.

Lirallen was last of the provincial rulers to kneel before them, as the most recently come to his title. Saskia stared in surprise as after him came Iskia. She knelt.

"I offer to you both my fealty, as Heir to the Icelands and the senior representative here today," Iskia said in a clear voice. "In addition I offer to you my heartfelt congratulations and also my thanks."

"We accept your oath, Princess Iskia Cevaria," Aleks said. "And we are glad to see you here today as Heir."

Iskia moved away to stand by Lirallen, who nodded approvingly to her. The procession of Lords continued, their Ladies standing beside them. A few ladies stood in their own right and offered fealty for their lands. The Lady of Iridia City and ruler of Erinea province was one such, Lady Asfahalia. She had been her father's only heir and was now his successor. In her middle age now, she was straight-backed and sharp-eyed, though her pleasant smile softened her face into attractiveness. Her consort bowed at her side.

The procession continued. Saskia stiffened in her chair as Liara walked up to face the thrones. She gave the barest minimum of a curtsy to Saskia.

"My lady Empress," she said coolly, "Congratulations upon your elevation." She turned to Aleks and smiled.

"My lord Emperor," she said sweetly. "I have no land upon

which to offer fealty. But I offer to you my services in any way you see fit." She curtsied extremely low, almost falling out of her dress, leaving Aleks in no doubt as to what services she was offering.

Aleks could not see Saskia's face, but he could almost feel her distress. He decided that his lovely wife was far too lenient with her former friend. Liara obviously had no intention of giving up, even now that Saskia and Aleks were married.

"Lady Liara," he said pleasantly. "As my bride's foster-cousin, I am pleased to claim you as my family. As the senior member of your family, I am free to do with you as I see fit, am I not?" Aleks caught Lirallen's eye. Lirallen, having no particular love for his younger half-sister, nodded in acceptance of whatever Aleks chose.

Liara heard Aleks' meaning differently. "I would be pleased to accept a position in your household, if you should so desire, my lord," she said breathily.

"Oh no, my lady. As my kin you are far too valuable to be wasted on something so menial. You are eighteen, are you not?"

"Yes, my lord, of age."

"Indeed. Of age and more, to be wed. Clearly you are unable to choose for yourself a man. And thus I give you as a gift, and a gift to you. I'm going to make you a princess, Liara ca'Berenna. You could do no better. My wife's brother is in need of a bride for his province. You are to wed Sasken Cevaria before Midsummer."

Liara's body went taut with shock. Whispers broke out around the throne room. Was Liara formerly Aleks' mistress, that he should make her such a prize gift? Was it to appease Sasken for the loss of his sisters' guardianship?

"No!" Finally the scream burst from Liara's lips.

"Do you defy me, daughter?" Aleks said softly.

"I was supposed to marry *you*! She put you up to this, that scheming bitch-whore!"

Saskia gasped, to hear her former friend speak of her so, and flinched back in horror from the venom in Liara's words.

"You dare to speak against the Empress!" Captain Evan was instantly between Liara and Saskia, his sword drawn.

"Empress!" Liara sneered. "She's not fit to be an Empress. You can't do this to me! I am a Clanlord's daughter!"

Aleks flicked one bored look at Evan. Evan's men surrounded Liara and escorted her firmly from the room, still screaming abuse.

Aleks looked at Saskia. She was staring at him, shocked.

"I am not sure how clever that was," Saskia said softly.

"Why?"

"You have just put our two greatest enemies together. They have common cause against us. I fear they will cause us more trouble now."

Aleks shook his head. "Not if they do not leave the Icelands. I think they will not be able to find many valid reasons to leave there soon."

"Do you really think Liara will marry Sasken?"

"She has no choice, Sass. The penalty for direct disobedience to an Imperial command is death. I would not enforce that on anyone, but Liara doesn't know that. Only if her male guardian appealed would she have a way out, and I don't think Lirallen has much sympathy for his sister."

The procession of lords and ladies continued, after the brief break, until its end. Aleks stood and escorted Saskia down the steps. She suddenly realised she was very hungry: in the panic of having to make a new dress she had entirely missed breakfast, and it was now late afternoon.

The feast began. The high table, to Saskia's delight, was not by order of rank but chosen by Aleks. Aleks, with no living kin, had chosen a few close friends. Thus, at the circular table with the royal couple sat Lirallen, Mairi, Erhallen, the Icelander princesses, Enniskarin of the Desert and Captain Evan of Saskia's Guard.

Saskia smiled up at Erhallen, seated on her other side. He grinned back at her and patted her shoulder.

"You're married now, princess, how does it feel?"

"I don't think it's quite sunk in yet," Saskia admitted. She smiled at Iskia, seated beyond Erhallen. "How about you, Issy, has it sunk in yet that you're next in line to the Icelands?"

Iskia smiled back. "Only if someone murders that thieving

brother of ours."

Captain Evan, seated on Iskia's other side with Ria beside him, looked quite shocked. Captain Evan had protested in horror at being included among such august company, but Aleks had snorted rudely.

"Nonsense. How can you get to know your new lady unless you share meals with her? I've given you this job because I want her guarded every minute, Evan – and the easiest way to do that is for you to make friends with her. Besides," Aleks shrugged artlessly, "We need you to even up the numbers. I'm already swamped with Icelander princesses – for Light's sake, man, help!"

Ria, busy helping Enniskarin pour some milk, did not even hear the banter between her sisters. Beyond Enniskarin sat Liaskia, and Lirallen and Mairi between Lia and Aleks completed the circle.

Aleks would not let go of Saskia's hand. He kept lifting it to his mouth and kissing her fingers gently. Saskia turned to smile at him.

"I love you," Aleks said softly.

The smile that spread across Saskia's face astounded him. Her eyes turned soft, and she lifted her free hand to stroke his cheek.

"I love you, Aleks," she responded.

"Oh, don't look at me like that," he said.

"Why not?"

"Because I shall cause a scandal by sneaking off early from my own wedding feast. And people will say that I am entirely in love with my own wife."

"You better had be," Saskia said indignantly. "As for sneaking off early, well, I might have been having a few thoughts in that direction myself."

Mairi, overhearing them, was a little bit shocked. Lirallen thought it was funny. He leaned over.

"I would if I was you," he told Aleks with a grin. "Just chuck her over your shoulder and walk out."

"I think I had best feed my bride first, though, I would not want her to faint."

Everyone at the table was listening to the banter now, and grinning. Even the abused young princesses thought it was funny, as their older sister blushed into her winecup.

As it turned out, the couple stayed through the meal, and for half a dozen songs by the musicians while the tables were being cleared, and then danced once together and a few times with other people.

Saskia was dancing and laughing with Erhallen when Aleks came by with Iskia, paused, and switched partners smoothly. Erhallen took Iskia's hands with a smile and whirled her away.

"Are you ready, princess?" Aleks asked.

Saskia gulped and nodded. She knew the ritual of what happened next: she would be taken upstairs and put into bed by her ladies-in-waiting, and then Aleks' attendants would escort him to her.

To her surprise, Aleks led her to the side of the room, leant against the wall with a brief, flashing smile, and led her through into a secret passage.

"What!" Saskia exclaimed. "I didn't know this was here!"

"Arryn has shown me some of the Citadel's secrets. The place is riddled with secret tunnels and passages."

"Where does this lead?"

Aleks just smiled and led Saskia up through the dark passage and out into a corridor she didn't recognise. Finally he drew her through another door, then closed and bolted it behind them.

Saskia gasped, looking around the room. It wasn't Aleks' suite, but rather a beautiful guest room, with a huge four-poster bed. The bed had been strewn with white rose petals. On a table beside the bed was a wine pitcher.

"Oh, Aleks, you did this for me?" Saskia asked, amazed at his thoughtfulness.

"Of course, my love. Here." He poured her a glass of wine. Saskia drank, glancing sideways at Aleks as he sat down on the edge of the bed and began to unlace his boots. He looked wonderful to her, crown long put away, his dark hair flopped slightly curly on his forehead. Saskia stood undecided for a moment, wine cup clutched in her hand. Aleks discarded his boots, got up and came to her to take her in his arms.

"Did I tell you yet how incredibly beautiful you look today?" he murmured against her hair.

Saskia shook her head mutely.

"Then that was most ungentlemanly of me." He played with her hair a little, freed now from all restraint, it flowed long and straight down her back. "That's a fabulous dress."

"You're going to have to help me," Saskia said. "It buttons all the way up the back."

Aleks nodded. He stepped around behind Saskia and stared in horror at the long row of tiny buttons. "Oh, Light," he said.

Saskia grinned slightly. Then she heard Aleks take a deep breath and begin to unfasten the first buttons at the nape of her neck.

The buttons were almost beyond his big hands, and as he unfastened each one a little more of Saskia's smooth back was revealed to him. He bent his head to kiss the nape of her neck.

Saskia sighed a little and shifted against him. A button popped off in Aleks' fingers. Saskia glanced over her shoulder.

"Try not to ruin it, my love," she said.

Aleks sighed, frustrated. Fortunately a few buttons further down he found that Saskia was wearing a white silk chemise under her dress, or he thought that he would just have given up and ripped it from her. As it was, he was having difficulty breathing by the time he unfastened the last button. Saskia gave a slight gasp as the dress fell to pool around her feet. She turned to look up at Aleks, and he saw fear in her eyes.

"My angel, my angel," he murmured. "It's all right," he put his arms around her and held her for a long moment.

Hesitantly Saskia's hands came up to unfasten the buttons on his sleeveless jacket. She eased it open and wonderingly touched her fingers to his chest. As her fingers trailed lightly down to his stomach, Aleks stifled a groan.

Finally, they were both naked, and looking curiously at each other. Aleks took Saskia's hand and drew her gently down on the bed.

* * * *

116

The following morning, Saskia woke feeling more comfortable than she ever had in her life. Her head was rested on Aleks' broad chest, his arms wrapped around her. She stretched and then stifled a yelp of pain. Carefully she disentangled herself from Aleks. He slept on, an angelic smile softening that hard, dark face into youth.

Grunting slightly with pain, Saskia climbed out of bed and found a robe. Shrugging it on, she went to the door and peered out. Mairi was sitting in a chair by the window opposite, reading quietly.

"Mairi?" Saskia said softly. The older woman looked up with a start.

"Saskia." She set down her book and came over. "How are you? Are you in much pain?"

"A bit," Saskia admitted. "I thought it was supposed to hurt during, not after. My legs are so sore!"

Mairi grinned. "Don't worry, lass, it won't last long. Come, there's a hot bath for you waiting in your suite."

"Aleks – I should wake him."

"Don't worry about him, honey, Lirallen and Erhallen will be along in a minute."

Saskia relaxed into her bath with a sigh, feeling the warm water relaxing her muscles. "Mmm, that feels good," she told Mairi.

* * * *

Aleks woke cold and alone. For a moment he wondered if he had imagined everything, but he could still smell Saskia's sweet perfume on his pillow, and found one of her long silvery hairs wound around his fingers. He sat up, wondering where she had gone, and then his eyes fell on the bloodstain on the sheets.

Lirallen and Erhallen barged in through the door a moment later, followed by Enniskarin of the Desert and a couple of Aleks' other young squires.

"Did you sleep well, my lord?" Enniskarin inquired innocently.

"I certainly hope not," said Lirallen, and burst out laughing.

Erhallen saw the small blood spots on the sheet.

"Did you count them?" he asked.

"What?" Aleks replied.

"The drops, Aleks. When a Clan maiden is taken to bed, her man must give her one jewel for each drop of blood she sheds for love of him. A clansman would give his bride red glass if he could afford nothing better. Saskia may be Icelander by blood but she is Clan in her heart."

"Then, I shall buy her a necklace of – seven rubies," Aleks said, peering at the sheet carefully.

Erhallen nodded, satisfied, as Aleks climbed out of bed.

"Where is she?" Aleks asked.

"With Mairi, gone to take a bath," Lirallen replied. He began to laugh as Aleks turned away to take the clothes Enniskarin was offering.

"What's funny?"

"Saskia should cut her nails. She's left very visible evidence all down your back that she enjoyed her wedding night."

Aleks tried not to grin smugly, peering over his shoulder. "Guess I'll be working with my shirt on in the practice yard the next few days," he said.

* * * *

Saskia actually felt shy about seeing Aleks again. Mairi, knowing just how she felt, had made arrangements for them to have lunch together in private.

Saskia was sitting in the library waiting for Aleks when he came in from the practice yard. He was hot and sweating, wearing only black trousers and a thin white lawn shirt unlaced to his waist. He tossed his sword into the corner and stopped at the sight of Saskia, seated by the fire. Even the Citadel was cold at Midwinter.

Saskia looked up at Aleks shyly, a blush staining her cheeks. She smiled hesitantly.

"Hello, beautiful," Aleks walked over and leaned down to kiss her. His nose was cold against her cheek.

"Oh: you're cold!"

"Not really. I was just practising with Erhallen. Light, the man's a demon with a sword!"

"He was the Master of Swords before becoming Berenna's Lord," Saskia reminded him.

Aleks groaned slightly, sitting down. "Don't I know it!" Still, he looked pleased: Saskia suspected he had held his own.

Saskia was a bit nervous about looking Aleks in the eye. She served him food and a cup of lightly spiced wine before sitting down to eat herself. She found that for some reason she had no appetite.

Aleks, watching his beautiful wife pick at her food, lost his own appetite. "Are you not hungry, beloved?" he asked.

Saskia raised her eyes to his. "Not really," she admitted.

"Me neither." Aleks paused, biting at his lip, then got up and held out a hand to Saskia. "Want to come out riding?"

"Oh, I'd love to!" she brightened instantly.

They went out to the stables and Aleks ordered Sandstorm and Dawn saddled. Saskia had forgotten about her sore muscles, and had to hide a slight gasp as she swung up into Dawn's saddle. The little mare had not been out for a few days and frisked impatiently.

Riding in the huge park below the Citadel, no one so much as gave them a second glance. Saskia marvelled at how easy it was for Aleks to stay hidden in plain sight, especially when his face was stamped on every coin out of the City mint.

"I am surprised no one recognises you," she said to Aleks.

"Why should they? I'm just a man riding a good horse. They're far more likely to recognise you: fair hair is not all that common here in the south and there are stories being told all over the city of the Icelander princesses."

Saskia looked around a little nervously. Indeed, a few people were looking at her curiously.

"I should have worn a scarf to cover my hair," she said.

"No one will bother you, princess," Aleks said firmly. He touched the hilt of the sword sheathed on his back. "I swear it."

"Still," Saskia looked around. "I want my own sword, Aleks. I am not some pampered lady of the court. I might be a princess by birth but I am a Clan warrior by raising."

"Not very conventional." Aleks looked disapproving for a moment. Belatedly Saskia remembered that the Desert valued women more than most, and that the great Desert army did not send women into the front line.

"I do not want to offend, Aleks, or to make either of us a laughing-stock," she told him seriously. "But I do not feel safe, with my brother still on the loose. I need to be able to defend myself, and my sisters also if it comes to that. I have the training and the ability: Erhallen has every confidence in my skills and you have seen for yourself how good he is."

Aleks nodded. "All right. Have him get you a sword: ten swords, if you wish. Humour me in one thing, though: do not wear them openly on formal occasions. Swordbelts and dresses, they don't go well together."

Saskia laughed. "All right. I promise, no steel and diamonds. But I do want to hide a few swords around the palace, places where I can get to them easily."

Aleks smiled. "As many as you want, my love. The Citadel has a few built-in secrets that it might come in handy to show you. Arryn has given me the secret plans of the palace: you'd be amazed just how many hidey-holes and tunnels there are."

Later on, they returned to the palace, laughing and smiling together. Instead of going back into the keep after dropping off their horses, Aleks took Saskia's hand and led her around to the gardens.

"The palace has a secret here that I want you to have for your own."

Saskia followed, bemused, until they came to a wall that seemed to be part of the castle wall itself. Aleks grinned over his shoulder at her, pushed aside a hanging sheet of ivy and opened a gate in the wall.

"Only a few gardeners and myself know about this," he said. "The only windows that look out over it are the Emperor and Empress' private quarters."

Cunningly made, the wall fit seamlessly into the castle itself. Inside, the little garden was very quiet and tranquil. A little stream splashed over a few rocks, a tiny path wound between old, gnarled apple trees to a little bench under a willow. The

120

grass was thick and plush, but kept neatly cut, and the ferns at the side of the stream were tamed so that the water could still be seen. A few plants were there that Saskia recognised as flowering, but in Midwinter they were just green leaves.

"Oh, but this is beautiful!" she said.

"Not so lovely in Midwinter, I fear," Aleks said. "But in the summer, this is a beautiful refuge: it is sheltered from the sun most of the day and the stream never dries out. It is the Empress's Garden, and no one may come here without your permission."

"Even you?" Saskia said playfully.

Aleks smiled down at her. "Well, my lady Empress, I should hope that you would give me your permission always." He gathered her close into his arms and bent his head to nuzzle at her hair. Saskia turned her face up and they shared a long, deep kiss.

"Mmm," Saskia said when he released her. Aleks wanted to kiss her again: she looked so beautiful, eyes half-lidded with passion, lips a little apart. "Oh, I can hardly wait for tonight." She flushed a little at her own boldness.

"Let's not, then," Aleks said.

"What?" Saskia said, surprised.

Aleks grinned. "Lovemaking does not all have to be done under cover of darkness. No one will disturb us today. Come on." He led her back out of the garden into the keep, and up to his private quarters.

Saskia had never been in Aleks' suite before and looked around her, impressed. The room was tastefully decorated, in blue and cream. The bed was magnificent, the biggest she had ever seen, with cream hangings and sheets.

"I'll lose you in that bed," she said, laughing.

"You certainly won't," Aleks replied. "You won't have a chance, because I won't be letting go." He drew her down beside him and they began to kiss again.

Afterwards, Saskia lay wrapped in Aleks' arms, head on his broad chest. Outside the window, the sky was rapidly darkening towards night. Listening to his steady breathing, Saskia thought that Aleks had fallen asleep. Silently, she slipped out of his arms and bent to dress. She could not find one boot, and with exasperation lit a ball of wyrdfire on her hand.

"What in the Light is that?" Aleks exclaimed.

The witchlight went out instantly. Saskia could still see Aleks, sitting up now and staring at her intently. She sat back down on the edge of the bed.

"Witchlight, or wyrdfire," she said. "All Power-Gifted can make a witchlight, those Gifted with Fire use wyrdfire."

"Show me again," Aleks demanded. Saskia relit the wyrdfire for him. He leaned close. "It's actually touching your hand, does it not burn?" he asked.

"No," Saskia said. "I cannot be burned by fires of any kind."

"Would it burn me if I touched it?"

Saskia looked surprised. "I don't know. Put your hand close: does it feel hot?"

Aleks stopped when still a good handspan away. "It feels *very* hot," he said. "Could you throw this?"

"I suppose so," Saskia said. She followed Aleks' train of thought. "Yes, I could certainly use it as a weapon, if it came down to that. It wouldn't really be necessary, though, I could just set fire to a man's clothing, or his hair or beard, at a distance."

"How remarkable," Aleks said. He looked at Saskia. "I didn't really expect to get a witch for a bride when I asked for a princess."

"Well, I am both," Saskia said a little haughtily. "And I'd rather you didn't call me a witch, either. That's rather an insulting term. Sorceress is more acceptable."

"Sorry," Aleks said meekly. "I didn't want to be rude. Don't be upset with me, Sass. I need your help."

Saskia smiled at him. "I'm not really upset. You couldn't know. And what do you mean, you need my help?"

"I'll show you." Aleks scrambled out of bed and dressed hastily. Saskia wasn't sure where to put her eyes and eventually just walked over to the window to look out.

When Aleks was dressed, he led Saskia down to his study, a small quiet room next to the library. The secretary Arryn worked in the anteroom, and nodded pleasantly to them both as they entered.

Aleks' desk was piled high with papers, in three separate stacks.

"What's this?" Saskia asked.

"This pile is new stuff I haven't sorted through yet. This one is the stuff I have finished and haven't yet given to Arryn. And this is the pile of stuff I think I can deal with." The first pile was about as tall as Saskia's forearm was long, and the second two were pitifully small. It looked as though Aleks was struggling.

"That you *can* deal with? What about that which you can't?" Saskia asked, suddenly realising what he had not said.

"That's over there." Aleks waved at a table across the room. It was stacked high with more paper than Saskia had ever seen.

"Can't anybody help you with that?" Saskia asked, raising her eyebrows in horror.

Aleks shook his head miserably. "Almost all of it is things left over from the old Emperor's reign. Many of them refer to private agreements and the like. It's only polite of me to fulfil them if I can. Arryn does his best to help, but what I really need are the old Emperor's journals. He kept a daily log of all the people he talked to and petitions and documents that he signed."

"Well, where are they?" Saskia asked.

"Over there." Aleks pointed at a shelf of thick brown books, each one with a year date on the spine. He pulled out the most recent, last year's. "The only problem is, the Emperor had an Icelander nurse when he was young. They're all written in the Icelander dialect. To keep anyone from nosing, I suspect."

Saskia could not help but smile. She took the book from his hands and set it down on a table. Looking through, she found that the journal was very organised, each entry neatly dated on a fresh page.

"Get some of those petitions, we'll have a look," she suggested.

The very first one Aleks brought referred to the date of a conversation. Saskia looked it up and translated. The look of relief on Aleks' face was wonderful to see.

"I understand this one now!" he said. "Oh, what a relief, Sass! Do you think you could translate that whole section? Then

I wouldn't have to bother you every time I want the same part."

On request, Arryn found a new book for Saskia, and she seated herself and began to translate while Aleks sorted through his new pile of papers. Every now and then he would bring her another reference to look up, but mostly they worked in companionable silence.

"I want to go away for a few days," Aleks said a little later on.

"Where to?" Saskia asked, lifting her head from the books.

"Just away from all this. I want a little time just for the two of us, just being the two of us. Arryn told me that the last Emperor and Empress Asparia went away after they were married, to a place called Moon Lake."

"Where's that?"

"I'm not entirely sure," Aleks admitted. "There's a Sun Lake, near Highfort, and Arryn said he thinks that Moon Lake is near there somewhere, perhaps on the Summerlands and Eastphal border."

"It sounds lovely," Saskia said enthusiastically. "Why don't you ask someone about it?"

And so it happened that four days later, they left the Citadel with a small party of guards, heading first into Eastphal and then on over the Summerlands border to Moon Lake, skirting the high mountains of the Roman'ii since the weather there was appalling in winter.

Chapter 8

Moon Lake, the Summerlands. Late Winter, the year 2716 after Founding

Saskia thought Moon Lake was the most beautiful place she had ever seen. The lake curved gently along the floor of a small valley, just a few miles from where the Grain River began. The entire valley was an Imperial retreat: local farmers grazed their sheep there to keep the grass down, but they were gone before Saskia and Aleks arrived. There were two small, low buildings for guards and servants, and the main lodge itself.

The lodge was a marvel: built partly out on stilts over the clear icy waters of the lake. There was a wooden deck that caught the afternoon sun, and inside, only one room, and a tiny cupboard for the necessary. The main room was large, however, with two fireplaces. Near one stood a big copper bathtub, big enough for two. In front of the other fireplace was a thick fur rug, and beside that, a big, soft-looking bed. The rest of the furniture was sparse, but well made: a comfortable sofa, a table with two chairs, and a small bookcase with a few well-thumbed leather-bound books in it.

Saskia looked around, laughed, and tossed herself onto the bed with a whoop of joy. "I love it!"

A servant was carrying in their things. They would be left to their own devices mainly, only to call for servants when they wanted some food.

They spent fifteen long, lazy days at the lodge, relaxing and getting to know each other. Several mornings they sat out on the deck, feet dangling down towards the water, fishing with roughly made poles. Saskia caught a trout one morning and squealed with delight. Aleks, who had little luck with the fish, just sighed and shook his head.

"Witch," he accused. "You must have used sorcery somehow."

"How could I?" Saskia said. "It's a Water creature and my Power is of Fire: I would have driven it away, not called it to me. It looks delicious: let's cook it for dinner."

* * * *

They returned to the Citadel happy, laughing and at last comfortable with each other. Huge piles of papers awaited Aleks on his desk, and invitations drifted like snow on Saskia's. There were more for her than for Aleks: for her to go riding, visiting, shopping, for tea. There were some for both of them: for dinner, for dancing, for parties at Spring Equinox.

Saskia's sisters were glad to see her. They had been a little lonely in the Citadel. Lirallen and Erhallen had gone back to their holdings in the Clanlands and there were not really any other people in the Citadel who knew their true situation. There were noble children by the dozen for them to play with, but all three girls had grown up too quickly. Their outlook was far beyond children of their own age, and so they mostly stayed together. But with Saskia back, they came out of their shells again, and socialised with her.

Despite their youth, the princesses were accepted totally into society: no one would dare to refuse the sisters of the new Empress, and they were also extremely eligible. Aleks, however, frowned severely on the few who were foolish enough to suggest contracting a betrothal. Erisien of Forstport asked for betrothal for Iskia, to be consummated in a wedding when she was sixteen.

Aleks leaned back in his chair and looked at Erisien. The Forstian noble was a good enough man, a little older than Aleks but handsome and wealthy. Iskia probably could not do much better.

"No," Aleks said flatly.

"But why not?" Erisien half begged. Aleks remembered Saskia telling him the young lord had thought himself in love with her and knew a little pity.

126

"Erisien," he said, "Iskia is very different from my wife. Saskia has been hardened by years of living in the Clanlands. Iskia is younger, and far more fragile. She has suffered emotional abuse for some years. I am her guardian, not her owner. It is not for me to parcel the princesses out for useful alliances. They have suffered enough: I want them to be happy. I mean for all of them to chose their own husbands when the time comes. I will give you permission to pay court to Iskia, Erisien, because I believe you to be a good man. But if I hear so much as a whisper of you trying to compromise or force her, I'll see you dead for it. Are we understood?"

Erisien nodded, wide-eyed. "I am not entirely sure I understand your reasoning, my lord. Surely the princesses are yours to use as you see fit?"

"That's what their father and brother thought also," Aleks said. "But I will not see these princesses forced into slavery to anyone. Their marriages will be their choice and theirs alone."

That night, in bed, Aleks repeated the conversation to Saskia. She approved heartily.

"Erisien is such an ass," she said disapprovingly. "Fancy just asking for Iskia. I don't believe she's so much as looked at him twice."

Aleks shrugged. "He didn't want Iskia, anyway. He wanted you, and thought he'd take the next best thing."

Saskia shook her head disapprovingly. "Fool. He always was too stupid to take no for an answer."

"Yes." Aleks hugged her fiercely. "You're *mine*. I won't share you, and I'll never let you go."

"What?" Saskia laughed. "Feeling a little possessive?"

"Very possessive. I'll deal with men admiring you, but that man coveted you, and thought he'd take Iskia because he could not have you. I'll kill him if he tries anything without her permission."

As it turned out, Aleks had nothing to worry about. Erisien, perhaps sensing the Emperor's animosity towards him, headed promptly home to Forstport. A few weeks later they received notice of his betrothal, to the daughter of another minor Forst lord.

* * * *

Time moved on and soon it was Midsummer, Saskia's seventeenth birthday. Aleks threw a small party for her, just family and friends, and Lirallen, Erhallen and Mairi came back from the Clanlands to see them. The day of the party was beautiful, they held a small picnic in the Empress' Garden, and all sat on the soft, springy grass by the little stream.

Aleks wrapped Saskia in his arms and pressed his face into her hair for a moment. She hugged him back, tilting her head to smile up at him.

"Why don't we go away for a few days?" Aleks suggested. "I can't take a long enough break for us to go out to Moon Lake again, but I could probably spare a ten-night or so."

"Where would we go?" Saskia asked.

"Perhaps just a little tour. Take a boat up the river for a day or so, and ride around a little bit of South Erinea: get a feel for the locals. I have not done enough of that yet: I know what the Desert people are like, and I know enough of the Clanlands and Icelands now. But the people from these central, farming lands are different and I would like to get to know them."

Saskia agreed: she had travelled through Haven and ForstMarch on the way to the Clanlands, but had never been into Erinea and its massive farmlands.

They headed out at dawn a few days later, with Erhallen, Evan and two trusted Imperial Guards. They spent several days riding around small villages and market towns, rarely recognised. Often Saskia and Aleks would ride into the town alone, and walk around the market, have a meal in the inn, and not be recognised until the Imperial Guards showed up.

* * * *

The royal couple arrived back in the Citadel late afternoon on the seventh day. Aleks and Saskia rode into the Citadel's courtyard, laughing together, Evan and the other men behind them with Erhallen. Aleks lowered Saskia gently down from his saddle and jumped down beside her.

128

Lirallen, Mairi, Liaskia and Riaskia came out to greet them. They smiled and greeted Saskia. She noticed that Ria and Lia were looking around strangely.

"What is it?" Saskia asked.

"Where's Iskia?" Ria asked curiously.

"What did you say?" Aleks said, turning to stare.

"Where's Iskia?"

"Why, she's here with you. Is she not?"

Ria stared at Aleks horror-struck. "Oh, Light, no," she said in a whisper.

"Ria, Ria, what is it?" Saskia clutched at her sister's hands as Ria swayed.

"We – we found a note in Iskia's room after you left. Some of her things were gone – packed neatly, no sign of trouble. The note was in her handwriting, it said simply that she was going with you, that you decided at the last minute that you wanted a girl's company. It made sense, no maids along to attend you or anything."

Saskia swayed too. Aleks caught her, fearful that she would faint.

"Sasken," she whispered.

"I know. Come on, everyone inside. Mairi! Take Saskia upstairs, get a hot drink into her. And the other two, they both look shocked. Evan, Lirallon, Erhallen, come with me."

The four men went up to the library. Aleks, upset, poured himself a small glass of brandy. He offered the decanter round. All three of the other men nodded.

"That was damnably clever," Evan said after they had all sat in silence for a minute or two. "There would be no reason for the younger girls not to believe such a plausible story."

Lirallen nodded, shame-faced. "I never even thought to question. Riaskia just told me Iskia had gone on the trip. It didn't occur to me that anything untoward could have happened."

Aleks nodded. "I don't see what Sasken's doing, though," he said. "Surely this will serve only to make me angry. He still does not have Saskia, and now she will be guarded more closely than ever."

Erhallen frowned, shaking his head. "It doesn't make sense.

Why take Iskia, the weakest of the sisters? Surely she will only slow him down."

Aleks all of a sudden understood, and didn't like it. "Iskia is the oldest sister," he said.

"No, that's Saskia," Evan said, mystified.

"Not any longer, not as far as Sasken is concerned. She is wed: no longer virgin, impure and of no further use to him. He could not guarantee that any child she bore would be his. Iskia is the second choice for his princess."

"Bastard," Erhallen said through gritted teeth. "And she's ill, too, Princess Iskia."

"I am going to kill him if he's harmed so much as a hair on her head," Aleks snarled.

"No, you're not," Saskia said, walking in at that moment followed by the two youngest sisters. "I've told you, Aleks, he's not for you to kill. And not for either of you, foster-cousins, or you, Captain."

"What is this?" Lirallen asked, confused. "Why can't we kill him?"

"My mother had the TimeSight: she told Rianna who must kill Sasken. The time is not right."

"Who is it?" Aleks demanded.

"Me," Riaskia said in a clear voice. The four men turned to look at her. She stood straight-backed under their curiosity, just twelve years old and small still.

Saskia was gaping at her sister. "How do you know?"

"Don't be a fool, Sass. You already knew I had the TimeSight too. These last years, Mama using the Gift has triggered the Sight in me also. I saw everything she saw, and other things she did not." Ria's eyes were shadowed.

"You knew she would never return to Iceden," Saskia said, understanding suddenly. "You knew you were saying goodbye forever."

"I was the one who saw the other possibilities," Ria responded.

"We're going to have a long talk about this quite soon," Saskia said with a penetrating look at her younger sister. Then she turned back to the others.

"I daresay Ria won't tell you what will happen if you do kill Sasken," she said, "but take it from me, it won't be good. Ria has to kill him and she will do that when the time is right. In the meantime, I don't intend to leave Iskia with our brother."

"I'm going after him," Aleks said.

"No!" they all shouted at once. Aleks looked indignant.

"You must not," Lirallen said definitely. "He has Luck, you know that. You beat him in a fair fight last time, but this time he may not fight fair. The Empire cannot afford to lose another ruler so soon. Let me go."

"The same goes for a Clanlord," Aleks snapped back.

"I will go," Evan said eagerly.

Aleks considered that a moment. "No," he responded finally. "This might – just possibly – be a diversion, to have us looking for Iskia when the real target is still Saskia. I want you beside her."

"Then it's me," Erhallen said. He shrugged. "Berenna will be safe in the hands of our cousin Erifennen a while longer. Forever if need be. There is no reason for me not to go."

"Iskia is my ward, my responsibility," Aleks said. "But Lirallen is right. If I cannot go myself I would not trust anyone more than you, Erhallen, to bring her back safe."

Saskia nodded. "If anyone can get her back, Erhallen, it's you. I want to go myself, but somehow I think I would not get out of the Citadel without you all trying to stop me." Definite nods were her answer before they all turned back to Erhallen.

"Take some of my men," Evan urged. "Or some Imperial Guards from the North, at least: you do not know the land."

Erhallen shook his head. "I don't think so. Give me a fast horse and a good map, and I will manage. Other men would only make me more visible and slow me down. I cannot go in through Iceport, I must cross the Haven border, so I suppose someone could come with me until then."

"One of my men is half Havener, half Icelander," Evan said. "I will have him make ready."

Evan's man, Jerik, was a tough, competent sort. Erhallen liked him at once.

"Are you ready? Do you have everything you need?" Saskia

asked, when finally the two men stood in the courtyard, holding the reins of their horses. They would not be riding far for now: just to the docks, to take the riverboat for Iridia, from where they would catch ship for Terrport, then travel upriver a ways before crossing into the Icelands. Aleks had put two ships at their disposal, the riverboat *Windsprite* was waiting for them at the Citadel's docks, and the fast clipper *Emperor Kerabian* would wait for them at Iridia.

Goodbyes were swift: no one wanted to waste any time. Sasken was a week ahead of them, he would be at Iridia by now. They were unlucky in that this year had been wet, and the river was still flowing deeply enough for the boats to come all the way to the Citadel. Otherwise, Sasken would have been forced to travel much more slowly and they might have had a chance of catching him, or of getting a message ahead by pigeon.

* * * *

Erhallen chafed at the slowness of the riverboat: but it still travelled faster than a horse, since it moved constantly, even by night. Sometimes in the day, though, it seemed slow and he could not keep himself from pacing the deck.

The air grew colder as they headed north. Jerik revelled in it, but Erhallen grew chilled, his hot Clanlander blood too warm for the colder north. Fortunately Saskia had anticipated this, and sent along a pack of warm clothing for him, for which Erhallen was extremely grateful.

Finally the riverboat reached Iridia. Jerik and Erhallen unloaded their horses and headed across to the open-sea docks. The *Emperor Kerabian* was there, the captain none too pleased about having to wait for them. The mention of Aleks' name silenced him, and they cast off for Terrport within the hour.

"Trouble at Iceport this week," the captain commented once they were safely out at sea.

"What sort of trouble?" Erhallen asked quickly.

"Lots of ships and cargo being searched. Some people have been turned back, not allowed to enter the Icelands."

"Is that legal?"

"Sort of. The Prince has declared some sort of quarantine."

"There's a plague?"

"I doubt it. No, for his own reasons the Prince has decided to restrict entry to the Icelands. A lot of ships are docking at Terrport instead: we may have trouble docking. It could take a day or two: you might have been as quick riding from Iridia."

Erhallen shared a quick, worried glance with Jerik.

"What about with this?" Erhallen handed a letter to the captain. He unfolded it and read.

"Whosoever aids this man, aids me, and whosoever hinders him, hinders me. Signed in the Light by Aleksandr von Chenowska." The captain goggled at the letter. "If this cannot get us a berth in the docks, I do not know what will, my lord."

The captain was proved right. When the assistant harbourmaster was rowed out from the port to check their papers for priority, they gave him the letter. He instantly directed them into the first available berth. They were docked within an hour. Erhallen and Jerik paused only long enough to unload their horses and collect fresh supplies, then set out, heading fast upriver along the Iceflow.

Beyond Terrport, the Iceflow was not navigable by boats bigger than rowboats, since it almost immediately branched off into three much smaller tributaries. The main stream was the one they followed, the one Saskia had come down with her mother four years earlier. It marked the Icelands – Havener border.

"I grew up about ten miles from here," Jerik said one day as they negotiated a tricky shallow ravine.

"You're half Icelander yourself, aren't you?" Erhallen asked.

"That's right. I wish you'd let me come over the border with you. I speak the language, I look like one of them. I can get you in, my lord, trust me."

"All right." Erhallen nodded. "You said the crossing place in the river is further up?"

"Another mile or two from here. The river is too fast and too cold to cross just anywhere, and all the places further up are too close to Iceden and may be heavily patrolled."

The ford looked rather deep to Erhallen, but Jerik sent his

horse confidently across and was soon waiting on the other side. Erhallen followed, sucking in a sharp breath as the icy water swirled around his legs.

"Light, that's cold!" he gasped, as he reached Jerik on the far bank.

Jerik grinned. "You'll soon warm up. Come on. We've got to move fast now, get away from the river and cover our tracks. We'll come to Iceden from the north, so it doesn't look like we're approaching from the Empire."

It took them another two days to get around to a good place to approach Iceden. They had been stopped once by a patrol, but Jerik lied glibly and told them that they were on their way to Iceden to volunteer into the Icelander Guard. The patrol sent them on their way at once.

Erhallen was tired as they approached Iceden in the evening, but not too tired to marvel at the beauty of the strange city. The white needle of Iceden soared high into the sky. The low buildings around its foot were a shambles, however.

"What a mess," Erhallen said in a low voice.

"The prince lives in luxury while the Icelanders struggle to win a living from this hard land," Jerik shrugged. "That's how it is here, how it has been for a long time."

"Since the Icelander princes became obsessed with their own sisters and daughters, I daresay," Erhallen snarled.

At that moment, bells in the tower began to ring.

"What is that?" Erhallen asked.

All the blood drained out of Jerik's face as he listened to the pattern of the bells. "It's the wedding bells," he said. "It's Autumn Equinox today, Princess Iskia's fourteenth birthday. I suppose that adds almost legality to this."

"Somehow I don't think it's my sister Liara that Sasken's marrying then," Erhallen said grimly.

"No."

"Do you know the protocol? What will they do?"

"The wedding will be in the Temple of the Light: there's one inside the tower, about half way up." Jerik took a plan of Iceden, drawn from memory by Saskia and the others, out of his saddlebag and looked at it. "Here, look. It's an evening wedding, so they will already have had the dinner. He'll probably take the princess straight to his bed after the ceremony. This, here, this is the prince's bedroom."

The two men looked thoughtfully at the map. "Then we have perhaps one hour to get into Iceden and up to the prince's bedroom," Erhallen said.

"Bit of a tall order," Jerik agreed.

"Let's go."

The town gates were unguarded. The two men left their horses tied among a dozen others in an inn yard and headed for the castle at speed. Saskia had drawn on the map the approximate location of the secret door her mother had brought her out through. They found the place quickly and searched for the mechanism.

"Think this is it?" Jerik tugged on an iron ring set into the wall. With a grating sound a section of wall swung aside.

"Come on!" The two raced inside and up through the cobwebby passage. Swords drawn, they were heedless now, desperate to find Iskia before Sasken forced her.

Finally they reached the end of the passage, in the room that Saskia had shared once with her sisters. The prince's bedroom was just down the corridor. Out in the passage they found two guards. They were dead with two swipes of Erhallen's sword and then the two men hastily headed for Sasken's room. Erhallen flung open the door.

Iskia was lying on the bed, naked. She sat up slowly as Erhallen opened the door, and smiled at him vaguely. Her eyes looked glassy and unfocussed.

"Look out!" Jerik shouted as Erhallen started towards Iskia. He pushed Erhallen in the back, forcing him down.

There was a <u>thrum</u> sound, and a crossbow bolt whizzed over Erhallen's head and buried itself in Jerik's chest. He gasped out once, but the bolt was true to the heart.

Erhallen saw Sasken in the shadows beside the bed, wearing only his trousers, crossbow empty now in his hand. Erhallen lunged across the room, sword out. At the last minute he remembered Riaskia's warning, reversed his sword and hit Sasken hard just above the ear with the hilt. Sasken went down like a felled tree.

Erhallen ran back across the room and shut the door. He knelt beside Jerik and closed the dead man's eyes.

"May your soul walk in the Light now and forever," he whispered. "Goodbye, my friend." He bowed his head for a moment, then got up.

Princess Iskia lay on the bed, shifting about and sighing restlessly. Erhallen frowned. He went over and tasted the dregs of remaining wine in the two cups by the bed, making a face. One contained a powerful dose of a calming potion, the other a huge dose of aphrodisiac.

"Oh, Light," he murmured, looking at the princess. Obviously Sasken had wanted her quiet and willing. "Bastard."

Erhallen looked around for something to dress Iskia in. He found only a shift, and a wedding dress that he could not possibly take her out in. With a sigh, he opened Sasken's wardrobe and took out some trousers and a cotton shirt. He slashed off the bottom of the trousers to make them a reasonable length for the tiny princess, and forced her into them. She sighed and writhed under his hands. Erhallen found himself shaking: Iskia was after all beautiful, and fully formed as a woman. He hated himself for the urge to take her, and was perhaps a little rough as he tied the trousers closed and dragged the shirt over her head. With a whispered apology he took Jerik's long coat and put it onto Iskia. She kept moaning and trying to kiss him.

"Light, give me strength," Erhallen said in a strangled voice as one of her slim hands closed over his crotch. He removed the hand and swung Iskia up over his shoulder. She was quiet, stroking his back.

Erhallen headed out into the corridor and back to the secret passage. Iskia weighed almost nothing, a feather. He was worried about her, knowing that some of the drugs she had previously been given had triggered fits when they wore off. He had to get her away from Iceden and back over the Haven border.

Outside it had started to snow again, an early autumn snowfall. Erhallen cursed luridly and raced back though the streets to the inn where the horses were. After a moment's deliberation, he decided to leave Jerik's horse: Iskia was light enough that his could carry them both, and he suspected she was not strong enough to ride alone even when she regained coherency. He settled her before him, wrapping his cloak around them both.

"Erhallen," Iskia said softly as he rode quietly out of town. He looked down at her in surprise: surely she was not coherent already?

Iskia's beautiful amethyst eyes were turned up to his face, and she gently stroked his cheek, heavy with beard he had not shaved since before Terrport.

"Princess, how are you feeling?" he asked.

"Safe now with you, my love," she said.

"Uh-oh," Erhallen said aloud.

"You came for me, I knew you would. Can we be wed soon?"

"Princess Iskia, you and I are not betrothed."

She began to struggle at that, and to cry out.

"Hush, hush," Erhallen begged, terrified she would bring pursuit down on them. He dared not gallop while she was fighting him. "Princess, yes, we will be wed as soon as we get back to your sisters."

Iskia quieted at once, and wrapped her arms around his neck. "Kiss me," she demanded. When Erhallen hesitated, her beautiful amethyst eyes hardened and darkened. She tensed in his arms. Convinced she was about to fight him again, Erhallen kissed her.

Erhallen almost lost himself. Iskia's mouth was so soft and sweet, her body pliable against his. They rode through the snow kissing fiercely.

It was the cold that brought Erhallen back to his senses. Iskia had nothing on her feet, and he was sure they must be freezing. He persuaded her to sit quietly while he found spare socks in his saddlebag and put them on to her feet. He wrapped his cloak more securely around them both.

"Sleep, my love," he whispered into her ear. "Sleep now, I have you safe."

Iskia obeyed, finally, head resting against his chest. Erhallen turned his face up to the dark, snowy sky and sucked in a few ragged breaths. What in the Light had he been playing at? Saskia would have his guts with a dull knife if she ever found out. Iskia was barely fourteen, under Clan and Icelander law a legal age for wedding and bedding, but as an Imperial ward she would either have to be sixteen or have Aleks' specific permission to wed.

Why was his mind off down <u>that</u> track, Erhallen wondered. Iskia was far too young for him anyway. Why in the Light would he want to marry her?

"You're an idiot," Erhallen reproached himself. "Now get moving, you've got to make the ford before dawn, or the hunt will be on."

He picked up the pace and they headed south and along the river, the falling snow covering the tracks behind them.

They reached the ford just after sunrise. Erhallen lifted the still-sleeping Iskia's legs high, not wanting her to get wet in the icy water. They crossed and instantly turned due south, away from the clear trail Jerik and Erhallen had left coming up the river. Erhallen hoped Sasken would follow that when he found it, and head back for Terrport or for Haven.

Iskia woke a couple of hours later, as they cantered smoothly across a snowy meadow. Erhallen felt her stirring and drew the horse back to a walk.

Iskia opened her eyes and looked around her. "Where in the Light am I?" she said. She looked up at Erhallen, and after a moment recognition dawned. "My lord Erhallen?"

"Princess Iskia. How are you feeling?"

"My head hurts. Where am I?" Iskia looked around, puzzled.

"Haven Province, and heading south as fast as we can go. They will have started after us at sunrise, and that's if your brother didn't wake before then. Although I hit him pretty hard."

"I don't remember," Iskia said dazedly. "I remember being made to drink things and put in a wedding dress. I think I remember the temple. But then it's all black."

Erhallen breathed a silent sigh of relief. "We broke in just before – just before, um, your brother took you to bed. He killed my companion and I knocked him out and took you."

* * * *

Iskia felt quite content resting against the Berenna lord's chest. She had spoken to him a few times, sat beside him and danced with him at Saskia and Aleks' wedding. He was a fine figure of a man, and his strong arm held her securely against him while his free hand guided the horse.

"I need to stop at the next town and change horses," Erhallen said after a while. "My map says that we are not too far from the Haven to Whiteport road: there are staging posts all along it. I do not want you to be seen."

They crossed the road a few minutes later. Erhallen decided that the nearest town was a few miles east, and turned that way. When they came in sight of the town, a tiny place of about thirty houses and an inn, he left Iskia hidden in a small thicket of trees and went on alone.

Iskia was frightened and hungry. She dared not move, and stayed hidden in the low scrub around the trees. She peered out at the sound of hoofbeats a while later and saw Erhallen returning on a fresh horse.

"Why only one horse?" Iskia asked as he reined in beside her.

"Just how good are you on horseback?" Erhallen said pointedly. Iskia flushed slightly. "I thought so. We have to move fast, princess. I do not think you could handle a fast enough animal to keep up." He leant down. "Up you come."

Iskia was settled and they were moving again before she could think of a response. Then her nose twitched. "Bread! You brought fresh bread?"

Erhallen smiled and handed her a small loaf, already cut in half and buttered, with a thick chunk of ham in it. Iskia tore into the bread ravenously.

"Eat slowly!" Erhallen cautioned. "I'm not sure what was in the drugs Sasken gave you, but they could make you sick. Be careful."

Iskia obeyed, chewing a few mouthfuls down slowly. Her stomach seemed all right, but her head still pounded abominably, and the bright morning sunlight only made it worse. Once she had finished eating, she closed her eyes and let her head fall back against Erhallen's chest. She was soon asleep again.

That evening, Erhallen stopped in a tiny village away from any roads. There was a small inn there, and he made Iskia keep her head covered until they were safely in the only guest room.

"We are registered as husband and wife," Erhallen said as he shut the door. "You are nothing like me, not enough to pass off as my sister. And though I could be your bodyguard, you are too scruffy to be a fine lady. I have told them you are ill. I am going out now to find some clothes, and something to disguise that hair of yours. Do not answer the door to anyone except me."

Iskia found a mirror over the washbasin and stared at herself in horror. Somewhere she had got mud on her face, and the cut-off clothes of Sasken's she was wearing made her look like a boy. She looked horrible. What must the handsome Berenna lord think of her? She washed her face, and tugged the comb on the washstand through her hair, but could do nothing about the rest.

A little while later there was a knock on the door.

"Who is it?" Iskia asked.

"Erhallen."

Iskia opened the door and Erhallen slipped inside. He was carrying a large bundle, which he unrolled to reveal a dark travelling dress with divided skirts, that looked almost small enough for Iskia. There was a bundle of underclothes and a night-shirt too.

Iskia reached for the clothes, but he stopped her. "Just a few minutes. I want to disguise that hair of yours. I bought these off the village wisewoman, and she gave me some stuff that will turn your hair brown. Not permanently!" as Iskia's eyes widened in horror. "It will wear off in a couple of weeks."

Erhallen rubbed the sticky brown syrup into Iskia's hair, and made her sit for an hour. He brought her some food and she ate a little listlessly.

"Right, rinse your hair off in the basin," Erhallen said. Iskia obeyed him, and then sat by the fire to comb out and dry her hair. A thought had occurred to her and she kept glancing at Erhallen, and then at the bed. He interpreted the look correctly.

"You need not fear, princess, I will be sleeping in the chair," he said, almost amused.

Iskia flushed. "Yes, my lord," she said.

Erhallen went out while Iskia changed into her night-shirt. When he came back in she was tucked up in bed with the covers up to her chin.

Erhallen pushed the chair, a large, comfortable armchair, he was pleased to note, back up against the door. Then he removed his shirt and belt and unsheathed his sword, laying the naked blade across his lap. Iskia stared, eyes wide.

"Sleep, princess, I will guard your rest," he said, amused again. He reached out and turned out the lamp.

Iskia lay still, listening to his breathing. Suddenly she began to feel afraid. The dark closed in on her and she began to breathe harshly with panic.

"Princess?" Erhallen said in a low voice. "Are you all right?"

His voice calmed her a little. "It's very dark," she said. "When I was taken from the Citadel to Iridia – I was shut in with no lights and no windows. The only time I saw light was when they brought my food. I did not even see their faces: saw nothing until I was brought out at Iridia and saw Sasken there."

Erhallen's hatred for Sasken grew with each word. "You're safe. I swear it, princess, I swear on my life he will not have you back again!"

He heard a sniffle, and realised that Iskia was crying. Erhallen's heart ached for her: she had been so brave. Putting his sword down, he crossed to the bed, sat beside her and put his arms round her in a big comforting hug.

Iskia clung to Erhallen, crying desperately at last. She had been so afraid, so humiliated, convinced that Saskia would not be able to mount a rescue attempt in time. She had thought it was too late right up until she woke up on Erhallen's horse.

"It's all right, princess, just hold on tight," Erhallen said comfortingly. She did, clinging to his shoulders in a death grip and sobbing. He held her for a long time, until her sobs quieted and she relaxed against him.

Iskia could not remember ever feeling so good. Erhallen's

chest was warm and muscular under her hands, his massive shoulders shifting as he held her against him. She let out a little sigh.

Erhallen suddenly didn't like the reaction his body was having. In the darkness he could not see Iskia at all, only feel her, and she didn't feel like a child. She felt like a woman, warm and willing in his arms, and his body wasn't listening to his brain telling him he was a fool.

Erhallen set Iskia away from him gently. "Will it help you sleep if I talk to you, princess?" he asked.

"Yes," Iskia said, regretting the loss of his warmth but accepting it. "Tell me about Saskia, about the Clanlands and everything."

"That might take a while, princess."

"Don't call me that!" Iskia regretted the outburst at once.

"Why?" Erhallen asked simply.

"When you say it, it sounds like 'child'. I'm not a child."

"No, you are not." Erhallen paused a moment. "We have a long way to go, my lady. You outrank me by birth. It is for you to choose what I will call you. I would be pleased for you to call me Erhallen."

"I want you to call me Iskia, then."

"Then, Iskia, lie quiet and I'll tell you about the day I first met your sister. She was all sweaty from running around Clanhold's walls, covered in dust." Erhallen talked on, pausing occasionally to listen. Finally Iskia's breathing quieted and slowed into the pattern of sleep.

Erhallen sighed and sat back in his chair, pulling his blanket around his shoulders. Sleep was a long time coming.

In the morning, Iskia awoke first. She lay in the sunlight pouring in through the small window, and looked at Erhallen. Sleep had softened the dark face, smoothing the hard lines. He looked younger, less fierce. He had shaved off his beard last night while they were waiting for the colour to soak into her hair, but already she could see a faint stubble forming again. The urge to touch it surprised her.

Iskia lay back and tried to think objectively. Was she just grateful to Erhallen for saving her? Or were these feelings some sort of youthful crush? She put a hand to her head, the headaches at last were gone, but confusion had taken their place.

"I'm fourteen years old," Iskia whispered to herself. "My marriage to Sasken will be annulled, for reasons of both consanguinity and consent. But unless I'm married, I'm still a target for Sasken. And marriage may be a problem now: what man would have me? No one could be sure my brother didn't take my virginity." She paused. "No one except Erhallen. He would be sure. He's not wed. And a Clanlander, so wedding me at fourteen would be legal." She wondered for a moment about her status as an Imperial ward, but shrugged it off. It was a problem that could be dealt with.

Iskia slipped silently out of bed and moved over to Erhallen. His sword leant against the wall beside him, within easy reach of his hand. His legs were stretched out in front of him. Iskia eyed him thoughtfully, then straddled his legs and climbed carefully onto him, putting one knee beside each hip and pressing her breasts against his chest.

Erhallen was having the most delightful dream. The woman in his arms was soft and willing. He strained to be inside her, feeling her sweet mouth press against his.

Iskia was delighted with Erhallen's response. He sighed against her lips and his tongue slid gently into her mouth. His hands came up to grasp her waist, and his thumbs slid up towards her breasts.

It was slow to dawn on Erhallen that the woman in his arms was real. His eyes snapped open and he stared at Iskia in shock.

Iskia found herself tossed unceremoniously off Erhallen. She stumbled back and sat down on the bed.

"What in the Light are you doing?" Erhallen yelled at her.

"I want to marry you!" Iskia shouted back, and then covered her mouth with shock.

"What? Why?"

"I've just been illegally married to my brother, and I'm about to spend weeks tramping all over the Empire with you. Who do you think will marry me after that?" Iskia said almost wearily.

She effectively silenced Erhallen. He had expected to be

able to send Jerik to collect a suitable escort as soon as they crossed the border. However, Jerik was dead, and he dared not leave Iskia for long, or take her into a large town where Icelanders could be looking for her. She was right. He sat down again heavily.

"Oh, Light," he said.

"If I am not married Sasken will be after me forever," Iskia said. "I am fourteen: legal under the laws of your people and mine. You know the truth about me: you know I am still virgin." She got up and walked towards him, and Erhallen found himself unable to look away from the sway of her hips in the thin night-shirt.

"You want me, Erhallen ca'Berenna. Don't deny it. I can make you happy, I swear it. Protect me."

"Saskia will geld me with a dull knife if I so much as lay a finger on you," Erhallen said as Iskia leant over him.

"No, she will not, Erhallen." Iskia raised her hands and slowly unbuttoned the front of her nightgown. "It was you who put those clothes on me. You've seen me naked. Don't you want to look again?" The nightgown fell to the floor, and Erhallen could not tear his eyes away.

"We're not wed yet," he said hoarsely.

"We will be," Iskia said. She leant forward and kissed him.

Erhallen's determination broke. He dragged Iskia against him and kissed her fiercely. She clutched at him, hands slipping down to unfasten his trousers.

Erhallen was almost frightened to touch Iskia. She seemed so small to him, so fragile, he was worried he might hurt her or crush her. Erhallen lifted her easily and carried her to the bed. Laying her down he searched her face with his eyes.

"Are you sure you want this?" he asked. "Stop me now, Iskia, or not at all."

"Not at all," Iskia said, reaching up to pull him down on her, and Erhallen was lost. He caressed her wonderingly. Iskia screamed once as Erhallen took her, and he froze.

"Iskia, Iskia," he stroked her hair, holding her carefully. A tear welled at the corner of one of her eyes. He kissed it away gently. "I'll never hurt you again, I swear it. Only relax now." He kissed her again and slowly Iskia relaxed in his arms.

* * * *

Two hours later, they rode out again, both with expressions of wonder on their faces. Iskia snuggled close to Erhallen's chest, and the arm he held her with tightened protectively every few minutes.

"Where are we headed?" Iskia asked as they rode on.

"The original plan was to cross into Erinea just above the ForstMarchian border. Aleks had patrols waiting for us there. But I'm not doing that: we're going to go on through ForstMarch and into the Clanlands, and be married under Clanlands law before your sister catches up with me."

"Saskia wouldn't really hurt you."

"Oh, yes she would, princess, she'd geld me with a dull knife. Aleks would probably kill me himself if he suspected what I'd done. He's not going to be best pleased as it is, but if we're married under Clanlands law at least it's mostly legal. We'll probably have to be re-married after your first marriage has been annulled and Aleks gives over your wardship."

"I didn't realise it would be so complicated." Iskia looked worried. Erhallen could not help but kiss her.

"Don't worry. It's all going to be all right."

They headed south at speed. Aleks and Sasken would no doubt be hunting all over Haven and Erinea for them, but Erhallen kept away from main roads and travelled fast. Once over the ForstMarchian border he relaxed somewhat: they were now well away from any direct route back to the Citadel. Saskia would be worried sick but he could not help that.

Chapter 9

The Clanlands, late winter,
the year 2717 after Founding

The journey to the Clanlands border was uneventful. On New Year's Day, a couple of miles over the border, Erhallen recalled the location of a Hold with a Temple of the Light, and turned east. They arrived at Clan Wastrahold an hour or so before sunset.

The colouring on Iskia's hair had faded. She looked absolutely beautiful in the setting sun as Erhallen set her down from his saddle, and a whole group of young Clansmen stopped in their work to stare. Then Erhallen dismounted and put his arm round her, and the young men all sighed and turned away.

The priest of the Light was happy to perform a marriage for the lord of Clan Berenna, after all one of the most powerful men in the Clanlands.

"And you are, my dear?" he asked Iskia.

"I am Princess Iskia Cevaria of the Icelands."

"How old are you?"

"I am fourteen. Legal under both Icelander and Clanlander laws," Iskia added when he hesitated.

"All right." The priest nodded.

"Get on with it, man, we've got to be off," Erhallen said firmly.

"As you wish." Most of Clan Wastra had come in to witness the ceremony. They were to be disappointed by its briefness.

"Does anyone hear know of any reason why these two should not be married? If so, let them speak now or forever hold their peace." Silence was the only response. Iskia and Erhallen shared a look, but did not speak. The priest continued.

"Do you, Erhallen ca'Berenna of Clan Berenna, of your own free will take in the Light this day Iskia Cevaria of the Royal Blood of Iceden, to be your bride, until death may part you?"

"I do," Erhallen replied.

"Do you, Iskia Cevaria of the Royal Blood of Iceden, of your own free will take in the Light this day Erhallen ca'Berenna of Clan Berenna, to be your husband, until death may part you?"

"I do," Iskia said clearly.

"Then be you joined in the Light as man and wife. What this day has been put together, let no man put asunder."

They both stared. "You may kiss your bride," the priest added.

"That was quick," Iskia said as they headed for the Erinean border not an hour later. They both began to laugh.

"Quick or not, it was legal." Erhallen patted the copy of the marriage certificate in his pocket.

* * * *

Three days later, they returned to the Citadel. Erhallen strode right into the palace, waved through by the guards who recognised him. He and Iskia went to look for Aleks and Saskia.

They found their families all together, the three sisters, Aleks, Lirallen and Mairi eating their lunch and talking quietly. Liaskia was the first to reach them. She threw her arms around her sister, and sent a Healing probe right through her. An instant later Lia screamed.

"No! You were too late, you were too late!"

"What!" Saskia cried. "How do you know?"

"She's pregnant! Pregnant with Sasken's foul spawn!"

"No!" Erhallen shouted. They all turned to look at him. He took a deep breath and looked at Iskia. She looked back at him with a soft smile. "I didn't know – but it's not Sasken's. It's mine."

Erhallen had expected it to be Saskia or even Aleks, but to his shock it was Lirallen's sword that levelled at his throat.

"Explain yourself," his brother said in a deadly quiet voice.

147

"Erhallen and I are married under Clanlands law," Iskia said, pushing the sword away. "I am fourteen, old enough under the law of both the Clanlands and the Icelands."

Saskia and Lirallen both looked at Aleks, the most legally knowledgeable among them. After a long moment, he nodded reluctantly. "Yes. With Iskia's freely given consent, she can be legally married as long as she marries a Clanlander or Icelander under their law. As a ward of the Empire, consent of the Crown must be received, but can be given after the marriage." He shrugged. "As far as the law is concerned, her marriage to Sasken never even took place, and so does not have to be annulled, since it was prohibited under the consanguinity laws."

Saskia and Lirallen both wavered. But then they reluctantly acknowledged his words. Saskia went to Iskia and put her arms around her wordlessly.

"Are you well, sister?" she asked.

"Never felt better in my life," Iskia said agreeably.

Lirallen finally stuck out his hand to his brother. Erhallen shook it, and then knelt before Aleks.

"I offer you my apologies, your Grace. I should not have done what I did, but I have done my best to make it right."

Iskia, hearing him, thought her heart would break. She loved Erhallen, had fallen deeply in love with him on their journey. And now he was saying he was only trying to do the right thing by her?

"Do you love her?" Saskia queried, hand sliding to her sword hilt again.

Erhallen turned his head to stare at his tiny wife. "Yes," he said, sounding surprised. "Yes, I do love her. More than I know how to say."

The smile that spread across Iskia's face made it clear how she felt. She pulled away from her sisters and went to her husband.

"I am as much to blame as Erhallen," she told Aleks bluntly. "I was forced into an illegal marriage with Sasken, and then had to traipse over half the Empire alone with Erhallen. What chance of a husband did I have after that?"

Aleks had to acknowledge the truth of that. "And Erhallen

did the noble thing and asked you to marry him," he said.

"Well, that's not actually how it happened," Iskia said. "More like, I demanded that he marry me and then seduced him."

"Out," Saskia ordered Liaskia and Riaskia. When they were gone, she turned on her sister. "You did what?"

Iskia blushed and took Erhallen's hand. He sighed, exasperated. "It's the truth, Saskia. Not that I was unwilling, which is about the only thing in all this that I am truly ashamed of. I could not control myself."

Saskia just shook her head in disbelief. "Well, now I <u>am</u> shocked," she said.

Mairi had begun to laugh. After a moment or two they all joined in. Erhallen put his arms round Iskia and hugged her close to him.

"I love you," he whispered into her ear. Iskia smiled adoringly up at him.

"I can't believe I'm pregnant," she said, hands pressed to her stomach. Erhallen grinned delightedly.

"Didn't take long, did it?" he said.

* * * *

Their happiness was destined to be short-lived. Iskia slipped and fell one day walking across one of the marble floors in the great halls of the palace. The tearing pains began almost at once in her belly and she lost the baby within a few hours. Afterwards, she cried in Saskia's arms while Lia worked to heal her.

Finally Erhallen was allowed in to see his wife. He had been pacing the corridor outside, worrying. As he folded Iskia in his arms, Lia beckoned Saskia out.

"What is it?" Saskia asked.

Lia frowned. "I'm not sure, Sass, but the scarring is terrible. I do not think she will ever be able to conceive again."

"Oh, Light," Saskia said in horror. "How am I going to tell them?"

Lia shook her head. "I do not know, Sass, but you must: or she will be forever trying to conceive, and forever blaming herself for not being able to."

"Erhallen will be blaming himself too, thinking that Iskia is too young."

Lia disagreed. "But that's just not true: Mama was younger than Issy is now when Sasken was born. It's because of Issy's illness, and she will have that all her life. Her age has nothing to do with it, and probably not the fall either. It's quite likely that she could never have carried this child to term, quite possible that they would both have died."

Saskia told Erhallen, too worried over his reaction to leave the task to anyone else. Lia broke the news to Iskia that she could have no more children. Iskia cried for days, unable to deal with the fact. Erhallen was in shock, stumbling around like a ghost. The fact that Mairi was pregnant and just beginning to show almost destroyed him. Only Lirallen could get through to comfort him.

"You could set her aside," Lirallen suggested, to provoke a reaction. "She's barren, legally you have grounds."

"Never," Erhallen spat. "I don't care that much about children. Your children can inherit the Berenna clan. It's Iskia I love, Iskia my wife, she whom I nearly lost when I put a child in her belly. I promised her I'd never hurt her again and I did, I destroyed her womb."

"From what Lia said, Erhallen, it's unlikely Iskia could ever have borne children, to you or any other man. Lia was frankly surprised that she was able to conceive at all."

Erhallen shook his head. "It's more for her that I grieve than for me. I'm selfish enough not to want to share her with children. But for Issy never to know the love of her children – that's a terrible thing for a woman to live with."

Lirallen nodded understandingly. "I am taking Mairi home to Clanhold," he said. "Our firstborn should be born in the Clanlands at least, and I have not spent enough time there this last year. Saskia has asked me to take the younger princesses with me, to give them the Clanlander education she benefited from. She wants them to be able to defend themselves. It would be no bad thing for Iskia to learn the same."

Erhallen nodded. "But not at Clanhold," he said firmly. "I

will teach Iskia myself: at Berennahold. I don't want her around Mairi right now."

Lirallen nodded. "Saskia and Aleks need some time without all of us in the way," he said. "Riaskia and Liaskia cannot be safer than in the Clanlands, where no Icelander can go without everyone seeing them. Aleks is sending six of his best men to keep a constant watch over them, and I will be assigning six Clansmen to work with them also. Send me a Berenna warrior to be one of the six."

"Of course," Erhallen agreed. He frowned briefly. "I must get back to Iskia, Lirallen, it is nearly noon. I do not like to leave her for long just now."

Iskia's body was slowly healing, accelerated by Liaskia's skill. Her mind, however, was slower to mend. Every child she saw, she would weep over. Saskia had virtually confined Iskia to the Icelands Tower, and kept everyone with children or who was pregnant away. Erhallen was the only one who could calm Iskia if she caught sight of a child.

Lia and Ria left for the Clanlands with Lirallen and Mairi, and a week later Erhallen and Iskia left for Berennahold. At last the Citadel was quiet, and Saskia and Aleks could settle into their daily routine of working together.

* * * *

Liara was at Berennahold when Erhallen and Iskia arrived. Furious with her for hiding away for so long, Erhallen sent her back to Aleks under guard.

Frightened, Liara behaved herself pretty well on the journey. When she was escorted into Aleks' throne room, she was back to her old confident self again, having charmed her guards easily, and convinced herself she could do the same with Aleks.

Aleks was rather relieved that Saskia was not present, having gone out visiting that afternoon. He looked Liara over grimly, wondering how one small girl could be so much trouble.

"I gave you an order, Liara ca'Berenna," Aleks said coldly. "Why did you choose to disobey it?"

Liara threw herself to her knees in front of Aleks, artfully ensuring that her body was displayed to best advantage. "Oh, Aleks, please! Don't make me marry a man I don't want!"

Aleks felt a stir of doubt, looking down at her. "What do you want, Liara?" he asked tiredly. "Have you some suitor you wish to wed? Do you wish to be a priestess of the Light? If I free you from this obligation, what do you want?"

Aleks was astonished by Liara's speed. One moment she was kneeling at his feet, and the next she had somehow scrambled onto his lap, arms locked around his neck. "I want you, my lord," she whispered breathily. "Set aside that skinny Icelander witch and marry me."

Aleks' guards were heading rapidly towards him to remove Liara. Aleks himself tried to push her away, but she clung like a limpet. At that exact moment the door swung open and Saskia came laughing in, Evan at her side.

Saskia took in the scene, ripped her sword from its sheath and ran for the throne, letting out a Clan war yell. Aleks' Guards turned to face her uncertainly, not too sure about whether they would have to defend their Emperor against his own wife. They stood aside at last as Aleks finally managed to push Liara off and throw her to the floor.

"I'm going to kill you this time, Liara!" Saskia yelled at the top of her voice, losing her temper at last. "You would try to steal my husband?"

"Aleks was just glad to see me," Liara stuttered, retreating behind Aleks' broad back. "Weren't you, darling?"

Saskia could not help herself from casting a suspicious look at Aleks. He shook his head firmly.

"It's a lie, my lady," one of the Guards said. "The lady threw herself on my lord just before you came in."

"I am sick and tired of this," Aleks snapped. Grabbing Liara by the arm, he pushed her towards Evan. "Take her. Get her out of my sight. Liara, I will not rescind the command I gave you. Sasken has already received the warrant. You will marry him."

Evan took hold of Liara's arm firmly. "An escort of female Guards, I think," he told Aleks. Saskia nodded approvingly: Liara had little chance of charming any of the hard-bitten

152

Guardswomen to her side.

Evan loaded Liara and her escort onto a boat to Iridia with orders that she was to be married to Sasken Cevaria immediately on her arrival in the Icelands. He returned to the palace to report to Saskia, who felt nothing but relief.

* * * *

Aleks was throwing a surprise party for Midsummer for Saskia, to celebrate the anniversary of their betrothal as well as her birthday. With no family present, it was a very formal occasion in the Hall, but they both enjoyed themselves immensely.

Saskia was mildly upset by the frequent questions about whether she was pregnant or not. She said nothing to Aleks, but he guessed what was troubling her. He too had become tired of the constant questions and insinuations.

Six days after Midsummer, word came back that Sasken Cevaria had been married to Liara ca'Berenna in Iceport. Aleks heaved a sigh of relief. "Finally, safely disposed of," he said to Saskia.

"I hope so. No doubt *she* will be breeding within weeks," Saskia said sadly.

"Oh, sweetheart," Aleks put his arms around her. "Maybe we should send to Clanhold, ask Lia to come back."

"She can't help me. She looked at me before she left, and said there was nothing wrong with me."

"Maybe it's me, then," Aleks said.

Saskia shook her head and looked a little bashful. "I had her check you, too."

"Well, you're still young, Sass. Maybe your body just isn't ready to conceive yet."

"I'm eighteen! Iskia conceived at fourteen!"

"And she lost it, too, and will never conceive again. Don't push, Sass. We've plenty of time. I know the whispers that you've been hearing, that the Emperor is required to set aside a barren wife. But you're not barren, I'm sure of it. And even if we never have children, I'll not set you aside."

"Even my mother could not See my children, though," Saskia said.

"Did you ask Ria? Her Sight is far stronger than your mother's was."

"N – no, I didn't."

"There. Perhaps you should have done."

"It's too late, now. She won't be back for a fair while."

"No, I told Lirallen I wanted them to have a proper Clanlands education. Ria's just the age you were when you went there, and Lia a little younger. A couple of years will do them the world of good."

"I will miss them," Saskia said, a little sadly. Then she brightened. "But I have you, Aleks." She put her arms around her husband and hugged him.

In late autumn, Iskia and Erhallen arrived for a visit.

"Why don't we ask the others here for Midwinter?" Iskia asked one day. She and Saskia were out riding in the city park, Captain Evan riding watchfully behind them with one of his men.

Saskia brightened a little. She had been very depressed of late, watching her second wedding anniversary approach with her womb still empty. "Yes, why not?"

And so it was done: Aleks sent out a messenger the following day. The girls arrived just before the Midwinter festival, though without Lirallen and Mairi, since the baby was due at Midwinter.

Lia and Ria had both grown: not so much in height but in stature. They had both gained some muscle and some understanding of fighting: though Mairi had insisted on teaching them many other skills as well.

Lia hugged Saskia with a delighted grin. "Oh, congratulations!"

"What?" Saskia said.

With a frown Lia put her hands on Saskia's stomach. "For sure, sister, but you're finally pregnant!"

"Am I? Truly?" Saskia clutched hands to her stomach in pleased delight. Ria laid her hands there too, and her eyes glazed over as she Saw the future.

"A fine son!" Ria exclaimed. "Light, Saskia, this one will be

154

an Emperor to make you proud!"

"You saw him crowned?" Saskia said, surprised.

"Yes." Ria frowned. "But he was still young. About the age Aleks is now, and so like him."

Saskia turned to look across the room to Aleks, greeting Lirallen. "Aleks will die young, then," she said sadly.

Ria touched her sister's arm gently. "I'm sorry. I never wanted you to know that."

"You have seen his death?"

"When I first met him. You have another twenty years or more, Sass, value it."

Saskia bit her lip for a long moment before nodding. "You're sure I'm carrying a son?" she said.

Lia shrugged doubtfully but Ria's nod was emphatic.

"I must tell Aleks," Saskia said. She went across the room to join her husband. He smiled down on her. A moment later as she whispered to him, his expression turned incredulous and he let out a shout of joy.

The Citadel was filled with celebration. Aleks wanted to let the whole world know, and so a proclamation was sent out to the far corners of the Empire by carrier bird.

Liara ca'Berenna, now Cevaria, had never left Iceport. Sasken had married her there, then put her in a fine house in the town centre and left her there. This probably had something to do with the way he had eyed her with distaste throughout the wedding. Afterwards, when they were alone, Liara had pulled a long knife from her skirts.

"Touch me and I'll geld you," she hissed.

"Why would I want you?" Sasken responded. "You weren't good enough for von Chenowska, after all: he wanted my sister. You're not good enough for me either. Keep your precious virginity." He left for Iceden within hours.

Liara screamed with temper when she read the message about Saskia's pregnancy. Her fondest wish had been that Saskia would prove barren and be set aside. Perhaps Aleks would then come for her, Liara. But now the bitch was breeding.

"I'll kill her son inside her womb," Liara snarled, pacing up and down. "I'll twist the knife myself." She sat down and began to pen a letter to her husband.

Sasken read his wife's letter with mounting interest. She seemed a surprisingly bright girl, this Clanlander woman. Certainly this was an intelligent plan. With Iceden snowbound, the river was frozen, so he called for horses to be saddled and headed for Iceport to set his plans in motion.

Liara was surprised when Sasken walked in on her unannounced. He unnerved her: not as big as Aleks or her brothers, still he had an air of menace about him.

"My lord," she bowed her head submissively, not wanting to anger him.

"Wife." His tongue curled around the word. "It seems that you are more intelligent than I thought. Foolish enough to anger von Chenowska, yet clever enough to come up with a plan to destroy him."

"For you, too, my lord: I want revenge on Saskia and you want your younger sisters back. I'll kill Saskia and the filth she carries, and you can have Riaskia and Liaskia, to do with as you please. As a virgin, I can have our marriage annulled and marry Aleksandr myself. It will be my son who sits on the throne." Liara's eyes glittered at the thought.

Sasken nodded thoughtfully. "I want no son of my sister's on the throne, she has the Power and a child of hers would be likely to inherit it. A sorcerer Emperor will make our worst nightmares into reality."

"Saskia will pass the Gift on to her children?" Liara asked.

Sasken shrugged. "I don't know, but I do know she is dangerous. She will kill to protect her child if she must. Neither you nor I can enter the Citadel safely, but I have plenty of trusted men. You spent quite a bit of time in the Citadel: I have only spent a few days there. Tell me about it. We shall make a plan."

Saskia became more relaxed, now that she was pregnant. She took to swimming a lot, in the heated pools under the palace, kept warm by a hot underground spring. It would be a little while yet before she started to swell, but the baby was taking its toll on her strength, making her sleep a lot more.

Ria and Lia were staying in the Icelands tower, Iskia and Erhallen in the Clanlands with Lirallen's family. The family all tended to eat at least one meal a day together. Saskia spent several days in the Great Market with her sisters. They were always recognised and welcomed at the stalls, given cups of warm mead to stave off the chill and honeycakes to munch. The stallholders all knew about the baby by now and the old women were always stopping Saskia to give her advice.

* * * *

One day, Saskia was relaxing in the pools. She was more tired than usual, drifting off in the warm water. Finally she swam to the edge of the pool and climbed out. She wrapped her robe around herself and turned for the doors. Just as she reached them the door swung open and four armed men walked in. Seeing her, they grinned wolfishly.

"Hello, Saskia," one said.

Saskia stared. He was familiar. Then she placed him: he had been a guard in Iceden, one of her father's trusted men. Her eyes widened and she took a step back, too shocked to attack.

"Oh, I'm going to enjoy this," the man said. He was the oldest of the four: they were all tough, competent looking men in plain livery. Two of them caught Saskia's arms and the third placed his sword against her belly. Saskia dared not struggle now: if she wriggled that sword would go right in to kill her child. She silently cursed herself for not acting more quickly when she first saw them.

"We're going to have you now, Saskia," the leader said. "We were never allowed to touch you royal bitches in Iceden. But you've sullied yourself with that Desert wolf, and so you're spoils for the taking." He began to unlace his breeches.

Saskia could not believe what was happening in her own home, with her husband not a few floors away. Silently she screamed, not daring to open the Power in her for fear the jewel on her hand would unleash its telltale glow.

Saskia was forced down onto the floor and the leader knelt between her legs and grasped at her breasts.

"Far lovelier than her mother," he commented to his men. "And the brat in her is making her breasts grow just sweetly." He

157

ripped open her robe, bent his head and bit her nipple.

Saskia could still feel the sword point pressing against her side. "Why are you doing this?" she demanded.

"Why do you think, Saskia? It's your punishment for marrying that Desert wolf. And now you're carrying his spawn. So after we've done with you, we'll pin you through the belly with a sword, and leave you for von Chenowska to find. Not even your sister can bring back a dead baby."

The rage swelled inside Saskia until it almost choked her. She could see a red mist rising in front of her eyes. Just as the Icelander positioned himself to force into her, she unleashed the Power and burst into flame.

The four men drew back, shocked. The ones touching her let go with screams, beating their hands together. At that precise moment the door crashed open and Aleks charged in, Evan and a handful of Imperial Guards at his shoulder.

The Icelanders were slaughtered to a man. Aleks turned to look at Saskia, struggling to damp down the flames. The baby inside her was grasping greedily at the Power.

Finally Saskia managed to put the flames out. She gathered the tatters of her robe around her, shaking with reaction. Aleks dropped his sword and came to her.

"Did they hurt you?"

"No," Saskia clutched at her belly. "They – they were going to. They were going to rape me and kill the baby." She snarled fiercely at the bodies. "That was too quick a death!"

"My love, my love," Aleks drew Saskia into his arms. "Deal with that filth," he told Evan.

The Citadel was in an uproar. Lia came running from the Icelander tower. Ria stayed behind, feeling a little unwell. Little did she know that her tea had been drugged that afternoon. By the time Lia returned to the tower the following morning, after a night spent making sure Saskia suffered no bad dreams, Ria was missing.

* * * *

Lia hardly knew what to do. She was quite sure that Ria had

not just gone out. Since Iskia's kidnapping, it was simple policy for the sisters always to let each other know where they were. Ria had been taken, and was probably a day upstream on the fastest riverboat by now. In the end Lia walked back to the palace and went to look for Captain Evan.

"Ria is missing," Lia said without preamble. "The last time she was seen was midday yesterday when I came here to look after Saskia."

Evan went white. "So Saskia was not the target after all," he said.

"I think that was a diversion," Lia responded. "I think this was carefully planned to get Ria away, and killing Saskia's baby would have been a bonus."

"Come with me," Evan led Lia to Aleks' study. He had barely slept the night before, and looked up hollow-eyed now.

"Lia? What is it?"

Lia did not know how to tell him. "Ria is gone," she said eventually.

"Gone? Gone where?"

"Just gone," Lia replied. "I think she was taken just after I left the Icelands tower yesterday."

"Not again," Aleks' expression turned ugly. "This time it's war!"

A party of men set out that night on a fast riverboat, to try and catch the boat carrying Ria. The Irldla port authorities were alerted too, and two days later half the army was on the march, gathering in. The Clanlanders, outraged, sent a massive band of men on horses, marching hard north, gathering war parties in ForstMarch and Haven on the way. Aleks himself rallied men from Erinea and Eastphal. The whole continent was outraged at what Sasken had dared to do, and soon there were ships on their way from the Summerlands and the Desert too, as much to avenge Saskia's honour as to rescue Ria.

* * * *

Ria woke with a groan. Her head was pounding and there was an abominable taste in her mouth. She tried to lift her hands

159

to her head and found them restrained, out to her sides, velvet–lined shackles around her wrists. Carefully lifting her head, she looked down, and found herself in a large four-poster bed. Not only her hands but her feet were also shackled, legs spread apart, stark naked. With growing horror, Ria screamed.

Liara Cevaria came in. She was gowned regally in Icelander white and purple with a silver circlet on her head. She looked down at Ria chained to the bed.

Liara smiled down at Ria, a triumphant, nasty smile. "I'm so glad we caught you. My husband was getting a little too frisky for his own good. I need to keep my virginity. Then when I kill your bitch sister I will be Empress."

"Being a Princess isn't enough for you?" Ria said.

Liara laughed, a little madly. "I don't give a damn about the title, you fool. It's Aleksandr von Chenowska I love. When Saskia's dead he'll marry me. But in the meantime I have you to occupy Sasken's bed. Better learn to please him quickly, little Riaskia. He doesn't have much patience any more." With that, she walked away. Ria lay there, frightened, trying not to cry. She could not believe that no one had come for her. Erhallen had saved Iskia right out of her marriage bed. Surely if they had broken into Iceden once they could do it again?

Little did Riaskia know, she was not in Iceden. Sasken had guessed Aleks would come after him, and had pulled back into the Icelander mountains. They were in Borkenfort, a mountain stronghold. Ria could remember nothing at all of the journey. She racked her brains, but her last clear memory was of the Icelands Tower in the Citadel.

Riaskia slept a little, fitfully. She woke when the door opened again. This time it was Sasken who came in.

"Hello, Ria," he said. Ria stared at him, incredulous. He sounded as casual as if they were just sitting down for tea. He started undressing and Ria tried desperately not to cry out.

"Are you hungry?" Sasken inquired, still in the same conversational tone.

"Yes," Ria said after a moment. "More thirsty than hungry, though."

Sasken nodded as though he had expected that. "I'm not

going to let you loose just yet," he said. "I don't like using the calming drugs any more. A little maid died of it. I don't want anyone to be hurt. I don't want you to fight me, Ria."

Ria tensed as he leant over her. "So beautiful," Sasken murmured wonderingly. "So like Saskia. You'll learn to please me, Ria. You must."

"Never!" Ria hissed at him.

Sasken laughed, and for the first time sounded unpleasant. "Never is a very long time, sweet sister. What do you think you will say when you must beg me for every drop of water and scrap of food that passes your lips? My wife says I should make you work for your keep. A sensible woman, Liara: she sees much that is to our mutual advantage. And so, in the day you will work for her, and by night you will work to please me. My needs will take precedence, naturally."

Ria could not help but scream. Sasken laughed. "My dear, who do you think is going to hear you? There is no one to help you here."

"You bastard!" Ria shouted at him. "I'll kill you, I swear it!" The look that came over Sasken's face suddenly terrified her. Then he smiled, and that was more frightening still. He stooped down under the bed and came up with a long whip in his hands.

"I wouldn't want to scar that beautiful skin," he said purringly, "but I'm an expert with the whip, sweet sister. I'll break you to my will yet."

The first stroke was across Ria's thighs. The pain was incredible. She screamed in agony. Sasken worked on down her legs with the whip until she was crying out.

"Beg me to stop," Sasken said through gritted teeth. "Beg me!"

"Please, please, please!" Ria screamed. Sasken carried on for a few more strokes and then stopped. Tossing the whip aside, he knelt on the bed beside Ria and began to kiss her legs gently. The pain was slowly dying down. Ria lay, gasping, eyes squeezed shut at the sheer horror of what was happening to her.

Sasken flung himself down on Ria and forced himself into her. Ria screamed again at the sheer agony of it. He grunted and pounded atop her, and Ria felt as though she was being torn in half. At last he gave a convulsive shudder and a groan, and collapsed on top of her.

Ria lay still, trying not to cry with pain and horror. At last Sasken lifted himself off her. Tears of shame ran hot down Ria's cheeks. Sasken smiled down at her, and then he climbed off, put his clothes on and walked away.

Ria cried and cried. She felt sick, weak, and shaky. A little maid came in with a damp cloth and wiped her up. Ria begged before she began, and the maid was able to squeeze a few drops of water from the cloth into Ria's mouth. She swallowed greedily, but got little relief from it.

"I need to go to the bathroom," Ria told the girl shakily. The little maid ducked her head and ran out.

Sasken came in a few minutes later. "Are you going to behave yourself?" he asked.

"Yes," Ria whispered, unable to summon the strength to defy him.

"Yes, master," Sasken corrected her.

"Yes, master," Ria said compliantly. Sasken released her, and she struggled to her feet with a groan.

Ria concluded that it would be simpler and less painful not to fight. She would end up doing what Sasken wanted anyway, but it would only earn her pain, and hunger and thirst, if she disobeyed him. She must keep him happy and then, one day, he would let his guard down, and she would fulfil her vision and kill him. Ria felt quite calm at the thought. Sasken had raped her, his own sister, under-age even by Icelands law. Sasken would be sentenced to choose: castration and a life of slavery, or death. Ria would remove his choice, and no court in the world would find her guilty of murder.

Ria was smiling to herself when she came back and found Sasken sitting naked on the bed. She faltered for a moment and her resolve weakened. Sasken frowned at her.

"Must I chain you again, Ria, or will you try to please me?"

Ria took in a deep breath and gathered all her courage. She knelt at Sasken's feet. "I will please you in any way you desire, master," she said submissively.

Sasken laughed in delight. "I knew you'd come around.

162

More intelligent than Saskia, she is far too stubborn for her own good."

When he demanded that she go on top of him, Ria obeyed and gritted her teeth against the pain. She knew enough from Iskia and Saskia to know that there would be no pleasure in sexual activity if there was no desire. So she endured the pain, and Sasken's cry of joy. She endured him holding her in his arms afterwards, kissing her hair. Then he made her get up.

"Put this on." He tossed a scarlet dress at her. It was a whore's gown, cut low in the front and with sides split to her hips. Ria looked for underwear, and then saw the smile on Sasken's face. Reluctantly she put on the dress.

"Oh, I like you in that," Sasken murmured when she came out to join him. She stood, eyes cast down.

Liara walked in at that moment. "Pleasing yourself already, Sasken?"

"Of course, sweet wife. She belongs to me, after all. Unless you were wanting to take her place? You're not as beautiful as Ria, but bear in mind she'll be unavailable for one week a month. Maybe I'll need you to give me some relief."

Liara paled with temper. "I gave you your precious sister, Sasken. We have a bargain."

Sasken shrugged. "What do I care for bargains?" He smiled nastily. "I'll leave you your precious virginity, Liara."

"Why didn't you want me to take Liaskia as well?" Liara asked, ignoring Ria as though she were not even there.

Sasken shook his head. "Lia is too dangerous," he said. "She has the Healing. My father had that, and he used it to cause pain. Lia has a great deal of that Gift, she could perhaps even kill with it. I wouldn't want her stopping my heart while I took her."

Liara nodded. "What Gift does this one have?" she asked, gesturing to Ria.

"The TimeSight, so I hear."

Liara laughed. "Did you See that you would become a slave, Ria? A plaything for your brother? Did you?"

Ria's cheeks flushed with shame and temper. She had never seen that, and she silently cursed the TimeSight.

Sasken laughed. "Work her hard, Liara. She needs to earn

her keep."

Ria had never imagined such humiliation. Liara set her to the most degrading tasks, scrubbing floors and polishing hearthstones. By night she had to please Sasken however he wished, and by day slave from dawn until dusk. She was exhausted, broken. The worst times were when Sasken came to look for her in the daytime, driven by his urges. He would take her wherever he found her and then wander off again, leaving her battling with the pain and the exhaustion.

Sasken tormented Liara too, though. He insisted that she sit in the room while he took Ria and made her please him, insisting that Liara must study if she was to learn to please a man. Liara was somewhat revolted at first, but after a while she began to watch with interest, studying what Ria had done when Sasken let out a groan.

"What does that feel like?" Liara asked avidly one time, when Sasken cried out.

Sasken looked at her thoughtfully, pushing Ria away for a moment. "I'll show you," he said. Liara flinched back. "It's all right, wife, I swear in the Light I'll not touch you myself. Ria can do the work. Get undressed and get on the bed with her."

Liara obeyed, not daring to cross him. Ria looked at Sasken, puzzled. "I don't understand, master," she said.

Sasken smiled, sitting back to lean against one of the posts. "I'm going to enjoy watching this. Kiss her breasts, Ria. Just relax, Liara my dear."

Ria obeyed reluctantly. Out of the corner of her eye she saw Sasken reach down for his whip and began to obey with a will.

Liara moaned and shifted. Ria closed her eyes in humiliation, but obeyed the orders Sasken gave.

Sasken liked to watch. When he decided Ria had finished, he grabbed Ria and took her roughly. Ria struggled not to cry, but dared not fight. She lacked the strength to survive another beating.

Afterwards, Liara and Sasken both smiled on Ria, in the way that one would smile on a dog that has just learned a new trick.

And so a new humiliation was added to the list of what Ria must endure. Liara was insatiable, calling Ria to her several times a day. Even in the one week a month she did not have to endure Sasken inside her, she still had to please them both in other ways. For two months this went on, and Ria began to wonder if anyone would ever come for her, if Sasken would ever let his guard down enough to let her near a weapon. Even the TimeSight seemed to have abandoned her: She was so weak and tired the visions would not come.

Then she overheard Sasken shouting at Liara one day. "That bastard von Chenowska's after my guts. He's taken most of the lowlands, his damned slut Saskia is sitting in Iceden. I tell you he's after me. He's declared me a criminal under Imperial law and my lands forfeit – to Iskia, that bitch!"

Ria could almost see the smile on Liara's face. "My lord, this is the perfect opportunity. Iceden is riddled with secret passages. Have someone sneak in and kill Saskia. Aleks will be so overcome with grief he will leave. Then I will show up and throw myself on his mercy, and he'll be so relieved he's saved one person from you, he'll forget all about Ria. I'll marry him and I'll keep him so occupied he'll forget all about you. You can keep Ria in peace and father your next generation on her."

To Ria's ears that sounded like an incredibly shaky plan. Aleks was far more likely to burn the Icelands to bare rock to find Sasken if Saskia was killed, and Liara's idea of keeping him away sounded like pure fantasy to Ria.

"All right," Sasken said, and Ria shook her head in amazement. Was he mad, or stupid, or both? It was an idiotic plan.

That night, Ria had to share the bed with both of them again. But this time, as Liara cried out with ecstasy, Sasken pushed Ria aside.

"A little gift for von Chenowska," he said, and drove hard into Liara. She screamed as he pierced her maidenhead.

"No! Damn you, Sasken, no!"

"Too late," he laughed. Ria huddled on the edge of the bed, privately rejoicing. Aleks could not marry Liara any time soon now. It would be difficult for her to get the marriage annulled.

Liara wept afterwards, but Ria could not find any sympathy for her. An escort of soldiers left with Liara the following day.

Chapter 10

Borkenfort, Spring, the year 2719 after Founding

Ria was mistress of Borkenfort now. Looking out of windows facing toward the lowlands, she could see smoke, and guessed that battles were being fought down there. Someone had finally come for her. She hugged herself, rejoicing. She might be utterly ruined, but she'd be free of Sasken at last. No one would marry her. She shed a few silent tears: she would never know the happiness her two older sisters had. She hoped Saskia would be all right when Liara's men tried to get into Iceden. And there, standing at the window looking down, the TimeSight finally came back to her.

The scene in front of Ria disappeared and she saw Iceden, and Saskia sitting in an upper room in the tower. A secret door slid open behind her, but Saskia did not seem to notice. Three men emerged, blades in their hands. Not until the first one was only inches from her did Saskia move. Ria could not hear, but her sister's mouth opened in a war yell as she whirled, ripping a sword from a sheath on her back, and decapitated the first assassin with a single stroke. The other two were quickly dead also.

Ria's vision cleared. She glanced quickly about her but there was no one near. She leaned against the wall for a moment. So, Saskia would survive the assassination attempt. Ria's mouth curled in a tight, vicious smile.

Sasken was worried. The tide of battle was clearly turning against him. Even some of his own Icelander lords were rebelling, turning against him and fighting with the Emperor in Princess Iskia's name. That enraged Sasken even further, but he dared not venture outside Borkenfort's walls.

Sasken took to abusing Ria increasingly, demanding that she please him. But as Aleks advanced and there was no word of Saskia's death, Sasken's panic grew and he became impotent. He beat Ria, shouting at her that it was her fault.

And then, one morning, Ria looked out of the window and saw an encampment of men below Borkenfort's walls. Aleks had arrived.

That was the day Ria found the knife. It wasn't a long knife, the blade no longer than her hand, and it was blunt. She suspected Liara had been using it to cut wool for her tapestry.

Ria sharpened the knife in secret, she had plenty of time. Liara was no longer making demands on her time and working her to the bone. The siege dragged on as well, for Borkenfort was old and tough. Then one day Sasken's few remaining loyal supporters finally turned on him.

"Get up on the walls and talk to von Chenowska," a grizzled old lord said forcefully. "Find out what he wants, Sasken. The man will never leave us alone and Borkenfort cannot hold out for many more days."

Reluctantly Sasken obeyed. He stood on top of the battlements with his men behind him.

"What do you want, von Chenowska?" he shouted down.

There was a stir in the ranks. Finally Aleks rode out on Sandstorm. "Give me Princess Riaskia," he shouted back. "You have illegally kidnapped a Ward of the Empire, Sasken. I am within my rights coming here to get her back."

"She's my dear sister," Sasken said, not wanting his lords to know what had been going on. "Riaskia is entirely safe with me."

"Bring her out where I can see her," Aleks ordered.

"In one hour," Sasken shouted back.

Ria was ordered into one of Liara's courtly dresses. It was too short and showed her ankles, but would have to do. She was virtually dragged up on the wall beside Sasken.

"Are you all right, Ria?" Aleks shouted up.

"I am alive, my lord," Ria called back.

Aleks closed his eyes in horror, knowing what she was telling him. He had already known: it had taken them too long to realise Sasken was not at Iceden and find him.

"Do you want to come back to the Citadel, Ria?" he called.

"Yes!" Ria shouted, unmindful of Sasken's hand gripping her arm. He shook her fiercely.

"You're not leaving!" He dragged her away from the battlements and down into the castle. Back in his suite, he tore the clothes off her and whipped her back until she screamed, heedless of the cuts he was putting on her, then raped her mindlessly. Ria's hand closed on the knife under the pillow, and she brought it out in a wide arc and rammed it into the side of Sasken's neck.

Sasken was the one born with the primary Gift of Luck, but Ria had some too. As she forced the blade into Sasken's throat, she cried out to the Light to guide her hand. And her Luck answered. Sasken was dead with the first slash. Ria struggled out from under him and stood panting by the bed, naked and covered with blood, knife held ready to strike again if Sasken so much as twitched.

* * * *

Aleks had seen Ria dragged off the wall and had gestured to Captain Evan, who was leading a secret attack. Eight men rappelled onto Borkenfort's roof from the mountain behind, which it had taken them days to climb.

Evan himself was the first man down into the castle. Icelander lords who had gone over to Aleks had given him plans, so he knew exactly where he was going. He ran heedlessly through the corridors, letting his men handle the guards, and threw open the door to Sasken's suite.

Evan took in the scene with a single glance and stopped dead in horror. Ria snarled at him, the small knife bloody in her hand, and he lowered his sword carefully and sheathed it.

"Princess Riaskia," he said formally. "I am Captain Evan of the Empress' Guard. Your sister sent me to rescue you."

In Ria's eyes was the pain and madness of a wounded animal. She stared at him uncomprehendingly for a few moments. Then slowly her fingers uncurled and the knife fell to the floor.

"I killed him," she said brokenly. "He hurt me – he hurt me so many times – and she hurt me too – but she's gone. I killed him."

Evan had no idea what to say. Ria turned away and he saw the lash marks on her back. She had been whipped hard: he had only seen those kind of wounds on common criminals, thieves and muggers.

"Princess," he said softly. Slowly, as those huge, fearful amethyst eyes locked on him, he unrolled a bundle that had been tied to his back. "I have brought some clothes for you."

The clothes were familiar, riding things that Ria had used in the Clanlands. Evan waited while she dressed. He had to get her out of Borkenfort: even with Sasken dead there would still be trouble, and no one knew that he was dead yet. Princesses Iskia and Liaskia waited outside the walls and Saskia was on her way from Iceden.

Ria followed Evan docilely. He led her back on to the roof where his men were waiting and they put her into a special harness attached to a rope. Ria screamed when they began to lower her over the edge.

Evan cursed. "I'll go with her," he said to his second in command. "I think she trusts me." He took a rope and went down after Ria, talking to her, making her look at him instead of down at the ground. Once they were down, willing hands released them. Ria screamed again as hands touched her.

"Get off me! Don't touch me! I won't, I won't be hurt again!"

"Get back," Evan ordered. "Give the princess some room."

They obeyed, falling back. "What's wrong with her?" a young Guards officer asked.

"That's none of your business. This is: Sasken Cevaria is dead. I saw it with my own eyes. Tell the Emperor."

Evan was the only one who could get near Ria without making her scream. She was too weak to walk, and he could see the blood soaking through the shirt on her back.

"Will you let me carry you to your sisters?" he asked gently. "We have to get away from the walls – it is not safe here."

Ria hesitated for a long moment, and then nodded. Evan

lifted her carefully in his arms, trying not to touch her wounds. She sucked in a pained breath, but did not cry out.

Evan carried Ria through the camp to the command tents. Looking at his grim face, the soldiers parted to let him through. Even Aleks' own guards just stepped aside.

"I have her," Evan announced, walking into the tent. Aleks was not there: gone to talk to the Icelander lords now that Sasken was dead.

Liaskia ran to her sister's side as Evan laid Ria down on the couch. Ria had fainted: she groaned now and her eyelids fluttered.

"She is badly hurt," Evan told Iskia and Erhallen. "Sasken had whipped her."

"They said that Sasken is dead. Did she – did she do it?" Iskia asked.

"Oh, yes," Evan said grimly. "And the bastard deserved it, too."

There was a commotion outside, and into the tent burst Saskia, dragging Liara by the hair. Aleks was right behind them.

"Look who I found skulking about a mile away," Saskia said grimly.

Riaskia's eyes opened and she saw Liara. She began to scream.

"Get her out of here!" Aleks snapped to a guard. "She's no longer a princess: with Sasken dead the title goes to Iskia. Liara bore no heirs. Under Icelander law she is barren and entitled to nothing: not even to keep her husband's name."

"I'm pregnant!" Liara screamed even as the guard dragged her out. There was a pause, and even Ria quieted. Then she began to laugh hysterically.

"Liaskia, find out if she speaks truth," Aleks requested. Liaskia left Ria's side for long enough to touch Liara's belly.

"It's true," she said in revulsion. "The bitch is carrying Sasken's hellspawn."

"What does this mean?" Saskia asked desperately.

"Under Icelander law, if the child is a boy it will inherit. Otherwise, the princedom is Iskia's, to be inherited by the next born male heir in the Icelander line," Aleks said after a pause to think. He gestured to the guards. "Lock her up. Feed her and treat her gently, but she is to have no freedom. In the meantime, I confer the Regency of the Icelands on Princess Iskia of the Royal Blood of Iceden."

The circlet he offered Iskia was made of gold. Iskia accepted it with a nod of thanks. Then everyone turned back to Ria.

"Can you help her?" Saskia demanded of Lia.

"The physical is not so damaged. I can heal her and not leave so much as a single scar, no pain at all. But I can't heal her mind, Sass. I don't even want to think about what Sasken and Liara have done to her, but I think it may have driven her mad."

Captain Evan was still there: he felt strangely reluctant to leave. Ria opened her eyes again and looked around her: she screamed at the sight of Aleks and Erhallen, but when her eyes fell on Evan, she quieted again.

"It's men. Out, you two," Saskia ordered. "Evan, for some reason you don't bother her: I suppose she sees you as her rescuer. Will you stay?"

Evan felt awkward, but he sat down by Ria and held her hand. He talked to her of things far away, things that could not possibly make her think of her brother and the Icelands. He spoke of his youth in the Summerlands, growing up on his father's apple farm, and joining the army.

Ria quieted as he talked, and as she drifted off to sleep, Lia laid hands on her and did the Healing. The bruise on Ria's cheek faded, and Evan guessed that everything else was gone too. She was still too thin, too pale and exhausted. Finally she slept peacefully.

Saskia beckoned everyone away. "Evan, you saw. How did she kill him?"

Evan hesitated, but in the end did not want to try to hide the truth from them. "I did not see it happen," he said. "But I think she had just done it when I came in. From the look of the body, he was – he was on top of her, and she put a knife in his throat. It was quick. Too quick for that bastard," he added viciously.

"He raped her," Saskia said dully. "I knew – I knew when we did not find them at Iceden, but somehow I hoped."

"I think worse was done to her than that, my lady, I think they tried to break her." Evan's face softened as he looked back at the sleeping princess. "I think they nearly succeeded."

"She's ruined," Iskia said despairingly. "Who will marry her, Sass? She'll never be happy."

Evan looked at Iskia in surprise. "She might not marry a great lord, my lady, but there are plenty of good men out there who would take a wife like Princess Riaskia. Surely that would suit her better: some quiet life in a little country manor, than being constantly on display at court, where everyone would know what was done to her."

Saskia looked thoughtfully at Evan. That was an insightful thought from any man, never mind from a hardened soldier like this one.

"Are you married, Evan?" she asked suddenly. "I never asked."

"No, I'm not, my lady. I was betrothed, but my Careen died of the red fever, and that's when I joined the Army."

"You can't think – Sass!" Iskia exclaimed. Evan's eyes widened at the same moment.

"What are you saying, my lady?"

"Ria needs a husband, and as quickly as possible."

"No," Evan said firmly. "What she needs, my lady, is time to heal. You cannot take this choice from her too. If she chooses to wed, let her wed whom she wants. She might never want to. The Priestesses of the Light would be glad to take her, with her Gift of TimeSight. She could go into a closed female cloister, and never have to lay eyes on a man again."

Saskia nodded slowly. "Right again, Evan. I begin to think you a perfect choice. You are now Princess Riaskia's personal guard. I want you no more than twenty feet from her side."

"Saskia!" Iskia was outraged. "You can't do that, you can't throw the poor man into Ria's path. Besides, she couldn't marry him: she's not fourteen yet, and he's a Summerlander, bound by Empire laws. They couldn't marry until she was sixteen anyway."

"Plenty of time for her to get to like him then," Saskia said, eyes still searching Evan's face. He flushed red, then went pale, then red again.

"You love her, don't you?" Saskia said. "I should have known back in the Citadel, when you were so upset after she was taken. But of course then you thought it was hopeless."

Evan struggled for the words to say. Finally he fell back on formality. "As my lady wishes, I will remain by the princess's side."

Saskia nodded with a slight smile, and drew Iskia out of the tent with her. Lia gave Evan a considering look, and went back to check on her sister.

"Do you truly love her?" Lia asked.

"Why do you ask?" Evan hedged.

"Because if you do there could be no man better to look after her. Ria may become dependent on you after this: you rescued her after all. If you love her you can save her from the madness that will haunt her. I know Ria better than anyone, and I know that when she is feeling stronger the Gift will be burning in her, she will see the future. Ria has TimeSight so strong she can *shape* the future, sometimes. If she wants you in it, that will be that. If you don't love her, then you had better run now."

"I don't know," Evan said despairingly. "She's so young, Lia, and by birth she is far, far above me. And yet, she needs someone to take care of her now."

"Forget about the age difference, Evan. If you love her, you're probably the only man in the world who can make her happy, make her forget. Do as you told Saskia: marry Ria and take her off to some quiet little country manor. Take her home to the Summerlands and grow apples."

"Don't you think you should ask me?" said a weak voice. They both turned in horror: Ria was awake.

"Oh, Light," Evan said, not knowing where to put himself.

"You need a husband, Ria," Liaskia said, leaning over her sister. "Evan loves you."

"Do you?" Ria queried, turning her beautiful eyes up to his face.

"I don't know," Evan said. "I have always admired you, princess, but it has always been as one who could never have you. I would not have thought you would want to know."

"That idea about growing apples in the Summerlands sounds appealing," Ria sounded drowsy, she was drifting back to sleep. "Talk to me some more about the Summerlands, Evan: I have never been there."

Evan obeyed, talking until long after she slept soundly, her small, frail hand gripped in his.

* * * *

Liara was petrified. She was not entirely sure about being pregnant, but the moment she heard that Sasken was dead she knew that she would be next. Saskia had almost killed her outside the camp, had only been stopped by her escort, who insisted that the Emperor must be the one to give justice.

For the first time, Liara thanked Sasken for forcing her. Without the child growing in her belly, she had no doubt that she would be dead now, condemned by Ria and executed. She clutched at her belly, praying silently for the child to stay alive and safe, and to be male. If it was a boy, the Empire law declared that the closest living relative – Liara – would be regent. If a girl, she would have no rights at all. Saskia would probably take the child and Liara would be tried and executed for her crimes.

Finally, as Liara lay on the bed in the small, dark tent, listening to the soldiers moving around outside, she came to the realisation that Saskia had won. Aleks would never love Liara. He wanted her dead, now: she had seen it in his eyes when he pronounced the law. He would do everything in his power under the law to see her executed.

* * * *

Liara remembered with rage how Saskia had caught her. Liara had left her two-man escort a little distance back and gone on foot to see if she could get back into Borkenfort. After the assassination attempt on Saskia failed, Liara was frightened and decided she would be better off with Sasken, trying to appeal to Aleks' mercy. She also needed to kill Riaskia before the princess could denounce her.

174

It had been a long time since Liara had practised the skills she had learnt in the Clans, but she was still a Clandaughter and she remembered what she had been taught. She was creeping quietly through the low scrub, towards a secret tunnel that led to a cave just below the fort, when there came a shout behind her. Liara spun, pulling her bow from her shoulder and stringing an arrow. She saw the black uniforms of the Imperial Guards and let fly.

The arrow burst into flame in mid-air. Liara stared disbelievingly as it fell harmlessly to earth.

"Well, well," said a voice. "What have we here?"

Liara stared as the Guards rode forward. Saskia rode in the middle, heavily pregnant now, but still dressed as they were in the black uniform, silver lightning bolts on her shoulders. Liara snatched another arrow, but that one caught fire even before it left the string, and she dropped both bow and arrow.

"Witch!" Liara screamed at Saskia. The men laughed.

"That I am," Saskia responded. She flicked her fingers. "Seize her. I've no doubt she's up to no good."

As a Guard dismounted to approach her, Liara drew her sword. Clan-trained by her brother Erhallen, she was competent with it. The Guard paused and looked back at Saskia.

"Would you face me, Liara?" Saskia drew her own sword and dismounted gracefully. She gestured the Guard aside.

Liara hesitated. She had never seen Saskia fight, but she had heard her father and brothers praising Saskia's talent. Surely she could not be as good as one trained in the Clan arts since birth? Liara set her jaw and stepped forward.

Seconds later, Liara's sword spun out of her hand. Saskia laughed and swung the sword up to her throat.

"You challenged me," Saskia said, deadly soft. "I am carrying the heir to the Empire. Your life is forfeit for that, Liara, if for nothing else."

"Not here, Empress," said the senior among the Guards. He had golden crowns on his shoulders: Aleks' man. They were half and half, Liara noticed, three of each, but this man seemed to be in charge.

"Why not?" Saskia said, blade hovering dangerously close

to Liara's throat.

"It is for the Emperor to pronounce justice and to set her penalty," the soldier responded. "I have no doubt that he will agree with you and order her death. But even you, my lady, have not the right to pronounce summary justice here."

Saskia paused for a moment. Then she nodded and sheathed her sword decisively. "Bring her," she ordered. She shot a look at her Guards. "Don't be gentle."

Liara was tied up and slung roughly over a horse. She still could not believe Saskia's ability: how could a heavily pregnant woman move that quickly and easily?

* * * *

Liara's hate for Saskia knew no bounds as she sat in her dark prison. "I'll destroy her," she vowed. "I swear I'll destroy the pale bitch. And Aleks too: for loving her and not me. I'll destroy them both. I'll kill their children and I'll make sure none of their blood ever sit on the Imperial throne. I swear I'll bring them down if it's the last thing I do." Liara chuckled to herself and hugged her flat belly. "And you'll help me do it, sweetheart. After all, they killed your father."

Anyone who saw Liara at that moment would have feared her. Her eyes glowed with the fire of madness. Her obsession had finally tipped her over the edge.

* * * *

Ria woke several times in the night screaming. Each time, Evan was there to calm her.

"You're safe, princess, you're safe. It's all right. Sleep now."

Unknown to him, the word "princess" was what reassured Ria. Evan said it in the same voice she had heard Aleks use so many times to Saskia. No one had called Ria princess since she was taken, and to hear it spoken in such gently reassuring tones made her feel very safe and secure.

Ria woke feeling ravenously hungry. She had not eaten

properly in many weeks. Looking at her wrists, she saw how thin they were, like sticks lying on the bedcovers.

Evan was asleep in a chair beside the bed. Looking at him properly for the first time, Ria saw that he was a handsome man, with his hard face and short, dark blond hair. He was not particularly tall, barely just above Ria's own height, and whip-thin. But she remembered the strength of him as he carried her easily last night: he had lifted and cradled her as though she weighed no more than a feather. She had felt absolutely safe in his arms.

Just like that, Ria's vision filmed over and the TimeSight came on her, over in moments and leaving her gasping. When her vision cleared, Lia was standing at the end of the bed.

"What did you See?" Lia asked softly, coming around and placing a tray of food on Ria's lap. Ria's stomach growled at the smell of freshly baked bread.

"A farm," Ria said in some surprise.

"A farm?"

"Yes – *my* farm. And he was there." Ria turned to look at Evan, sleeping. "He was my husband." She looked astonished.

"You could do worse. Here. Eat!"

Ria wasted no time, grabbing a chunk of bread and spreading honey onto it. She groaned in bliss, taking a large bite.

"Not too quick," Lia cautioned. Ria slowed down and Lia put her hands on her sister's shoulders,

"There. Now you won't be sick. But still, eat slowly."

Lia stepped around the bed and peered into Evan's face. "Tired," she said softly with a shrug. "But healthy: there's nothing I can do for him. Some breakfast, perhaps, when he wakes."

Evan stirred then, and his eyes opened. He looked into Lia's face for a moment, then turned his head to look at Ria. She smiled at him.

"Good morning, princess," Evan said. "How are you feeling?"

"Weak, and very hungry!" Ria said with a smile.

Lia went out, and returned a few minutes later with another tray of food for Evan, who fell to like a starving wolf.

After Evan and Ria were done eating, Evan put the trays aside. Sitting back down by the bed, he hesitated when he saw Ria staring at him. Then he took a deep breath and offered her his hand. Ria accepted it gladly, and the smile on her face lit up Evan's world.

* * * *

In another tent not very far away, Saskia and Aleks were having a fight.

"I want her dead!" Saskia screamed. Borkenfort had surrendered before darkness fell, and the Guards had been up most of the night questioning the inhabitants. One Guard had brought a maid to Saskia not long before dawn. The Guard, a hardened soldier, was grey and shaking. A few minutes later, as the maid repeated her story, Saskia felt sick to her stomach. The maid had been the one who tended Ria after Sasken first raped her, and she had been witness to many of the indignities visited on Ria by both Sasken and Liara.

"You will speak of this to no one," Saskia said to the maid.

"No, my lady, no one will hear of this from me," the girl replied. She was young, and plain, but not plain enough to have escaped Sasken's attentions. He had left her alone after Ria arrived, but the girl could find only pity for the princess.

"Take her away," Saskia said to the Guard, one of her own. "Make her comfortable." She did not need to repeat her warning about silence. The Guard knew well enough that he should speak of this to no one.

Aleks came in, tired after a sleepless night talking to the Icelander lords, to find Saskia sharpening a long knife with icy, methodical slowness.

"Good morning, sweetheart," he said quizzically. "Are you well?"

Saskia's eyes frightened him suddenly. They were burning orange, and he suddenly realised that she was filled with the Power and holding it in check.

"I'm going to kill Liara this morning," Saskia said calmly.

"Oh, I don't think that's a good idea," Aleks said, having to make an effort to keep his voice steady. "Why don't you give me that knife?" For perhaps the first time since he had known Saskia, she genuinely frightened him.

So Saskia told him. She told him what Liara had helped to do, how the pair had tried to break Ria and nearly, so nearly succeeded. If Ria had not been certain that she would kill Sasken, she would have been destroyed before rescue came.

"I don't know how Ria found the strength," Saskia said, shaking her head in wonder. "I would have hurled myself from the walls long hence."

Aleks was pacing, his face furious. "I can't order her death," he said, almost pleadingly. "I cannot, it is against the law, and I cannot let you either."

"What, then?" Saskia demanded. "I will not have her where Ria can ever set eyes on her again."

"No, we are agreed on that!" Aleks thought for a minute. "Once her child is born, I can banish her. I can insist that she stay in the Icelands, that she may not leave here without specific Imperial permission. For now, we will take her to Iridia. There she will stay where I can have her watched until the child is born. If it is a girl, it will be taken from her and she will face Imperial justice. If she bears a boy, I have no choice but to make her the Regent. Until the child is twenty-one years of age, and then she must face justice, if she is ever foolish enough to leave the Icelands without my specific permission. Should she disobey her banishment, I will order the Law down upon her."

Saskia did not look satisfied. Aleks frowned, and shook his head at her. "You will not kill her, Sass," he said. "I will not have her blood on your hands."

Saskia bit at her lip. "I will not illegally cause her death," she compromised. "But should she break her banishment, I will pursue her to the extent of the law. I will not have her tormenting Ria, either. You send Liara away *now*, under guard to Iridia. Ria cannot travel just yet, and we will go another way, anyway. I want to be out of the Icelands as soon as possible to bear my child."

Aleks' face softened, as it usually did when he thought of their son. "How is he?" he asked eagerly.

Saskia laid hands to her belly, and a dreamy look came over her face as she communed with their unborn child. "He's awake," she said. "He doesn't like it that I'm upset. But he does like the Power in me, oh yes. I think he will be Power-Gifted, Aleks."

"Then he will be the first Emperor so Gifted," Aleks said. "It will be a heavy burden for him to bear."

"The Light will provide, Aleks, trust in the Light."

Aleks nodded, and put his arms around Saskia, hands on her belly. "Love you, princess," he said.

Saskia responded with a weary smile. "Love you too," she replied, leaning against him for support.

Chapter 11

Haven City, late summer,
the year 2719 after Founding

Two weeks later they arrived in Haven. Saskia could no longer ride and Aleks had ordered a litter rigged for her. Ria rode in the litter with her, still too weak to handle a horse. She was, however, improving daily, though she would not speak of what had happened inside Borkenfort to anyone. Evan stayed close to her side at all times, and Ria's TimeSight came thick and fast, showing her future visions of their life together. Evan was caught in a trap of his own making, and was surprised to find how much he liked the idea. They could not be married until Ria was sixteen, but that was no bad thing: she needed time to forget what Sasken had done to her.

In Haven, the Duke opened his house to the Imperial party. Saskia was given a comfortable bedchamber of her own. Aleks slept in an adjoining room; Saskia got little enough sleep now and did not need him disturbing her. They had celebrated Midsummer on the road and arrived in Haven ten days later.

Saskia was not sure exactly when the baby was due, but from the size of her belly she was sure that it could not be long. Lia worried over her: her long, slim bones seemed so fragile to bear a weight such as this baby. But Saskia was strong, with hard muscles overlaid on her slender frame. Her back ached abominably, though, and her slim ankles swelled so she could barely walk. At last the day came when Lia ordered her to bed, not to get up again until the baby was born.

Three nights later Saskia awoke suddenly, a tearing pain in her belly. It was terribly dark in the room, and she dared not so much as light a spark with the Power. She had been unable to do anything much with Fire since the attack on her in the Citadel, for fear she would lose control as the baby grasped at the Power.

Saskia reached out in the blackness and cursed as she knocked the unlit candle beside her onto the floor. Another pain doubled her up for a moment.

"Help!" she called weakly as the pain passed.

A moment later, Aleks came barging in through the door to the adjoining room where he was sleeping. He slept like a cat, Saskia knew: still, she was surprised that he had heard her.

"Sass?" he called.

"A light, Aleks, please," Saskia begged. A few moments passed, then a candle bloomed in the darkness. Aleks came over to the bed.

"Are you all right?" he asked.

"I think the baby may be coming," Saskia replied. "Get Lia, quickly!" She gasped as another pain ripped through her.

Aleks bolted. A few minutes later he was back with Lia in tow, and the Duke's wife, Lady Elyria, a handsome woman in her middle years who smiled down at Saskia.

"Never you mind, my lady," she said warmly. "I've got four children older than you: I know what it is to birth a child, never fear."

Lia laid hands on Saskia's belly and nodded approvingly. "Things progress well, sister: I cannot speed up the process but I can help ease your pain a little."

Indeed, a blessed coolness was already washing through Saskia, the pain diminishing. She sighed.

"Oh, bless you, Lia, that is so much better!"

"It will get worse again before it is over," Lia warned. "You are going to have to be brave."

Saskia nodded, then caught Aleks' eyes. He was watching with a horrified look on his face.

"Get him out of here," she said weakly.

Elyria turned on Aleks at once. "Out, out! This is surely no place for a man!"

"I want to stay with her!" Aleks protested.

"Go, Aleks," Saskia begged weakly. "I'd not have you see me like this. Find Erhallen, go out."

182

Aleks went to her side and stooped to gently kiss her brow. "I love you," he told her, and then went out.

* * * *

Erhallen had been woken by the commotion as Aleks woke Lia, sleeping in the next chamber. Iskia did not wake, and Erhallen, guessing what was happening, left her to sleep. He got up, dressed silently, and arrived at Saskia's door just as Aleks came out, wild-eyed. Evan looked up from his post outside Ria's door, but he would not leave that place until she woke, and just nodded to Erhallen.

The Duke of Haven, Drefanel, arrived a few minutes later. He was a gruff, middle-aged man, who liked Aleks generally but disapproved of him because of his youth, and for his hastiness in marrying Saskia. It was fairly obvious why: his youngest daughter Drefala was a beauty, and just a few months younger than Aleks. Shortly after Aleks and Saskia married, Drefala was sent off to Zahennarra as a bride for the Prince. By all accounts Prince Zaren was a good man, but he was already near forty years of age. Saskia, who had made friends with Drefala in the Citadel, was furious, insisting that Drefala would never have married such an old man of her own free will. But Drefala's signature was on the marriage certificate, and though Aleks suspected Drefanel of coercion on his daughter he could not prove anything. The two men had a wary respect for each other, no more.

Now, however, Drefanel was merely a concerned man, a man with four children himself, and he recognised what Aleks was going through in a way that Erhallen did not.

"Come on, son," Drefanel said gruffly. "My library's downstairs, and I have a decanter of good Summerlander apple brandy. It's not yet midnight, and it's going to be a long night."

Aleks let the other two men lead him downstairs. Still dressed only in the light breeches he had been sleeping in, he shivered slightly as his feet touched the bare stone floor. Drefanel noticed and beckoned a servant over.

"Go find an Imperial Guard: have them bring some clothes

183

and boots for the Emperor to my library," he ordered.

A little while later, the three men sat in front of a hastily stoked fire, sipping quietly at brandy. Aleks was restless and kept jumping up to pace.

It was about an hour later when the first scream ripped through the house. Aleks was racing for the door at once. Erhallen tackled him and held him back.

"You can't go in there!" Erhallen shouted.

"Let me go! Saskia!" Aleks howled. Drefanel came to help Erhallen, and together they literally dragged Aleks back to his chair. Another scream sounded out and he flinched, crying out in sympathy.

"We need to get him out of earshot," Erhallen said desperately. Together, the two men struggled to get Aleks out of the living quarters and into one of the keep's gardens.

"I pray none of the Guards see us manhandling the Emperor so," Drefanel said, almost amused. "It would be worth my head, for sure!"

"I wish they would," Erhallen groused. "Aleks isn't coherent, and he's fighting us. They could help. I'm only glad he can't get his hands on a weapon. Where are those damn Guards when you need them?"

"We are here, Lord of Berenna," a soft voice said. Before the astonished eyes of the two lords, four black-clad figures materialised out of a dark, barely visible doorway.

Drefanel was far more shaken than Erhallen. "Are there Guards all over my palace?" he demanded.

"No, my lord," the leader replied. "Only here, where the Emperor is, and upstairs, the Empress' Guards watch Saskia's door." He gestured, and the other three came to take Aleks. He seemed calmed by their familiar uniforms and they were able to lead him outside.

* * * *

The Guards kept Aleks walking. He seemed to calm down after a while, but kept begging to go back in and see Saskia.

"They'll come for us when it's time, my lord," one of the

Guards insisted, and Aleks quieted.

Dawn came, and then sunrise. It was the day of Harvest Festival, but all the preparations were taking place in a very subdued manner. If things went well, far more than just the harvest would be celebrated in Haven.

The day wore on, and it was after noon when finally Lady Elyria came for them. Her eyes were tired and her skirt marked with blood, but she was smiling. She stopped before Aleks and curtsied low.

"My Lord Emperor, the Light has blessed you with a son," she said.

"Saskia?" Aleks asked anxiously.

Elyria hesitated imperceptibly. "She will be well," was her response.

Aleks was gone at once, Erhallen on his heels and Drefanel not far behind.

Aleks burst into the birthing chamber and stopped, frozen at the sight of his wife. Saskia looked ghastly: her skin was the colour of bleached paper and her breathing shallow. Clean sheets had been put on the bed, but there was still blood on the floor.

"Oh, Light's mercy," Aleks whispered. "What have I done to you?"

"Aleks!" Lia saw him and grabbed his hands. "She will be all right, Aleks. She nearly died, I think if I had not been here you would have lost her. But she will get better, and her womb is undamaged, the second birth will be easier."

"What are you talking about?" Aleks said. "I cannot put her through this again!"

Lia grinned. "You might change your mind. Don't you want to meet your son, Aleks?"

Another woman came forward, and put a bundle of white cloth into his arms. Aleks looked down for the first time into his son's face.

Electric blue eyes stared back. Dark hair already curled over the small pink scalp. Aleks had no one to tell him, but the baby looked exactly as Aleks himself had done at birth.

"Hello," Aleks said a bit awkwardly. "I'm your papa, I suppose."

185

The baby surveyed him for a moment. He opened his mouth, and Aleks winced, anticipating a scream. But there was only a small yawn.

"He's your son, right enough," Lia said, grinning. "I've never seen a new-born so like his father."

"Sasskandr," Aleks said to the baby. "Your name is Sasskandr." He kissed his son very gently on the brow, and then let the woman take him back to his wet-nurse.

Aleks sat by Saskia until she woke, a couple of hours later. Lia insisted that Saskia drink some beef broth before she talked.

"I Named him Sasskandr," Aleks said, "for both of us. I was waiting for you to wake before I announce it to everyone."

Saskia smiled weakly. "It is a fine name," she said softly.

"I am so proud of you both," Aleks said, leaning over to kiss her. "Sleep now, beloved. I will speak with you tomorrow."

Saskia did not sleep for a while, but lay looking down at her new-born son. She was completely awestruck: the Power had surged as he was taken from her womb, and she had to struggle for a moment to control it. The jewel on her hand had flashed exultantly, and on some instinctive level Saskia had known that it heralded the birth of one of her blood with the Power.

Saskia had researched the strange jewel after she had discovered that she could use it to channel the Power. It was originally an Icelander heirloom, given to an Emperor as a token of fealty many years ago. The Icelanders had named it the Ice Tear, and claimed it was linked somehow to their royal house. Saskia thought it was rather appropriate that it had somehow come back to an Icelander princess.

Saskia touched the Ice Tear gently to her sleeping son's forehead. It glowed softly, but Sasskandr did not wake. With a sigh, Saskia snuggled down beside him and fell asleep.

Down in the Great Hall, the feast was in full swing, though still strangely quiet. Aleks walked in and up to the high table. Long before he had reached his empty chair beside Drefanel a total hush had fallen.

Aleks stepped up onto the chair so that everyone could see him. He had no need to call for attention, every eye was already fixed on him.

"I would like to share with you all tonight," he began, "the best news any man can receive. My wife the Empress is resting safe and well, and our first born son Sasskandr is whole and healthy."

The cheer was stupendous. Everyone wanted to shake Aleks' hand and congratulate him. Within minutes bells were ringing out over the city to announce the birth of the Heir to the Empire.

* * * *

The news reached Iridia two days later. In her cell, Liara shivered. She had been given quite a comfortable room, really, in Lady Asfahalia's fortress. The lady knew what Liara had done, though, and there were no luxuries for her, not even any men to work her wiles on. The guards were all female, and a tough and forbidding bunch at that.

Liara pressed her hands to her belly desperately. "Live," she whispered. "Be male!" It had been made quite clear to her that a daughter would bring her death. Suddenly, Liara felt a motion under her hand. It was the first time she had felt the baby move. "That's right," she whispered. "Grow strong, my son. One day you'll kill Aleks and his son for me, and I'll cut out Saskia's heart myself."

Frost Festival had passed, and Saskia and Aleks long returned to the Citadel, when Liara herself went into labour. She was astonished to find that the midwife was Icelander, and even more incredible, a sympathiser. She did not think it was right that the rightful Princess should be locked up, no matter if her Prince had been crazy.

Liara was astounded when she gave birth to twins. The first child born was a girl, and she had despaired, thinking she was sure to die. But the second was a son, and though puny, he cried and breathed well.

"My daughter," Liara took the little girl into her arms. "What a weapon," she whispered, her mind working furiously. "I have to get you out of here."

"I could take her, my lady," the midwife said. "I will make

187

sure she is kept safe until you call for me."

"I will reward you with more gold than you ever imagined," Liara promised. The baby girl was quiet. She looked like Liara: small and compact, with brown hair. The boy had white hair and violet eyes already.

"For sure they're Icelander," the midwife said fondly. "You'll name them in the proper way, of course. Liarken for the little prince."

Liara smiled at that. Her smile disappeared at once when the midwife said:

"And Saskara for the little princess."

That sounded far too much like Saskia for Liara's liking. There was nothing she could say, not when she depended on this woman's goodwill.

And so Saskara was smuggled away in the night, and it was announced that a new Prince was born for the Icelands.

* * * *

Saskia raged when she heard. Aleks would have no choice but to make Liara Regent, provided that her son survived to his first birthday. Until then, Liara would have all the privileges of the Regent, but none of the power. Saskia was also a little concerned: on the night that Liarken was born, she had been woken in the middle of the night and seen a flash in the Tear on her hand. Liarken must have the Power.

Saskia was delighted when she herself became pregnant again that spring. However, her delight vanished when she realised that Aleks would have to travel to Iceden without her to proclaim Liara as Regent, since Saskia would be only about a month from her time by then.

* * * *

Aleks insisted everything would be fine, and since it was winter he would be able to make good time on the river and only be away for a couple of months. He set off at Autumn Equinox, hating to leave Saskia but knowing that she would be able to check on him since Iskia was staying in the Citadel, able to use her powerful LongSight.

Aleks made good time on the journey north, and arrived the day before Liarken's birthday. He had cut it fine, but intended to be in Iceden no longer than absolutely necessary. Liara welcomed him and threw a huge banquet in his honour.

Aleks was exhausted after a full day of travelling and the long banquet. They would be leaving again right after the ceremony in the morning, so he went to sleep quickly, trying to get as much rest as he could.

* * * *

Saskia was restless again. The baby was kicking violently, and it was cold in her wide bed without Aleks. She woke up early, got up and put on a robe, then sat down by the fire. She sewed for a little while, then on impulse, decided to check on Aleks. She called for Iskia, and they sat together, Saskia channelling the Power so that she could share Iskia's LongSight.

At once they saw that Aleks was asleep. Saskia was just about to withdraw from the vision when she saw a secret door slide open in the wall. Saskia could only watch, helpless. Iskia tried to pull away, but Saskia hung on to the vision and broadened it to see the rest of the room. They saw a room in Iceden, richly furnished.

With a shudder of horror Saskia recognised the room as the bridal chamber, where Icelander princesses spent their wedding nights. It was redecorated now, but she could feel the pain of women burned into the walls.

Aleks was awake. A woman came into view, walking quietly to the end of the bed. Saskia thought it was one of her sisters for a moment, then stared in horror. It was herself. Aleks smiled.

"Saskia, my love," he said. Saskia realised he had been drugged somehow, and someone was using the Power to maintain the illusion. Aleks was absolutely convinced it was Saskia before him.

Back in her room, Saskia's hand clenched around the Tear.

A tiny extra current of Power raced through. She strained to see the woman for who she really was.

The woman wearing Saskia's face seemed to blur around the edges. She did not change completely, but rather seemed to be two women in one place, one much shorter and plumper, with long dark hair, and a smug smile.

"Liara!" Saskia screamed in rage. She could do nothing but watch helplessly as Liara climbed into bed beside Aleks and began to touch him with clever fingers.

"No! No! Noooooooooo!!!!" Saskia screamed, but somehow could not bring herself to look away.

When it was over, Liara got to her feet and stretched languorously.

"Oh, I enjoyed that," she purred. "Such a shame it's only for the one night."

"And he cannot be used too hard, or he will be too tired tomorrow," said a voice. Another woman stepped into view, robed in long, dark clothes. "Well, Liara, you had what you wanted. Happy?"

"No," Liara said. "He thought I was that slut. I swear one day he'll come willingly to my bed. But I'll have to bring her and that damned bloodline down first."

"You've made a fair start tonight," the woman said. She laid a hand on Liara's naked belly, and smiled unpleasantly. "Ah, yes. Twins, I think."

Liara laughed. "Well, that's one thing I've proved. I've been bedded twice in my life, and caught with child both times. I'm certainly more fertile than the Icelander whore."

Liara leant back over the bed. "Can I have him again?" she asked the sorceress. "Make him believe again."

"It's not a good idea, Liara. You could shake the babes loose from your womb."

"That's Princess Regent Liara to you. Get out! Aleks would actually be suspicious if I didn't make some effort to seduce him."

The sorceress shrugged and left, smiling a little to herself. Lifting her hands, she wove Power through Aleks' body, taking the last residue of the drugs away, and carefully removing the

190

memory of what had happened. Saskia knew a moment's respect for the sorceress: she was very skilled, and must have at least a little of the Healing Gift along with the Power. Her control over the mind of a man, even an exhausted, sleeping one, was impressive.

Liara slid into bed beside Aleks. She began to move over him, kissing his long, hard body. She looked like herself again. Aleks sighed and put out his hands. As soon as they closed around her waist he snapped awake. His eyes focussed on her face, then he gave a yell of disgust and physically threw Liara away from him. She landed on the floor with a cry.

"You slut," Aleks got to his feet. "My wife is giving birth to my son back home, and all you can think about is your own gratification?"

Liara said nothing, just ran out of the secret door she had entered by. Aleks piled a couple of small tables against it to wedge it shut.

* * * *

Once the vision was gone, Saskia gave in to racking sobs. She could never tell Aleks what Liara had done. Iskia did not know what to say to her, just sat staring in horror. There was only one person who would understand: only one who had been afflicted with Liara's temper too.

Saskia rang the bell for her maid and asked for Riaskia. Iskia had to explain when their sister arrived, Saskia could not find the words. Afterwards, Iskia felt sick and had to go out for a few minutes.

"Oh, dear Light," Riaskia said, reaching out to hug her eldest sister. "I am so sorry."

"Why? Aleks has not been unfaithful to *me*."

"But you had to watch: Sass, that must have been dreadful for you."

Saskia shrugged. "Aleks must never know," she said simply.

"How? If Liara really is pregnant, she'll declare them as his one day. Aleks will deny it, the priests will prove him wrong, and he'll be absolutely crucified."

191

"Liara will never have the chance."

"What are you going to do?" Riaskia said in sudden horror. "Sass, what are you planning?"

"I won't have her raising Aleks' children. This is my thought. Iskia can never have children, but no one except us family know that. We'll declare her pregnant. Erhallen will have to know, of course, but I don't think he's likely to have a problem with it. When Liara gives birth, we'll steal her children. She cannot make an outcry: after all, she cannot declare herself pregnant. She's not married, and cannot be while she is Regent."

"And Iskia and Erhallen can raise them. Sass, that's brilliant. Erhallen looks a bit like Aleks, and even if the children take after Liara, he's her half-brother after all: the colouring is similar enough that no one can prove anything."

Saskia grinned. "I wanted to raise them myself, but I can hardly fall pregnant today with Aleks a week away and Iskandr yet to be born."

Riaskia laughed. "That would stretch the bounds of belief. One question, though: how are you going to steal them?"

"Easy. We'll declare Iskandr's naming ceremony about the time they're due to be born. Liara cannot decline. She'll have to set out and give birth on the road. I might even be able to influence things so she gives birth just before arriving. In the hustle of the arrival, no one will notice two babies are stolen until Liara looks for them."

"It's a bit sketchy," Riaskia said dubiously.

"Give me time: I only just came up with this plan."

Both sisters laughed. Then Riaskia sobered.

"Are you sure you want to do this? Steal Liara's children?"

"Has she not stolen them from Aleks? They aren't hers, Ria. Aleks' children are *mine* to raise. When she stole his seed she wore my body. They are *my* children. I may not be able to raise them myself, but Iskia is my first choice for their mother."

Riaskia nodded in acceptance. "Can I steal them?" she asked.

"What? What are you talking about?"

"I owe that bitch. We've a score to settle. She had me kidnapped so that Sasken could vent his brutality on me while she went on her merry little way. It's true he only used her once, the night before she left Borkenfort. Thank the Light it was her who caught with his filthy seed and not me."

"How could *you* do the kidnapping?"

"You want as few people as possible to know, don't you? I bet you were going to ask Erhallen to do it." Ria's eyes narrowed. "If you tell me you were thinking of doing it yourself, I will smack you very hard."

Saskia blushed slightly. "Well, Erhallen seemed the obvious candidate."

"That's the problem, sister dear. Erhallen's a great soldier, but he's a Clansman first of all. He's used to rushing in, sword drawn, giving a battle cry. Evan, on the other hand, is a trained Imperial Guard. He can move without being detected in any territory."

"Are you sure, Ria? Liara will kill you if she catches you."

"She won't. You just worry about keeping the sorceress off our backs."

Saskia nodded. "Thanks, Ria," she said simply.

"So, who's going to know? You and me, obviously, Evan, Issy and Erhallen. Liaskia?"

Saskia thought for a long moment. "I'm reluctant to tell her," she admitted. "You know how naive Lia can be. She might let something slip."

"She doesn't *need* to know, but how are we going to fool her about Issy? They're really close. Issy might want to tell her, anyway."

Saskia frowned, biting her lip. "I know," she said, her face clearing. "She's been on about becoming an officially trained Healer. We'll send her off to their Collegium. It's right out in North Envetierra. We'll send her off before Issy announces her pregnancy, and by the time the message catches up and she could turn round and come back, the winter storms will have started. She'll be stuck."

"Perfect," Ria agreed. "Light, Sass, we could really pull this off!"

"We have to," Saskia said, suddenly deadly serious. "I will not have Liara raise my children. I will not. I'll kill her first, and that would be breaking a promise I made to Aleks. We have to succeed. He will never know, and neither will she. I'll wrap so many Believe spells around them, and make them part of them using the Tear, no one will ever even want to question. No one will ever see anything but children born to Iskia. Even if they're girls and grow up into the spitting image of Liara, people will still see nothing but daughters of Erhallen."

At that moment Iskia came back in. "What about Erhallen?" she said.

"We have a plan," Saskia said. "Have a seat."

Iskia was very dubious at first. But her desire for children of her own soon overcame her doubts.

"Do you really think we could get away with it?" she asked, desperately wanting to believe.

"Definitely," Riaskia said. "But we have to have your complete co-operation, and Erhallen's. Can you guarantee him?"

Iskia bit her lip. "I think so. It might be better if it came from you, Sass. You've known him a lot longer than I have, after all. I think you must heavily lay the argument that otherwise he will never have his own children. I know he longs for them. It almost destroyed him after I miscarried and we found out that I would not be able to bear."

Saskia nodded. "I will do my best. Bring him to me."

* * * *

Erhallen listened carefully to what Saskia had to say, then looked at his wife, sitting beside him, eyes downcast.

"Iskia, are you absolutely sure you want this?" he said.

"I'm sure, Erhallen. How can I ever have children, otherwise? Saskia is right, they are not Liara's to raise."

"Not ours, either."

"No, that's right," Saskia said. "They are Aleks', and therefore mine. If he could know of this, he would agree with me. He would want to raise them as his own. But he cannot know, and so it is for me to decide. If he ever finds out it would destroy him, you know that. He must never know."

Erhallen nodded, agreeing. "Then I thank you from the

bottom of my heart, Saskia."

"Two good things in one," Saskia said, smiling. "I will take from Liara what she has stolen from me, and I will give my dearest sister the joy she could never otherwise have."

Iskia smiled, and for the first time true hope was in her face. "I can hardly wait. When should I announce my pregnancy? Sass, you must help me stuff my dresses. We must arrange for Lia to go to North Envetierra soon too."

* * * *

Saskia continued to plan. When Aleks arrived back she seemed very distracted, but he put that down to her being so close to her time. In fact, she was now a few days late.

Riaskia brought Evan into the plan. And then, one night, as Saskia was sitting talking quietly with Ria and Evan, Iskandr decided it was time to be born.

Saskia dropped her needlework into her lap and bent over with a groan.

"Sass! Oh, Light!" Ria turned to Evan. "Fetch Liaskia, quickly, run!"

Evan was gone. Ria helped Saskia to stand, and to walk. Shortly after, Liaskia came running in, Iskia not far behind her.

"Out, you two," Liaskia ordered Iskia and Riaskia. "You're neither Healers nor mothers. Go!"

Outside the door they found Aleks, pacing nervously, both Erhallen and Evan trying to get him to go away with them. Ria took charge and marched everyone down to the library.

"She nearly died birthing Sasskandr," Aleks said, panicking. "I want to be with her. I don't want it to happen again."

No one could give him comfort. But it was only four hours later, midnight not even arrived, when Liaskia came in, smiling.

"Iskandr is born, my lord," she said. "Both Saskia and your son are doing just fine."

The relief on Aleks' face was wonderful to see. He raced up the stairs two at a time and burst into the birthing chamber. Saskia was resting in the bed, her son held in her arms, a beautiful smile on her face. The Tear had flashed again, an even brighter flare than at Sasskandr's birth, so it was confirmed that Iskandr would have the Power too.

Aleks knelt beside the bed in wonder. The baby was sleeping, but he looked just as Sasskandr had at birth, rather pink, but with his mother's fair skin and his father's dark hair.

"Another son," he said in wonder. A few minutes later Liaskia came in with Sasskandr.

"Hello, son," Aleks took the child from her. He was a little fractious, having just been woken up. "Meet your new brother Iskandr."

"Skan," Sasskandr said cheerfully, reaching out to grab at his mother. Saskia took him, smiling.

"That's right, darling, Iskandr."

"Skan," Sasskandr repeated, nodding.

"He'll figure it out," Aleks said with a laugh. "Come, give him to me. I'll put him back to bed."

Sasskandr didn't figure it out. Upon continued pressing, he modified his brother's name to "Iskan" but there it stayed. Soon enough Saskia and Aleks found themselves abbreviating their younger son's name too. Sasskandr's endearing habit of calling himself "Kandr" caught on too.

When Lirallen and family came to visit, young Mirallen, a year older than Sasskandr, promptly became "Mirri". Sasskandr's seriousness was quite infectious and everyone picked up his nicknames, at least for the other children.

* * * *

The time passed quickly. Aleks, puzzled by Saskia's insistence, nevertheless gave in and requested Liara and Liarken's presence at Iskandr's Naming Day. Liaskia was hustled off to North Envetierra, protesting slightly, but reassured that the family were all healthy and could well do without her.

Iskia waited until Lia's boat was long gone up the Empire Water and then announced her pregnancy. Everyone was astounded, and delighted: Iskia had mourned so long she had virtually given up the idea of having her own children. This was nothing short of a miracle.

196

There would have been too many questions if no healer had been brought in to look Iskia over, so Saskia did her homework. She found the Healer who had done her best in Rianna's last days, Kersuna, a very old lady now. She listened to Saskia's story: to the whole truth of it, and nodded finally.

"As you will, my lady. I mislike lies, but one lie deserves another. I doubt not that the Emperor's children will have a far better life with Princess Iskia as their mother than with that nasty little baggage."

"Thank you," Saskia said sincerely. "Name whatever you will as your reward."

"I'm not long for this life, my lady, another year or two perhaps. I'm still healthy, but old age takes its toll. All I ask, is that when I'm gone, you donate a trust in my name, to the city. That *any* child born with the Healing Gift, no matter how small, have their passage paid to go to the College to learn."

"That I will do, and right gladly," Saskia said. "In truth, I will do my best, not just for the city, but for any child born in the Empire to have that right."

Kersuna smiled, and nodded. "You're a good girl, Saskia. I told Rianna as much before she died."

Saskia smiled back at the old lady. The following day, Kersuna announced that Iskia was pregnant with twins, just as the sorceress had told Liara. It would be easy enough if they were wrong, to state that one twin had died.

Chapter 12

The Citadel, Midsummer,
the year 2721 after Founding

Liara cursed and ranted when she read the letter, but it was
clearly penned as an order. Aleks wanted to see that Liarken
received the proper upbringing, and that included meeting his
Heir, for so Iskandr technically was until Liarken himself
fathered children. Liara raged over that, sure that her daughter
Saskara should be Heir. But a woman could not rule the
Icelander royal line unless there were no male heirs at all, and
even then she would only be allowed to be Regent for her sons.

That had occurred to Iskia also. The children she would
adopt would be acknowledged as second and third in line to the
Iceden throne, though they would have no blood right to it. She
decided to renounce the throne and declare herself no longer of
the Icelander blood. Thus her children would be not of the blood
also, and have no possible claim on the throne.

"What do you think I will have?" Iskia queried. She was
sitting in Saskia's chamber with her hands on the stuffing under
her dress. Saskia laid aside her sewing and smiled at her sister.

"I don't know, my dear. Come, let us link: you can see
Liara."

They linked and the Sight carried them out and up to the
river. It was a few days before Midsummer. Iskandr's Naming
was to be held at Harvest, and Liara was well on her journey. It
had been a dry year, and the river was no longer navigable as far
as the Citadel. The group were having to travel by wagon, and
Liara's temper was fraying in the heat. She sat in her litter,
carried between two horses, curtains drawn to hide her from the

world. Of course, no one could know she was pregnant. She had brought only a small entourage, of loyal Icelanders who would be silent. Liarken sat beside his mother in the litter. Thankfully, the sorceress was not with the party: Saskia and Iskia had looked and seen that she had been left behind in Iceden to mind matters there.

A few more days passed. Liara steadily neared the Citadel. Eventually the Icelander group made camp for the last time before reaching the city, setting up their tents early one evening. There were only a few miles to go, but obviously Liara was panicky about her pregnancy being discovered. Saskia called for Evan and Ria, and asked for Kersuna also.

Evan and Ria left the Citadel an hour later. Saskia had used Earth skills to create four small bodies, two girls and two boys, to substitute for the babies they would steal. They were indistinguishable from real children. Saskia gave them all dark hair and blue eyes.

Saskia and Iskia watched until they saw Ria and Evan arrive, and creep on silent feet towards the camp. Ria had shown enormous trust in Saskia for this. She walked straight into the middle of the camp and headed for the guards' stewpot, tipping a vial of liquid Kersuna had given her into the pot.

No one took any notice of Ria: Saskia had wrapped a very clever Air illusion around her. People would only see Ria if they expected to. So when they saw a saddled horse walking down the street, they would see a girl on its back. But here in a camp in the woods, no one would be expecting to see her, and so she could move about without being observed.

An hour later, the guards all lay about snoring. Saskia brought Kersuna into the link, and then did something she had never tried before. She tried to use Power over a distance. She used the Healing ability of Kersuna to loosen the babies in Liara's womb.

Liara was in labour within minutes and yelling for help. Liarken's nurse was the only woman with the group, and never thought to look outside, but just attended to her mistress.

An hour later the babies were born. The nurse scooped them up and carried them into the other part of the tent to wash them.

A few moments later she returned to attend to Liara, who had fallen into an exhausted sleep.

Saskia again took a grip on the powers at her disposal. Silently she put an Air shield between the two parts of the tent, so that the sound of the babies crying would not penetrate. Then she reached out to Ria and used Fire to set a spark to the grass in front of Ria's feet. Ria jumped, stamped out the tiny flames, and beckoned to Evan. They dashed for the tent. Evan pulled up a couple of tent pegs and they crawled under the canvas.

Ria snatched up the children, who stayed remarkably quiet, and unwrapped them quickly from their blankets. "Both boys," she told Evan. Evan quickly handed her the two fake boy bodies, and Ria wrapped them back up. Then each of them grabbed up one baby, tucked them into the blankets they had brought, slipped out under the tent wall and forced the pegs back in. Moments later they had disappeared into the night.

Saskia took her time waking the guards up a few at a time. A few minutes later, they all jumped as a terrible scream sounded out from Liara's tent.

"What? What is it?" Liara demanded, struggling to sit upright. "Bring me my sons, woman!"

"Oh, my lady, my lady!" the nurse wailed. "My lady, they're dead!"

Saskia didn't watch. She broke the links instead and looked back at the other two women in the room. They were in Iskia's chambers in the Clanlands Tower. It had been announced earlier that Iskia was in labour, and Erhallen had gone off to find Aleks and have a few drinks together. Strangely, Erhallen was as nervous as though it really was Iskia giving birth.

Ria and Evan didn't arrive back for another three hours. Just as dawn broke, Ria came to Iskia's room. Evan had gone to burn the bodies of the other two fake babies.

The three women were all drowsing on the bed. As Ria burst in, they all leaped up.

"I have them," was all Ria said. She went straight to Iskia, and laid the children into her arms. Iskia, with shaking fingers, turned back the blankets to look on the faces of her sons.

Saskia leaned over to look at the children Aleks had

fathered. They had his dark hair: but that could as easily be Erhallen's. As yet, their round baby faces showed no resemblance to anyone.

"Let me check them," Kersuna said. A moment later she stepped back. "Perfectly healthy, my lady. Congratulations, you have birthed two fine sons."

The four women smiled at each other, in perfect accord. "Saskia, you'd better go find Erhallen," Iskia said.

Saskia nodded. "Thank you, Ria. You and Evan go to bed. Get some rest."

Saskia went to find Erhallen and Aleks. They were sitting in Aleks' study, both drowsing in their chairs. Saskia touched Erhallen on the shoulder, and he started awake.

"You have two fine sons," Saskia said. They looked deep into each other's eyes for a moment, then Erhallen nodded.

"Praise the Light," he said fervently. That woke Aleks. He stared around for a moment.

"Iskia has birthed twin sons," Saskia told him.

Aleks smiled with joy. "That's wonderful! Erhallen, you had best go to her directly."

When Erhallen was gone, Saskia sighed and sat down. She was exhausted. Up all night working with the Power, through a LongSight vision, was the one of the hardest things she had ever had to do.

"Was it an easy birth, sweeting?" Aleks asked.

"I don't think twins are ever easy," Saskia answered.

"Eh, I think you are right there," Aleks said. He leaned over to kiss Saskia, and then surprised her by scooping her up into his arms. "Come on, beautiful, I'm taking you to bed."

"To sleep, I hope," Saskia sighed.

"Surely. But maybe later, we'll have a try at making a little sister for all these strapping boys this family is producing!"

Saskia could not help but chuckle. "Not quite yet, I beg you," she said. "I could do with a couple of years off, to let the boys grow up a bit before I start having more than two underfoot!"

Aleks grinned. "You'd better keep drinking that brew of Lia's, then, for I've no intention of staying out of your bed!"

Erhallen leaned over Iskia, lying in bed cradling the babies. Everyone else was gone, leaving them for this private moment.

"What will you name your sons, my lord?"

Erhallen took them from Iskia. The older boy had a red thread tied around his wrist. They were so perfect as they slept, so small. Erhallen was terrified he might drop them.

"My oldest son shall be Iskallen," he said. "And my younger son shall be Saskallen, in honour of our lady Empress." His eyes met Iskia's and she nodded in perfect accord.

From that moment on, neither of them spoke of the fact that the boys were not theirs. As far as they were concerned, the two boys were as much their children as if Iskia had given birth to them. Though they were not of Iskia's blood, she could not have loved them any more. They were her sons, and she would be as fierce as any mother to protect them.

Just a few weeks later, Iskia and Erhallen left for Berennahold with their sons. They intended to stay away for a while, to give the boys a chance to grow up a bit in their home. Saskia missed her sister, but Iskia wrote regular letters.

* * * *

Some months later, Lia returned from the Healers' college, having learnt as much as she could there. She had sailed directly to Berennahold to see Iskia and the children, and never suspected a thing.

Saskia was pleased to welcome her youngest sister home. Ria was glad to see her too: she and Evan had announced their betrothal formally just before Iskandr was born and now that her favourite sister was home, Ria was ready to get married.

The wedding was a small affair: Aleks had knighted Evan and bestowed some land upon him but he was still only a minor member of the nobility and Ria wanted no fuss made on her account. They intended to head down to Summerlands immediately after the wedding, to spend some time together. They would return to the Citadel in time for Midsummer the following year.

* * * *

Saskia had never known so much happiness. She doted utterly on her sons, and Aleks adored them also. All the days seemed to be filled with sunshine and laughter. Liara sulked and plotted in her northern stronghold, but Saskia had no intention of letting her anywhere near Aleks again. Liara would conceive no more children to curse them.

All the family came back to the Citadel for Saskia's twenty-third birthday. Ria was pregnant, due for her first baby around Frost Day. She had somehow concealed it from Evan for fear he would not let her travel to the Citadel, but Lia let the cat out of the bag at once. Lia checked her over, and insisted that Ria should not travel any more, but must remain in the Citadel until her baby was born. Iskia wanted to stay too, and Erhallen, always happy to indulge her, agreed. And so the sisters were together again, and happy to spend time with each other and with the children.

Saskia sat in the garden and watched the four boys playing. Sasskandr at four was the biggest and strongest by far, but gentle with his strength. Iskandr at not yet three and the twins at two were all much of a size, big and strong for their age.

Saskia looked yet again at Iskallen and Saskallen and wondered how anyone could possibly miss the resemblance to Aleks. Sasskandr was the most like his father, but the twins were spitting images of Iskandr, save for their dark eyes. It was astonishing, really, almost as if Saskia really could have been their mother and Liara no kin to them at all.

Logically Saskia knew that no one could break her spells. No one ever so much as remarked on the resemblance between Iskandr and Iskia's boys.

Saskia had no difficulty thinking of them as Iskia's sons. Only rarely did she ever remember they were Liara's sons.

"They're so like him, aren't they?" Liaskia's voice said as she came to sit by Saskia.

"Who?" Saskia said, hearing the almost-panic in her tone and cursing herself.

"Erhallen, of course. I don't think I've ever seen two

children more like their father. Even Sasskandr isn't that much like Aleks."

"Oh," Saskia said. It was hard for her to see such a resemblance, but she supposed it was there to see. After all, Erhallen was Liara's half-brother: there was no reason why the boys should not be like him.

"Where's Issy?" Lia asked.

"Gone shopping with Ria. Ria is getting very broody now she's so close to time, and is buying lots of baby clothes!"

"Do you think she'll have a son?"

"I truly don't know, Lia. I did try with the Tear, but whatever the child is, it is not Power-born. You would think that perhaps one of us might have a daughter, though!"

Lia laughed. "Perhaps it will yet be you." She paused and gave Saskia a strange look.

"What? What is it, Lia, why are you looking at me like that?"

Lia shook her head. "I'm not entirely sure. Just – recently, you feel different. I was wondering if you were pregnant again."

Saskia looked astonished. "I had thought I was, but was not sure myself yet! Come, give me your hand. We shall try a little look, perhaps."

The link between them was always hard to establish, since of all the sisters, their powers were the most different. Saskia's raging torrents of Power always threatened to utterly hide Lia's Healing, but they needed both and struggled to meld them. At last Saskia put her free hand on her flat stomach and directed the melded query through the Tear.

One tiny part of Saskia's mind watched the Tear for the telltale flash of Icelander sorcerer blood, but none came.

When Saskia had perceived Iskandr at two months old, he had been a bright flare in the darkness of her womb. Now this child should be about the same age, but she had to strain. Finally there was a flicker in the dark. Then another, then a third.

"I *am* pregnant!" Saskia exclaimed.

"Wait," Lia said. "There was something odd about those flickers: they were all different."

They looked again, and the flickers came again, in a slightly different order this time, and distinctly apart from each other.

"What does *that* mean?" Saskia said, bewildered.

"I think it means there's not one child growing in you, but three."

Neither of them had TimeSight, but Saskia had linked with Ria once or twice and thought she knew how it worked. They both stared into the Tear on Saskia's hand, by far the easiest thing to try and project into. And there they saw three little girls like flowers, laughing and clustered around Aleks' knee.

Saskia was gasping. She let go of the vision and the Tear's light blinked out.

"Daughters," Saskia breathed. "Oh, Light, Lia, I'm going to have daughters!"

"Three of them," Lia said, delighted. "You'll have your hands full for a few years."

"Hello, beauty," said a deep voice. "What are you looking so happy about?"

Saskia jumped up and ran into Aleks' arms, bursting into tears.

"What in the Light..." Aleks said, holding his wife carefully. "Sass? Lia? What's going on?"

"That's not for me to tell, my lord," Lia said, bowing. She smiled a little wistfully.

"I'm pregnant," Saskia sobbed into Aleks' neck.

"What?" He held Saskia away to look at her, astonished. "And this is not a good thing?"

"Oh, yes, yes it is! I'm going to have a little girl! Well, three, actually."

"What?" Aleks looked flabbergasted. "Three? How do you know?"

"Lia helped me and we saw them in the Tear."

"Three little girls with golden hair," Lia confirmed. "I saw them, my lord, with you, very clearly."

"Oh, Sass," there were tears in Aleks' eyes too. "You've given me such wonderful sons, to follow me and carry on my work. But daughters...."

Of course, Lia thought. Daughters were very special to a father under Empire tradition. They represented his name: only a first born son could be more precious.

"When are you going to get married and have some babes of your own, Lia?" Aleks asked, after the two of them had finished hugging and laughing.

"Oh, I'm young yet," Lia said with a slightly forced brightness.

"Lia, when I was your age I was two years married with Sasskandr on the way," Saskia replied pertly.

Lia only flushed slightly. Saskia shook her head tolerantly. She knew what the problem was. Lia had idolised Aleks for too long and could find no man to match up to him. She adored Aleks, and envied Saskia greatly. But Lia's heart was pure, and she would never try to steal Aleks for herself as Liara had done. She would live out her life lonely if need be, rather than betray her sister.

Later on, alone in their chamber, Saskia spoke of her worries about Lia.

"At least Ria is married and pregnant now. But Lia may never have children if she goes on like this, and she has too much love to give for that to happen. We've got to find her a good man."

Aleks shook his head at her. "She's met every eligible man in the Empire, just about. She's the highest born unmarried lady in the Empire at the moment, quite apart from being almost as beautiful as you are. Not even considering her abilities as a Healer. Did you know they've begun to call her the White Lady?"

Saskia nodded. "A hard reputation for her to live up to." She laughed suddenly. "Almost as hard as the Ice Witch some fools name me!"

Aleks kissed her, grinning. "I prefer Flower of the North, for you," he said. "I do have one more idea for Lia, though."

"Who?"

"Well, that's the problem: you'll hate him."

"How could I? Who is he?"

"He's a Roman'i."

"A what? You want to marry my sister off to some vagabond traveller? Certainly not!" Saskia glared at her husband indignantly.

"No vagabond, this one, my love. Isulkian is the prince of all the Roman'ii. He rules virtually the whole of the Roman'ii Territories. He's a rich man, and we buy a lot of livestock off him. He breeds the best cattle in the Empire."

"Still, Aleks, to send Lia off to the hills...."

"You listen to me. Little Lia is the strongest woman I've ever met, apart from you. You could handle it easily."

"Well, yes, but..."

"Just because Lia is tiny doesn't mean she's fragile. She's hard as nails, and her experience with Healing will make her a treasure to the Roman'ii. She will probably be treated more gently than you have been here."

Saskia changed tack. "What's this Isulkian like? Is he a complete barbarian like the Roman'ii we see at the fairs?"

Aleks laughed. "Wait and see. You'll meet him tomorrow. I had word today that he arrived in the city."

"Oh, you are the most *exasperating* man!" Saskia exclaimed.

Aleks just laughed again, caught her two braids in his hands and pulled her to him for a kiss.

* * * *

Saskia was dying of curiosity about Isulkian. She was in the Court the following day when he was presented, and had persuaded the other sisters to come along with her, ostensibly to keep her company.

It was the Frost Day festival, and the formal court was quiet, only a few people wanting to see Aleks. Some of the nobility who showed up regularly looked a little surprised to see Saskia sitting alongside Aleks, but she came sometimes to these courts. The sisters chatted quietly at the back of the hall, wondering curiously what Saskia would have them see.

The crier entered the room.

"Your Imperial Graces," he said with a flourish. "I have the honour to present Prince Isulkian of the Roman'ii."

"Yeah, yeah, get out of the way," said a voice. In stomped

the handsomest man Saskia had ever seen. He was perhaps only a little taller than she was, still quite tall. His eyes and hair were black as a raven's wing, his skin darkly tanned. Perfectly white teeth flashed in that perfect, high-cheekboned face, and he moved with the grace of someone who spent their life on horseback.

"Aleks, you bastard!" he yelled in delight, and charged up to the throne. Aleks leapt up to meet him, and they hugged tightly.

"It's bloody great to see you, Isulkian," Aleks said, thumping his friend's back.

Isulkian freed himself from Aleks' hug and stared at Saskia. "Light of heaven, strike me blind!" he cried out. "For surely now I have seen the most perfect creature in the world!"

Saskia could not help but like him. She grinned.

Aleks was frowning furiously. "Isulkian, that's my wife!" he hissed.

"Damn it all, I knew I should have killed you years ago," Isulkian said laughingly. He bent over Saskia's hand, holding it far too long. "How in the Light did you manage to catch this exquisite creature?"

Aleks grinned. "I stole Saskia from her mad Icelander brother."

"Oh, then this must be the Ice Witch!" Seeing Saskia's eyes narrow, Isulkian immediately corrected himself. "The Flower of the North – damn me, you always were a lucky pig, Aleks!" He shook his head. "Which brings me to the real reason I'm here, Aleks, I need a wife, and fast."

Saskia blinked at the sudden change of subject, and so did Aleks. "What?"

"The Old Ones have decided it's time I wed. They've picked out three girls and told me to choose among them."

"So? Roman'ii girls are very pretty, as I recall." That earned Aleks a fist in the ribs from Saskia.

"That's not the problem. One is the daughter of my greatest enemy, one is his sister, and the other is my cousin. Marrying either of the first two would guarantee my death as soon as I fathered a son, and marrying my cousin would be a fate *worse* than death. I *hate* her."

"And because you cannot overrule the Old Ones, you've come to me." Aleks rolled his eyes.

"Exactly!" Isulkian beamed. "If you command me to wed, not even the Old Ones can object."

"I'm not just going to pick some girl and order you to marry her, Isulkian. I have to make sure she doesn't hate you."

Saskia's sisters had drawn closer, curious. Isulkian, hearing steps behind him, whirled, hand dropping to his hip. In a moment he sized up the others: Iskia with Erhallen bulking massive beside her, Ria heavily pregnant, hand held by whip-thin Evan. And Lia, tiny, incredibly beautiful and alone.

Isulkian's eyes widened. He forgot about everyone else in the room and stared at Lia, completely tongue-tied.

Aleks began to laugh. "Isulkian, I think this is the first time I've ever seen you speechless," he teased. "Allow me to introduce my wife's sisters, the Princesses of Iceden."

"Princess Iskia and her husband Lord Erhallen, Warlord of Clan Berenna," he began. Isulkian recovered his manners enough to bow over Iskia's hand. "Princess Riaskia and her husband Lord Evan."

"My congratulations on your forthcoming blessing," Isulkian said charmingly.

"And Princess Liaskia. You may have heard of Lia, Isulkian: she is sometimes known as the White Lady? Lia has been to North Envetierra to study at the Healers' College there, and has returned a very fine doctor."

Isulkian looked impressed. He took Lia's hand and lifted it to his lips. She was staring at him like a frightened doe, completely overawed by his charisma.

No, Saskia amended to herself as she watched, his Charisma. That was why Isulkian reminded her so much of Aleks – he was born with the same massive instinctive Charisma, completely uncontrollable. With such looks and such abilities, it was no wonder he had united virtually the whole of the hillmen under his leadership.

Isulkian was still holding Lia's hand. He turned to Aleks and gave him a look full of meaning.

"Aleksandr von Chenowska, you have been entirely selfish to keep such beautiful women to yourself," he said.

Saskia could not help grinning. She caught Ria's eyes and saw laughter there. A moment later Ria paled and clutched at her belly.

"Ria!" Saskia leapt to her sister's side. "Is the baby coming?"

"Ah – I think so. That was a contraction."

Lia whirled away from Isulkian and placed her hands on Ria's stomach. "We need to get her to the birthing chamber," she said after a moment. "I think this is going to be a quick one."

Evan picked his wife up carefully. Despite his slim frame he was incredibly strong, as Saskia had found out more than once in the practice yard.

Isulkian followed along. No one told him to leave, he reasoned, and if he was to marry Princess Liaskia he ought to see just how good a healer she really was. However, when they got to the birthing chamber, Erhallen and Aleks both stepped firmly in front of him.

"Not a cat's chance in hell are you going in there," Aleks said firmly.

"But my lord..."

"*No*, Isulkian. If you want to see Lia's Healing in action, you'll just have to wait for someone to get injured – or go and follow her when she visits the city hospital."

Isulkian looked sulky, but finally nodded his assent. A moment later, Evan came out of the chamber, his eyes a little wild. Aleks took one look at him. "The library," he said. "I have some brandy there."

The four men sat in the library, well out of earshot of any cries. Evan could not stop pacing. Aleks kept grinning at him.

"I was just the same when my sons were being born," he said.

"What about you, Erhallen?" Isulkian asked innocently. Both he and Aleks wondered at the odd tightness about Erhallen's mouth.

"I was very worried about my wife," Erhallen said after a moment. "Iskia is the most fragile of the sisters by far, and at one stage we thought that she could not have children at all. She will have no more. But we have two fine, strong sons, and I thank the Light for it every day."

And my lady Empress, Erhallen added silently to himself. He looked at Aleks, and vowed once again to guard Saskia's secret with his life. The truth could break their marriage.

* * * *

Ria was not having a fun time with labour. She hissed with the pain and clutched at Saskia's hands. Only Liaskia could calm her, and she was too busy to do more than lay an occasional hand on Ria's brow to quiet her.

Ria's TimeSight was raging loose as well, and she kept seeing fragmentary visions. Everyone she looked at, she saw their future children as strange shadows around them. Every time she looked at Saskia, she saw so many children her eyes blurred with the daughters and sons yet to be born to her sister.

Lia would bear one son only, and Ria's mouth twisted with amusement as she saw the spitting image of Isulkian in the boy's face. Iskia of course was barren. Ria lost the vision and let out a groan as a terrific contraction ripped through her.

"It's coming, Ria, it's coming," Liaskia said. "Just one more push, come on."

Ria groaned, the tendons standing out in her neck. Liaskia let out a cry of triumph, echoed a few seconds later by the wail of a healthy baby.

"You have a daughter!"

Saskia had automatically glanced down at the Tear, but there was no flash to indicate sorcerer's blood. The child was normal, quite probably Gifted, but not with the Power.

"Evaskia," Ria said weakly. "Give her to me." The midwife was massaging Ria's belly to help expel the afterbirth.

"I'll go to Evan," Saskia said. She kissed her sister's brow. "You had a far easier time of that than I did, sister dear! Perhaps there's something to be said for having a skinny husband!"

Evan was up the stairs in a few swift leaps. He shot in through the door of the birthing chamber and clutched Ria to

211

him.

"I love you, I love you," he babbled. "Are you all right?"

Ria was crying softly. Saskia, arriving behind Evan, winced at her next words.

"I so wanted to give you a son!"

Saskia gestured to Iskia to come away. The sight of them, both of whom had two sons, even though Ria knew Iskia had not given birth to hers, would not help her now. Only Evan could reassure Ria.

"Oh, my love," he said softly, stroking Ria's hair. "If you had given me no children at all, still I would count myself a lucky man. A daughter will be a blessing to us every day. We have years yet ahead to try for sons. But if you bear me no more children at all, I'll still be the happiest man alive."

Ria wept into his shoulder as he held her. "I love you," she choked. "I was so frightened."

"You and me both, princess." Evan held her close, closing his eyes and pressing his cheek against her hair.

Liaskia and the nurse were cleaning the baby and now Lia picked up her niece and carried her over to the bed.

"Your daughter, my lord," she said.

Evan reached for his firstborn. "Evaskia," he said softly, turning back the blanket to look at the sleeping child's face. "Oh, she is so beautiful!"

Indeed, the child was lovely: the first daughter born to any of the princesses, she had the Icelander royal looks: silver hair and eyes already a clear amethyst.

"She'll be a heartbreaker in a few years," Aleks said, coming in and peering at the baby. "You'll have your work cut out fending off all the suitors!"

Evan grinned down at his firstborn. "It'll be a pleasure," he said, gently stroking his daughter's soft silvery hair.

Chapter 13

The Citadel, Frost Day,
the year 2723 after Founding

Lia went out to wash her hands and stretch her tired body. She was just arching her back, hands raised above her head, when there was a gasp behind her. Lia whirled to see the Roman'i prince, staring at her wide-eyed.

"My lord Isulkian," Lia bowed her head slightly, wincing as her muscles pained her. "Were you looking for me?"

"All my life," Isulkian said softly. Then a little louder, he said; "My lady Liaskia, you look most exhausted, and must be famished too, in truth. Allow me to escort you back to the Icelands tower so you may rest."

Lia smiled genuinely at the thought of getting some sleep. Her Empathy made it very hard for her to rest around other people: their emotions were constantly crowding in on her. But the Icelands tower was empty save for a few guards posted at the entries, and the quietness inside was an emotional haven for Lia.

"Thank you very much, my lord," Lia said. "That is most kind of you, I would appreciate it very much."

Lia was surprised to find it was still dark outside, not yet dawn, and quite chilly. She shivered slightly. Isulkian, noticing, at once pulled off his leather coat and wrapped it around her shoulders. He took a torch from the palace gate to light their way.

"Thank you," Lia said, pulling the coat around her. She glanced sideways to smile shyly at Isulkian. He looked absolutely lovely, wearing only a black sleeveless shirt and dark trousers. The impossibly high cheekbones looked higher than ever, the hollows beneath them dark in the flickering light.

They reached the door of the Icelands tower and Lia slipped off Isulkian's coat, offering it to him.

"Thank you," she said shyly.

"Rest well, princess," he said softly, taking his coat. He handed the torch to the door guard.

"But – you won't be able to see your way, surely!" Lia objected, as he turned to go.

Isulkian turned back to grin at her. "My eyes are used to the night, princess. Never fear, I won't trip." And he was gone, melting silently into the darkness.

Lia shrugged and headed eagerly for her bed, staying awake only long enough to eat an apple. She was so tired, she slept until almost sunset. Waking, she hurried back to the palace to check on Ria, ate with Saskia and Aleks and then returned to her bed. She had been half hoping to see Isulkian, but there was no sign of him.

Saskia barging into her room awakened Lia just before dawn. "Lia! Lia, wake up, we need you!"

"Wussat?" Lia struggled awake. "What's wrong? Is it Ria?"

"No! Aleks just had word. A mine has collapsed, about a day's ride from here. They're digging it out but they need a Healer, and fast! Now move!"

Lia was on her feet and dressing at lightning speed. She snatched up her bag of useful things, bandages and ointments. Then the two girls were racing down the stairs. Outside twenty horses were waiting, Aleks and a handful of guards, and somewhat surprisingly, Isulkian and five Roman'ii. Lia had no time to question. She jumped into the saddle of the mare a groom was holding for her, made sure her bag of medical supplies was securely tied behind her, and they were gone, racing out through the city.

"What's he doing here?" Lia asked Saskia, gesturing at Isulkian.

"He showed up while we were trying to get the horses ready. When he found out where we were going, he said he'd been there. None of us have, he can lead us straight there. And he and the other Roman'ii with him are trained to find their way in the dark: they can lead us safe where no one else could."

Saskia cast a sideways look at her sister, as they both bent low over their horses' necks. "Do you object to his coming along?"

Lia's blush was thankfully hidden by the darkness. "Why would I?" she said in a voice that sounded abnormally high.

On fast horses, they reached the collapsed mine in mid-afternoon. Lia's legs were shaky when she slid off her horse: she had not ridden so fast or so far since leaving the Clanlands.

The diggers had managed to open up another collapsed section and were carrying the wounded out. Saskia left Lia to see to the wounded outside and went into the mine at a run to see if she could help open anything up using the Power.

"Sass, be careful!" Aleks yelled after her. Then he shook his head angrily. "Lia, come on. I'll carry your bag. Where do you want to start?"

The rescue workers had put up a hospital tent. Lia pointed, and Aleks followed with her bag. Inside, the scent of blood and death appalled them both. They paused, and then Lia sucked in a ragged breath. "There. A man's dying over there." She could *feel* him, and only hope that she would be in time to save the miner from the crushed chest that was making his breathing slower and more laboured by the minute.

* * * *

In the mine, Saskia used Earth Power to clear debris. She pulled out two men who had been trapped. The mine was for silver, and so there was little dust in the air, but the tunnels were small and narrow.

Isulkian had followed Saskia in and made sure she kept her footing steady, well aware that sometimes Saskia's concentration was the only thing that stopped them from being buried alive too.

At last Saskia was certain that there was no one left alive inside. She headed back out, going to look for Lia, so that Saskia could enhance her Healing with the Power.

Liaskia lay on the grass and closed her eyes. The sick spinning feeling slowly faded as she rested, but the deep, bone-weary ache in her body would not go so easily. The horror of what she had seen that day stunned her: the men broken almost

215

beyond recognition as they were pulled out of the collapsed mine.

Saskia had fed Power-enhanced strength to Lia until she could use no more. Finally no one was left in danger of dying, and Lia had fled the camp, running hard across the grass, desperate to get away from the emotions that crowded in on her.

Now Saskia went alone around the camp, using the Power to fix what crude wounds she could. Without the fine touch of a Healing gift, she dared not attempt anything tricky. Finally, she had done all she could. Feeling unaccountably tired, she headed for the mess tent. Maybe the babies were leaching her strength: she was only a few weeks pregnant but she had heard of it happening.

* * * *

Lia finally slept. When she woke, it was still dark, and she stretched. With surprise, she found that someone had tucked a thick blanket around her as she stretched. "Sass?" she said. Silence was the only answer. Sitting up, she saw a dark shape seated against a nearby tree trunk. "Sass, is that you?"

"No, my lady," said a low male voice.

Lia scrambled to her feet, feeling at her waist for her knife. "Who's that?" she demanded, fear putting an edge into her voice.

"It is I, my lady, Isulkian."

"Oh! The Roman'i." Lia relaxed and dropped her hand from her knife.

"Yes, my lady. Here, would you like some bread and cheese?"

Pulling the blanket around her shoulders, Lia walked over and sat down beside him. The sky was gradually beginning to lighten, and she could just make out his face. "That would be very nice, thank you," she said.

Isulkian put a thick slice of bread and a wedge of cheese into Lia's hands. She could not finish it, though.

Isulkian shrugged and wrapped the remainder back up. He offered Lia his water bottle to wash the food down, and was mildly encouraged when she didn't bother to wipe the neck before drinking.

"You're very tired, my lady," he said.

"Yes," Lia agreed. "Healing that hard, it takes all the strength out of me. Yet still, there were some I could not save. Not even Healing backed with Power can bring a man back to life, or reconstruct a crushed chest or skull. One of those men died in my arms."

"Then he must have thought the Light's angel had come to take him to the Afterworld," Isulkian said gently. "You did everything you could, my lady. I watched."

"It's not enough." Lia was trembling. "I did everything I could, so did Sass. She's the strongest sorceress in a thousand years, and they say I'm the finest Healer ever born. But it still isn't *enough*!"

Isulkian was unsure what to do, but when the first agonised sobs burst from Lia, he abandoned propriety, took her in his arms and rocked her like a small child.

Lia wept for them, for the men she had not been able to save. She cried for the pain of their wives and children. One of the men had died with his wife's name on his lips, fearful that she would not be able to care for their children without the money he brought in. Lia's Empathy had made her feel every instant of his pain and fear.

Another miner had slipped peacefully away even as Lia worked her Healing on him, trying to stabilise a failing heart. The others were killed in the mine, or died before Lia got to them, and there was nothing she could do for them.

Lia rested her head on Isulkian's broad chest and sobbed. She was only dimly aware of his holding her, but her Empathy, stretched painfully during the day, was sensing the emotions he gave out, comforting and gentle. It was a similar sensation to being wrapped in a warm furry rug. At last she quieted, and stayed where she was, comfortable at last.

"My lady," Isulkian said at last. "Come, I should take you back to camp."

"Don't want to go." Lia cuddled closer to him, like a kitten seeking warmth.

Isulkian sighed a little exasperatedly. He could not resist

stroking the moonlight hair. "Princess," he said a little more firmly. He was greeted by silence. She had fallen asleep again.

After a few minutes, Isulkian rearranged Lia in his arms and stood up, carrying her easily. She was not tall like Saskia and did not weigh much.

* * * *

Saskia was awake before dawn, and out in the hospital tents to check on the wounded. She was absolutely shocked rigid when Isulkian walked into camp carrying a sleeping Lia in his arms.

"What in the Light..." she began. Isulkian shook his head at her.

"It is not as you think, my lady. The princess needed a little time and space. She walked away from the camp last night, and I followed to watch over her. She woke a little while ago, but rests again now."

"Bring her in here," Saskia said, opening the flap of Lia's tent. She watched the way Isulkian laid her sister down gently, and then covered her with a blanket. He paused and stroked Lia's hair very softly, then followed Saskia out of the tent.

"I trust your intentions towards my sister are honourable," Saskia asked, tapping her fingers on her sword hilt.

"I would be advised to keep them so, my lady, I have heard of your prowess with the sword."

Saskia, unused to Roman'ii humour, gave him a filthy look.

Isulkian quickly realised his mistake. "I apologise, my lady: I meant only to joke. I assure you Princess Liaskia is safe with me. Although – " he gave Saskia a thoughtful look. "By Icelander customs, you are now the head of your family, are you not? Your sisters are given into your care?"

"Until they are married, yes," Saskia nodded.

"Then by the customs of my people, I must ask your permission formally to court Princess Liaskia for my bride." Isulkian bowed his head to her.

Saskia hesitated. She knew enough of Roman'ii customs to know that if she refused now, Isulkian would leave the camp within the hour and never be caught in her sight or Liaskia's

218

again. Saskia knew she had to think of Lia's benefit: would Lia live a comfortable life among the Roman'ii? She didn't doubt that Isulkian would treat her sister well.

"I give you my permission," Saskia said after a long moment. "But you hear me well, Isulkian: if I ever get even a hint that you are not treating her as she deserves, I *will* come after you. Lia has had a hard life and she deserves better."

Isulkian looked shocked. "My lady! I swear on my own life! I would never, never let the slightest harm come to my princess!"

"Your princess?" Aleks' voice said. "So you've changed your mind about stealing my wife away from me?" He walked around the tent and put his arm around Saskia.

"Nay, my lord, for the Empress Saskia is surely the most beautiful woman in the world, but until she sees the light and falls in love with me, I could not steal her away. Sadly, the poor deluded lady is clearly quite in love with her husband, so I must turn my attentions elsewhere while I wait."

Saskia got the joke this time and laughed. Isulkian smiled and bowed over her hand. "My lady. With your permission, I will watch over Princess Liaskia's rest?"

"From outside the tent," Saskia said firmly. Isulkian's face dropped a little, but he nodded. "As you command."

"What was that about?" Aleks asked as they walked away. "Why wouldn't you let him sit in the tent?"

"Lia might decide she doesn't want him, Aleks. Just how many men would be entirely happy to take a bride who had once spent many hours alone in a tent with a Roman'i?"

Aleks frowned. "I see your point."

"Let me handle this, my love. Lia is my sister, and I want her to be happy. I'll not have her forced into any decisions. If she decides she wants Isulkian then my blessings on them both. But I will not let him push her too hard."

Aleks nodded. "Fair enough, but sometimes being forced into something is the best thing. Don't you agree?"

"It was for us, my love. But I was sixteen years old, and truth be told, I had no other options. I'll never regret a minute of *my* choice, but I don't want Lia believing she has no options."

Aleks kissed his wife, smiling. "I'll try to make sure

Isulkian doesn't get too pushy." He looked up at the sky and sighed himself.

Saskia touched his arm in sympathy. "You should get some rest. Is the weight heavy?"

It had been Aleks himself who realised something was wrong, even before the messenger from the mine had ridden in. The Ceremony of Earth had given him odd abilities where the Empire was concerned, and the collapse of the mine so close to him had suddenly increased the weight of responsibility he had to carry. Not since the weight had first fallen on him at his crowning had Aleks been overwhelmed by it, but at the moment of the collapse he had felt as though his chest was being crushed.

"I'm not doing too badly now," Aleks replied. He rubbed thoughtfully at his shoulders. "The weight is decreasing again."

"You had best get some sleep, though," Saskia said firmly. "Go, rest. I'll take care of everything that needs doing."

Aleks obeyed her without argument, and was soon deep in a blissfully dreamless sleep. Saskia sighed wistfully at the thought of joining him, then rolled up her sleeves purposefully and headed back to the hospital tent to help.

Lia woke, and stretched. She felt wonderfully rested. Remembering the day before, she sighed, got up and frowned down at herself, still in her clothes from the previous day. She washed her face, then took out a clean shirt and trousers and changed.

Outside, the sun was shining. Lia began to walk purposefully towards the hospital tent.

"Ah, no, my lady," a deep voice said. Lia whirled to see Isulkian. Her face coloured slightly as she remembered breaking down and crying on him.

"My lord Isulkian?" she said formally.

"The Empress ordered me to see that you eat before going back to work, my lady. I have bread and fruit: would you care for some?"

Lia paused for a moment, but if Saskia had given the order, she had best obey it.

Lia sat down by Isulkian and ate ravenously. Afterwards, he placed a gentle hand under her elbow and accompanied her to the hospital tent.

Once inside, Lia was all business. Yesterday had been spent healing the more serious hurts: today she had time to care for other things. She stopped to look at one man with his wrist heavily bandaged, unwrapping the bandage and pursing her lips over the arm, the bones of the wrist bent at an unnatural angle.

"It's broken," the man told her. "Her Grace the Empress put a bandage on to stop me moving it about, but she said I would have to wait for the White Lady for the Healing."

Lia stroked the man's forehead. He was not young, but he lay back and looked up at her with the trusting eyes of a child.

"Hush," Lia whispered. "Hush." As the man's eyes closed, she laid her other hand on his arm and her fingers tightened for a moment. Isulkian heard the audible click as she snapped the bone back into place, seemingly using no strength at all. The she ran one slim finger along the forearm. The man shivered convulsively.

Lia released him, and the miner opened his eyes in wonder. He pulled the rest of the bandage away from his arm and flexed it.

"White Lady," he whispered in awe.

Lia smiled. "Rest," she said. "The strength for that came from you. You will need to regain it. Eat well, and sleep."

She walked away, and Isulkian followed quietly behind her to the next bed. The man there had been one of the most critically injured yesterday: Lia had restructured a fractured skull and restarted his heart when it stopped from shock. Today he lay in a deep sleep. Little more than a boy really, he could not have been more than eighteen and looked much younger while sleeping.

Lia stooped over the young man and stroked his brow. He did not stir. Carefully she touched her fingertips to various places: his head, chest, legs and arms. She frowned over his left shoulder.

"There is another fracture here," Lia said softly to Isulkian. "Not all the way through the bone, but it could break easily if he moved around much." She clenched her hand around the shoulder, and the man woke.

"White Lady!" the man cried out. Lia smiled down at him.

"It is all right, lie quiet," she reassured softly.

"I love you, White Lady," the man said trustingly.

Isulkian felt a sudden wave of jealousy. He pushed it down fiercely, aware that should he win Lia's love, he would still always have to share her with her patients. But it was hard, seeing a handsome lad like this one, so obviously adoring her.

Isulkian followed Lia all day. By the time she was finished, the sun was falling towards the horizon again. Lia turned away from her last patient and smiled wearily at Isulkian.

"May I escort you to dine, my lady?" Isulkian asked, offering his arm.

Lia smiled. "I'd like that," she said wearily.

To Lia's surprise, Isulkian led her to a tent she hadn't seen before: blue and silver silk, guarded by two tall, forbidding Roman'ii warriors.

Inside, a feast was laid out on a low table. Isulkian seated Lia on a silver cushion, and then sat down opposite her.

Lia looked with interest at the food: she had never seen anything quite like it. There were many small bowls, containing different meats, vegetables, sauces, rice, and some odd stringy white things.

"What are those?" Lia asked.

"Rice noodles. Here." Isulkian picked up two slender sticks in front of Lia. Deftly he picked up some noodles, dipped them in one of the sauces and lifted them to Lia's lips. She ate them a little doubtfully, then gasped.

"That's delicious!"

"This is a traditional Roman'ii feast. We do not eat like this all of the time, of course, we are nomads and such food takes a great deal of time to prepare. But for special occasions, this is how we eat."

"What is the occasion?" Lia asked, experimenting with the sticks. To her surprise, she found they were quite easy to use.

"I am eating dinner with a princess: is that not occasion enough?"

Lia could not help but smile. "You are a disgraceful flirt, Isulkian."

"And you love it, don't you, princess? Everyone treats you as though you were made of glass: worshipping at your feet and calling you White Lady. When was the last time a man called you Liaskia and dared to whisper that you were beautiful?"

Lia stared at him, open-mouthed. Isulkian turned his head away.

"Eat, princess, or the food will grow cold."

Lia obeyed, her mind running over what he had said. One tiny thought kept intruding. "He thinks I'm beautiful." Lia looked at the dark head bent opposite her. Isulkian looked up, sensing her scrutiny, and his black eyes flashed with something Lia could not interpret. Carefully, Lia felt out towards him with her Empathy and met a solid wall. He was unreadable to her: like Aleks, his Charisma stopped anything but raw Power getting through.

Lia frowned down into the little bowl of rice in front of her. She carried on eating, delighted by the food: it had so many different tastes, spicy, nutty, or sweet. She sipped at the wine Isulkian had poured for her.

Isulkian watched Lia. Light, but she was lovely, so graceful, even skilled with the eating sticks that outsiders never seemed able to learn. She seemed almost born to be a Roman'i.

When they had finished eating, Isulkian led Lia to another pile of cushions, beside one wall of the tent, and sat down beside her.

"Thank you for dinner, my lord, it was absolutely delightful," Lia said sincerely.

"You are very welcome. Lia."

Lia stared up at him in surprise. Always before he had called her my lady, or princess. Hearing her name from his lips shocked her.

"My lord?" she said.

"Name me. I want to hear you say it."

"Isulkian," Lia said hesitantly.

Isulkian sighed softly. "Ah, Lia, you don't know what it does to me, to hear you speak my name so sweetly." He seized her hand and held it to his cheek.

Lia rubbed her fingers against Isulkian's jaw, surprised by

the roughness of his stubble. His dark eyes held hers, and for a moment she forgot to breathe. He reached his other hand up and stroked her hair.

"Kiss me, *kerishna*," he begged.

Lia knew the word: one of the few Roman'ii words that had found its way into the common language. It translated roughly as "heart's blade". It meant the love of one's life, the one person who could destroy the heart with words alone. She hesitated, hearing it: a Roman'i did not name a *kerishna* lightly, but then she leant forward and pressed her lips against his.

Isulkian savoured every instant of the short kiss. The feel of Lia beside him, ah, but he ached so to take her in his arms and hold her. Nevertheless, he was quite sure that if he were to do anything without Lia's express permission, the Empress would take it as a violation of their agreement and would be after him with a gelding knife.

Lia sat back after a few moments and looked at Isulkian. He looked back at her through heavy-lidded eyes.

"Princess," he murmured softly. "My princess." He said it in an oddly possessive tone of voice, and suddenly Lia felt nervous.

"I should go," she said.

"As you wish, princess," Isulkian stood gracefully and offered a hand to help Lia up. She accepted.

"Thank you for a lovely meal," she said stumblingly.

"Perhaps you will consent to dine with me again once we have returned to the Citadel?" Isulkian suggested.

"Perhaps," Lia nodded, suddenly desperate to get away. Her Empathy was letting her know that there were dangerous emotions swirling in the air, hungry emotions – and Lia was not quite sure whether they came from Isulkian or from herself.

* * * *

On the way home, Lia rode beside Saskia for much of the way, and Aleks rode up ahead with Isulkian and most of the men. Saskia's Honour Guard surrounded the two women.

Saskia glanced often at her younger sister as they rode. Lia was very quiet, fiddling with her reins and gazing often at the group riding up ahead.

"What do you feel for Isulkian?" Saskia asked suddenly.

"What?" Lia blushed fiercely.

"Isulkian? Your pet Roman'i? He asked my permission to court you."

"He did?" Lia brightened.

"Yes, and I agreed, on the condition that anything that occurred between you was to be by your choice and yours alone."

"Oh." Lia fiddled with her reins a little more. "I don't know, exactly. He makes me feel – funny. When I'm not with him, the time seems to crawl until I see him again."

Saskia sat back in her saddle, a little surprised. That would have been her response exactly in the months leading up to her marriage.

"Maybe it's love," Saskia said, a little mockingly, to test Lia's response.

"I don't know." Lia's eyes lifted to the group up ahead. "He makes my head ache and my heart sing. He's the most complicated man I ever met, and yet he named me his *kerishna*."

Saskia's eyebrows shot up. "No Roman'i would name any woman his heart's blade unless he intended to wed her," she said definitely.

"Really? I didn't think it would be said lightly."

"I think you can be sure of his heart, Lia. Just make quite sure you know what you want before you agree to wed him."

At that moment Aleks came galloping back to join them. "Come ride with me, wife, I miss your company," he said laughingly to Saskia. She moved Dawn to join him, but with a laugh he reached down from Sandstorm and lifted her to sit before him. One of the Guard caught Dawn's reins.

"I want no less than this for you," Saskia called to Lia, leaning back against Aleks' broad chest as he urged Sandstorm on to rejoin the others.

Lia leant over her little mare's neck and raced after them. She pulled up, laughing, beside Isulkian.

"Good morning, princess," he said, bowing to her from the

225

saddle.

"I wish you'd call me Lia," she said impulsively.

"You honour me. Lia," he said softly.

Lia shivered slightly. Her name on his lips sounded like a caress, almost indecent in daylight. She looked at Saskia and Aleks, just a little way in front of them. "That's what I want too," she whispered silently.

Isulkian saw her lips move, saw the direction of her eyes, and guessed what she was thinking. She wanted the kind of love Saskia and Aleks shared: to love each other all the days of their lives. After seven years of marriage, they were quite clearly still deeply in love with each other.

"I will love you like that," he promised silently. "I'll hold you every day of our lives and love you more with every hour."

Lia turned back to Isulkian and smiled up at him. He caught his breath at the sudden beauty of that smile, at the sunlight reflecting off her silvery hair. Leaning towards her, he held out a clenched fist.

"I have a gift for you, my lady."

"Oh!" Lia reached out her hand, and he opened his fist and laid something small into her palm.

Lia gasped at the beauty of the tiny ornament. No longer than her thumb, it was a little wooden swallow, wings spread wide, perfectly carved and polished. "Oh, Isulkian, it's beautiful!" she exclaimed. "Where did you get this?"

"I made it for you," he responded. When she looked up at him, surprised, he smiled. "Fly free, princess. Spread your wings."

Lia wrapped the bird carefully in her handkerchief and put it in her cloak pocket. "Thank you," she said sincerely.

Isulkian laughed, and swung his mare away to join his men. Lia watched him go, fingers straying to the hard lump in her cloak that was the wrapped bird.

They were back in the Citadel by nightfall. Lia was exhausted when they finally rode into the palace courtyard.

"Sister, you look dreadfully pale," said a warm voice. Lia turned her head to see Erhallen.

"I'm deadly tired," she responded with a smile.

226

"Let me help you down," he offered. Lia consented gratefully, and as he set her on her feet, smiled.

"Thanks, Erhallen. Lord, I need a bath."

"Issy guessed: she had the servants heat hot water for everyone. I have no doubt that it was being carried to your room as soon as they saw you riding in."

Lia smiled dreamily. She thanked the groom who took her horse, and headed for the doors with haste.

Isulkian had overheard the conversation, and leant against his mare trying to breathe. He had thought he could control his lust for Lia, but hearing her speak of a bath, all he could imagine was her pale nakedness all slick and shining with water. Ai, but the very idea could drive a man wild!

Lia felt greatly refreshed after her bath. She dressed and went down to the dining hall for dinner. On the way in she met Ria and Evan.

"How's Evaskia?" Lia asked at once.

"Oh, she's just wonderful," Ria replied cheerfully. "Last night she never woke up at all. She's got such a sweet temper."

"Obviously inherited from my side," Evan jibed.

Ria dug her fist into his short ribs. "Behave, you," she said, laughing.

"Yes, *kerishna*," Evan replied. Lia's head snapped round at the word, and they both stared at her.

"What is it, Lia?" Evan asked. "What did I say?"

"Ah," Ria said, suddenly understanding. "That's a Roman'ii word, isn't it, beloved?"

Lia darted into the hall ahead of them, blushing, before either could say anything more.

The following day Lia could not seem to find interest in anything. Saskia had barred her from the infirmaries for the day, insisting she needed to regain some strength.

Lia did a little sewing, then felt bored, so she walked down to the royal library to borrow a book. She found Aleks there, looking something up. He smiled when he saw her.

"Good morning, little sister. How are you feeling?"

"Bored: I want something to read. Any recommendations?"

Aleks smiled. "Oh, plenty. What do you feel like reading?

History, romance, tragedy?"

Lia shrugged. "A bit of all three?"

Aleks snapped his fingers. "I have just the thing." He walked back among the shelves and reached a book down from a top shelf. "I always liked this one as a boy. There's plenty of drama and derring-do, and I could always just skip over the soppy bits."

Lia took the book without even looking at it. "I'm sure it will be fine, thanks," she said and left him to work.

Back in her room, Lia looked at the book and felt her face grow warm yet again. It was titled *Wanderings with the Roman'ii*.

Lia opened the book and began to read. She was quite soon caught up with the tales, a series of short stories on Roman'ii life and history. Aleks was quite right, there was plenty of action, romance, a little tragedy. The Roman'ii, it seemed, were a passionate people.

Lia read several of the stories. Her favourite was about Jeleifa, who ran away from a marriage her father had arranged for her. She took a job working in a keep stables, and the keep's lord, Isfahan, fell in love with her. Jeleifa fell in love with Isfahan too and consented to wed him. No sooner had she accepted, than Jeleifa's father arrived at the keep, full of apologies for the lord because his daughter had run away and he would have to break the betrothal.

Jeleifa refused to believe that Isfahan had not known who she was. She ran away a second time, but she was already carrying his child (having anticipated the marriage somewhat) and ended up returning to the keep just in time to hear Isfahan agreeing to take her younger sister Jeleina as his bride in her place.

Jeleina did not want to marry Isfahan. Jeleifa met with her sister in secret, and on the day of the wedding it was Jeleifa behind the veil. Isfahan went down on his knees when she took off her veil and begged her forgiveness. Jeleifa's father had told him she was dead.

Lia closed the book, smiling, at the end of the story. She jumped at a knock on the door. "Come in!" she called automatically. She stared in surprise when Isulkian entered, carrying a parcel.

"Oh, my lord!" she jumped to her feet in surprise.

"Princess, please: sit down."

Lia obeyed and smiled up at him. "Will you sit? I will ring for tea, if you like."

"Thank you."

Lia rang the bell, and ordered tea when her maid arrived. Isulkian's eyes were drawn to the book, forgotten in her lap.

"Reading about my people, princess?" he said teasingly.

Lia blushed slightly. "Yes, my lord. They are most fascinating stories. I was just reading about Jeleifa and Isfahan."

Isulkian smiled. "Ah, my favourite story. They are my great-grandparents."

"Truly?"

"Truly, princess. Jeleifa and Isfahan's firstborn son Isfeihan married the Roman'ii princess Terula, and their son Isulan was my father, my mother being Lady Kalukian of Eastphal." Seeing Lia's frown, he explained, "We name in the opposite way to the Imperial convention. For a son, it is the father's name and the derivative of the mother's, and for a daughter, the other way about. We do cheat, to make them sound more musical: the Imperial way is stricter."

"I think I would have liked to have known Jeleifa," Lia said. "She sounds like a strong woman."

"My grandmother would tell you better: she was married to Isfeihan as a child bride and spent many years in Jeleifa's house before living with her husband. Light willing you will meet her."

"Your grandmother – Terula – is still alive?"

"Indeed, she leads the Old Ones, a council of wise people who make many of the decisions among my people."

"They are the people who ordered you to get married."

"That's right, princess." They stared at each other for a long moment. The tea arrived, breaking up the silence. Lia fussed a little, pouring tea for Isulkian. He set it on a table at his elbow, and leant forward, offering her the parcel.

"I brought a gift for you, princess."

"Oh, you shouldn't have!" Lia opened the parcel carefully,

and gasped as she drew out a shawl made of silver lace. It was utterly beautiful, catching every scrap of light.

"I wanted to buy you a jewel, but the Empress said it would not be proper," Isulkian said. "So I went to the Market, and found this. It comes from the Desert."

"It's fabulous." Lia turned the shawl in her hands, admiring. "Isulkian, this is a princely gift. I know what Desert lace is worth: almost as much as their diamonds!"

"Hardly, princess," he laughed. "Will you wear it tonight at dinner? There is a formal meal. I would be very honoured if you would consent to partner me this evening."

"I should be delighted," Lia said with a smile. Inwardly she panicked, wondering what she would wear. As soon as Isulkian had left, she went through her wardrobe, dismissed the whole thing, and headed off to the Clan tower and Iskia's rooms. Saskia undoubtedly had more suitable clothes, but Saskia was a head taller than Lia. Iskia was roughly the same size.

* * * *

Saskia walked in as the two sisters were despairing over the inadequacies of Iskia's wardrobe.

"What in the Light is wrong?" she said, seeing Lia on the brink of tears.

"Isulkian's given me this beautiful shawl, and I haven't a thing to wear it with, and he asked me to wear it tonight!"

Saskia looked at the shawl. "My word," she said reverently. "That's glorious, Lia. I've got loads of Desert lace, and I've never seen anything as good as that."

"I know!" Lia wailed.

"All right, all right, don't panic. I'm sure I've got something."

"But it won't fit me!"

"That's why the Power comes in handy. I made my wedding dress in a couple of hours after Sasken ruined the first one, remember?"

An hour later Lia had a new dress, made of soft silvery silk. Plain yet daring, it had neither sleeves nor shoulder straps, but ended just above her breasts. The long straight skirt swept the floor, and the whole thing clung to her small body.

"I feel positively exposed," Lia said, hand to her throat. "Most of my dresses have collars or high necks."

"Then it's high time you showed off your other assets," Iskia said with a grin.

"What about jewellery?" Lia asked in sudden consternation.

Saskia shrugged. "Come and have a look in the strongroom. I'm sure there's something."

A few minutes looking through jewellery cases and Iskia gave a cry of triumph, holding up a simple silver circlet set with pale opals. "This would be perfect for you tonight, Lia!"

Lia agreed, delighted. She decided she needed no other jewellery: anything else would only detract from the beauty of the shawl.

The evening could not come fast enough for Lia. She was busy getting ready but time still seemed to crawl. At last there was a knock on her door.

"Enter!" Lia called.

Isulkian walked in and stopped dead. The lamps were turned down low, but still Lia caught every ray of light. She shone like the moon. Isulkian took two long strides forward and fell to his knees before her.

"*Kerishna*, I beg you, do not go down dressed like that," Isulkian begged.

"Why not?"

"Every man in the room will try to steal you away for a dance, and I will die of jealousy should another man so much as touch your hand."

"Then I'll just have to make sure no one does," Lia laughed. "Come on, Isulkian. It's my new dress and I want to wear it."

"As you wish, princess." He stood and offered her his arm. Lia looked him up and down first.

Isulkian's height and broad shoulders were well set off by his clothes. He was formally dressed all in black, the collar and cuffs of his coat embroidered in silver. He looked marvellously handsome, and yet somehow primitive at the same time, his long black hair tied back with a strip of leather.

Lia accepted Isulkian's arm. His free hand came up to clasp possessively over hers.

* * * *

In the hall, everyone gasped at Lia's dress. The other sisters had all dressed quite plainly, not wanting to upstage her on such a night.

Isulkian's predictions proved correct. Every young lord in the room was flocking around Lia, begging for a chance to dance with her. Lia could feel Isulkian's temper fraying as he stood beside her. Increasingly she felt as though she was holding a dangerous dog on a very thin leash.

At length Lia managed to dismiss all her suitors. The poisonous glares coming from Isulkian helped, as did the fact that he firmly refused to relinquish her arm.

"Come my lord, why don't we take a walk in the garden?" Lia said sweetly, feeling the leashed temper in him. She had to get him out of the room before he lost what little control he seemed to have.

Isulkian followed her docilely. Lia led him through the formal gardens, then stopped in front of an ivy-covered wall, pulled aside a sheet of ivy and beckoned him through a small gate.

"What is this? I did not know this was here," Isulkian said.

"It's Saskia's private garden. It was built for the last Empress, and Aleks gave it to Sass. Hardly anyone knows about it."

In the moonlight, Isulkian could see quite well. The garden was small and quiet, neatly cut grass, a little stream set among rocks, a few fruit trees and benches to sit on. "It's lovely," he said. "Are you sure Saskia won't mind us being here?"

"Oh, quite sure. She only comes here when she and Aleks need to escape and have some time alone. There are always a few Imperial Guards wandering round the outer gardens then."

Lia seated herself on one of the benches, beneath a blossoming tree. The silver and opal circlet on her head shone faintly in the moonlight. A petal of pale blossom fell and landed in her hair.

Isulkian stepped forward and gently lifted the petal. Lia looked at it in surprise, then smiled and reached up for Isulkian's hand. He dropped the petal and sank to his knees at her feet, laying his head in her lap. Lia stroked his sleek dark hair.

"You truly do love me, don't you?" she said wonderingly.

"Why do you sound so surprised, princess? Surely many men have wanted to love you."

"No. Many men have wanted me. Big difference. None of them have wanted me for anything other than what I could be for them. A princess, an alliance with the Imperial family, a Healer, a trophy to look beautiful on their arm. Only you have seen through to who I am, and still loved me. Only you have seen me weep for what I could not do."

"Only I have dared to call you Lia," Isulkian said softly.

"Yes. They did not even call me princess as you do. When you say it, it is the same way that Aleks says it to Sass. Possessive and loving all at the same time."

"That is what I want to be to you, princess," Isulkian said. "Your master and your slave. I want to sweep you up and carry you off, and sometimes all I want is to kneel at your feet, and worship, Light help me. I've never met anyone like you." He lifted his head and looked into her eyes.

"I love you, Liaskia Cevaria," he said simply. "I want you to be my bride. I want to love you all the days of your life, to have children with you, to grow old beside you. Will you consent to wed me?"

Lia smiled down at him and said "Oh, yes. Yes, please."

Isulkian's smile was blinding. He kissed her hands and drew something from his pocket. "I know among your people it is tradition to give a ring to seal a betrothal," he said, "so I have bought you one. But among the Roman'ii, we give what is called a wedding necklet." He opened his hand, and from his fingers dangled a rippling river of silver, glittering with white Desert diamonds.

Lia's mouth fell open, and she stared. She lifted wondering fingers to touch the necklace. The links were made in the shape of snowflakes, every one different, the centre of each set with a diamond.

Isulkian stood and stooped to fasten the necklet around Lia's neck. It hung beautifully above the silvery dress. Then he reached into his pocket again and produced a ring topped with a fine blue sapphire. It was too big for Lia's finger.

Isulkian shook his head in despair. "I told the jeweller you had tiny delicate hands. He did not believe they could be smaller than this. I will get it adjusted for you."

"I need no ring, Isulkian, my necklace is so beautiful!" Lia said.

"It was Jeleifa's wedding necklet," Isulkian said. "Isfahan gave it to her when he still believed her a stable girl."

Lia understood: it had represented the purity of their love before other things had come between them. She lifted her hand to her throat to stroke the necklace.

"I will not dishonour it," she told Isulkian.

Isulkian drew Lia to her feet. "I'm going to kiss you now," he told Lia seriously.

"We have kissed before," she said quizzically.

"No, Lia. You have kissed *me* before." He enfolded her in his arms and bent his head to hers.

Lia clutched at Isulkian's shoulders as his mouth came down on hers. The kiss was gentle yet demanding, hot and passionate. After a long moment Lia let out a faint moan and Isulkian's hands slid down to her hips. He pulled her hard against his body and Lia gasped.

"My princess, my princess, I love you," Isulkian moaned against her throat.

"Love or lust, put her down right now," said a voice dripping with ice. Both of them turned to see Saskia there, Aleks behind her. Saskia as usual had pulled out a sword. Lia wondered irrationally just how many swords Saskia had hidden around the palace. It looked incongruous with Saskia's long green dress.

"Lady Empress," Isulkian bowed to Saskia, his exuberance undimmed. "Princess Liaskia has just agreed to be my wife."

Saskia turned sharp eyes on Lia. "*Vrai*?" she said.

"*Eis endeyah*," Lia replied. She babbled off a long stream in the Icelander dialect. Aleks tried to follow what she was saying but it was too quick for him.

Saskia dropped the sword and ran to put her arms around her youngest sister. The two women hugged, laughing, chattering away in their own tongue.

"Congratulations," Aleks said, offering his hand. Isulkian grasped it in delight, grinning.

"I am the happiest man alive!" he exclaimed.

Aleks shook his head. "In seven years, you will understand why *I* am the happiest man alive right now," he said.

Isulkian nodded, understanding. "Such joy every day – how do you bear it?" he said wonderingly.

Aleks grinned in reply. "You'll understand."

Saskia wanted to arrange a big wedding for Lia, but her sister refused.

"No," Lia said flatly. "What would be the point? I am a princess in name only: heir to nothing, no strategic alliance."

"But Isulkian is the lord of his people!"

"And we will be married in the way of his people. I want to do this, Sass: you read the same books I did as a child, about the brave Roman'i warrior who stole away his bride. Amongst the Roman'ii, it is expected that their princes will live up to the reputation of the tribes."

Saskia frowned. "But you should have a celebration!"

"We will. But," Lia smiled, "we will have some time together first. A Roman'i must keep his bride with him for at least a moon before she is his. *Then* we will celebrate, with Isulkian's people. We can celebrate here too, if you wish: have a betrothal party. But one morning when you wake we will be gone. The Light will shine on us even if we do not marry in a temple, Sass: our temple will be the sky and the mountains."

It took a few minutes, but Saskia finally accepted what Lia wanted. She hugged her youngest sister. "I just want you to be happy," she said.

And so it was. They threw a big party for Lia and Isulkian on Midwinter's Eve, and that very night the two disappeared. Aleks knew where they had gone: Isulkian had said it was too late in the year to take Lia into the Roman'ii mountains and the weather was too poor. They would head east instead and spend some time in a house on the Dawn Water coast, just a little way north of Grainport. The house belonged to a cousin of Evan's who had lent it willingly. Evan and Ria were staying in the Citadel for a while because Evaskia was as yet too young to travel, and Evan's cousin was coming to spend the winter with them.

Chapter 14

The Citadel, after New Year,
the year 2724 after Founding

Four days after New Year, Aleks and Saskia were in the nursery one evening, playing with their sons. Without so much as a knock the door flew open and an Imperial Guard and Aleks' secretary Arryn came in.

Aleks was on his feet in a moment, seeing the look on Arryn's face. "What? What is it?"

Arryn held out a piece of paper. "This just came in by carrier pigeon."

Saskia was removing the two boys, taking them through to their nurse. Iskandr, upset by the noise, was yelling his head off, but Sasskandr was frowning, a serious look on his handsome little face.

Aleks unrolled the paper swiftly and read. He looked up at Arryn incredulously, then read the paper aloud as Saskia returned.

"Ships came on the Day of the Dead. Eastport has fallen."

"What?" Saskia snatched the message paper. "What ships? What do they mean, fallen?"

Arryn shrugged. "I cannot say, my lady. It is only six days since the Day of the Dead. That must have been a fast pigeon, to have flown here so quickly. Perhaps more messages will come in the next few days."

"If Eastport has truly fallen and this is an invasion, we cannot afford to wait," Aleks said. "They could be halfway to Highfort by now."

Arryn shook his head. "We have no other way of getting information, my lord."

"Yes, we do," Saskia said.

"What?" Arryn and Aleks demanded together.

"Iskia." When they stared at her, Saskia frowned. "She has the LongSight, Aleks. It might not control her like the TimeSight does Ria, and it might not be as obviously useful as the Healing or the Power. But she has it, and a lot of it. She could probably See as far as Eastport unaided. If I back her with the Power, she will See beyond the furthest reaches of the Empire."

Aleks turned to the Guard. "Get Erhallen and Iskia ca'Berenna. Now." The Guard set off at a dead run.

Erhallen and Iskia arrived within fifteen minutes. Saskia and Aleks were in the library with Arryn. Arryn had led them to the back of the room, and then surprised them both by swinging around a bookcase to reveal a massive map of the Empire set on the back. It was beautifully made of bronze inlaid into the wood, with engravings on to show the borders, rivers, principal towns and other landmarks. It was kept polished and bright.

Iskia arrived trying to pull her hair into a tidy braid. "What, sister? What is wrong?"

Aleks explained succinctly. Both Erhallen and Iskia stared at him in shock.

"But – who?" Iskia said.

"That's what we need you to find out," Saskia said. Arryn was pulling two heavy armchairs right up in front of the map. "I'm going to back you with the Power: your vision should be clearer and then I will see the same as you do."

The two women were just seating themselves when Ria came rushing in with Evan.

"Ria, I'm going to be using the Power," Saskia warned. "You'd better get out of here if you don't want the TimeSight taking over."

"What are you talking about?" Ria exclaimed. "It's been taking over all day! What in the Light is going on?"

"What have you been Seeing?" Saskia asked quickly.

"It doesn't make sense. I keep getting flashes of Lia. In some kind of trouble?"

"Oh, Light – Lia!" Saskia said. "We will look for her first: it should be easy to lock on to her. Ria, you'd better take a seat."

238

Ria found another chair and sat down at the back of the room. The moment Saskia grasped the Power, Ria's eyes glazed over as the TimeSight took her again. Evan sat down beside her to wait.

Saskia, mindful of the trouble she had been having lately using the Power, used the Tear to focus at once. The hand with the Tear grasped Iskia's, and with the other Saskia leaned forward and touched the map, on the coast above Grainport.

"Lia," she said.

Iskia's eyes blanked. She and Saskia shared the vision. They seemed to be high above the land. There was no sea in sight, just rolling hills. Lia and Isulkian must have gone inland. The view swooped down, and they approached a farm cottage. Inside, Lia lay asleep on a bed. Through a door, they could see Isulkian, standing with three other Roman'ii, talking.

"Safe enough for now," Saskia said. "Iskia, can you take us out towards the coast?"

"No," Iskia said slowly. "It's hard to move. When I get to a place I can focus, but moving is too hard."

"All right." Saskia dragged herself out of the vision just enough to see the map, overlaid on the place where Lia slept. To her surprise she found that her finger had moved, inland from Grainport, to a place near Moon Lake, where the foothills started. "They must be here," she said,

"All right, we have it," Aleks replied.

Saskia lifted her finger from the map with an effort. She placed it down again. "Eastport," she said.

This time they did not zoom down. They did not need to, Saskia could see enough. She had never been to Eastport, but quite clearly it should not look like this. The great docks were crowded with masts, but they were masts on ships of a type Saskia had never seen. Parts of the city still smoked after burning, and over the house that had been the Governor's a strange flag flew, a red ship on a black banner. At the edge of the city, a massive corral had been put up, and was filled with horses, many obviously brought in from the surrounding countryside.

Saskia changed the view again. "Grainport," she said.

Grainport was the same. The situation was repeated at Pearlport, Wineport and Silkport. Fireport, Summerhold and Highfort were as yet untouched. There was a battle actually going on at Furport, and looked as though it had been running for a few days now. Parts of the city were afire, but so were two of the invaders' ships in the harbour. They burned slowly, sluggishly, as though they had been soaked in water.

The Seal Islands were too sparsely populated for them to be able to look at in much detail. They checked Zahennarra and Iridia, but nothing was happening there. Saskia was feeling the strain of the Power now, and Iskia's teeth were gritted as she fought to control the vision.

"Just a few more," Saskia said, struggling for breath. "Here, on the Grain River."

That was one blessing. Though the Grain River was deep and wide, just three leagues upstream they found one of the invaders' ships stuck in the middle of the river. They were deep-water ships and could not go far upstream. However, on the Wine River, clearly there was a more intelligent commander. There were riverboats moving upstream packed with men. With the last of the Sight, the women zoomed in to look at one of the boats.

The men were swarthy and dark, short, wearing armour made out of leather with steel plates sewn on to it like scales. Their swords were curved and they had small round shields. At last Saskia realised what she had been seeing all along. Just then the Power died within her, and they were both flung headlong out of the vision as Iskia lost the Sight.

The men jumped as the two women's eyes cleared and they groaned aloud. Saskia's hand dropped away from the map and she fell back in her chair. She felt totally drained. The Power was completely beyond her.

Iskia was a bit quicker to recover. She reached for Erhallen's hand and he helped her over to the table where Aleks and Arryn were marking maps with the places Saskia had touched. Ria groaned as Iskia got to the table, finally coming out of her TimeSight vision. Evan crouched beside her with a pen and paper to write down anything coherent that she could tell him.

Iskia took a blank sheet of parchment and a pen and began to sketch. She had a good hand, and quickly a ship began to take shape.

"What an odd ship," Aleks said. The men were all clustered around the drawing, and did not see Saskia get up and walk back among the library shelves. They all jumped a minute or so later when she threw an open book down on the table.

"I knew I'd seen them before," Saskia said. Indeed, there in the book was a drawing of a ship very like the one Iskia had sketched.

Aleks picked up the book. "*Trading with the Southron Tribes*," he read. "Oh, Light." He looked down at the drawing in the book. "A Southron war corsair," he read from the description. "The smallest of these may carry a hundred men, and the largest as many as a thousand."

"There were at least twenty in each of the ports," Iskia said, wide-eyed. "And they all looked big."

"At least ten thousand men," Aleks said bleakly. "In each port. The smaller ships are probably being used to scout, and to subdue coastal villages."

Aleks and Erhallen shared a look. Evan came to the table and took the book to see for himself. "I am going," he said in a flat voice.

"No!" Rla cried out.

"I must. They are my people, Aleks. The Summerlanders need our help. I am the only one you have who can raise the countryside against these people." Evan looked down at the map on the table in front of them, a paper copy of the wall map, now covered with scribbles, as Iskia wrote on it numbers of ships and men.

Evan tapped the map. "Summerhold is lost. Those men in barges on the Wine River, they will be at Summerhold in three, maybe four days. If they come in from the Grain River too – Summerhold will not hold out for so much as a week, it is not a fortress. You *can* save Highfort, you must. North Market and Iridia, too. If they have taken Furport those two will be next. Iridia is the key. If you can keep Iridia you can harry them from the North, and if you can keep the Empire Water open you will win this war."

Aleks nodded. "Highfort?"

"Highfort is too close to the Citadel. If they can take Highfort and North Market they can come to the Citadel on two fronts. Make no mistake, Aleks, they mean to take the Empire. They had to take the Summerlands first: after all, the Summerlander ships were the biggest threat to them. But I would bet that there are no Summerlander ships left unburned."

Aleks agreed. "We need more people here." He looked around. "Arryn, get a couple of Guards. Send them for the Captain of the Guard and the Chief of the Army."

"Tonight?" Arryn queried. "It's nearly midnight."

"I mean to march in the morning. Let's go!"

* * * *

The Captain of the Guard arrived first, from the Imperial barracks. It was a woman: tall and as strong as any man, her dark hair cut short. Evan recognised her.

"Carlene!" he exclaimed. The two shook hands vigorously, and then bent over the map, Evan explaining in a low voice.

The Army chief took longer to arrive, from the headquarters in the city. He was old, but straight-backed: a veteran of several minor wars.

"General Dirk," Aleks greeted him. "Thank you for coming."

"Well, well. Hello, Carlene. What's all this then?"

Evan ran through a quick briefing. Saskia noticed that Aleks had moved away and stood staring at the bronze map in the wall. He reached out his hand to cover the Summerlands and eastern Erinea as Saskia reached him.

"Gone," Aleks said in a dull voice. "Gone: and Envetierra must be gone also. Two and a half provinces lost, and I had no idea. What use the Ceremony of Earth if I do not know when there is something wrong? How did I not feel this? I feel it now, the weight, almost driving me down. What good is that *now*? So many are dead!"

Saskia did not know what to say. She reached out and put

her hand over Aleks' on the map.

"We'll get it back," she said, trying to sound sure. "We have to make it right."

"It should never have gone wrong!" Aleks shook his head furiously. "I *swore*! I swore, and all unknowing I broke my oath!"

The others turned to look at him. Aleks pulled his hand away from Saskia's and dragged out his dagger. "I promised," he said. "I said that my sword would be the first raised in her defence and my blood the first spilled in her service. For seven days and more my people have been fighting." He slashed the dagger across his palm, ignoring Saskia's cry of horror.

Carefully, Aleks smeared his blood across the Summerlands, and across the Envetierran islands, and Eastport and Furport. Turning, he caught Arryn's eyes. "Let that be the mark of the land that the enemy has gained. It shall not be wiped off from any place until that place is back in Imperial hands."

Saskia ripped a strip of cloth from the hem of her shirt and used it to bind Aleks' hand. "At least you had the sense not to cut your sword hand," she muttered.

They worked all through the night. The General sent men to rouse the army out of their barracks and to call back every soldier on leave. Several hundred Summerlanders were to be separated off, given under Evan's command to go home and raise a resistance.

Erhallen wrote a message for Lirallen and had it sent by several pigeons. Aleks did the same for Enniskarin of the Desert and the other Empire lords. At last, it was nearing dawn and they looked at the map.

"We're not going to be able to move fast enough," the general said soberly. "The fighting men will be needed, to dig them out of the towns. But if we can't stop those corsairs, we're lost. They'll take Iridia and Zahennarra, and after that all they have to do is head slowly west. And if more ships come, they'll start on the ports in the west too, and it will be all over."

"Damn them for taking the Summerlands," Aleks said angrily. "Those ships were our only chance."

"Not the only chance," Saskia said slowly.

"What other ships are there?" Aleks said.

Saskia nibbled her lip. "There's the Icelander war galleys," she said.

"Hah! You think Liara will order them to sail? Even if they would sail in her name, they would not leave the northern waters. They will be needed to stop the Southroners taking Iceport."

Saskia shook her head. "But, don't you see? If they can stop the invasion at Iridia, Iceport will not need defending."

"Still, Liara will not order them to sail," Erhallen said. "Even if they would listen to her."

"They would listen to me," Saskia said.

There was an instant clamour, insisting that she not go, that she was too valuable, that she was pregnant and too fragile. Only Carlene nodded slowly.

"Quiet!" Carlene shouted. "Let her speak!"

Saskia sucked in a deep breath. She would not meet Aleks' eyes, but instead looked at Carlene.

"It has to be one of the Icelander Royal Blood," she said. They all nodded to that: for sure the Icelanders would not follow anyone else.

"Iskia as second in line would be the best choice, but she is too necessary here. She *must* stay by Aleks: even without the Power to boost her she can still See far enough to check on the progress of battles and such." Iskia nodded in agreement.

"Lia is lost to us for now. Isulkian will be trying to get into the Roman'ii mountains to raise his own people for the fight. And besides, it is on the front lines that she is needed: if the men know that the White Lady is there to heal them it will be worth many lives in morale."

"Ria could go," Evan said, looking at his wife, who nodded.

"No," Saskia responded. "I too have made a promise: I promised Ria that she need never again set foot on Icelander soil. I will not break that. And besides, I think she should go with you, Evan."

"Into resistance territory?" Carlene gasped.

"Yes. Your Gift works best in small ways, Ria. You cannot see the outcome of this invasion, but you could tell Evan the number of men who will die if you set up an ambush. I think you must go to Summerlands, sister. My sons are too young. And so, that leaves only me."

Aleks shook his head furiously. "It is too dangerous."

"No," Ria said. Her eyes glazed over briefly with the TimeSight, then she turned to Aleks. "Saskia *must* go to Iceport, Aleks. Or the war will be lost."

Aleks bit his lip, and shook his head again. "Are you telling me the whole truth, Ria? Your mother went willingly to her death to save you all. Am I sending Saskia to die for the Empire?"

"If that is what is required, that is what I will do," Saskia said before Ria could reply. "I have given you two male heirs, Aleks – I am expendable."

No one could disagree with that, though Aleks certainly didn't like it. Aleks still looked at Ria, awaiting an answer. In the end she shrugged doubtfully.

"I just don't know. You might die if you go, Sass. But if you *don't* go, we will *all* die."

That effectively ended the argument, though Aleks was still not happy. Saskia refused to hear any more arguments, though, and they began to make plans.

Saskia was to be on the first boat to Iridia. A ship would be waiting there to sail her to Iceport. Erhallen and General Dirk were going to Highfort, to try and save it, with the greater portion of the army. Aleks, Iskia and Carlene were heading for North Market, and from there Aleks would lead a detachment of men for Furport, their first objective to take back.

Carlene would continue north to try to save Iridia. Evan and Ria would be going into the Summerlands, with all the Summerlander soldiers they could find. Somewhere along the way they would try to contact Isulkian and get the Roman'ii down to fight with them.

The Desert army would protect Fireport, after all the only viable landing place in the whole Desert, and Lirallen would be marching the Clans across to join them. From there they would try to press east into the Summerlands, to take back some of what was lost. Arryn would remain in the Citadel, to take up the post of chamberlain and wait for Aleks' return.

* * * *

When dawn came, Saskia was ready. Messengers had been running all night. All the boats in the docks had already been commandeered by the military, their cargo rapidly unloaded, and fresh supplies put on board. The first boat to go was Saskia's, Aleks to sail a day behind her after setting everything else in motion.

Saskia wept over her two sons as they lay still sleeping. They must stay here for now. Mairi was on her way from Clanhold and would take all the children back to Clanhold with her: there could be no place safer for them.

Aleks sat beside Saskia, holding her hand. He hated having to leave the children, and hated even more being separated from Saskia. They held each other for the single hour they had before Saskia had to go. She was already dressed in a smart dress for their farewell, and maids were hastily packing for her.

The children were soon awake, and looking for their breakfast. Iskandr, a sunny child, was not much affected by his parents' misery. Sasskandr, though, was quiet and withdrawn, sensing trouble. Finally Saskia kissed him one last time.

"I'll see you soon, my love," she said.

"Mama," Sasskandr said piteously. It broke Saskia's heart, but she pressed her cheek to his dark curls one more time and went quickly out into the hall to join Aleks as the boy's nurse took the children. The scream behind her tore her in two.

Saskia doubled over, clutching at her stomach as her emotions jarred her daughters and they decided to struggle. Aleks grasped her arm. "Sass! Are you all right?"

"Yes, yes," Saskia straightened. "They just know I'm upset. Come on, we'd better get down to the docks."

A carriage waited outside for them. Saskia's things had already been taken to the boat. They held each other in silence all the way to the docks, both of them knowing they might never see the other again.

At the boat, they stepped out of the carriage. Everyone was there to see Saskia off, knowing that the success of her mission could mean the difference in the outcome of the war. Iskia and

Ria kissed their sister, weeping, and Evan and Erhallen both hugged her roughly to hide their emotions. The ship's captain, a naval officer, came up and bowed to Aleks and Saskia.

"My lady, I am Captain Arbis. Your cabin is prepared, if you are ready to board."

"Take good care of her, Arbis," Aleks said gruffly.

"Your Imperial Grace, I swear by my hope of Light eternal that the Empress will be safe with me," Arbis said formally.

"Good enough," Aleks said. He looked up at the ship's rail and saw two familiar faces: two of the Empress's Guard who nodded back at him. They would make sure she came to no harm, if they could.

Saskia looked up at him, tears brimming in her eyes.

"Don't cry, my love," Aleks whispered. "This is not the end, I swear it."

Saskia swallowed her tears with an effort. Reaching up, she pressed her lips to Aleks'. "Next time we meet, my lord, perhaps I will be able to present you with your daughters," she said, trying to smile.

"Please the Light I'll see you before that," Aleks said. Gently he stroked her shining hair and kissed her once more. "Go now, before I cannot let you leave me."

Saskia took a few steps back. Then she curtsied low to the ground and said clearly. "My lord Emperor, I go with your charge, to rouse the Icelands to our aid. May the Light shine upon you until we meet again."

Aleks bowed in response. "My lady Empress, carry with you our best wishes for your success."

Arbis offered Saskia his arm. She accepted it, and they boarded the boat together. Even as they stepped aboard, the lines were being cast off. Saskia took her place at the rail beside Arbis. Everyone waved as the boat slid away from the quay, but Saskia had eyes only for Aleks. His lips moved, and she knew what he said.

"I love you too," she mouthed back, touched a hand to her heart, then to her lips. She could not step away from the rail, but stood watching until the dock was gone from sight.

"My lady?" Arbis said gently. "Would you care to see your

cabin?"

"Thank you," Saskia said. She followed Arbis mechanically. The cabin was pleasant, small but neatly furnished with a small bed, a trundle for the single maid Saskia was taking, and a cupboard for her clothes.

Saskia's maid Lirris was folding clothes neatly into the cupboard. She was a tough woman, no longer young, but still handsome. Citadel born and bred, this was a great adventure for her.

"My lady," Lirris curtsied to Saskia. As soon as they were alone she would be less formal, but in front of Arbis Saskia must be the Empress: someone to respect.

"I will leave you to make yourself comfortable, my lady." Arbis bowed briefly.

As soon as the door closed, Saskia sat down on the bed. Her face crumpled and she finally gave in to tears. She had no idea that it would be so hard to leave her children, and being parted from Aleks was a cruel wrench.

Saskia had not realised before just how much they depended on each other for everything. Aleks was always there when she needed to talk, and she had always been there to support him when the weight of the Empire became too heavy for him to bear alone. She worried that he would not be able to cope without her, that the weight would crush him down.

Aleks might seem strong and determined, but Saskia knew the real man and understood that even after several years, he was still uncertain that the decisions he made would be the best thing for the Empire.

Lirris sat down beside her mistress and put her arms around Saskia. "Don't cry, Saskia. It's all going to be all right when we get to the Icelands."

Saskia was not nearly so confident. Despite her assurances, she did not truly know whether the Icelander captains would follow her. They could fall back on protocol and insist on having Liara's countersignature as Regent. Liara would gladly let the Empire burn to spite Saskia. Saskia was actually taking a huge risk, putting herself into Icelander hands as she must. Liara could have made standing orders for an "accident" to be arranged should Saskia ever fall into Icelander custody.

Being late winter, the snows were melting up in the mountains and the river was fast. It took only a few days to reach Iridia, then Arbis took charge of an ocean-going ship, the *Snow Raven*, and they headed for Iceport.

Saskia prayed that no spy had sent word of her coming to Iceden, or she might receive a deadly welcome. But in Iceport they sailed into the harbour and raised not a murmur. At least not until Arbis' men went out on the streets and starting talking to the ships' captains, asking them to be at the harbour hall at sunset.

* * * *

Saskia leaned on the ship's rail, breathing in the strong sea air. She looked around the harbour and docks and counted the ships. There were eleven of the massive Icelander galleys, built for trade but equally equipped to deal with pirates. Saskia lost count of the smaller ships very quickly, but one she did recognise.

The slender ship looked like a splinter beside the massive galleys, but she bore the scars of battle on her side. From her mast, a tattered green and gold flag flew. It was a Summerlander ship. She must have escaped the fighting somehow, perhaps outrun the Southron corsairs at sea, and somehow escaped as far as Iceport.

Saskia wondered if there were any others that had escaped: after all these light ships were very fast. Perhaps there were others, in Iridia or Zahennarra, or hiding out amongst the Seal Islands. Maybe some had fled west and reached Fireport. She must find that ship's captain.

When Arbis returned, he brought a man with him. Thin and tired-looking, with light brown hair, Saskia guessed him at once to be the Summerlander ship's captain.

"This is Captain Kerr," Arbis introduced. "Captain, our Lady Empress."

The man went to his knees in front of Saskia. "My lady," he said. "Thank the Light you have come to save us!"

Saskia bent with a grunt to raise him up. "No, my good man, do not kneel to me. I must talk with you. Come, we will go and sit at table. Arbis, will you join us, please?"

Kerr was visibly shaky as he walked. Saskia was having difficulty herself now. The triplets were so massive that she was struggling to carry their weight. Lirris thought they might be born early. Saskia had calculated that they were due just before Flowers, but it was only a few days past Light's Day and already she was bigger than she had been before the boys were born. Saskia tried to work it out: there must be at least forty more days before the girls could be born. She groaned quietly: how could she bear getting any bigger?

Arbis held Saskia's chair for her and then the two men sat down.

"Tell me about your ship," Saskia said, to try and put Kerr at his ease.

Kerr only looked more worried. "She's the *Asparia's Dance*, my lady, named for our former Empress. She was not my ship before we sailed: I was the second mate."

"Second mate? What happened to the captain and first mate?" Arbis demanded.

Kerr sighed. "Perhaps I'd best start at the beginning. We were late sailing out of Zahennarra, bound for Grainport with a cargo of seal fat and jewels. The Captain was furious: he'd wanted to be home by New Year. He was newly married and had promised his wife he'd bring her a Zahennarran sapphire as a New Year gift. But there was floating ice in the harbour and we could not sail until some days after we planned."

Kerr bit his thumbnail. "The quickest way back to Grainport is through some channels in the Seal Islands: though the charts are available for anyone to use most will not, for the channels are shallow and liable to rip the bottom out of a boat. It was the day before the Day of the Dead: we came out of the passage not too far north of Eastport, making good time, and saw one of those black ships with her stern to us."

"What did your captain do?" Arbis asked.

"We wasn't sure what to do. None of us had ever seen or heard tell of a ship like that one. They could not have seen us,

250

because we just came out from behind a high island. So the Captain figured we'd turn south and head for Grainport: after all that ship looked like she was headed in for Eastport. So south we turned, and about twenty minutes later the lookout came screaming down telling us there were many masts on the horizon. The captain gave orders to turn about, and we headed back towards the passage. But the first ship had seen us after all and turned back, and we were caught."

Kerr swallowed convulsively. "That ship turned to match our course, and she matched our speed, too. The captain hailed her, and he'd barely spoken when, when, he caught on fire."

Saskia sat forward. "A fire arrow?" she asked intently.

"No, my lady. Then the mainmast caught on fire. The first mate panicked and jumped overboard, and a lot of men went after him. The black ship carried archers, and then they started shooting, picking off the men in the water, like it was just fun for them."

"Someone was using the Power," Saskia breathed.

"Yes, my lady, they were. But," Kerr looked sheepish, "well, I have a little of the Power myself."

"You do?"

"Enough to put out the mainmast fire and put enough wind into our sail to get *Asparia's Dance* back into that channel. The black ship tore out her bottom coming after us. Unless they've got her out, that channel's blocked now."

"And so you were now in charge," Saskia said.

"Yes, my lady. We fled back up through the Seal Islands. We saw two more ships, but they were small ones. One of them must have carried an Earth Power, for the ship's sides began to crack and age, and the water to come in."

"What did you do?" Saskia asked, somewhat impressed by the nondescript little man's resourcefulness.

"My primary power is in Air, but I have some in Water and a little in Fire. I set fire to their mainsails, and we fled again. The next ship we saw, I think carried no sorcerer, but they clearly wanted to board us and chased us. I could not shake them off using the Power, so we had to run. We wanted to go back to Zahennarra, but there was floating ice and we dared not slow down enough. So we headed out into the northern sea and thought we'd make for Iridia. But the black ship tried to board us not far from Iridia, and we had to keep going. Finally we ran into an Icelander galley. She sank our pursuer and escorted us into Iceport. We've been laid up here ten days making repairs."

Saskia nodded, thinking hard. She found it hard to believe that the invaders were using the Power in battle. Most people in the Empire believed the Power, like the other Gifts, was a Gift from the Light.

Most people who discovered that they had a Gift went into the priesthood or, occasionally, special service to the Emperor. Still, Saskia was sure from talking to the chief priests in the Citadel, there could not be more than one or two hundred people Power-Gifted in the whole of the Empire. How could the Southroners have so many? From what Kerr said, she guessed that all the large ships probably had a sorcerer assigned to them, and as many small ones as possible. That meant at least a hundred.

"How is it that you remained a sailor when you discovered you had the Power?" Saskia asked curiously.

"I did not, my lady, as soon as my family found out the priests came for me. But even in port I pined away from the sea – my family were all fishermen. The priests decided to let me go. But they commanded me not to become a solitary fisherman as my father was, but to sign on as a ship's officer and to use my abilities for the good of my ship."

Saskia nodded. "Well, Kerr," she said. "I'm giving you a chance to do more than good by your ship. Do good by your Empire: sail with me when the time comes, and use your Power to help me stop the invaders."

Kerr nodded, eyes shining. "Aye, my lady, I will. *Asparia's Dance* will be no use to you except perhaps as a messenger's ship. I cannot sail her anyway, once I had made port I am bound to keep her there until her owners confirm me as captain."

"I suspect her owners are dead," Saskia said bluntly. "Grainport is gone, Kerr: half burned. All of Summerlands is lost, and so is Envetierra, Eastport, and almost certainly Furport. Zahennarra may be lost too, and perhaps even Iridia by now."

"Still, the law states she cannot be moved until her owners command it."

Saskia shrugged. "We'll deal with that when the time comes. Some other man can be captain, I care not. I need you with me."

"Your pardon, my lady," Kerr hesitated, "but I thought you were very strongly Gifted with Fire?"

"I was," Saskia said. "The babes I bear are not, though, and every day I carry them my own Power recedes. My first two sons are Power-Gifted, and my Power was the stronger for carrying them. These children are not. The Power should return, but they are not due to be born for many days yet."

Kerr nodded. "I understand. So you need me to be the Power for you until you get it back."

"Exactly," Saskia replied.

Arbis shook his head. "Wait a moment. Kerr, who knows that the invaders use sorcery?"

Kerr looked puzzled. "Well, everyone, I daresay."

Arbis and Saskia shared a look. "You'd better have a damned persuasive speech, my lady," Arbis said.

Saskia nodded. "I think I can demonstrate enough Power to convince," she said. "I need to think. Arbis, why don't you take Kerr into town, buy him a good meal on me. Any of his shipmates who fancy sailing with us, too."

At sunset, Saskia sat on a chair on a small dais in the harbour hall. The room was freezing, and she watched as the ship's captains and their officers filed in and sat down. She knew that unlike Summerlander ships, Icelander galleys were owned by their crews, with the captain owning the largest stake. A majority of the officers for each ship would have to agree before that ship would sail.

At last they were all there. Saskia surveyed the room as Arbis closed the doors to keep the draught out.

"Cold in here, isn't it?" she said in a conversational tone, speaking in the Icelander dialect. She lifted her hands, gathered the Power and wove Fire and Air to warm the room up.

There were audible gasps as the men removed their coats in the now pleasantly warm room. "Ice Witch," a few murmurs went up.

Saskia nodded. "Everyone comfortable? Good." She stood up and walked forward. She had dressed very carefully indeed for this occasion. She wore black breeches, for comfort and for her allegiance to the Clanlands. Over that, she had a white-and-purple tunic, hanging loose, for her Icelander blood. But on her head the circlet was of gold, and the gems on her hands flashed.

Glittering on her wrists, Saskia wore the bracelets Aleks had bought for her at the boys' births, diamonds for Sasskandr and sapphires for Iskandr. On her back was strapped her sword, and sewn into the belt across her chest were thirteen small flags, each edged in gold, the colours of all the provinces. Thus she clearly represented the Empire here, but showed that she had not forgotten from whence she came. These men would respect that.

Saskia waited while they looked her up and down. Then she spoke again, still in the Icelander tongue.

"I am Saskia von Chenowska, once a di'Berenna but born a Cevaria of the Royal Blood of Iceden. My second born son is the Heir to the Icelands." She paused, and smiled down at them. She walked along the front of the stage, and they followed her with their eyes as though hypnotised.

"Your Prince is a baby," she said. "Your Regent is a soft southlander who does not understand the hard rules of the Icelands."

The men were nodding at that and grinning ruefully. Saskia suspected some of them had already encountered Liara's high-handed ways.

"The overlord to the Icelands is my husband, Emperor Aleksandr von Chenowska," she said. "He is a southlander, but a warrior, forged in the hard Desert. He is a worthy sire to the Icelands Heir."

They were all nodding, agreeing with her. Even here word of Aleks had reached them, and of course they had heard the story of his fight with Sasken.

Saskia stopped and looked down at them, her eyes hard and dark. "The Empire has been invaded," she said. "I have no doubt you already know: most of you will have heard from Kerr here about the black ships that have come, carrying sorcerers. I tell

254

you now. Eastport, Grainport, Silkport, Wineport, Pearlport, and Furport: they have all burned and been lost. Envetierra is gone entirely. There has been no word from Zahennarra and we are hoping the floating ice will have protected them." Saskia paused briefly to rake the room with her eyes. No one made a sound.

"The Seal Islands are in little danger because of the shallow passages between them: in the winter they mostly freeze. But Iridia will be next, and perhaps Fireport. The invaders are already marching on Highfort and North Market. The whole of the Summerlands is lost: Summerhold will have fallen by now."

The Icelander sailors were all staring at her, shocked. Perhaps they had not really had any idea just how widespread this invasion was.

Saskia took a deep breath. "If we cannot stop them from taking both Iridia and North Market, the Empire Water will be lost to us. The Citadel will be next, and for the first time since the Founding a man will sit on the Emperor's throne who has not been Chosen."

Gasps of horror went up around the room at that. The Emperor was Light-chosen – for a usurper to sit on his throne was blasphemy, even for Icelanders.

"What can we do, my lady?" one man, a tall, gruff sailor, asked.

Saskia gathered her courage, and wished mightily for just a little of Aleks' Charisma. "You can follow me," she said. "A group of soldiers followed me up the Empire Water to reinforce Iridia's garrison. I am going to help them. The ships will strike there next for sure, Iridia is both the gate to the Empire Water and the key to the North. If Iridia is lost, the war is lost. I have to go to stop it. I cannot command you, I am not your province ruler, nor your Emperor. But I am a Princess of the Royal Blood of Iceden, and a representative of the Empire, and as such I can ask you to follow me."

"But these ships carry sorcerers!" a voice shouted from the back of the room.

"As will yours," Saskia responded. "This is a province capital city. You have a major temple here, and in every major temple is at least one priest with the Power, and many others with other Gifts. Captain Kerr here will be sailing with us. He too is Gifted with Power, and he has faced the invaders and survived, destroying two of their ships in the process. And I, I your Princess and your Empress, the Power is also mine to command." She lifted her left hand, and a gust of Air extinguished all the torches.

Kerr was the one using the Air Power, but the sailors need not know that. Then Saskia linked with Kerr and took his Power to channel into the Tear. The wyrdfire ignited above her hand, bright enough to illuminate her in a fiery glow. With her other hand, Saskia reached back and drew her sword.

"I am your Princess and the mother of your Heir. I am the Emperor's Bride and I ask you now: who will follow me?"

Saskia could not know, but as she stood there, lit by the wyrdfire, sword in hand, she looked just like a statue of a woman in the city. It stood in the main square, cast in white marble. In one hand the woman held up a lantern, in the other, a long knife, used to gut fish or cut nets. Her hair was blown back as she peered out to sea.

The sailors called the statue the Storm Watcher, and every Icelander who sailed out of Iceport would touch the statue for luck before a voyage, and in thanks on their safe return home.

"Storm Watcher – she's the Storm Watcher," men whispered at the back of the hall. Then a voice spoke out.

"I'll follow you, Princess. Whether my men choose to bring our ship or not, I'll lift my sword beside you to fight for Iridia." It was the tall sailor who had first asked her what he should do, getting to his feet. Beside him, men shared glances, and then stood. All over the hall, men were standing.

"We'll sail for you!"

"Aye, *Wind Dancer* will sail!"

"*Wave Runner*!" "*Storm Song*!" "*White River*!"

Saskia lifted her sword for silence. The room quieted. "We sail on the high tide, two days hence," she said. "You have that time to provision, fill your crews, and bid your wives farewell. I will take no man who does not volunteer: I have no wish to anger your Regent by conscripting men. Every man must make his mark on a paper at the temple."

Saskia had already been to the temple that afternoon. The priests were with her, convinced she herself was Light-blessed, and had drawn up the volunteer agreement. Many of them were Gifted in useful skills and had agreed to sail with her: there were three with some degree of the Power, including the chief priest.

In addition, the priests knew of four other Power-Gifted within a day's fast ride, and had sent messengers to summon them. There were other useful Gifts like TimeSight, Healing, Luck and LongSight, though none with the strength in their Gift that Saskia and her sisters had.

Chapter 15

Iceden, early spring,
the year 2724 after Founding

Two mornings later saw the ships ready to sail. The captain of the biggest ship, the *Wave Runner*, was the first man who had stood for Saskia and as such she accorded him the honour of transporting her. She was absolutely astonished to arrive at the quay and look up at the ship.

Men lined the rail, each one in their standard clothing, generally plain workmanlike gear. But on each man's shoulder had been hastily sewn a patch, an Icelander white and purple flag, stitched on with gold thread to signal that they were fighting in the Emperor's name. The women of the town must have denuded the shops of gold thread to do so much so quickly.

Kerr and Arbis were sailing with them, to advise and assist Saskia in planning. Another man was sailing the *Snow Raven*, there being plenty of spare crew. Almost every man who could walk had been to the temple to volunteer, and all the ships were crewed to capacity. Saskia had also declared the *Asparia's Dance* crown property, then promptly gifted it to Kerr and told him to pick a captain and crew to sail her.

The fast little Summerlander ship was too valuable to waste: she could pass through narrow channels where the bigger galleys might ground, and could sail far faster than they could to carry messages and such.

With Saskia on the *Wave Runner* would also sail the chief priest from Iceport. Named Dendri, he was strongly Gifted with the Power in Water, very useful on the sea.

Saskia liked Dendri, who wasn't at all stuffy, and she and Kerr already had their heads together working out how to link all their Powers together.

But the biggest surprise awaiting Saskia was the ship's figurehead, turned out towards the sea. Arbis had deliberately brought her the long way down the quay so she would see it. The brooding visage of the Fisherman, the usual talisman for these ships, had been replaced by the Storm Watcher, and the face she wore was Saskia's own.

Saskia did not find out until later, but the figure had been made by Iceden's four best craftsmen, aided by a priest Gifted with Earth Powers, who had cut the tree for the figurehead himself. The five men had been working non-stop for the last two days, and the figurehead had been lifted into place the previous night, in the pitch dark and cold.

All the crews had seen the figurehead and were glad: while they had all been to touch the statue, they were pleased that their Watcher would be sailing with them, and the figurehead would make it easier for them to pick out Saskia's ship.

The Captain met them at the gangplank, his officers lined up behind him. "My Lady Empress," he said, bowing very low. "Our ship is yours. We dedicate her life to your service. In return, we ask a boon of you: that you lift from her the common name of *Wave Runner* and give her a better."

Saskia stood frozen for a moment. Then she smiled on the captain and his men. "I am not the Emperor, to bestow titles of nobility," she said. "I can give only of myself, and thus I offer you what I have. I name this noble ship, *Saskia's Heart*."

A chorus of cheering erupted around the docks as her words were relayed. The ships sailed within the hour, and as they went, a man was hanging from a rope below the ship's bow, carefully painting on her new name, where a new board had been fitted to receive it.

Saskia was standing at the bow rail, watching the sea. The weather was mild yet, no high winds, but still a little spray splashed on her.

"You are getting wet, my lady," Arbis scolded. "It cannot be good for your daughters. Come, let me aid you back to shelter."

Saskia could barely walk. "Oh, when will this be over?" she

groaned.

"Soon, I hope, my lady, for your sake," Lirris said, coming to aid her to a seat. "Praise the Light, before Iridia."

Dendri was looking anxiously at Saskia. He drew Arbis aside. "Sir, I think we should send across to the *Wind Song*. One of my people is there, a good Healer. Not in Princess Liaskia's class, but experienced with difficult births, and trained at the College on North Envetierra. I know he has seen twins and triplets born before."

Arbis nodded agreement. "Talk to the Captain: have them send a ship's boat over. We're only three days out of Iridia but I'm not sure the little princesses are going to wait that long to be born."

Arbis was right. The Healing priest, a very old man, arrived later, took one look at Saskia and hustled out everyone except Lirris.

"Who are you?" Saskia asked weakly as the old man bent over her.

"I'm here to help, little one. I think those daughters of yours have decided that there's no more room in there and it's time to be born."

Saskia's first daughter was born at the darkest hour of the night, her second in the pale light of dawn, and the third an hour later in the glory of a bright sunrise.

"It is for their father to name them," Saskia whispered when Lirris asked her what she would call them. "But I will give them names until he sees them: call them by the hour of their birth. Midnight, Dawn and Sunrise."

The Power had returned to Saskia in a huge rush as Sunrise was taken from her womb. She had to replace all the constraints she had once used to keep the Power in check to avoid everything around her catching on Fire.

* * * *

Kerr and Dendri, seeing her the day after the birth, both stared, astounded: to their Power-tinged vision, Saskia glowed with Power held in check. Even Dendri, Water-Gifted, could see the Fire nimbus glowing around her.

Saskia was fit and strong and on her feet within hours of the birth. Thankfully she had plenty of milk this time, for the babies were very small, though healthy. The old priest just shrugged over them.

"They are tiny, my lady Empress, but I doubt not that they will all be well. They just have some growing to do." He laid hands on Saskia, to help Heal her and to make sure her milk would flow well for the babies. They all seemed ravenous, and had distinct personalities already. Midnight was a quiet, serious little soul, who would tolerate no hands on her but Saskia's. Dawn was impatient and temperamental, liable to scream if she didn't get everything she wanted instantly, and Sunrise was a sweet, sunny little thing, seeming to smile already and only too happy to snuggle into whatever arms held her.

Saskia desperately wanted to show them off to their father. Even more desperately she wanted to know how Aleks was doing. She demanded anyone with the LongSight to come to her at once.

Three priests arrived within an hour. Saskia touched the Tear, and realised that two could barely See as far as Iridia. She sent them to Arbis, to try and link with Kerr and tell what they saw in the harbour. The third could perhaps See as far as Furport on his own, and Saskia made him sit down with her. He was young, and seemed nervous around her: not uncommon!

Saskia calmed him with a cup of tea, and then took his hand and used the Tear to boost his Sight. The young man gasped as Saskia took him further than he had known he could go without the vision dissolving.

"Aleks," Saskia said sharply. "Find Aleks."

Then she saw him. Though it was evening where she was, the sun had long passed that far east, and Aleks was asleep in a dark tent. He looked well, though a little thin, and was sleeping deeply. Saskia could not get an impression of anything but darkness and sentries around the camp, although they were clearly not in a town.

Saskia lost the link as the young priest drew back, clutching at his head. She was straining too hard, using too much Power, and hurting him. Carefully she helped him up and called for the Healer to see to him.

Saskia's radiant smile spoke for her when she reached Arbis and Kerr. "The Emperor is well, he sleeps," she said.

"Praise the Light, my Lady," Kerr said fervently.

"Kerr and the priests had a look at Iridia: there is fighting there," Arbis said. He pointed at a map on the table, showing Iridia and the coast for a good ten miles around it. "There are ships here, and here, and one beached here, two miles from the city. Iridia had good warning: they sank two big barges at the harbour mouth and nothing can get in. It looks like the invaders tried to burn the barges, but nothing will burn below the waterline, and the ships still could not get into the harbour. The city walls are safe, and the river still closed. But this beached ship carried many men, and they are marching on the eastern walls."

Saskia looked thoughtfully at the map. "Have they been trying to burn the town?" she asked.

"It would seem so, my lady, but I think they have been unsuccessful. Perhaps they do not have a sorcerer with much Fire."

"Most not Gifted with Fire cannot do anything with it at a distance," Kerr offered. "I can usually only set light to things within the reach of my hand. I have tried to throw fireballs, but they fizzle out before going more than a few feet. I normally have to touch something to set fire to it."

Saskia nodded. "Then they have no Fire Gifted." Her smile blossomed. "I shall give them quite a display."

To keep them safe, Saskia sent Lirris and her daughters to *Asparia's Dance*, put a Water-Gifted priestess on board and told the captain of the little ship to sail as fast as he could go should ill befall her. The Emperor's daughters must not fall into the hands of the enemy.

Saskia wept as she put Midnight into the arms of the priestess. This was the second time she had to leave her children to the safe-keeping of others. Without Iskia, she had no hope of seeing as far as Clanhold to check on her sons.

* * * *

Late at night, four days after sailing out of Iceden, they approached Iridia, all lights doused. They had waited below the horizon until dark fell, and now sailed as fast as the wind would carry them, wind speeded up by Kerr and two other priests Gifted with Air Power.

In total, there were four Gifted with Air Power sailing, three with Water, and three with Earth, plus Saskia with the rare Gift of Fire. On *Saskia's Heart*, the flagship, there was one with each kind of Power, the strongest in each, ready to counter whatever the Southron sorcerers might be able to do.

Saskia stood in the ship's bow, wearing black fighting gear, her only concession to rank the rings on her hands. Just behind her stood the other three, Kerr, Dendri and Lowri, the young Earth Power priestess.

"They're here," Kerr whispered. "I can feel them, can't you feel it? The air is carrying the scent: a boat too long at sea."

Saskia could not smell it, yet, but if Kerr could then the other ship could be no more than a few hundred yards away. She strained her eyes and saw a faint light in the darkness.

"Get ready," Saskia whispered back. The word went back along the ship. A horn sounded out, and every man and woman on the open docks of the Icelander fleet put one hand over their eyes and squeezed them shut.

Saskia's hands lifted, she alone could look on this and not be blinded. She hoped that not too many were looking over Iridia's walls out to sea.

To the men on the Southroner ship, it was a vision from their nightmares. The whole sky caught fire with a searingly bright light, so bright it was as though the sun had risen at midnight. They stared in horror upwards, never seeing the massive galley bearing down on them. When the light winked out suddenly, they were totally blind in the darkness.

There was a lot of yelling. Saskia lifted her hand again, and a witchlight ignited, very faint but quite enough for them to see the other ship by. Men were stumbling around, clutching at their eyes and crying out. It was only a couple of ship lengths away.

Dendri hooked his hand and the water swelled, lifting the black ship and swinging her easily in alongside *Saskia's Heart*. The *Wind Sprite* pulled in on the other side, and Arbis roared out the command to board.

In minutes the black ship was taken, her crew suppressed. A man was brought to Saskia, tied hand and foot and knocked unconscious. "The sorcerer, I think, my lady," the officer who delivered him said.

Saskia had two men tie the sorcerer to a chair. Then she and the other three sat down opposite him. Saskia woke him with two quick slaps of Air across his face.

The sorcerer awoke with a snarl. Seeing the four seated opposite him, he stared. That two were women, and young women at that, he seemed to find funny. Then he looked down at the ropes tying him to the chair, and sneered.

"Fools, that you think to bind me!" he snarled in a guttural accent. "I am a mage!"

"Really?" Saskia said in a bored tone. She lifted her hand, and the other three imitated. Each lit their witchlights. The mage stared in horror. Saskia's wyrdfire was bright red-gold, fiercely burning. Lowri's was greenish like swamp gas, Kerr's pure white, and Dendri's roiled blue-green like the ocean.

"You permit *women* to use magic?" the sorcerer said, recoiling as though they were poisonous snakes.

"Of course. You do not?" Saskia said.

The sorcerer smiled, a smile Saskia did not like. "If we find women who have any magic at all, whether true magic or Sight or Healing, they are Bound so they may not use their magic, and given to the mages to breed the next generation strong and true. I will look forward to Binding *you* myself."

"I wonder if this Binding would work on men?" Lowri mused.

The sorcerer glared. "Silence, woman! Dare you speak in the presence of your betters?"

"It is *you* who are in the presence of your betters," Saskia said icily. She stood up and walked towards the sorcerer. "I'm going to send those two out now. They are priests, and really should not be a party to this. Kerr here and I have stronger stomachs."

Dendri and Lowri left, with rather disapproving looks. They understood the necessity, but they did not like it.

"Lowri says that your Power is in Earth," Saskia said. "Kerr here is what you would call an Air mage. I have Fire. Now, we need information out of you. We can do this the easy way or the hard way. It's up to you." With that, she drew a long, sharp knife and brought it to the sorcerer's hand. "Tell me your name."

The man looked at the bright, sharp steel against his skin. He swallowed. Then he looked up into Saskia's eyes, terrifyingly hard, and at Kerr's granite-sharp face.

"My name is Vai'iyanta Ti'vihela," he said compliantly.

"Very good. What is the name of your ship?"

Vai'iyanta smiled proudly. "He is the *Hand of Chaos*."

"Did you command the ship?" Saskia said.

"Of course!" Vai'iyanta looked affronted. "Only one with the Blood may command."

"What is the Blood?" Kerr said.

Vai'iyanta nodded at his hands. They were marked with blue tattoos. "The Blood are those born of magic families. Those with true magic are marked with the blue, those of the lesser magics with green. Each child is marked when his magic manifests."

"Except the women," Saskia said.

"All females born of the Blood are marked at birth, with a family sigil tattooed on their forehead."

"Are they then kept by that family?" Saskia said, grimacing: that smacked of incest.

"Oh, no!" Vai'iyanta looked shocked. "When the girl-child turns ten, she would be given as a favour, to another family, and given to one of that family who felt he might father good sons on her."

Saskia made a face, not liking the idea. But this was not important. She would have plenty of time to get all the information she wanted from this man. Right now, she needed information about the ships and men around Iridia, so that when dawn came they would be ready. She knew that already men were coming from various ships to man the *Hand of Chaos*. A lot of Southroners would die after the sun rose.

Vai'iyanta, now he had decided to be helpful, told Saskia a great deal. At last Saskia rose, nodding. "I'm going to see Arbis," she said. "Put him to sleep." The clout of Air Kerr slapped against Vai'iyanta's head put him down again.

"Keep an eye on him," Saskia warned, and went to find Arbis.

The enemy had twelve ships near Iridia, not including the one beached and the *Hand of Chaos*. Saskia grimaced again as she said the name.

"I don't like that name, it sounds cursed. Get that man with the paint pot, we're going to rename her."

And so, before dawn came, the ship was renamed *Light's Victory*. Arbis selected a crew of reliable men to sail her.

Vai'iyanta had told Saskia that he had been detailed to watch for attack from the west. She suspected that was why he had been so co-operative: he had failed in his duties and his life was probably forfeit if he was ever caught. The crew of his ship had fought to the last man, and there were no survivors apart from Vai'iyanta.

The *Light's Victory* might not be a big ship by Southroner standards, but she handled like an unwieldy scow. Dendri sent his other Water-Gifted priest on board to try and get the waves to assist her passage, and Kerr made sure that the right wind blew in her massive sails.

"I'm glad we didn't get one of the really big ones," Arbis said to Saskia as they watched from the deck of *Saskia's Heart*. They sailed in the wake of *Light's Victory*, keeping well behind, watching her wallow along. "If *she* sails like a bathtub: imagine what the biggest ones handle like!"

"No wonder they need mages on board," Saskia said. "It's just to keep them from sinking!"

They both laughed, and then quieted as the LongSighted priest on board came up. "Sir, my Lady, there's a ship ahead," he said tensely. "Perhaps four or five miles. It's a bit hard to tell, in this fog."

"We're nearing Iridia, this is probably the first of the blockade," Arbis said. "Everyone ready!"

The signals were sounded. The four Power-Gifted gathered on the deck, the LongSighted priest with them. He had the most important job during this battle, to tell them what was happening out of their sight.

"There's two ships," he said after a moment. "Heeling round, swinging for us."

"Pick up speed," Arbis commanded. The signals were passed and the *Light's Victory* and *Saskia's Heart* were running alongside, others pulling in behind them, some swinging out to circle around the battle and hunt for other ships.

There was a *boom* ahead of them. The water began to swell suddenly in front of the two ships.

"Dendri!" Saskia snapped. She felt Dendri gather in his Power beside her, and could see across to the deck of *Light's Victory*, and the other Water priest there lifting his hands as he worked the Power. The two ships rocked and swung, but kept their course.

Saskia waited tensely. At length there came a shout out of the fog: the guttural Southroner tongue, hailing the *Light's Victory*. Or, Saskia supposed, they were probably calling to the *Hand of Chaos*.

"I wish we had Envetierrans on board," Saskia said in an undertone to Arbis. The Envetierran tongue was virtually identical to the Southroner, but it was so difficult to learn no one bothered if they did not intend to live on the Islands.

Arbis nodded, eyes straining into the fog. Then suddenly the fog blew away in a high wind, and the ships were left in clear blue seas and sky.

"Light," Saskia whispered. Everyone stared in stunned silence. One of the ships facing them was about the size of the *Light's Victory*. The other was the biggest ship any of them had ever seen, easily twice as high and three times as long.

"*Storm Dance!*" yelled the LongSeer suddenly. "The *Storm Dance* is on fire!"

Dendri knew where the ship should be and turned that way. They could barely see a spark, on the far side of the huge ship. The *Storm Dance* had sailed too fast in the fog. Even for Dendri, very strongly Gifted, that was a long way. He linked hands with

267

Kerr to take some strength.

While the two battled silently to put out the fire, Saskia started looking for the mage who had started it. That was at too long a range for anyone but a Fire-Gifted. With a snap of her hand she set the smaller ship's mainmast on fire as a distraction.

The Fire mage must have been tracking her strings of Fire. Saskia could feel them backlashing as the other mage used them against her, but Saskia had long ago learned how to use the Tear to stop backlash from hurting her. She grasped the Power again, Linked with Lowri and used their combined strength to set off an explosion in the side of the huge ship.

Lowri let out a yell of shock. Saskia was astonished too: she had only expected to be able to burn part of the ship, but using the Fire and Earth Power together made explosions. She vaguely remembered Rianna telling her that, but had never tried it since melding two completely different Powers was extremely tricky.

Saskia took Lowri's hand to make the Link stronger. A second explosion, below the first, rocked the huge ship.

Saskia could feel the Power rippling wildly. She had never known so much Power unleashed in one place, and of all the types. She counted herself lucky to have the Tear, to be able to feed the backlash into it and use the additional Power generated.

On the other ships, they could see men running, panicking, trying to deal with the flames springing up. Saskia was trying to set off the explosions where there seemed to be fewest people. Finally the huge ship turned away and sailed north, fleeing from them with her masts afire. The smaller ship was already sinking, burning low in the water.

Saskia sagged, exhausted, against Kerr, who caught her arm in a strong grip. "Are you all right, my lady?"

"I am." Saskia looked at Lowri. "That was tiring."

Lowri nodded, accepting a cup of water from a sailor. "You know, my lady, we have more Power at our disposal."

"How?" Saskia said.

Lowri and Dendri shared a look. Finally Dendri shrugged. "It's up to you. Perhaps she would have figured it out herself eventually anyway."

Lowri turned back to Saskia. "You have Linked many

times, both with those Gifted with Power and those with other Gifts."

Saskia nodded impatiently. "Of course. What is your point?"

"Always it has been with their consent. There is, however, a way of Linking without consent. The initial link is more difficult to establish."

Saskia frowned, trying to see what Lowri was getting at. "Vai'iyanta!" she exclaimed, understanding. "Do you think that's how they control their people?"

"I doubt it," Lowri said. "He seemed to imply their Binding was a permanent process, and this is not. The priesthood discovered it many years ago, and the secret has been closely guarded. We use it to restrain those who misuse their powers."

Saskia nodded. "Teach me how," she said. "We will need all the strength we can use before we take Iridia."

The battle for Iridia raged for days. Saskia and the others were hard put to it just to deflect the attacks launched on them by the Southroners. Most of the fighting ended up hand-to-hand, especially when a weird Power-storm prevented either side from using sorcery for two days.

Saskia herself was down on the docks in the fighting. The Southroners had taken the docks but not breached the city walls, and had not been able to penetrate more then a few hundred yards into the Empire Water. The Iridians came out to join the fight and Southroners were caught between the two forces.

Saskia's two Guards were horrified that she insisted on fighting alongside her men, but they could not stop her. Instead, they followed, determined to guard Saskia's back against the enemy.

Saskia led a charge towards the enemy. She had learned enough tactics to understand exactly where extra swords would do the most good, and led her party of men into a knot of ferocious fighting. Sword in hand, she looked like a warrior queen. Her very first swing decapitated a Southron soldier, and her backslash ripped the arm off another.

Screaming with rage and bloodlust, she killed ten men all by herself and severely wounded a dozen more. Not until later did she realise that was the first time she had killed hand-to-hand, and begin to shake with reaction.

Saskia had commanded anyone captured or killed that had tattooed hands to be brought to her, but there were none. Obviously all the mages were staying well back from the fighting. She felt a wave of hatred for them, working with Lowri as they tended to the wounded. Saskia could not stop herself from weeping over the men who had fought and died in her name that day.

"It's all right, Saskia," Lowri was saying softly.

"It's not all right!" Saskia said. "I brought these men here, to fight and die in my name, and we don't know if it's even worth it! The rest of the Empire could be lost by now and we have no way to know!"

Lowri rubbed Saskia's shoulder sympathetically. "I think that we would know, Saskia, I really do. If we were the only resistance left there would be many more ships than this here."

"It's not just that," Saskia half-sobbed. "I want my children, and Aleks. The Seers are too tired to See far, and even if I could use the Power to boost them I doubt any of them could see to *Asparia's Dance* to make sure the girls are all right. It would take Iskia and me at full strength to see as far as Clanhold to check on my sons. And Aleks is fighting somewhere far to the east, without even me to watch his back."

The emotions of the day had finally caught up with Saskia. She had finally run out of Southroners to kill: they could not stand before her and fled before the raging woman with her lethal sword. Saskia had started after them, and almost killed one of her Guards who stepped before her.

"Enough!" the Guard shouted. "Enough, my lady! They're dead – look around you!"

Saskia lowered her sword, and looked around. Southroners lay sprawled all around, and the dock was soaked in blood. Surprisingly few Icelanders and Iridians lay there, but it was the horror of the black and silver tunic that brought Saskia to her senses.

"Allen," Saskia whispered in horror, going to her knees beside her dead Guard. The other Guard knelt beside her, tears pouring unashamedly down his craggy face. They were two of the original men Evan had commanded as the Empress' Guards, and men more devoted to Saskia she could not have hoped to find.

"Oh, Devon," she said to the other Guard softly. "He's gone. Allen's gone."

"I know," Devon replied sadly. "I couldn't save him, my lady. It was him or you."

Saskia laid her head against Devon's shoulder, and he put his arm around her awkwardly. They were both blood-soaked, exhausted. Finally Saskia stood, scrubbing the tears from her eyes with one filthy hand.

"Make sure he is properly burned," she asked. "I must go now, Devon. There are men who still live that I may be able to help." She sheathed her sword and walked steadily away towards the hospital that was being hastily set up. Devon's heart ached for her, but he picked up his dead comrade gently and walked towards the squad of men who were collecting bodies to burn.

Soldiers of both sides had died. The Imperial forces gathered those of their dead that they could, set them adrift in captured Southroner landing craft, and burned them. The Southroners merely threw bodies into the harbour. It would take a lot of cleaning up before the water of Iridia's harbour would run clear again.

Chapter 16

Furport, summer,
the year 2724 after Founding

Aleks was bone-weary. He wished for Saskia at his side. There were sorcerers in Furport, and though the battle had started two days earlier, the Imperial forces had spent most of their time trying to avoid such magical terrors as they had never imagined. Lightning bolts hurled down on them, the rain pelted them constantly, and at night everything froze hard. The army was miserable. They kept asking where Saskia was, where was the Ice Witch to protect them with her sorceries?

Iskia did what she could. She used her Sight to scout the land ahead for them, to make sure there were no ambushes waiting. The Southroners did not always fight with sorcery: their soldiers seemed to enjoy a good scrap. But what Iskia saw them do to the captured Imperial soldiers ended with Aleks finding her being sick behind a tent one night.

"Iskia? What is wrong?" Aleks asked anxiously.

Iskia shivered convulsively as Aleks took her inside and made her sit. He pressed a hot drink into her hands, and offered to summon a Healer.

"No!" Iskia almost screamed. "No Healer!"

"Iskia!" Aleks grasped her hands. "What have you seen? You must tell me!"

The words stumbled off Iskia's tongue. "I saw – a woman of your forces who was captured today in the fighting. She wore the blue tunic of the Erinean forces. They killed all the men, but they had taken her back into the city. A man put his hands on her. He had green tattoos on his fingers. There were several of them there, with many common soldiers." Iskia paused.

"Go on," Aleks pressed.

"They raped her. The soldiers. All of them."

"How many? She must surely be dead!"

"No," Iskia shook her head. "That's the horror of it. The men with green tattoos were healers. Every time it looked as though she would faint, from the bleeding and the pain, they laid hands on her and Healed her. Healed the pain, but not the memory. And then it all started again."

Iskia bit her lip, bile rising in her throat. "Oh, Light, Aleks, she's still there! They will keep on using her and Healing her, a slave for any man to relieve himself on! She is half-mad already with the horror of it!"

Aleks stumbled away from Iskia and outside, gulping air to clear his throat. He felt as sick as Iskia, even though he had not seen as she had.

Outside, he gulped in the cool night air. A Healer paused by him. "My lord, are you well?"

"Yes. Wait." Aleks looked at the man, a young priest. "Are there any Power-Gifted among you priests?"

"Yes, my lord, but they are very tired. It is all they can do each day to fend off the worst of the magical attacks from the enemy."

"I need the help of you and one Power-Gifted. Find someone who is strong and not as tired as the others. Come back here as quickly as you can."

When the two priests, both young men, returned, Aleks greeted them and brought them inside. Iskia looked up in surprise.

"We're going to end her suffering," Aleks said gently. Briefly he filled the two priests in on the situation.

"Power-Gifted can Link with any other Gift, am I right?" Aleks said.

The priest nodded.

"Right. Iskia here has LongSight. I want you to Link with her and with this Healer here, and use the Gifts to stop this soldier's heart. She deserves better than this, and I think even if we could rescue her, she would kill herself with the madness."

Both priests nodded in agreement. The look of relief on

Iskia's face was incredible. "Oh, thank the Light! I can't stop myself from Seeing her." She lost focus for a second. "She's sleeping. If we do it now she will just never wake up."

A few minutes later it was done. The two priests nodded to Aleks with respect and left. Iskia leaned back with a sigh of relief.

"After every fight from now on, I want you to find any female prisoners," Aleks said. "Use those two priests and make sure that does not happen to any other women."

Iskia nodded. "Yes, Aleks."

"I will put the word out what happened. We already know they immediately kill any male prisoners they take. Everyone knows that death waits for anyone taken. The women will be glad to know that they cannot be subjected to that kind of treatment. They are soldiers: I believe every one of them would choose a clean death over rape and madness."

The soldiers agreed. Iskia wore herself out occasionally after the fighting, but no more women were subjected to torture. The Gifted in the camp began to make themselves known to Aleks, and started using their Gifts more for the benefit of the army. There were no strong Power-Gifted, but they could do enough to ensure that the army did not bear the full brunt of attacks with the Power.

* * * *

The battle for Furport wore on. Ten days later, they were fighting right up to the city walls, the Imperial forces gaining ground with every step.

Furport was built around a horseshoe-shaped harbour, but it was not possible to circle the walls and attack from the inside of the city, as the ends of the walls jutted well out into the sea and the currents were too strong to dare swimming.

Aleks was leading yet another attack on the walls. He had picked out a place he thought might break, a low section between two guard towers. Occasionally he cursed his predecessors, a series of rather paranoid Emperors who had insisted that most of the cities in the Empire had walls built of solid stone fifty feet high.

Only new cities, like Summerhold, did not have the walls. The old Summerhold had been wrecked by fire a hundred years or so ago, and the Lord of Summerlands had rebuilt the city as a pleasure palace, the whole place filled with beautiful houses and gardens.

Aleks made a face, thinking of it. Summerhold had no choice but to surrender immediately, but every adult male in the town had been put to the sword, and any women beyond childbearing age also.

Terrible things were happening in the Summerlands, from what Aleks heard. He only hoped that Evan and Ria could make a difference. At least North Market was safe: the Southroners did not seem to realise there was a city on the river yet. Or perhaps they intended to take it from the river after Iridia.

Carlene had sent word that she was on her way to join Aleks: as commander of the Imperial Guards, having Aleks so far from her made her nervous. She should arrive in a few days.

Aleks was glad of that: though he trusted the men with him, Carlene understood strategy far better than he ever could, and he needed her advice. In addition, she was loyal only to him, and would never breathe a word of what he said. He could confide his fears in Carlene. Though Aleks admitted to himself that what he really wanted was to confide in Saskia. Iskia was no substitute for her sister: she was too worried about her own husband, needing Aleks to be strong and convince her that the war would end quickly.

Aleks suddenly realised he was at the top of the siege tower and they were about to go over the wall. He tightened his grip on his sword and took the final leap from teetering wood to solid stone. A pike came swinging at him and he chopped the blade off the handle and took the wielder's head off with a swift slice of his sword.

It did not occur to Aleks for several minutes that there was less resistance than usual. But after a short fight, the Imperial forces found themselves in possession of not only the wall but also one of the guard towers.

Aleks grabbed the arm of one of his sergeants. "What's going on?" he yelled.

The sergeant pointed wordlessly over the other wall, into the city. Aleks looked, and looked again. The Southroner ships in the harbour were burning, and three Icelander war galleys were disgorging soldiers at the docks.

"It's the Empress!" a voice hollered, and the whole force atop the wall took it up. "The Empress!"

"Saskia," Aleks breathed. She had arrived at just the right moment to distract the enemy and allow them to break over the wall. They had to move quickly now, get more soldiers over the wall and pin the invaders between the two forces.

By nightfall Furport was back in Imperial hands. The Southroners were diminished to small pockets of resistance in various houses, now besieged.

* * * *

Aleks and Saskia met again in the main square. He was filthy, covered in blood, dressed as a common soldier. Only the gold circlet on his head marked him out. She wore black leather trousers with a light chainmail shirt and a plain helmet concealing her hair.

Aleks didn't recognise Saskia, expecting her still to be carrying the triplets. Only when Saskia stepped right in front of him did he pause. He had been heading relentlessly for the docks, to board the ships and find his wife.

Saskia pulled off her helmet and her hair fell down. Looking up into Aleks' face, she smiled.

"Sass?" Aleks said incredulously. "You? But – the babies?"

"Born days ago. Safe on a ship waiting outside the harbour. The city is ours, now, I sent one of my people to fetch them."

Aleks flung his arms around Saskia with an inarticulate cry. She clung on to him, burying her face in his shoulder. And then behind him, coming down the street, she saw Iskia.

"Iskia!" she yelled, tearing free of Aleks and running to her sister. "The boys – you have to help me See to Clanhold!"

Even as Saskia reached her sister, she gathered in the Power, and, unconsciously, that of Lowri, Kerr and Dendri, with whom she had been working so much in the last days. Since they were all currently busy forcibly withholding the Power from Southroner mages, the amount of Power available to Saskia was unlike anything she had ever known before. Iskia was equally as eager as Saskia to see to Clanhold: after all her two sons were there as well. As the two touched their minds ranged out, far across the continent, and into Clanhold.

It was still early afternoon in the Clanlands. There was a small garden in the centre of the great fortress, and there they saw light, laughter, and children playing. Mairi sat in the warm sunlight, her own baby daughter Liralli and Ria's Evaskia in her lap. Around her feet played the boys, in a rambunctious game of Tag.

Saskia and Iskia watched for a few minutes, hearts gladdened by the sight of their children safe. Then Saskia, feeling the sheer strength backing up the Sight, decided to check on their sisters.

"Lia," she said.

Night was not far away where Lia was, in the low hill country. Then they realised their other sister was there too: Ria sat a few feet away, quietly chewing on some bread. Beyond her, Evan and Isulkian were drawing plans in the dirt with a stick.

Saskia released all the Power she had taken in, careful to let it slip a little at a time. Aleks was beside her, watching anxiously.

"Everyone is fine," Saskia said. "The boys are safe in Clanhold with Mairi, Lia and Ria have met up and it looks like Evan and Isulkian are planning something."

Aleks put his arms around Saskia again. "I want to see my daughters," he said.

Iskia smiled, eyes turning blank again. "They're here, Aleks."

Three burly sailors carried the girls into the square at that moment. Two slept peacefully, but Dawn, as usual, was up and yelling her head off.

"What have you named them?" Aleks asked.

"They are for you to name, Aleks. I gave them baby-names; Midnight, Dawn and Sunrise, for the hours of their birth, but they are for you to choose their true names." Saskia hefted Dawn into her arms, where the child immediately silenced.

Aleks took Midnight from the other sailor. "Who is this?"

he asked.

"That's Midnight, your oldest daughter, my lord," the sailor responded.

"Then her name shall be Aleksia, for us both. And that shrieking demon?" he asked Saskia.

"Dawn, the second-born."

"Then name her Aleksella, for my mother. And this sweet little thing, she must be the one you have called Sunrise: let her be Aleksanna, for the noble Rianna, foster-mother to my wife."

Saskia smiled up at Aleks, and Iskia reached out and took Aleksanna gently from the sailor. "You should be in bed," Iskia scolded gently, smiling down into the beautiful little girl's sleeping face. "Come: I daresay quarters have been prepared for us all. We can make them comfortable, and get something to eat."

* * * *

For the first time since leaving the Citadel Aleks got a good night's sleep. He and Saskia had a room in a house that had been deemed to be entirely safe, that quarter of the city having been thoroughly searched. Lirris watched over the babies and Iskia slept not far away.

Within a few days, Furport was empty of Southroners. Two ships of surrendered Southroners had been permitted to leave the harbour, after Saskia had made sure there were none on board with marked hands. She spent several days questioning those that she found with the tattoos, though a lot had committed suicide rather than be questioned.

One night, Saskia was alone in the rooms she and Aleks were sharing. He had gone off to yet another tactical discussion, Iskia was out and the babies were sleeping in the next room.

At last, Saskia had a bit of privacy. There was something she had been wanting to try, and now seemed an opportune moment. Dendri had given her a book that had come from the Temple in Iceport's library. They had quite a good collection of books and discourses on the Power and its uses, and though Saskia had read quite a few in the Citadel's library, she had not seen this one, entitled *Uses of the Fire.*

There were several things in the book Saskia had not heard of, and one included the conjuring of visions. Apparently, if she used a real fire as opposed to a magical one, she could weave Fire threads through it so that she could make any image she wished appear in the flames. Saskia had already used that one, but could see few practical uses for it.

The spell Saskia really wanted to try was considerably more difficult, and the book warned that it should not even be attempted unless a very great amount of the Power could be used, preferably four or five Fire Powers working linked together.

Saskia was not sure how strong those sorcerers had been, but everyone insisted that she had more Power than most ever born, and with the Tear to help her, Saskia rather thought she might be able to do this on her own. Tonight she intended to open what the book called the Spirit Roads.

Saskia sat in a comfortable chair beside the fire, looking deep into the heart of the flames. She began to gather in the Power, as much as she could hold, and wove the required Fire.

Saskia was gasping with the effort by the time the spell was complete, and for a moment thought she had failed because nothing happened. Then the flames swelled strangely and changed shape, and Rianna's face appeared in the flames.

Saskia gasped. It had been a long time since she had seen her foster-mother.

"You have done well, heart's daughter," Rianna said gently. "I see that you are tired, and troubled. Never fear, you will win through. Your children will all be safe."

"I never knew you had the TimeSight, Rianna," Saskia joked to hide her shock.

"Not in life," Rianna smiled mysteriously. She seemed to glance over her shoulder. "Another waits to speak to you, child." And she flickered, and was replaced by Saskia's mother.

Saskia could not stop the tears that started in her eyes. "Mama," she whispered.

"Sweetest child," her mother smiled. "I watch over you all. Your children are beautiful, I am so proud of you. You have all done so well."

"I still miss you, Mama," Saskia said.

"Don't, child, for I am happier now than I have ever been." The princess looked upwards for a moment. "You should let this go now, Saskia. The Power you need for this is too great, you will be drained when you let go. You need not fear malevolent spirits on the roads – you will never find your father or brother here. They are not permitted access to the places of the Light. But still – you had best not hold for too long."

"Love you, Mama," Saskia said. Her mother smiled in reply, and then Saskia let the Power go. Immediately she collapsed: the Power in her gave her strength, but now it was gone she felt absolutely exhausted. She gathered herself up and went to bed before Aleks saw how tired she looked.

* * * *

The following morning, Aleks needed to review the situation and see where the army needed to go next. He called in all dispatches and spent several hours with his aides sorting through and discarding anything that was unsubstantiated or out of date.

"Right," Aleks said finally. He had taken over the city governor's offices, and sat with Saskia at his side. Iskia sat just beyond her, ready to help with the LongSight, and there was one representative from the Icelander ships and one from the priests, two generals Aleks had brought with him and Carlene, just arrived in the city.

"Let's summarise what we know," Aleks said. "Anything we need clarification for, we will try to use LongSight to see what can be seen. The Empress and Lady ca'Berenna have already spent some time this morning filling in gaps in our knowledge, and I do not wish to waste their energy, so there will be no frivolous checking."

There were nods of agreement around the table. Aleks tapped the map which was spread out in front of him. "All right. We'll start in the north. Iridia is clear and the northern sea is free of Southron ships. Zahennarra and the Icelands have escaped unscathed. The Southroners have ignored Zahennarra entirely, which has been to our advantage: they are able to send supplies out and we will be getting good supplies of steel swords and arrowheads now that Furport is open."

"Two galleys have remained in the northern sea to patrol," the Icelander captain said. "They will make sure that no one passes north of the Seal Islands without being challenged, and we left one LongSighted with them to be sure no one could sneak by."

Aleks nodded approvingly. "Excellent."

Carlene spoke up. "As you know, my lord, North Market has been untouched and Lady ca'Berenna cannot See any troops inland from us to the west. I felt secure in leaving the city with a competent commander."

Aleks nodded. "Good. Your troops are fresh and have seen no fighting: I intend to take them south with me. General Adman, I intend to leave you here as Furport *must* be held."

Carlene nodded. "We will leave two divisions of troops to garrison the town, a company of engineers to direct the rebuilding, and a company of trackers to get out into the countryside and start finding the refugees and getting them back to the city."

Aleks spoke again. "Supplies are going to be a problem this year with Summerlands in enemy hands so we have to make sure all the farms are fully staffed and working at full output. There will be Summerlander refugees fleeing north soon enough, and plenty of them will be farmers by trade. Make sure that they are used sensibly."

The General nodded with a surprised expression. It was more of a manager's job than a task for a military commander, but Aleks knew Adman was competent enough for it.

Aleks turned to the Icelander. "Captain, I want three ships left behind. One is to patrol the eastern side of the Seal Islands, from the southern tip of Zahennarra up to Zahennarra City. The second is to patrol the western side, from Iridia to Eastport. Naturally they will stay away from Eastport until we have taken it back. For the third ship, I want you to choose a quick ship with a knowledgeable captain. I want that one weaving in and out of the islands, making sure no one is hiding in there to come out and ambush us."

The captain nodded, wide-eyed. "But won't that make them try to land in eastern Zahennarra?" he asked. "Shouldn't we have another ship patrolling up there?"

Saskia smiled grimly. "I wish them luck of trying to land there," she responded. "Zahennarra City is about the only decent landing place on the whole Light-blasted island. There are a few fishing villages with tiny harbours, but anyone trying to land a Southron warship there would have to be insane. They'll be smashed to bits on the rocks, and any survivors will find a very rough welcome from the Zahennarrans. No, I don't think we need to worry about that."

Aleks nodded in agreement. "Right. Looking south, then." He looked down at the map. "The Summerlands is gone. We can do nothing for them right now. Evan and Ria are there leading the resistance fighters. Isulkian is desperately trying to keep the Southroners out of the mountains and so far seems to be succeeding: they seem to have got no further than the foothills." Aleks tapped the northern borders of Summerlands.

"They have been besieging Highfort for weeks. General Dirk got there in time but there is a huge fight in process. Some of the Clanlanders have arrived and are trying to lift the siege: many of the others have taken up positions throughout South Eastphal to keep the Southroners away from the Citadel."

They all digested this information. Then the other general, General Hiller, spoke up soberly. "You had best hope the Roman'ii can hold the mountains, my lord, or the Clans could find themselves flanked and Southroners in the Citadel."

Aleks nodded. "Lirallen knows that. He has sent as many men as he dares, though the Clanlands must keep their own ports fortified. Fortunately they only have a few, and there are men moving south from Haven and ForstMarch to help them."

Carlene spoke up again. "The Southroners seem to like to take one port at a time. We do not think they will try for anywhere in ForstMarch or Westphal if they cannot take the Clanlands. Nevertheless, those provinces are looking to their defences. But they too are sending men south to help."

"What of the Desert?" the priest asked.

"Yes, the Desert," Aleks said. He looked down at the map

again. "We do not have much information from there. Saskia and Iskia looked earlier, and Fireport has definitely fallen. The Southroners realised they could not navigate the Desert Water and so they tried to march through the desert. Whole columns of them are dead. It seems that the Desertmen decided to let them take Fireport and have the Desert do their killing for them. They put poison in the Desert Water and any Southroner who tried to drink it is dead too."

Everyone was looking astonished. "And the Desert army?" asked Hiller.

Aleks shrugged. "Split up into various groups. Some of them are keeping an eye on the routes through the Desert. Some others have gone to the mountains to help the Roman'ii, and are doing a good job of it. The largest group went east and is keeping the Southroners out of the Desert that way: it seems that they are winning back Summerlander soil one foot at a time. There are some tremendous battles being fought down there."

"Who in the Light is leading all this?" Hiller said disbelievingly.

"The Lord Enniskarin, it seems," Saskia responded.

"But he's just a boy!" Adman said.

"He's sixteen now," Aleks shrugged. "He's proven himself a very capable commander."

There could be no disagreement about that. Everyone looked down at the map. Then the priest spoke up for the first time. "So, my lord, what next?"

Aleks shrugged. "We have only two options as I see it: Eastport or Highfort."

Adman nodded. "But the question is, where then?"

"Indeed," Aleks nodded. "If we take Highfort, we risk getting surrounded by the enemy on all fronts. If we take Eastport, we then must fight inland to Highfort and risk them coming up on our backs from the sea again." Aleks shook his head, frowning.

The problem with taking back the continent one port at a time was obvious: they would be pushing the Southroners into a corner and they would not only fight like trapped rats, they might even decide to try to push for the Citadel. No, the invaders had to be pushed *outwards*, forced back onto their ships and driven away so decisively they would never return.

Aleks outlined this logic, and everyone agreed with him.

"So, we must lift the siege at Highfort," Carlene said. "And then drive outwards, as you say. Push them east or south, so they can get back in their ships and run away. South would be better, of course, because then they will be spreading tales of a defeat among their own."

Aleks nodded. "I do not really see any other course. We must march south and take Highfort as quickly as possible. Once we have reclaimed Eastphal, we can blockade the Summerlander borders. The Desertmen seem to be doing a damn good job on the western side and I intend to let them carry on doing it. Some of the Clans can go to reinforce them, especially once the Southroners have given up on Fireport. I intend to ask Lirallen to do that himself: he can assist Enniskarin better than anyone."

"What about the rest of the Clans?" Iskia asked intently.

"They are the most mobile among us and I need them to patrol the western and northern edge of the mountains," Aleks said.

Carlene nodded in agreement. "That is critical, I cannot emphasise enough how disastrous it would be if even small groups were able to get through somehow. I want to ask Erhallen to lead that."

Iskia raised her brows, but nodded. "I have a suggestion also," she said shyly.

"Go ahead," Aleks encouraged.

"You said it yourself, the Clans are the most mobile fighters. Why not set aside squads for messaging? We have no time to train new pigeons, and communication between the armies cannot depend on Sight because I would only be able to See, not tell them what to do."

Aleks nodded. "You're right. That is exactly the sort of work Clansmen are trained for, after all: we will set up squads to carry messages swiftly."

"What of the rest of the army, my lord?" Hiller asked.

"We're heading for Highfort, first of all. Then we're going to clear every last Southroner out of Eastphal and start for the

Summerlands. I intend to blockade the northern border and lead any man suited to it into the mountains. We'll drive them out on all three fronts."

Aleks turned to the Icelander captain. "You and yours have the most important job of all," he said seriously. "No more ships may go further north than Eastport. Once we have taken Eastport back we can keep them south of the Seal Islands, and then I'll want half the fleet to circle west and get round as far as Fireport. Make sure any ships leaving there head *east*, not west."

The captain shook his head. "You don't ask much, do you?" he said glumly.

"Captain, if you and your people can do this for me, I will reward you with more gold and land than you ever imagined," Aleks said. "I know how tough this is going to be, and for that reason I will be sending with you every strong Power-Gifted that we have." He heard Saskia's sharp breath, and turned to her.

"Except the Empress. I am sorry, Captain, but I cannot bear to let my wife out of my sight again."

They all grinned, understanding. Then Aleks got to his feet. "We're in it now, ladies and gentlemen. This will not be a quick war. We're going to have to dig them out of the Summerlands an inch at a time, and it's going to be bloody, especially if they start getting more reinforcements. We are not outnumbered – or not by much – but they can change that. And then when we've done that, we have to retake Envetierra and get rid of these bastards for good."

Aleks scratched unconsciously at the scar on his hand. It itched strangely. The weight pressing on him seemed less now too, now that he had retaken Furport.

Saskia nibbled on her lower lip, looking down at the map. She could not see anything that Aleks and Carlene had missed.

"One more question," Iskia said. "Why are they doing this? What do they want?"

"I can answer that," Saskia said with a grimace. "I have been questioning some of their leaders – those of Gifted blood. They have simply run out of space. Their religion commands them to breed as many children as possible – especially those of Gifted blood – and their Healers are good enough that they live long lives.

There is just no more space in their land – and it is a hot place, far to the east and south." She shook her head incredulously.

"They have been fighting wars over *water*. So their Council – they are led by a council of warlords representing the Gifted families – got together and decided to colonise the Empire. They seemed to think there was no one here, or no one of consequence: they intended to enslave the natives, and were pretty surprised when they had to fight for Envetierra and the Envetierrans told them they would have a serious fight of it on the continent. So they sent for reinforcements and worked out a plan to take the Summerlands, the most vulnerable part."

Aleks grimaced. "When this is over, I'm going to rebuild the Summerlands as a damned fortress," he said. "I'm not having this happen again. The Southroners can just find somewhere else to colonise." With that, he picked up the map. "Thank you for your assistance, ladies and gentlemen."

"What about the babies?" Saskia asked when the others were all gone.

Aleks frowned. "They are too young to leave you, Sass. I intend to have Carlene take charge of their safety, and when they are old enough to travel and the route is safe, she will take them to Clanhold personally."

Saskia nodded reluctantly. Carlene was utterly trustworthy, and she would make sure the triplets were safe.

"We missed our anniversary," she said regretfully.

"I know," Aleks acknowledged. "Midsummer is long gone and I pray it will be the only one I spend without you. I missed you so, Sass." He drew her into his arms. "But I do have a gift for you: it was made long before we left the Citadel, and is not for your birthday, but for the girls' birth. You remember the bracelets I gave you for the boys?"

Saskia nodded. The string of diamonds for Sasskandr had delighted her, and the sapphires for Iskandr matched perfectly the blue of her son's eyes.

"Well," and Aleks drew a flat box from his pocket, "because the triplets are girls, you aren't supposed to be gifted with bracelets, by Desert tradition. But I will treasure them as I do my sons, and so I had this made for you."

The bracelet was made of amethysts set in gold, three strings of them, linked by intricate thin chains. Saskia gasped in delight and let Aleks clasp it onto her wrist.

"Aleks, it's beautiful," she said. "So unusual!"

"The chains are traditional, to show that they are triplets," Aleks said. "And, I thought – if they're anything like you – the stones might match their eyes."

Saskia smiled, reaching up to kiss him. "Thank you, Aleks, so much. Light, but I've missed you."

They held each other close, both silently vowing that the war would not separate them again.

Chapter 17

Furport, Harvest,
the year 2724 after Founding

Harvest Festival passed while they prepared to leave Furport. Finally everything was ready and the army set off south, on a long gruelling trek to Highfort. They had barely gone twenty leagues from Furport before the scouts started encountering columns of Southroners.

Aleks gave the order to fight, not daring to leave so many behind him. It would be nerve-racking enough, knowing that troops could swarm in from Eastport at any time, without leaving these soldiers wandering around the countryside.

The general plans of the war were being expedited. The battles in the south between the Desert army and the Southroners occupying Summerlands was being bitterly fought. More ships had landed at Wineport to reinforce the Southroners, and the Desert men were now outnumbered.

At least the Southroners had finally abandoned Fireport as a dead loss, and the Clans under Lirallen were now hard on the march to back up Enniskarin and his men. But the Desert was losing ground.

Aleks shrugged over Iskia's report. "Enniskarin knows Lirallen is on the way. He's a sensible lad, he'll give way slowly until his reinforcements arrive and then start to push back." He scowled over his map of South Eastphal. "I'm more worried about this. We can't keep fighting these skirmishes. We're losing men we can't afford to waste. We need to make a show of strength and scare the Southroners into running. We haven't shown our hand until now, maybe it's time."

Therefore, the following day, when reports came in of a

large column of two hundred Southroner foot soldiers, Aleks gave new orders. When those soldiers trotted through a patch of woodland and out onto an open field they found an immense army waiting there.

A trumpet sounded, and a detachment of cavalry led by Carlene charged. The foot soldiers gawked, then turned and fled back the way they had come.

Within two days, the situation had changed. Iskia kept a constant watch, and was able to report that the Southroners were converging on Highfort, obviously intending to take the city and then make the Imperial forces fight for it.

"That's it," Carlene said when she heard. "That's what we wanted. We head south now with all speed and lift the siege on Highfort before it falls."

And so it was. They pushed south as fast as the infantry could manage, making sure everyone was on top rations and in good health. The wet weather was just holding off an extra week or two and they managed to make reasonably good time.

* * * *

Aleks' men tore apart the Southron army at Highfort. A large group of Clan arrived at the same time, and over three days they raised the siege. General Dirk came to report to Aleks at last, once they were safely inside the city keep.

The general looked exhausted. He was old and had been pushing himself hard. They had heard incredible reports of him leading a decisive charge in one of the early engagements, when the battle had seemed lost. But he had done his duty, though he was outnumbered: the Southroners had not been able to get a single man into the city.

Dirk knelt stiffly before Aleks. "My liege."

"General," Aleks acknowledged. "Please, do not kneel. Someone get the general a comfortable chair."

"I am sorry, my lord, I failed in my duty," Dirk said when he was seated.

"You did what?" Aleks said, astonished. "You saved Highfort!"

"I saved the city, my lord. But, my lord, I am so sorry – Lord Kethran died of the blood poisoning not two days hence. He took an arrow in his arm and lost the arm, but the poison had already spread."

Aleks bit his lip. "Who was the heir?" he asked. He had known Kethran only a little: the lord had been not much older than Aleks and not secure enough in his holding to travel much. "Was Kethran wed?"

"He was, my lord, but Lady Anya threw herself from the battlements after he died."

Aleks' lip curled with disgust. "Any children?"

"Only Lady Kethya, my lord, and she is but ten years old."

Aleks shrugged. "Ten she may be, but both Highfort and Eastphal are now hers." He looked at Saskia. "Find her, will you, Sass? I think little Kethya may need a mother very much right now."

Saskia went to find the girl while Aleks and Dirk planned.

Lady Kethya was a pretty little girl, with thick brown hair and hazel eyes. There was flint in those eyes, though, as she looked at Saskia.

"Are you the Empress?" she demanded.

"I am," Saskia responded. Only then did Kethya curtsy, though she did it perfectly.

"Have you come to give me away?" she asked.

"Give you away? To whom?" Saskia queried.

"You will need a strong lord for Eastphal," Kethya shrugged. "The only way to do that is to marry me off."

Saskia shook her head. "You are too young for that to be legal even if it were true," she replied. "Who said that to you?"

"My uncle Divar," the girl said, puzzled. "He's Mama's younger brother. He's very nice to me."

"I'll just bet he is," Saskia muttered to herself. Divar had undoubtedly hoped to wed the child himself and take Eastphal. Well, he would soon encounter her wrath. Kethya would have to wait another six years before she could marry anyone, even with the Emperor's permission. And she could not be held to any betrothal contract she might sign now: Aleks had not long had a new law passed stating that the signature of any child under the age of fourteen could not be legally binding.

At dinner, Saskia found herself seated next to Divar. She had done a little bit of quiet research and discovered that he came from a poor, though noble, family. Kethran had married Anya for love, and from the first few minutes of talking with some of the servants Saskia knew that Divar had resented his brother-in-law's wealth and power, despite the fact that Kethran had been more than generous.

Saskia surveyed Divar thoughtfully. He was about her own age, though he repelled her: a handsome enough man, the greedy glance he had run over her body when holding her chair made Saskia want to punch him.

Divar chatted pleasantly enough. When Saskia quizzed him about his niece, Divar smiled. Saskia did not like the expression. Looking across to where Kethya sat, slightly awed, beside the Emperor, Divar said:

"Kethya is a lovely girl. A little spoiled, but all she really needs is a firm hand. I'm very fond of her, and she of me."

"I'll just bet you are," Saskia muttered under her breath. Later on, she cornered Aleks.

"You are not to make Kethya's uncle Regent for her," she ordered.

Aleks' eyebrows raised. "Why not?" he asked.

"Divar intends to wed Kethya and take Eastphal for himself," Saskia responded bluntly.

Aleks shrugged. "I can prevent that easily enough. But I can't find another Regent, Sass, Kethya has no other relatives living."

"If you stop him from wedding her, he will kill her," Saskia said. "There will be an accident for poor little Kethya, and of course who better to be the Lord of Eastphal than the beloved Regent who has served so well and grieves so for his poor niece?"

Aleks nodded. "I cannot deny it's possible. But she must have a Regent, and it would seem very strange if I do not appoint her only relative."

Saskia shrugged. "Easy enough. Give him command of some element of the army – as a reward. Send him off to

Eastport. As for a Regent, I have the perfect man in mind."

"Who?"

"General Dirk. He's exhausted, Aleks: the man is too old for a tough winter campaign. He won't last it. Give him Eastphal to defend and Kethya to watch over. The man is capable, and he has grandchildren. He will know exactly what to do with her."

And so it was done. Aleks ceremoniously put Divar in charge of a company (with a very capable deputy commander) and sent him off with two other companies to scout the countryside between Highfort and Eastport, to make sure there would be no ambushes. A few days later, they heard that Divar had been killed in one of the very ambushes he was trying to clear out. Kethya grieved, but not for long. General Dirk's family had come to join him now that Highfort was safe, and his youngest grandson was a handsome boy just Kethya's age. Aleks rather thought it was a love match in the making.

At last Iskia and Erhallen were reunited. Erhallen had been fighting to the south of the city, trying to keep Southroners from circling Highfort and heading for the Citadel. Finally some of the Clans had arrived, and reinforcements from Erinea, and Erhallen was sent back to Highfort to report. Entering the council chamber Aleks was using, he ignored everyone else, stalked across the room and swept his wife up into his arms. They clung together for a long moment.

"The boys?" Erhallen asked when he could finally set Iskia away from him.

"Well. We checked last night."

Saskia frowned, remembering. They had indeed checked on the children last night, and then on their sisters. Ria was clearly with child again, and starting to show. She was probably due after the New Year sometime. At least with Lia she would stay healthy, and the two of them were way back in the mountains now, in a high stronghold. Saskia had been rather surprised by Ria in the last few months: while Lia had been using every hour to Heal, Ria had thrown herself whole-heartedly into the fight. She had killed, too: Saskia had seen her wield the sword in a skirmish and she was good with it.

* * * *

Ria was tired and grumpy. The babies were finally making her belly swell. She was pregnant with twin girls: the TimeSight had shown it to her clearly enough. She had hidden it from Evan as long as she could, but he had finally noticed, blown a temper fit and ordered her back into the mountains with Lia.

Lia was enraged about being ordered home, but there was no denying she was not safe on the front lines. Just the previous week, there had been an attempt on her life.

A Southroner soldier had stolen Roman'ii clothing and hidden among their wounded. In the hospital tents, he had waited until very late at night and then attacked Lia, with the clear intent to rape and kill her. Lia, struggling beneath him on a bed, finally went beyond the edge of sanity and stopped his heart with a touch of the Healing Gift.

Isulkian, coming to find his wife, found her huddled, clothing torn, in hysterics beside a dead man. Finally getting some sense out of her, he ordered the body thrown out for carrion well away from their camp and called Ria.

Ria understood rape and the emotional aftermath. It had not quite happened to Lia, but the trauma of using her Gift to kill was equally as great. Isulkian would not allow his wife back on the front lines until she had recovered. He insisted she take at least a month off.

Finally, bored of Lia's moping, Ria turned on her sister. "It was you or him, Lia," she said. "He would have died anyway. Isulkian would have caught him before he got away, and then you would have been dead. We would probably have lost the war: Isulkian would have fallen apart if he lost you, and the Roman'ii will not follow anyone else. You did what you had to."

"But I *killed* him!" Lia wailed.

"I've killed too, Lia, many times. I killed our *brother*, for Light's sake. Now get over it."

And slowly, Lia did. As winter crept on into the mountains, the fighting died off somewhat; not even Southroners were crazy enough to fight in the mountains in winter.

Evan and Isulkian led daring raids lower down. Information

293

was coming in now, that Highfort had been retaken and that all of South Eastphal was back under Imperial control.

* * * *

The Southroners had not yet evacuated Eastport, but Aleks was marching on the port and they would be foolhardy to stay, especially since they had no hope of reinforcements. Messages had been sent to the city commander, warning that any non-Imperial ships approaching Eastport were being sunk.

Aleks finally lost his patience when the Southroners showed no sign of moving after he had been camped outside the city for three days. He had to retake Eastport now. He sent in another message.

* * * *

The commander in charge of Eastport, a Tattooed with a small amount of Power in Earth, read the message and then exploded in rage. One of his aides quietly picked up the paper and took it to the other leaders.

"Usurpers," the note read, "You will evacuate Eastport within seven days. You will not be hindered in leaving this continent, provided that you sail east and return to your own lands. Do not attempt to follow any other course and do not attempt to communicate with any other Southroner forces within the Empire. Do not attempt to stop at Envetierra. Do not attempt to take with you so much as one single Imperial citizen. Should you disregard any of these commands, your ships will be sunk and every last man will be executed. Signed, Emperor in the Light, Aleksandr von Chenowska."

The aide fell silent. The commanders looked around at each other. Their leader had finally calmed down and joined them for a discussion.

"He means it," one of them said.

"What kind of a man is this?" another asked. "He makes no attempt to bargain, he issues only commands."

"He is impertinent," the leader said. "He would have only

green tattoos, if he were Southroner. He has no right to command me. And he is a weak fool – he has taken a woman of sorcery to wife, and permits her to wield it!"

"But she is strong," another with blue tattoos on his hands said. "She took Vai'iyanta. He was one of the strongest among us and he could not stop her. And she has killed many, many others."

"Unclean," spat one of the other commanders.

"She has borne five living children, though three were girls," came the reply. "She would be a great gift, if she could be bound. The Blue Hand himself would want to father her children."

"We cannot take her," the leader responded sullenly. "We can do nothing but leave, or we will be destroyed. It is a good idea, though, and we will try our best to pass the message on. She would be a prize indeed, and maybe then this Emperor would be willing to bargain."

"Not that he would ever get her back," another said with an unpleasant smile.

* * * *

Aleks watched with a satisfied smile as the Southroners began to evacuate Eastport. He had a whole group of LongSighted keeping an eye on what went on the ships, making very sure that the Southroners took nothing and no one that they should not. When one of the priests reported to Aleks that women had been loaded onto one of the ships in the night, Aleks exploded with rage and wrote a second message. It was delivered to the Southron commander an hour later.

* * * *

"How does this man know everything?" the commander raged. He waved the note at his deputies and then hurled it onto the floor. One of the deputies retrieved the note.

"Unload the women from the ships now," he read. "They are not to be harmed. You will not be permitted to depart the

Empire alive if you take Imperial captives or commit murder."

The commander was raging now. Those women were priestesses from the temple that he had selected and Bound away from their Gifts. He had intended them as gifts when he returned to the Southron lands, hoping to appease their ruler the Blue Hand for his failure.

The women were unloaded and left back at the temple. They were badly bruised, and distressed that they could no longer use their Gifts. But they were alive, and within one day there were no living Southroners in Eastport. They got on their ships and headed east, trailed by two Icelander galleys.

* * * *

The army marched in and took the town. The people, those who survived, were traumatised: they had all been made into slaves. The priesthood was of little help: all the male priests had been killed and the women Bound away from their Gifts.

Saskia was curious about Binding. She sent Lowri to investigate to see if it could be undone, and was relieved when Lowri reported back that it was a simple enough matter, requiring Power and Healing to be used together. Binding could also be done on men.

Lowri took the initiative and went to find all those Southroner prisoners with tattoos, performing a Binding on every one of them. Vai'iyanta had been enraged that they had discovered the secret. It was one of the few pieces of information that they had been unable to get out of him. Now he too was Bound, and had no more gifts than any normal man.

Aleks was now working on securing Eastphal. The Southroners seemed to be getting the message and were fleeing south as fast as they could, avoiding conflict with Imperial forces.

* * * *

The pressure was increasing on the Summerlands – Desert border. Enniskarin and his men were fighting hard. The Clans and Lirallen had thankfully arrived and were patrolling the border vigilantly. The fine Desert horses stood them in good stead now as there were always plenty of good remounts. It was getting more difficult for the Southroners to slip groups over the border and spring surprise attacks.

Enniskarin was overjoyed to have Lirallen there. He had good advisors who had helped him greatly, but Lirallen had both experience and authority.

Lirallen recognised the signs of exhaustion in the young Desert lord as soon as he arrived and sent him off to sleep. The advisors all seemed to expect Lirallen to just take over. Lirallen insisted they wait to confer until Enniskarin could join them. At that meeting, Lirallen announced that he had no intention of taking command.

"What!" Enniskarin jumped to his feet. "But you have to! I don't know what I'm doing, Lirallen, truly!"

"You've managed well so far, youngster, and that's exactly why I have no intention of taking command. The Clans are here under me, and I will be glad to work with you and advise you on the deployment of the Desert forces. But I have been out into that camp, and I know: those men will follow no one but you now. You've won their loyalty, Lord Enniskarin, and that is not something you can give away. I'll not command any man whose loyalty lies elsewhere."

* * * *

Further north, in the foothills, Isulkian and Evan were planning yet another daring raid. They had worked out a good system by now: they would ambush a village, kill any Southroner they found and get the villagers away. There were few enough left that would leave: mostly women and young children. They were taken back into the mountains and sent to the Citadel.

Isulkian did not have men to spare to escort the refugees, but there were merchant caravans that had no goods to transport and would happily take people.

Aleks was paying a price of one gold crown for any Summerlander refugee who arrived safely at the Citadel. That price would only be paid once the refugee had been registered. It was a good system: the merchants were happy to keep their caravans moving, and had to keep the people well fed in order to ensure they arrived healthy. The merchants brought food for the soldiers on the return journey.

* * * *

Aleks scowled over a pile of lists. Food was becoming difficult to come by. Luckily it had been a good summer and there was plenty of food coming out of Erinea, northern Eastphal, Haven, ForstMarch and the Clanlands. But grain, the primary export of the Summerlands, was not in great supply and they were having to ration it. Rice was becoming the staple base of many meals.

At least Eastphal was safe now. Moreover, winter had set in late: though the fields had not been as carefully tended as they would have been, the crops still grew. Farmers had been brought back in to take the harvest before the weather turned and much had been rescued.

Aleks shook his head over the lists. They could count on no harvest from Summerlands next year either. Even if they could take it back before summer, he did not know how many people would be left to work the fields.

Aleks sighed and rested his head in his hands. He was the first Emperor in nearly a thousand years to fight a major war. He had no idea that it would be like this: so many little concerns. He would be much happier out in the field with a sword in his hand, but somehow the army had to be fed, and he personally would have to authorise ration increases or decreases.

Saskia came silently and stopped just behind Aleks, resting her hand on his hair.

"Are you all right, beloved?" she said gently, making a mental note to have a Healer check him over.

Aleks smiled up at her. "I am well enough, dear heart: just tired and sick of all this paperwork. How are my little angels?"

Saskia smiled. "They are wonderful, Aleks, and growing so well! They are the darlings of the camp, truly. Everyone will be sad to see them go."

Aleks nodded. He had made the decision that the girls would go before Frost: he was taking a good part of the army up into the mountains to join Isulkian, and Saskia would be with him. It was no place for three baby girls. Carlene was already assembling the required escort to take them safely to Clanhold, and Iskia would scout their route regularly to make sure it was clear of Southroner forces.

* * * *

Winter was setting in hard by the time they reached the mountains and joined the Roman'ii. They struggled through to the fort where Ria and Lia were.

The reunion of the four sisters was joyous. Ria's belly was swelling now, she would be due in another couple of months, and with twins was even bigger than she had been with Evaskia. She was chafing at her forced confinement, though, and anxious for news of Evan.

A few days later, Saskia and Aleks left the fortress and went to find Isulkian. They were escorted to him by silent Roman'ii warriors, and eventually found him resting in a small hut not far above the snowline. Evan was there too, and the two were plotting yet again.

Saskia was horrified at the sight of the two men. Both had lost weight and looked gaunt. Saskia insisted that they eat a good meal of the supplies she and Aleks had brought. Lia was only a day behind them, and both men blanched at the thought of her words when she saw them in this condition.

"We haven't had time to eat," Isulkian sad plaintively. "We've been raiding every hour we could, and in winter we have more darkness, so we have been using the advantage."

"Well, no more," Aleks said firmly. "You have softened them up well, but it's time to start driving them back towards the coast."

* * * *

It was a long, hard winter. Saskia fought beside Aleks for most of it, but he sent her and Lia back to be with Ria when her time came, and gave Evan leave to go also.

Ria gave birth on Light's Day, to two beautiful little girls they named Evanna and Evanella. Ria at once declared that as soon as she was fit she intended to go back to the front line. Within a month they were all back on the lines, fighting hard and driving the Southroners further out towards the sea.

The Southroners were reluctant to give up the Summerlands, but they were being hard pressed on three fronts and simply could not match Aleks' numbers. The Icelander ships had moved south now and were out in the ocean, merrily sinking any Southroner ship heading for the continent.

Aleks kept sending messages to the Southron commanders in the various cities and ports. The messages were simple: leave now and you may live.

Finally Enniskarin found the pressure easing up, and pushed hard for Silkport. The port had already been evacuated when he arrived. Soon he had secured all of Summerlands west of the Wine River. From the north, General Hiller was marching south and had Grainport under siege.

Evan was the most driven of the leaders. Aleks, recognising that the Summerlanders would rally to one of their own, gave Evan all the men he needed. The resistance networks had been built up on word of the raids in the west, and now there was dissent in Summerhold. Evan decided that the best thing to do was to head straight for the city and try to retake it, trusting Aleks to make sure he was not ambushed from behind.

On the day of Flowers Festival, the Southron commander in Summerhold surrendered. He set his men on the march south to Wineport. Evan entered the city in triumph, Ria riding at his side. The streets were filled with people cheering his name.

Aleks arrived two days later and was horrified at the state of the city. There was no nobility remaining, and few enough merchants. Virtually all the men between fifteen and forty had been crippled in some way to prevent their joining the resistance. Only a few who had managed to stay hidden were whole.

Women had been taken for use by the Southroner soldiers

and were traumatised. Some of those who had been used were just girls, as young as ten. The one blessing was that there were no unwanted pregnancies: there was a herb that grew in the Summerlands that prevented conception, and if taken in large enough quantities would cause a miscarriage. The herb was everywhere: it grew as a weed and could be found in every back yard and even sometimes poking up between paving flags.

Ria understood rape, though what had been done to some of the Summerlanders made her relive her own worst memories. She was invaluable in bringing the women back to themselves, and when Lia arrived with some of the other Healers they were able to start dealing with the physical hurts too.

By Midsummer all the Southroners had gone. Enniskarin and Lirallen came to Summerhold, leaving their men in the south to watch the coast.

Aleks was overjoyed to see them. Lirallen looked the same as always, a hard, serious Clan warrior, his face tanned nearly black by the hot Desert sun, but Enniskarin had changed. He was no longer a boy, barely recognisable as the shy young squire that Aleks had taken from Firehold. He would never be very tall, but the dark eyes were as fierce as any eagle's, and he looked far older than his years.

* * * *

The leaders of the Imperial forces convened in Summerhold to discuss the next step.

"We have to go after Envetierra," Aleks said firmly. "I will not leave it in Southron hands."

"Winter will be on us soon, my lord, and the ocean will be rough," General Hiller warned.

Aleks shrugged. "I cannot abandon them. They are in straits as dire as the Summerlanders were. Besides, if we do not take it back, it merely leaves a staging post for the Southroners to make the next invasion. I want every ship that can sail the ocean ready in a month." He rubbed his shoulders. The weight was nearly gone now that the continent was back in Imperial hands. But whenever anyone mentioned Envetierra, or he saw a map of the islands, he could feel the weight of the invisible hands dragging at him. He would not be able to relax until the whole Empire was free of the Southroner yoke.

The discussions were finalised, and everything prepared. The Icelanders were still prepared to sail. They would be well paid for the work, and now the ships would be filled to bursting with soldiers from the Desert and Clans also.

Aleks sighed over a map. There were plenty of people saying that he should just leave the Envetierrans to their own devices. But he could not, the duty weighed on him too strongly. Even without that, he could not bear to leave innocent people as slaves to the Southroners.

He lifted his head from the paper and stared at the wall in front of him. Summerhold was mostly wrecked, but a few houses were in good shape, and he had managed to claim a small office in one. It had been a cloakroom or some such thing before, and there was a mirror on the wall.

Aleks was not a vain man, but he frowned at the grey hairs beginning to sprinkle his black hair at the temples and the lines forming at the corners of his eyes. This war was making him old. Not many Emperors tended to live to a ripe old age, and now Aleks understood why. The weight of duty wore them down. Responsibility for the whole Empire was an appalling burden to shoulder.

Aleks straightened his back, calling himself a coward. "What do I have to whine over?" he demanded of his reflection. "I have a beautiful wife, and five wonderful children. This will all soon be over and we can all go home."

"I hope you're right," a soft voice behind him. Aleks jumped, and turned. He had not seen Saskia in the mirror. She came over and put her hand on his shoulder.

Aleks looked up at his beautiful wife and marvelled, as he had every day for the past several years, at how lucky he was. She looked sad today, though.

"What's wrong, Sass?" he asked.

Saskia sighed. "I have some news, and you will not like it. I am pregnant again."

Aleks' eyes widened with shock. "How?"

Saskia could not help but laugh. "Well, pretty much in the same way that we conceived the others," she remarked dryly.

"But isn't it too soon after the girls?"

"Not at all. I probably conceived sometime after Spring. They're due about Midwinter."

Aleks looked at Saskia's stomach, still relatively flat, and did some quick sums. "Only three months to go?" he queried.

"I know." Saskia shook her head with a puzzled frown. "But Lia insists that's right, and they're healthy."

The plural registered finally. "They?"

"I'm carrying twins, this time. Two boys, Ria tells me."

Aleks frowned. "Well, there's no help for it. You'll just have to stay behind."

"I most certainly will not!" Saskia drew herself up, eyes flashing. "I said I would not be separated from you again, and I will not!"

"Saskia, be reasonable! It was one thing for you to go to the Icelands, but this time you don't *have* to go to war!"

"I will *not* stay!"

They glared at each other fiercely, neither willing to give in. In the end, Saskia relented slightly. "I will ask Ria to See the consequences of my going or staying. If she says it is safe for me to go, I am coming with you."

Aleks chewed his lip, but could find no good argument. "All right," he acquiesced. Then saw the gleam in Saskia's eyes. "And Ria will tell me her answer herself," he said firmly.

Saskia cursed under her breath. Aleks' Charisma made it virtually impossible to deceive him. She nodded eventually.

Riaskia was quite definite. She shook her head firmly at Aleks. "You will lose this war if Saskia does *not* go," she insisted. "She has to be there. I can't see why."

Aleks accepted this with rather bad grace. When he had gone to give some orders, Ria turned to Saskia. "You must take care, sister," she said seriously. "The war will be lost if you do not go, but I cannot see for any certainty that it will be won if you do. Something has to happen to you, and I think it may threaten your life. Please be careful."

Saskia hugged her younger sister. "I will, I promise. You be careful too. There's a lot of work here in the Summerlands – too much for any one lifetime. Don't wear yourself out. Evan needs you, and so do the children."

Ria nodded, eyes shadowed. "Aleks has sent to Mairi to bring them. They will all be safe here when you return."

* * * *

Aleks was confident that he was leaving the Empire in good hands. He made Evan Lord of Summerlands, to Evan's utter astonishment. The people were absolutely delighted: they had lost their nobles, some of the first to die, but had been saved by one of their own and were happy to have him as their lord. Aleks set the silver circlet on Evan's head in Summerhold one bright afternoon.

"Well, you did marry a princess, what did you expect?" Aleks grinned as Evan touched the circlet, dumbfounded. Ria smiled behind Evan.

The ships sailed the following day. There was no shortage of volunteers. Too many had seen what was done to the Summerlanders, and felt compelled to try and relieve what was left of the Envetierrans from the same fate.

The Southroners had grouped in force on Envetierra, though the Icelander ships had successfully prevented them from being further reinforced from their homelands. The battles fought were often harsh and bloody, sometimes just between opposing Gifted who sought to save people around them. Saskia chafed that she could not help much as her Power was virtually gone again.

Saskia and Aleks were regularly on separate ships, Saskia staying back with the observers while Aleks was determined to get into the thick of the fighting. Every village they relieved, every Southroner ship they drove off, was another lessening of his burden, and he fought like a demon.

* * * *

One day, Aleks sailed in to shore to try and retake yet another fishing village. The weather was appalling and even the

Power-Gifted were having trouble steadying the seas and keeping the winds from pulling them off course.

Saskia was questioning some prisoners when there was a roar and her ship rocked violently. Saskia was close to her time now and could barely feel the Power, but it had certainly been used. She turned towards the steps to go up on deck, when suddenly the floor seemed to lurch underneath her and she fell and hit her head.

Saskia woke to complete darkness. She groaned, and tried to summon the Power. A tiny flame lit the end of her finger and she looked around. She seemed to be locked in some sort of cupboard.

At that moment the door swung open and a man looked in. He called something behind him in the guttural Southron tongue.

A moment later Saskia cried out in pain as her hair was grabbed and she was dragged out. She was on a ship, she realised: and facing its commander, by his blue-tattooed hands. The tall man looked very pleased with himself.

Saskia straightened her back. "I demand that you release me at once," she said in her best icy tones.

The commander burst out laughing. "You are in no position to make demands, whore," he said in the common tongue, with a heavy accent. "Besides, the only place to release you is over the side. I don't imagine you can swim too well with your belly that big."

Saskia stood her ground. They must know who she was or they would not have bothered this much with her. "What do you want?"

"Oh, not much," the commander said with a smile. "Envetierra and your unborn sons."

Saskia's hands dropped protectively to her belly. "Why?" she demanded.

"You speak with a sharp tongue to your betters," he snapped, striking her across the face with a sharp slap. "I am Commander Vai'rilaga Ti'vihela."

Saskia rocked with the blow, but did not fall. She had taken harder blows on the training ground many times. Her hands itched to strike back, but the odds were against her, with her

305

belly hampering her movements and no sword to hand.

"Any relation to Vai'iyanta?" Saskia asked politely.

"He was my brother. He is dead. One of my men can see to your lands, and he says that Vai'iyanta threw himself from a building not long after you sailed."

"I am sorry for your loss," Saskia said.

Vai'rilaga shrugged. "It matters not. I intended to take your unborn child as payment for my brother's life. When my healer told me you were carrying twins, that was a bonus." He smiled evilly.

"You yourself are too valuable to waste. You are no danger to me now: I know you cannot use your Power while you carry the children. But once they are born, I will Bind you, and take you back to Southron. Some have proposed you as a gift to the Blue Hand, but I think you will do well enough to breed up my heirs. You are more beautiful than I had heard."

Saskia was exerting all her willpower to keep a scream from bubbling up inside her. Just let her get her hands on a weapon! She would turn this arrogant fool into mincemeat!

Vai'rilaga tilted his head thoughtfully. "Come to that, I cannot be bothered to wait for you. They must be about ready to be born." He shouted commands in his own language, and a moment later a man in a white robe with green-tattooed hands came in.

"Induce her," Vai'rilaga ordered, pointing to Saskia. "Once they're born, I'll Bind her, and then once you've healed her I can enjoy her all the way home."

Saskia fought to keep the healer from touching her, but Vai'rilaga hit her head again, and the last thing she knew was a tearing pain in her belly.

Saskia woke to agonising pain. Vai'rilaga was nowhere to be seen, but the healer had been joined by another and they were helping her to give birth.

"Light help me!" Saskia groaned as the pain began to build.

The birth was mercifully quick. Saskia reached for her first son but her hands were slapped away. Her second was born moments later.

Saskia felt the Power return to her in a huge rush and

immediately drew in as much as she could hold through the Tear, which had, astonishingly, been left on her hand along with her betrothal ring. There was no way Vai'rilaga could sever her from this much strength. The Healers were busily healing Saskia, and she let them, feeling herself grow stronger, watching them wash her newborn sons.

Suddenly the door crashed open and Vai'rilaga roared in. "We'll see if the damned Emperor will risk his unborn children!" His eyes rested for a second on Saskia's flat belly. "They've been born? You idiots – you were supposed to call me as soon as she got close!"

He tried to draw in his own Power – Air, Saskia felt – but erupted into flames before he got even a little drawn in. The two healers were next, and when they had finished burning there was not so much as ash left, and yet not even charring on the wooden floor.

Saskia got to her feet a little shakily and picked up her sons. "I don't even know which of you is older," she murmured. "Well, never mind. It's not like you're the first–born. Come along, we'd better go find your father, it sounds as though he might be on his way."

The deck was chaotic, with men running and shouting everywhere. Saskia wrapped a shield of Air around herself and the babies to make them invisible and slipped quietly to the rail. An Icelander galley was pulled up right beside the Southron ship, far smaller but making a lot of trouble. There were actually Imperial forces on the deck fighting.

Saskia made a cushion of Air for herself and floated across to the Icelander galley. Once on deck, she vanished her invisible shield and looked around for someone she knew. Aleks himself was there, practically frothing at the mouth and ready to jump over to the other ship.

"Aleks!" Saskia shouted. He turned, saw her and came sprinting over.

"Oh, Sass, thank the Light you're safe," he gasped, enfolding her and the twins in his arms. "They're born!" he exclaimed a moment later.

"Yes, beloved. Unfortunately I don't know which is older."

Saskia let Aleks take one of the children. Spotting one of the generals passing, she grabbed his sleeve. "Call our men back off that ship. I'll set it afire – that lot deserve to burn."

"Did they hurt you?" Aleks demanded.

"No – but they did induce the birth. I killed the leader, and his healers." Saskia caught Aleks' arm. "Don't you go rushing off! Look, our men are coming back, now."

* * * *

The Southroners stood at the rail of their ship, jeering as the Imperial forces retreated and their ship pulled away. The helmsman turned the Southroner ship in pursuit, but Saskia raised her hand.

Some Southroners gazed at her, then screamed in sudden, terrified recognition. A very few dived into the water, but all the others were far too late to react. Flames streaked from Saskia's hand, and the Southroner ship caught fire all over.

Saskia turned away from the burning ship with a long sigh. Aleks was staring down at her, as though wondering who she was, but when he saw the weary pain on his wife's face, he smiled. The baby in his arms struggled and let out a cry, and Aleks rocked the child with a gentle croon.

"What will you name them?" Saskia asked, as the Imperial forces began to crowd around them both, offering congratulations and wanting to see the babies.

"Riandr and Liandr, how about that? For your fine sisters, who have done as much to win this war as anyone."

Saskia nodded. She leaned close to Aleks and he tightened his arms around her. "I was so afraid when I found you were gone," he said, pressing his face into her hair, uncaring that it was sweat-soaked and matted. "Enough of this. We're going to finish it and go home."

* * * *

The last Southroner departed Envetierra on the Day of the Dead, Aleks' twenty-seventh birthday and exactly two years after the invasion of the continent had begun. Aleks hugged Saskia when he heard the news. "We're going home at last," he said.

The Imperial fleet sailed back into Grainport ten days later. The Icelander galleys would be leaving for Iceport immediately, stopping only to drop the Imperial soldiers off. Evan and Ria were waiting on the quayside, and the rest of the family with them. Saskia searched the quayside for her children. Then she saw them: the girls held in the safe arms of Imperial Guards, Sasskandr and Iskandr one on either side of Carlene, holding firmly onto her hands.

Saskia waved to her children as she disembarked, and moments after she stepped onto dry land Sasskandr was on her, throwing himself into her arms. "Mama, Mama!"

Saskia hugged her son's compact little body, pressing her cheek into his dark curls. She had forgotten how wonderful he felt. Iskandr was only a step behind his brother, and she knelt down so that she could hold them both. She did not realise the tears were falling from her eyes until Sasskandr said, puzzled:

"Why are you crying, Mama?"

Saskia hugged him tighter. "I'm just so happy to see you, my darlings," she whispered.

Aleks was kneeling too, waiting for his turn. Sasskandr spotted him and jumped into his father's arms.

"Papa, papa! Uncle Lirallen made me a sword! He's teaching me to fight like you!"

Saskia and Aleks' eyes met, and they both looked at Lirallen, grinning cheerfully down at them, his own son Mirallen sitting on his shoulders.

"They've been breaking quite a lot of furniture," Lirallen warned. "Beware that one, he's naturally talented but just a little too enthusiastic for his own good."

Saskia heard the indignant squeals of her daughters and turned to retrieve them. She had only spent a few short months with them, and now they were over a year and a half old and walking. Saskia had missed their first steps, and wept over the news of it from Mairi.

She stood now to reach for the girls. When the reunion was over, Saskia finally stood and smiled at her sisters. Iskia looked

309

weary, leaning against Erhallen, but her smile was radiant. Their sons stood beside them.

Ria looked radiant. She and Evan were absolutely adored by their people, and Evan had used his contacts in the army to invite retiring soldiers to settle in the Summerlands. There were men there now to husband the surviving women, and in a few years the population would begin to return to normal.

Liaskia and Isulkian were there, with a great crowd of Roman'ii, and Lia's belly was swelling with her pregnancy. Saskia had not known before she left and hugged her sister delightedly, vowing to stay until the baby was born.

The occasion was a joyous one, and there were great celebrations. Lia gave birth to a son, Lisulkian, with Isulkian's black hair and flashing blue eyes. Saskia rather thought he would be a heartbreaker when he grew up.

Finally everyone returned to their homes, and more than two years after they had left, the Emperor and his family finally returned to the Citadel. The people were rejoicing in the streets: life was finally returning to normal.

Epilogue

The Citadel, Spring,
the year 2726 after Founding

Saskia and Aleks rode through the streets of the Citadel together. Carlene rode behind them, beside a carriage containing all the Imperial children, save only Sasskandr, who sat in front of Aleks on Sandstorm and waved regally to the crowd.

Aleks held his son firmly, but need not have worried: the boy sat the stallion as one born to it. Aleks thought that perhaps Sasskandr might be able to manage the fractious stallion by himself. He had no intention of finding out, though! Sasskandr might be precocious, but he was far too precious to risk on anything more than a quiet pony for a few years yet.

Saskia was pelted with flowers. There were many in the crowds who had seen her fight, with both her sword and with the Power, and were firmly convinced that she alone had won the war for them. The cheering for the Ice Witch, a title Saskia no longer objected to, was almost as loud as that for the Emperor.

At last they reached the Palace, and the throne room. Arryn formally surrendered his chancellorship, with a look of visible relief.

"There is something you must see," Arryn said after things had quietened down. It was late evening, after yet another banquet, and the children had all been packed off to bed.

Arryn led Aleks and Saskia to the library. The great bronze map Aleks had smeared his blood all over was covered with a white cloth. Arryn reached up and pulled it down.

The map shone, polished bright. There was no trace of blood remaining.

"You had it polished!" Aleks said, pleased. "Not until it was all over, I hope!"

Arryn shook his head. "I did nothing, Aleks. But I have known the progress of the war. As every battle was fought, the blood advanced or receded – right in front of my eyes, sometimes. Your last dispatch said the last Southron ships left Envetierra on the Day of the Dead? Well, on New Year's Eve, long before I heard – I came in here and the map was as you see it now, shining like a newly minted coin. No one had entered in my absence."

"The Power!" Aleks exclaimed, turning to Saskia. She shook her head.

"Not my kind of Power, love. Another kind, I think. The same kind that puts a weight on your shoulders when the Empire needs you."

"Light's blessing," Arryn breathed, eyes wide.

"Something very close," Saskia answered softly. They both watched Aleks, staring at the map. He reached out to touch the Envetierran islands. "Safe," he said. "Safe at last. The weight is gone." He closed his eyes in relief as the last of it lifted from him. There was only the weight he had grown used to: the mantle of the Empire on his shoulders, familiar now and almost comforting after ten years.

Saskia put her arm around Aleks' waist and leaned against him, looking hard at the map. There was work to do, rebuilding and reinforcing what the Southroners had destroyed. The Empire would not be caught out again.

Thus ends the first book of *The Ice Witch*. The second book, *The Earth Prince*, tells of Sasskandr's succession to the throne and his feud with the children of Liara.